GIRL MEETS BOY

Also by Ali Smith

Novels

Like

Hotel World

The Accidental

Collections

Free Love and Other Stories

Other Stories and Other Stories

The Whole Story and Other Stories

Plays

Trace of Arc

Just

The Seer

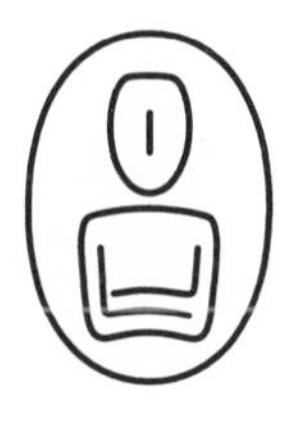

GIRL MEETS BOY

The Myth of Iphis

Ali Smith

CANONGATE

Edinburgh · New York · Melbourne

First published in Great Britain in 2007 by
Canongate Books Ltd., Edinburgh, Scotland

Printed in the United States of America
Published simultaneously in Canada

FIRST AMERICAN EDITION

ISBN-10: 1-84767-019-9
ISBN-13: 978-1-84767-019-9

Canongate
841 Broadway
New York, NY 10003

Distributed by Publishers Group West

www.groveatlantic.com

08 09 10 11 12 10 9 8 7 6 5 4 3 2 1

Myths are universal and timeless stories that reflect and shape our lives – they explore our desires, our fears, our longings and provide narratives that remind us what it means to be human. *The Myths* series brings together some of the world's finest writers, each of whom has retold a myth in a contemporary and memorable way. Authors in the series include: Chinua Achebe, Karen Armstrong, Margaret Atwood, AS Byatt, Michel Faber, David Grossman, Milton Hatoum, Natsuo Kirino, Alexander McCall Smith, Tomás Eloy Martínez, Klas Östergren, Victor Pelevin, Ali Smith, Donna Tartt, Su Tong, Dubravka Ugresic, Salley Vickers and Jeanette Winterson.

Τάδε νυν ἔταιραις
ταῖς εμαισι τέρπνα κάλως ἀείσω.

for Lucy Cuthbertson

for Sarah Wood

Far away, in some other category, far
away from the snobbery and glitter in
which our souls and bodies have been
entangled, is forged the instrument
of the new dawn.
E M Forster

It is the mark of a narrow world that
it mistrusts the undefined.
Joseph Roth

I am thinking about the difference
between history and myth. Or between
expression and vision. The need for
narrative and the simultaneous need
to escape the prison-house of the
story – to misquote.
Kathy Acker

Gender ought not to be construed as
a stable identity . . . rather, gender is an
identity tenuously constituted in time.
Judith Butler

Practise only impossibilities.
John Lyly

I

Let me tell you about when I was a girl, our grandfather says.

It is Saturday evening; we always stay at their house on Saturdays. The couch and the chairs are shoved back against the walls. The teak coffee table from the middle of the room is up under the window. The floor has been cleared for the backward and forward somersaults, the juggling with oranges and eggs, the how-to-do-a-cart-wheel, how-to-stand-on-your-head, how-to-walk-on-your-hands lessons. Our grandfather holds us upside-down by the legs until we get our balance. Our grandfather worked in a circus before he met and married our grandmother. He once did headstands on top of a whole troupe of headstanders. He once walked a tightrope across the Thames. The Thames is a river in London, which is five hundred and twenty-seven miles from here, according to the mileage chart in the RAC book in among our father's books at home. Oh, across the Thames, was it? our grandmother says. Not across the falls at Niagara? Ah, Niagara, our grandfather says. Now that was a whole other kittle of fish.

It is after gymnastics and it is before Blind Date. Sometimes after gymnastics it is The Generation Game instead. Back in history The Generation Game was our mother's favourite programme, way before we were born, when she was as small as us. But our mother isn't here any more, and anyway we prefer Blind Date, where every week without fail a boy chooses a girl from three girls and a girl chooses a boy from three boys, with a screen and Cilla Black in between them each time. Then the chosen boys and girls from last week's programme come back and talk about their blind date, which has usually been awful, and there is always excitement about whether there'll be a wedding, which is what it's called before people get divorced, and to which Cilla Black will get to wear a hat.

But which is Cilla Black, then, boy or girl? She doesn't seem to be either. She can look at the boys if she wants; she can go round the screen and look at the girls. She can go between the two sides of things like a magician, or a joke. The audience always laughs with delight when she does it.

You're being ridiculous, Anthea, Midge says shrugging her eyes at me.

Cilla Black is from the sixties, our grandmother says as if that explains everything.

It is Saturday tea-time, after supper and before our bath. It is always exciting to sit in the chairs in the places they usually aren't. Midge and I, one on each knee, are on our grandfather's lap and all three of us are wedged into the pushed-back armchair waiting for our grandmother to settle. She drags her own armchair closer to the electric fire. She puts her whole weight behind the coffee table and shoves it over so she can watch the football results. You don't need the sound up for that. Then she neatens the magazines on the underrack of the table and then she sits down. Steam rises off teacups. We've got the taste of buttered toast in our mouths. At least, I assume we all have it, since we've all been eating the same toast, well, different bits of the same toast. Then I start to worry. Because what if we all taste things differently? What if each bit of toast tastes completely different? After all, the two bits

I've eaten definitely tasted a bit different even from each other. I look round the room, from head to head of each of us. Then I taste the taste in my own mouth again.

So did I never tell you about the time they put me in jail for a week when I was a girl? our grandfather says.

What for? I say.

For saying you were a girl when you weren't one, Midge says.

For writing words, our grandfather says.

What words? I say.

NO VOTES NO GOLF, our grandfather says. They put us in jail because we wrote it into the golf green with acid, me and my friend. What's a young girl like you wanting acid for? the chemist asked me when I went to get it.

Grandad, stop it, Midge says.

What's a girl like you wanting with fifteen bottles of it? he said. I told him the truth, more fool me. I want to write words on the golf course with it, I told him and he sold me it, right enough, but then he went and told Harry Cathcart at the police station exactly who'd been round buying a job lot of acid. We were proud to go to jail, though. I was proud when they came to get me. I said to them all at the police station, I'm doing this because my mother can't write her name with words, never mind vote. Your great-grandmother wrote her name with Xs. X X X. Mary Isobel Gunn. And when we went on the Mud March, our grandfather says. Boy oh boy. It was called the Mud March because – because why?

Because of some mud, I say.

Because of the mud we got all up the hems of our skirts, our grandfather says.

Grandad, Midge says. Don't.

You should've heard the mix of accents coming out of us all, it was like a huge flock of all the different birds, all in the sky, all singing at once. Blackbirds and chaffinches and seagulls and thrushes and starlings and swifts and peewits, imagine. From all over the country we came, from Manchester, Birmingham, Liverpool, Huddersfield, Leeds, all the girls that worked in clothing, because that's what most of us did, textiles I mean, and from Glasgow, from Fife, even from right up here we went. Soon they were so afraid of us marching that they made brand new laws against us. They said we could only march in groups of no more than twelve of us. And each group of twelve girls had to be fifty yards away from any other group of twelve. And what do you think they threw at us for marching, what do you think they threw at us when we spoke in front of the great hordes of listening people?

Eggs and oranges, I say. Mud.

Tomatoes and fishheads, Midge says.

And what did we throw at the Treasury, at the Home Office, at the Houses of Parliament? he says.

Fishheads, I say.

I am finding the idea of throwing fishheads at official historic buildings very funny. Our grandfather tightens his hold round me.

No, he says. Stones, to break the windows.

Not very ladylike, Midge says from the other side of his head.

Actually, Miss Midge –, our grandfather says.

My name's not Midge, Midge says.

Actually, as it happens, we were very ladylike indeed. We threw the stones in little linen bags that we'd made ourselves with our own hands especially to put the stones in. That's how ladylike we were. But never mind that. Never mind that. Listen to this. Are you listening? Are you ready?

Here we go, our grandmother says.

Did I never tell you about the time when I was a really important, couldn't-be-done-without part of the smuggling-out-of-the-country of Burning Lily herself, the famous Building-Burning-Girl of the North East?

No, I say.

No, Midge says.

Well, I will then. Will I? our grandfather says.

Yes, I say.

Okay, Midge says.

Are you sure? he says.

Yes! we say together.

Burning Lily, he says, was famous. She was famous for lots of things. She was a dancer, and she was very very beautiful.

Always the eye for the lasses, our grandmother says with her own eyes on the television.

And one day, our grandfather says, on her twenty-first birthday, the day that the beautiful (though not near as beautiful as your grandmother, obviously) the day that the beautiful Burning Lily became a fully fledged grown-up – which is what's supposed to happen on the day you're twenty-one – she looked in the mirror and said to herself, I've had enough of this. I'm going to change things. So she went straight out and broke a window as a birthday present to herself.

Ridiculous present, Midge says. I'm asking for a Mini Cooper for mine.

But soon she decided that breaking windows, though it was a good start, wasn't quite enough. So she started setting fire to buildings – buildings that didn't have any people in them. That worked. That got their attention. She was always being carted off to jail then. And in there, in jail, in her cell, you know what she did?

What? Midge says.

She just stopped eating, he says.

Why? I say and as I say it I taste the toast taste again all through the inside of me.

Because she was like anorexic, Midge says, and had seen too many pictures of herself in magazines.

Because there wasn't anything else for her to do, our grandfather says to me over the top of Midge's head. They all did it, to protest, then. We'd all have done it. I'd have done it too. So would you.

Well *I* wouldn't, Midge says.

Yes you would. You'd do it too, if it was the only thing you could do. So then they made Burning Lily eat.

How? I said. You can't *make* someone eat.

By putting a tube down her throat and by putting food down the tube. Except, they put it down the wrong part of her throat, into her windpipe, by mistake, and they pumped food right into her lungs.

Why? I say.

Uch, Midge says.

Rob, our grandmother says.

They have to know, our grandfather says. It's true. It happened. And that thing with putting the tube into her windpipe had made her very very ill, so they had to let her out of the jail because she nearly died. And that would have been very bad publicity for the police and the jail and the government. But by the time Burning Lily got better they'd passed a new law which said: As soon as one of those girls has made herself better out there, and isn't going to die here in jail, on our hands, as if it was us who killed her, we can go straight back out and arrest her again.

But you know what?

What? I say.

What? Midge says.

Burning Lily kept on slipping through their fingers. She kept on getting away with it. She kept on setting fire to the empty buildings.

She was like a lunatic, Midge says.

Only empty buildings, mind, our grandfather says. *I will never endanger any human life except my own*, she said. *I always call out when I go into the building to make sure no one is in it. But I will carry on doing it for as long as it takes to change things for the better*. That's what she said in court. She used lots of different names in court. Lilian. Ida. May. It was before they knew what everyone looked like, like they do today, so she could slip through their fingers like water does if you clench your fist round it. It was before they used film and photos like they do now, to know who everyone is.

I hold up my hand, in a fist. I open it, then close it.

And she kept on doing it, he says. And the police were always after her. And next time, we knew, she'd surely die, she would die if they got her again, because she was too weak to do that starving thing many more times. And one day, now, are you listening?

Yes, we say.

One day, our grandfather says, one of our friends came round to my house and told me: Tomorrow you've got to dress up as a message boy.

What's a message boy? I say.

Shh, Midge says.

I was small, our grandfather says, I was nineteen, but I could pass for twelve or thirteen. And I looked a bit like a boy.

Yeah, Midge says, cause you *were* one.

Shh, I say.

And I checked through the clothes she'd brought me in the bag, our grandfather says, they were pretty clean, they didn't smell too bad, they smelt a bit leathery, a bit of the smell of boys.

Uch, Midge says.

What's the smell of boys? I say.

And it looked likely that they'd fit me. And lo and behold, they did. So I put them on the next morning, and I got into the grocer's van that stopped for me outside the door. And the girl driving the truck got out, and a boy took over the wheel, and she gave the boy a kiss as she got out. And before she got into the back of the van in under the canvas the girl gave me a rolled-up comic and an apple, and a basket of things, tea, sugar, a cabbage, some carrots. And she said, pull your cap down low and put your head inside the comic now, and start eating at that apple when you get out of the van. So I did those things, I did what she said, I opened the comic at random and held it up in front of me, and the pictures juggled up and down in front of my eyes all the way there, and when we got to the right house the boy driving stopped the van, and the front door of the house opened, and a woman shouted, All right! It's here! And I went round the back, that's where message boys were supposed to go, I was down behind the comic, and I took two bites out of the apple, which was a big one, apples were a lot bigger then, back in the days when I was a girl.

This time Midge doesn't say anything. She is completely listening, like I am.

And in the corridor of the big old house I saw myself in a mirror, except it wasn't a mirror, and it wasn't me. It was someone else dressed exactly the same, it was a fine-looking boy wearing the exact same clothes. But he was very very handsome, and that was how I knew he wasn't me and I wasn't him.

Rob, our grandmother says.

He was handsome, though he was very thin and pale, and he gave me a great big smile. And the woman who'd taken me through the house, she upended the basket so the groceries fell out all over her floor, like she couldn't care less about groceries, and then she handed the empty basket to the handsome boy and she told me to give him the comic and the apple. He slung the basket lightly on his arm and let the comic fall open in his hand, then he took a bite himself out of the apple in his other hand, and as he went out the door he turned and winked at me. And I saw. It wasn't a boy at all. It was a beautiful girl. It was beautiful Burning Lily herself, dressed just like I was, who'd turned and winked at me then.

Our grandfather winks over at our grandmother. Eh, Helen? he says.

Way back in the Celtic tribes, our grandmother says, women had the franchise. You always have to fight to get the thing you've lost. Even though you maybe don't know you ever had it in the first place. She turns back to the television. Christ. Six nil, she says. She shakes her head.

I want the French eyes, I say.

You've got all the eyes you need, our grandfather says, thanks to girls like Burning Lily. And you know what, you know what? She got as far as the coast that day, miles and miles all the way to a waiting boat, without the police who were watching the house even knowing she'd been and she'd gone.

Grandad, you're like insane, Midge says. Because if you work it out, even if you *were* a girl, that story would make you born right at the beginning of the century, and yeah, I mean, you're old and everything, but you're not that old.

Midge, my sweet fierce cynical heart, our grandfather says. You're going to have to learn the kind of hope that makes things history. Otherwise there'll be no good hope for your own grand truths and no good truths for your own grandchildren.

My name's Imogen, Midge says and gets down off his knee.

Our grandmother stands up.

Your grandfather likes to think that all the stories in the world are his to tell, she says.

Just the important ones, our grandfather says. Just the ones that need the telling. Some stories always need telling more than others. Right, Anthea?

Right, Grandad, I say.

Yeah, right, Midge had said. And then you went straight outside and threw a stone at the kitchen window, do you remember that?

She pointed at the window, the one right there in front of us now, with its vase of daffodils and its curtains that she'd gone all the way to Aberdeen to get.

No, I said. I don't remember that at all. I don't remember any of it. All I remember is something about Blind Date and there always being toast.

We both stared at the window. It was the same window, but different, obviously, nearly fifteen years different. It didn't look like it could ever have been broken, or ever have been any different to how it was right now.

Did it break? I said.

Yeah, it broke, she said. Of course it broke. That's

the kind of girl you were. I should have told them to put it into your Pure psychology report. Highly suggestible. Blindly rebellious.

Ha, I said. Hardly. I'm not the suggestible one. I nodded my head towards the front of the house. I mean, who went and bought a motorbike for thousands of pounds because it's got the word REBEL painted on it? I said.

That's not why I bought it, Midge said and her neck up to her ears went as red as the bike. It was the right price and the right shape, she said. I didn't buy it because of any stupid word on it.

I began to feel bad about what I'd said. I felt bad as soon as it came out of my mouth. Words. Look what they can do. Because now maybe she wouldn't be able to get on that bike in the same innocent way ever again and it would be my fault. I'd maybe ruined her bike for her. I'd definitely annoyed her, I knew by the way she pulled rank on me with such calm, told me I'd better not be late, and told me not to call her Midge at work, especially not in front of Keith. Then she clicked the front door shut behind her with a quietness that was an affront.

I tried to remember which one at Pure Keith was. They all looked the same, the bosses with their slightly Anglified accents and their trendily close-shaved heads. They all looked far too old for haircuts like that. They all looked nearly bald. They all looked like they were maybe called Keith.

I heard her taking the cover off and folding it neatly, then I heard her get on the bike, start it up and roar out of the drive.

Rebel.

It was raining. I hoped she'd go easy in the rain. I hoped her brakes were good. It had rained every day here since I'd got back, all eight days. Scottish rain's no myth, it's real all right. I ain't got nothing but rain, baby, eight days a week. The rain it raineth every day. When that I was and a little tiny girl, with a hey, ho, the wind and the rain.

Yes, because that was another thing that made Midge furious when we were little tiny girls, that he was always changing the words to things. If you can keep your head when all about you. Are losing theirs and blaming it on you. If you can bear to hear the truth you've spoken. If you can force your heart and nerve and sinew. If you can fill the unforgiving minute. With sixty seconds' worth of distance run. Yours is the earth and everything that's in it. And – which is more – you'll be a woman, my daughter NO NO NO GRANDAD IT DOESN'T RHYME she used to squeal, she used to stand on the linoleum right there, where the new parquet was now, and shout in a kind of amazing rage, don't change it! you're changing it! it isn't right! it's wrong! I had forgotten that too. Amazing rage, how sweet the sound. And *Midge, can I have that book? You can if you say the magic word, what's the magic word?* Imogen was the magic word. *Midge, can I finish your chips? Midge, can I borrow your bike? Midge, will you say it was you who broke it? I will if you say the magic word, what's the magic word?* Something about Midge had changed. Something fundamental. I tried to think what it was. It was right in front of my eyes and yet I couldn't quite see it.

They'd had a teak coffee table. I remembered now how proud they'd been about it being made of teak. God knows why. Was teak such a big deal? The teak coffee table was long gone. All their things had gone. I had no idea where. The only real sense of the two of them still here came from the way the light fell through the same glass of the front door, and the framed photo Midge'd put on the wall next to where the dinette door used to be.

Dinette. What a word. What a long-gone word, a word sunk to the bottom of the sea. Midge had knocked through the walls of the dinette into the living room to make one huge room. She had had central heating put in. She'd knocked through from the bathroom into the littlest bedroom where I used to sleep on the Saturday nights we stayed here, to make a bigger bathroom; now there was a bath where my single bed had been. She'd tarmacked over the front garden where our grandmother used to have her roses and her pinks. Now Midge's bike was kept there.

They looked old in the photo, I could see that now. They looked like two old people. Their features were soft. He looked smooth, sweet-faced, almost girlish. She looked strong, clear-boned, like a smiling young man from some Second World War film had climbed inside an older skin. They looked wise. They looked like people who didn't mind, who were wise to how little time was left. Come in boat number two, your time is up. Five years ago they went on holiday to Devon. They bought a trimaran at a boating shop on a whim, and they sent our father a note. Dear son, gone to see the world, love to the girls, back soon. They sailed off on their whim. They'd never been sailing in their lives.

Wise fools. They'd sent us postcards from the coasts of Spain and Portugal. Then the postcards stopped. Two years ago our father came up north and put up a headstone in the cemetery above their empty plot, the plot they bought before we were born, with their names and a photo on it, the same photo I was looking at now, and the words on the stone under the trees, next to the canal, in among the birdsong and the hundreds of other stones, above the empty square of earth, were ROBERT AND HELEN GUNN BELOVED PARENTS AND GRANDPARENTS LOST AT SEA 2003.

On the backs of the dolphins. Acquainted with the waves.

Then he gave the house to us, if we wanted it. Midge moved in. Now I was here too, thanks to Midge. Now I had a job too, thanks to Midge.

I didn't particularly want to be thankful to Midge.

But I was home, I had a home here in Inverness,

thanks to Midge. Well, thanks to the two of *them*, full fathom five, seaweed swaying round their unbound bones shifting on the sand of the seabed. Was the seabed dark? Was it cold? Did any light get down there from the sun? They'd been kidnapped by sirens, ensnared by Scylla and Charybdis. Cilla and Charybdis. That was what had got me thinking about Blind Date. That was why I'd remembered what little I hadn't completely forgotten of those Saturdays, the Saturday toast, the Saturday television. That, and the fixed and fluid features on the wall, of the old, the wise.

I wished I was old. I was tired of being so young, so stupidly knowing, so stupidly forgetful. I was tired of having to be anything at all. I felt like the Internet, full of every kind of information but none of it mattering more than any of it, and all of its little links like thin white roots on a broken plant dug out of the soil, lying drying on its side. And whenever I tried to access myself, whenever I'd try to click on me, try to go any deeper when it came to the meaning of 'I', I mean deeper than a single fast-loading page on Facebook or MySpace, it was as if I knew that one morning I'd wake up and try to log on to find that not even *that* version of 'I' existed any more, because the servers all over the world were all down. And that's how rootless. And that's how fragile. And what would poor Anthea do then, poor thing?

I'd sit in a barn. And keep myself warm. And hide my head under my wing, poor thing.

I wondered if Midge would remember that song, about the bird in the barn and the snow coming. I remembered it as something to do with our mother. I didn't know if that was a true memory or if I'd just made it up.

I sat down on the kitchen floor. I traced a square in the parquet with my finger. Come on. Get a grip. I should have been on my way to work. I should have been on my way to my next new day at the new Pure. I had a good new job. I would be making good money. It was all good. I was a Creative. That's what I was. That's who I was. Anthea Gunn, Pure Creative.

But I stared at my grandparents in their photo, with their arms round each other and their heads together, and I wished that my own bones were unbound, I wished they were mingling, picked clean by fish, with the bones of another body, a body my bones and heart and soul had loved with unfathomable certainty for decades, and both of us down deep now, lost to everything but the fact of bare bones on a dark seabed.

Midge was right. I was going to be late for work. I was late already.

Not Midge. Imogen. (Keith.) (What's the magic word?)

At least my sister had a Shakespearian name. At least her name meant something. Anthea. For God's sake.

Weren't people supposed to get named after gods and goddesses, rivers, places that mattered, the heroines of books or plays, or members of their family who'd gone before them?

I went upstairs and put on the right kind of clothes. I came downstairs. I got my umbrella. I put my jacket on. I stopped and looked in the mirror on my way out the front door. I was twenty-one years old. My hair was light and my eyes were blue. I was Anthea Gunn, named after some girl from the past I'd never seen, a girl on a Saturday evening tv show who always gave things a twirl, who always wore pretty frocks, and whom my mother, when she herself was a little tiny girl, had longed with all her heart to be like when she finally grew up.

I went outside mournful, and I hit pure air. The air was full of birdsong. I went outside expecting rain but it was sunny, it was so suddenly so openly sunny, with so sharp a spring light coming off the river, that I went down the side of the riverbank and sat in among the daffodils.

People went past on the pavement above. They looked down at me like I was mad. A seagull patrolled the railing. It eyed me like I was mad.

Clearly nobody ever went down the riverbank. Clearly nobody was supposed to.

I slid myself down to the water's edge. I was wearing the wrong kind of shoes to do it. I took them off. The grass was very wet. The soles of my tights went dark with it. I'd be ruining my work clothes.

There was blossom on the surface of the Ness, close to the bank, lapping near my feet, a thin rime of floating petals that had blown off the trees under the cathedral behind me. The river was lined with churches, as if to prove that decent people still believed in things. Maybe they did. Maybe they thought it made a difference, all the ritual marryings and christenings and confirmings and funereals, all the centuries of asking, in their different churches each filled with the same cold air off the mountains and the Firth, for things to reveal themselves as having meaning after all, for some proof the world was held in larger hands than human hands. I'd be happy, myself, I thought as I sat in the wet grass with my hands in the warmth still inside my shoes, just to know that the world was a berry in the beak of a bird, or was nothing more than a slab of sloped grassy turf like this, fished out of cosmic nothingness one beautiful spring morning by some meaningless creature or other. That would do. That would do fine. It would be fine, just to know that for sure.

The river itself was fast and black. It was comforting. It had been here way before any town with its shops, its churches, its restaurants, its houses, its townspeople with all their comings and goings, its boatbuilding, its fishing, its port, its years of wars over who got the money from these, then its shipping of Highland boy soldiers down south for Queen Victoria's wars, in boats on the brand new canal then all along the lochs in the ice-cut crevasse of the Great Glen.

I could, if I chose, just walk into the river. I could stand up and let myself fall the whole slant of the bank. I could just let the fast old river have me, toss myself in like a stone.

There was a stone by my foot. It was a local stone, a white-ridged stone with a glint of mica through it. I threw it in instead.

The river laughed. I swear it did. It laughed and it changed as I watched. As it changed, it stayed the same. The river was all about time, it was about how little time actually mattered. I looked at my watch. Fuck. I was an hour and a half late. Ha ha! The river laughed at me again.

So I laughed too, and instead of going to work I went into town to hang out at the new shopping centre for a while.

We had all the same shops here now as in every big city. They had all the big brands and all the same labels. That made us, up here, every bit as good as all the big cities all over the country – whatever 'good' meant.

But the shopping centre was full of people shopping who looked immensely sad, and the people working in the shops there looked even sadder, and some of them looked mean, looked at me as if I was a threat, as if I might steal things, wandering round not buying anything at half past ten in the morning. So I left the new mall and went to the second-hand bookshop instead.

The second-hand bookshop used to be a church. Now it was a church for books. But there were only so many copies of other people's given-away books that you could thumb through without getting a bit nauseous. Like that poem I knew, about how you sit and read your way through a book then close the book and put it on the shelf, and maybe, life being so short, you'll die before you ever open that book again and its pages, the single pages, shut in the book on the shelf, will maybe never see light again, which is why I had to leave the shop, because the man who owned it was looking at me oddly, because I was doing the thing I find myself doing in all bookshops because of that maddening poem – taking a book off a shelf and fanning it open so that each page sees some light, then putting it back on, then taking the next one along off and doing the same, which is very time-consuming, though they don't seem to mind as much in second-hand shops as they do in Borders and Waterstones etc, where they tend not to like it if you bend or break the spines on new books.

Then I stopped to have a look at the big flat stone cemented into the pavement outside the Town House, the famous stone, the oldest most important stone in town, the oldest proof of itself as a town that the town I grew up in had. It was reputedly the stone the washer-women used to rest their baskets of clothes on, on their way to and from the river, or the stone they used to scrub their clothes against when they were washing them, I didn't know which was true, or if either of those was true.

My mobile was going off in my pocket and because, without looking, I knew it would be Pure, and because I thought for a moment of Midge, I decided to be a good girl, whatever good means, and I made for Pure instead, up the hill, past the big billboard, the one that someone had very prettily defaced.

Matchmake.com. Get What You Want. In smaller writing at the bottom, *Get What You Want In The First Six Weeks or Get Six Months' Free Membership.*

It was a massive pink poster with little cartoon people drawn on it in couples standing outside little houses, a bit like weather people. They didn't have faces, they had cartoon blank circles instead, but they were wearing uniforms or outfits and holding things to make it clearer what they were. A nurse (female) and a policeman (male). That was one couple. A sailor (male) and a pole-dancer (female). A teacher (female) and a doctor (male). An executive (male) and an arty-looking person (female). A dustman (male) and a ballet dancer (female). A pirate (male) and a person holding a baby (female). A cook (female) and a truck driver (male). The difference between male and female was breasts and hair.

Underneath the Get What You Want line someone had written, in red paint, in fine calligraphic hand: DON'T BE STUPID. MONEY WON'T BUY IT.

Then, below, in a kind of graffiti signature, the strange word: IPHISOL.

Iphisol.

You're late, Becky on Reception said as I went past. Careful. They're looking for you.

I thanked her. I took off my coat and hung it up. I

sat down. I switched my computer on. I got Google up. I typed the strange word in and I clicked on Search: the web.

Well done, Anthea, on finally getting in, one of the shaveys said behind me.

In what? I said.

In to work, Anthea, he said. He leaned in over my shoulder. His breath smelt of coffee and badness. I moved my head away. He was holding one of the customised plastic coffee tubs with the clip-on tops. It said Pure on it.

I'm being sarcastic, Anthea, he said.

Right, I said. I wished I could remember his name so I could use it all the time like he was using mine.

Everybody else managed to get here by nine all right, he said. Even the girls doing work experience from the High School. They were on time. Becky on Reception. She was on time. I won't even bring your sister into this as a comparison, Anthea.

Good of you, I said.

The shavey flinched slightly in case I was daring to answer back.

I'm just wondering what could have caused you not

to be able to meet the same standards everybody else manages to meet. Any idea, Anthea?

Your search – iphisol – did not match any documents. Suggestions: Make sure all words are spelled correctly. Try different keywords. Try more general keywords.

I've been working quite hard on the concept, I said. But I had to do it off-site. My apologies. I'm really sorry, eh, Brian.

Uh huh, he said. Well, we're waiting for you. The whole Creatives group has been waiting for you for most of the morning, including Keith. You know the pressure Keith's under when it comes to time.

Why did you wait? I asked. Why did you not just go ahead? I wouldn't have minded. I'd not have been offended.

Boardroom two, he said. Five minutes. Okay Anthea?

Okay Brian, I said.

He *was* called Brian. Thank you, gods. Or if he wasn't, he didn't complain, or didn't give a fuck what I was saying, or maybe wasn't actually listening to anything I said.

★ ★ ★

Okay, ladies and gents, Keith said. (Keith sounded American. I'd not yet met Keith. Keith was the boss of bosses.) Let's do it. Get the lights, ah, ah, Imogen? Good girl. Thank you.

Midge wasn't speaking to me. She'd ignored me when I'd come into the room.

I want you to look at these slides, Keith said. And I want you to look at them in silence.

We did as we were told.

Eilean Donan Castle on a cloudy day. The clouds reflecting in the water round the castle.

The old bridge at Carrbridge on a snowy day. A ridge of snow on the bridge. The water under it reflecting the blue of the sky. Ice at its edges.

A whale's back rising out of very blue water.

An archaeological site with a stretch of blue water beyond it.

A loch in a green treeless valley with a war memorial at the front of it.

An island rising out of very blue water.

A Highland cow in an autumnal setting, behind it a thin line of light on water.

The town. The river I'd just thrown a stone into,

intertwined with that of America. (And the images in turn echo suggestively Whitman's own 1860 self-description—"Behold this swarthy face, these gray eyes, / This beard, the white wool unclipt upon my neck" [*LGC*, 126]—back in the "Lucifer" days, when he could conceive of his identity slipping across racial boundaries, when he could imagine his own face "swarthy," his own beard "woolly.") This 1870 edition of *Leaves* is the one that Whitman reissued as the Centennial Edition in 1876, an edition that marked not only the first hundred years of the nation's independence but also the end of Reconstruction, the withdrawal of federal troops from the South, and the "turning back of the clock," as blacks experienced a new disfranchisement through poll taxes, literacy requirements, and the reinstitution of Black Codes. In this edition, Whitman began the dismantling and dispersion of the poems in *Drum-Taps*, scattering them throughout *Leaves*, tinting his entire book with the war's crimson. He would work now, as M. Wynn Thomas has noted, "to turn *Leaves of Grass* itself into a veteran's testimony, into a centenarian's song, as it were."[40] In other words, Whitman, by the 1881 edition, was playing the role of the old soldier, seeking out ways to make the country pay its obligation of memory to those who had sacrificed so much in the Civil War so that the nation could endure.

Whitman not only scattered the *Drum-Taps* poems throughout *Leaves of Grass*, he also added poems to the "Drum-Taps" cluster that had not originally been in the group, thus altering his poetic representation of the war. In 1881, in one of the most significant reconstructions of his Civil War poems, he moved both "Ethiopia" and "Delicate Cluster" into "Drum-Taps." Five years after national Reconstruction had ended, Whitman's poetic reconstruction reached its conclusion: his 1881 arrangement of his poems would stand as the definitive one, and "Ethiopia" would, for generations of readers, simply be a "Drum-Taps" poem, serving to suggest that Whitman always considered the issue of the emancipation of the slaves to be at least a part of his significant memory of the war. In the original *Drum-Taps*, however, no black had been given any voice, and the question was never raised about the place of the freed slaves in American culture.[41]

In *Memoranda During the War* (1875–76), however, Whitman

had begun asking some troubling questions: "Did the vast mass of the blacks, in Slavery in the United States, present a terrible and deeply complicated problem through the just ending century? But how if the mass of the blacks in freedom in the U.S. all through the ensuing century, should present a yet more terrible and deeply complicated problem?" (*PW*, I:326). This was the surprising pair of essential questions for Whitman: one, the question before the Civil War, the question of slavery, the other, the question after the war, the question of African-American citizens. Before the war, he had been for freedom for the slaves; after the war, the very nature of that freedom became the problem.

In a way, Whitman, by 1858, had begun his retreat from his radical representation of rebellious blacks in the 1855 and 1856 *Leaves*. In the *Brooklyn Daily Times*, he argued for resettlement of blacks outside of the country.

> Who believes that the Whites and Blacks can ever amalgamate in America? Or who wishes it to happen? Nature has set an impassable seal against it. Besides, is not America for the Whites? And is it not better so? As long as the Blacks remain here how can they become anything like an independent and heroic race?[42]

Whitman here sounds like Lincoln—who also favored colonization of blacks—at about the same time:

> I have no purpose to introduce political and social equality between the white and the black races. There is a physical difference between the two which in my judgment will probably forever forbid their living together upon the footing of perfect equality, and inasmuch as it becomes a necessity that there must be a difference, I . . . am in favor of the race to which I belong, having the superior position.[43]

Clearly, Whitman underwent, along with much of white America, a difficult reassessment of his relationship to black America, starting in the years before the Civil War and extending long after it. As George Frederickson has said, before the end of the war, "Northern leaders had been able to discuss with full seriousness the possibility of abolishing slavery while at the same time avoiding the perplexing and politically dangerous task of incorporating the freed blacks into the life of the nation."[44] It was one thing to espouse the end of slavery but quite another to claim equality between whites and blacks. Whitman was therefore wildly ambivalent about the racial changes Reconstruction had brought about, and his most common way of dealing with his uncertainty was to turn away from it, to erase blacks as a subject of his poetic project.

This absence, of course, makes "Ethiopia" all the more remarkable, and Whitman's gradual insertion of it into "Drum-Taps" as a kind of ex post facto acknowledgment of emancipation makes it all the more interesting. For, while Whitman was aggressively silencing himself in his poetry about the issues that preoccupied the country during Reconstruction, he was struggling with them everywhere in his prose.

Forgetting to Answer Carlyle

I've noted that "Ethiopia" was written at the same time that Whitman was composing the essays that would come to be *Democratic Vistas* and that the poem and the essays were both originally scheduled to appear in the same journal. The *Galaxy*, in fact, thought the "Ethiopia" poem would most effectively work as a follow-up to "Democracy," the first essay in *Democratic Vistas* and the essay that Whitman conceived of as a "rejoinder" to Carlyle's "Shooting Niagara." The pieces begin to fall together, for Carlyle's harangue against democracy was most viciously directed toward the multiracial experiment that America had newly embarked on, what Carlyle liked to call "the Nigger Question."[45]

> —Half a million . . . of excellent White Men, full of gifts and faculty, have torn and slashed one another into horrid death, in a temporary humour, which will leave centuries of remembrance fierce enough; and three million absurd Blacks, men and brothers (of a sort) are completely "emancipated":

> launched into the career of improvement—likely to be "improved off the face of the earth" in a generation or two! (Carlyle, *Essays,* V:7)

Here it was in its starkest form: Lincoln's grand ideal of emancipation as the fruition of democracy reduced to a costly and silly scheme to free and thus to destroy an inferior race. This, pronounced Carlyle, was what America fought its Civil War for—not worthy ideals but blind stupidity. No wonder that Whitman was, as he says in a footnote to "Democracy," "roused to much anger and abuse by this essay from Mr. Carlyle, so insulting to the theory of America" (*PW*, II:375).

As Whitman began his own diagnosis of "the theory of America," he seemed at first to be ready to tackle the very problem so baldly stated by Carlyle. Again and again in the opening pages of "Democracy," Whitman edges toward a confrontation with the issue of interracial democracy, of black suffrage. He talks of "the priceless value of our political institutions, general suffrage, (and fully acknowledging the latest, widest opening of the doors)" (*PW*, II:364), and he talks of how "so many voices, pens, minds, in the press, lecture-rooms, in our Congress, &c., are discussing intellectual topics, pecuniary dangers, legislative problems, the suffrage" (*PW*, II:365). "I will not gloss over the appaling [*sic*] dangers of universal suffrage in the United States," he vows (*PW*, II:363). In the original *Galaxy* essay, which Whitman had thought would be accompanied by his "Ethiopia" poem, he did go on to directly engage Carlyle, using an uncharacteristic and uneasy sarcastic tone.

> —How shall we, good-class folk, meet the rolling, mountainous surges of "swarmery" that already beat upon and threaten to overwhelm us? What disposal, short of wholesale throat-cutting and extermination (which seems not without its advantages), offers, for the countless herds of "hoofs and hobnails," that will somehow, and so perversely get themselves born, and grow up to annoy and vex us? What under heaven is to become of "nigger Cushee," that imbruted and lazy being—now, worst of all, preposterously free? . . . Ring the

> alarum bell! Put the flags at the half mast! Or, rather, let each man spring for the nearest loose spar or plank. The ship is going down! (*PW*, II:749)

It's hard to tell how much Whitman's strained tone here is hiding his own deep reservations about universal suffrage, even as he tells Carlyle to "spare those spasms of dread and disgust."[46] Whitman sees the "only course eligible" as the swallowing of the "big and bitter pill" of Carlyle's "swarmery." He does not directly mention blacks again, though they are implicitly included in his disdainful embrace of the new masses: "By all odds, my friend, the thing to do is to make a flank movement, surround them, disarm them, give them their first degree, incorporate them in the State as voters, and then—wait for the next emergency" (*PW*, II:750). Then, Whitman brings himself back to the Carolinas, perhaps anticipating the originally planned juxtaposition of this essay with his "Ethiopia" poem. He tells Carlyle that his "comic-painful hullabaloo" is worse than the primitive cries of those whom the new suffrage will be recognizing as citizens; Whitman says he "never yet encountered" such "vituperative cat-squalling . . . not even in extremest hour of midnight, in whooping Tennessee revival, or Bedlam let loose in crowded, colored Carolina bush-meeting" (*PW*, II:750). Apparently aware that his edgy and emotionally uncontrolled outburst was betraying more than he felt comfortable with, he simply removed the whole passage from his published version of *Democratic Vistas*.

So, while he says he will not "gloss over" the issue of universal suffrage, in the final version of *Democratic Vistas* that is exactly what he does. He discusses equality between the sexes, but, after obliquely raising the issue of race in the opening pages, Whitman's essay veers away, never to return except in some small-print notes at the end, notes that he did not republish with *Democratic Vistas* after the initial printing, moving them instead to his "Notes Left Over." It is a stunning avoidance, especially given the "anger" Whitman claims he felt when he read Carlyle's harangue, and we hear all the more loudly Whitman's admission, in his footnote on Carlyle, that he "had more than once been in the like mood, during which [Carlyle's] essay was evidently cast, and seen persons and things in the same light, (indeed some might say there are signs of the same feeling in these Vistas)" (*PW*, II:375).

Some recently discovered manuscripts indicate that Whitman may have started out with the intention of breaking his silence on the race question. In one manuscript, perhaps notes for a section of *Democratic Vistas* that he never wrote, Whitman counseled himself to "Make a full and plain spoken statement of *the South*—encouraging—the south will yet come up—the blacks must either filter through in time or gradually eliminate & disappear, which is most likely though that termination is far off, or else must so develop in mental and moral qualities and in all the attributes of a leading and dominant race, (which I do not think likely)."[47] Here, Whitman sounds indeed like he sees "things in the same light" as Carlyle, predicting the same eventual disappearance of the black race and expressing some contempt for the notion that the black race could progress enough to hold an equal place in American society. Such applications of evolutionary theory, resulting in the prophecy that the black race was "destined to disappear in the South," were common in the postwar years (see Frederickson, *Black Image*, 237.)

Another Whitman manuscript from around the same time (it refers to the "Acts of Congress" and the "Constitutional Amendments" that Whitman was then attending the debates on) reveals a similar faith that evolutionary laws will solve America's race problem, that all the talk ("the tender appeals") about suffrage and equality will give way to the inexorable laws of "Ethnological Science," which settle "these things by evolution, by natural selection by certain races, notwithstanding all the frantic pages of the sentimentalists, helplessly disappearing [when brought in contact with other races, and] by the slow, sure progress of laws, through sufficient periods of time."[48] Frederickson in *The Black Image in the White Mind* has delineated in detail the various theories of race that "ethnological scientists" came up with in the nineteenth century, and, at one point or another, Whitman seems to have subscribed to most of them. But his evolutionary stance in these manuscript notes suggests that, at the time of Reconstruction, he believed the problems of race would eventually vanish as blacks somehow "filtered out" or disappeared or—less likely—became, through amalgamation, white.

Finally, in an essay he published in 1874, Whitman offered his most direct statement about black suffrage, but then—as he did with the black suffrage passages in *Democratic Vistas*—he removed the key passage before reprinting the essay.

> As if we had not strained the voting and digestive calibre of American Democracy to the utmost for the last fifty years with the millions of ignorant foreigners, we have now infused a powerful percentage of blacks, with about as much intellect and calibre (in the mass) as so many baboons. But we stood the former trial—solved it—and, though this is much harder, will, I doubt not, triumphantly solve this. (PW, II:762)

It is difficult to figure out what to make of this passage. Whitman seems once again to express some sort of faith that the future will simply take care of the problem, presumably either by improving the quality of black Americans or by filtering them out of existence. It is not an edifying passage, but it is consonant with a number of comments Whitman made in his later years. By 1888, he was capable of comments like the following to Horace Traubel, who had asked Whitman his views on racial amalgamation: "I don't believe in it—it is not possible. The nigger, like the Injun, will be eliminated: it is the law of history, races, what-not: always so far inexorable—always to be. Someone proves that a superior grade of rats comes and then all the minor rats are cleared out" (*WWC*, II::283). In the final year of his life, he was still arguing that "the horror of slavery was not in what it did for the nigger but in what it produced of the whites," and he was quick to propose that the reason "niggers are the happiest people on the earth" is "because they're so damned vacant" (*WWC*, VIII:439). Perhaps more dispiriting is Whitman's late affinity with the South, as if he were still speaking for the slave masters but no longer for the slaves and certainly not for the freed slaves.

> I know not how others may feel but to me the South—the old true South, & its succession & presentation the New

> true South after all outstanding Virginia and the Carolinas, Georgia—is yet inexpressibly dear.—To night I would say one word for that South—the whites. I do not wish to say one word and will not say one word against the blacks—but the blacks can never be to me what the whites are. Below all political relations, even the deepest, are still deeper, personal, physiological and *emotional* ones, the whites are my brothers & I love them. (*NUPM*, VI:2160)

Like virtually all such statements by Whitman, these are "off the record," either unpublished, excised from the book versions of the essays, or recorded only in conversations. He kept such statements out of his enduring books, almost as if he recognized his own retrogressive position on race, and deferred to the earlier days of "Lucifer," when he had been more progressive—even radical—in his notions of crossing racial boundaries. In his old age, he supported an exclusive racial identity, even a white America, but he kept erasing all his statements that tended in that direction, working against himself to keep his books—and the Walt Whitman that lived in them—more open to diversity than the old Walt Whitman who lived in Camden, New Jersey, was.

The "Ethiopia" poem thus becomes a key document in understanding Whitman's struggle with the issue of race, for it is the last place in which he still tries to work out some possible future for blacks in America, in which he gives voice to a hope for African Americans. There are vestiges, to be sure, of an evolutionary racialism in the poem; the ancient woman is "hardly human," is caught "as the savage beast is caught," and, as she approaches the soldier, she "ris[es] by the roadside," all suggestions of her low evolutionary position and her primitiveness. But Whitman balances these suggestions with her "high-borne" dignity, her mannered "courtesies to the regiments," and her "ancient" past. "Ancient" offsets primitive, modulating the "hardly human" so that it could suggest either "subhuman" or "superhuman," primitive or mythical. Or both. In his poem, then, as was often the case for Whitman, his ideas of race and of racial assimilation are not as stark or as reductive as in his prose. The poem exists in a realm of ambivalence and confusion, carefully avoiding categorical judgment.

Whitman's confusion and ambivalence occasionally emerge elsewhere, as when he wrestles with the migration of southern blacks north, a movement he calls a "black domination," which was fine as a punishment for the secessionists but had no place in the nation's capital: "The present condition of things (1875) in . . . the former Slave States— . . . a horror and dismay, as of limitless sea and fire, sweeping over them, and substituting the confusion, chaos, and measureless degradation and insult of the present—the black domination, but little above the beasts—viewed as a temporary, deserv'd punishment for their Slavery and Secession sins, may perhaps be admissable; but as a permanency of course is not to be consider'd for a moment" (*PW*, I:326). Whitman worked cautiously, very cautiously, when he put on record anything about his views of race or emancipation. As we have seen, many of his statements on race are parenthetical or in small print in notes at the ends of texts, literally reduced and marginalized, including some of his most progressive-sounding later statements. In the notes following the original book publication of *Democratic Vistas*, for example, Whitman makes his clearest statement of the role of emancipation in the "Secession War": "the abolition of Slavery, and the extirpation of the Slave-holding Class, (cut out and thrown away like a tumor by surgical operation,) makes incomparably the longest advance for Radical Democracy, utterly removing its only really dangerous impediment, and insuring its progress in the United States—and thence, of course, over the world" (*PW*, II:756). Slavery, Whitman says, was one of the "vast life-threatening calculi" in the world, and he celebrates its demise. And still, whispering in notes he would soon move to smaller print as "Notes Left Over," he approaches the giant new question of freed blacks' role in the reunited states: "As to general suffrage, after all, since we have gone so far, the more general it is, the better. I favor the widest opening of the doors. Let the ventilation and area be wide enough, and all is safe" (*PW*, II:530).[49]

"Ethiopia," then, was not an uncharacteristic Whitmanian gesture. Exactly in keeping with his delicate approach to the volatile issue of his day, Whitman loaded much into little, and; in 1881, he floated this small and oddly over-formed poem into the midst of his "Drum-Taps" so as to reconstruct his own view that the abolition of slavery was one of the main purposes for which the war was fought. Nearly two decades after Lincoln had redefined the purposes of the war for the nation, Whitman followed his dear, departed president and inserted the image of a black woman saluting the American flag into his poems of the war to preserve the Union. But he did so only in the most contingent way, through the perspective of a Union soldier who could not understand her gesture. Whitman, finally, shared the soldier's confusion and ambivalence about what emancipation meant.

At the end of the war, when abolitionists came to Charleston harbor to raise the Union flag over Fort Sumter, a black man with his two young children in tow approached William Lloyd Garrison to thank him. In the harbor, a ship decked with American flags was filled with celebrating black people. A white officer said, through tears as the American flag was raised, that "now for the first time [it] is the black man's as well as the white man's flag."[50] Whitman never shared this officer's emotional pride in sharing the flag among the races, but he gradually accommodated himself to the new reality. One of the last works he published in his lifetime was a prose piece he had written during the war but had never printed, an admiring recollection of the "First Regiment U.S. Color'd Troops." Whitman, at the end of his life, returned to his Civil War notes and recalled "a visit I made to the First Regiment U.S. Color'd Troops, at their encampment, and on the occasion of their first paying off, July 11, 1863." He comments positively on the black troops' fighting ability and notes that "few white regiments make a better appearance on parade" than the black troops.[51]

But what he remembers most is the calling out of the names of the black soldiers as they are being paid: "The clerk calls George Washington. That distinguish'd personage steps from the ranks, in the shape of a very black man, good sized and shaped, and aged about 30" (*PW,* II:588). Whitman is fascinated and notes, "There are about a dozen Washingtons in the company. Let us hope they will do honor to the name" (*PW,* II:588). Then he watches another company get paid: "They, too, have great names; besides the Washingtons aforesaid, John Quincy Adams, Daniel Webster, Calhoun, James Madison" (*PW,* II:588). "These, then, are the black troops," Whitman concludes. "Well, no one can see them, even under these circumstances—their military career in its novitiate—without feeling well pleas'd with them" (*PW,* II:589). This scene, which Whitman carefully *does* incorporate, even if belatedly, into his permanent books, offers one of the only glimpses he gives of young black men—former Lucifers—taking their place in America, carrying the revered names of American history and tinting that history with a new shade, suggesting an amalgamation of black and white, of a young black "novitiate" carrying the name of George Washington into America's future. "The officers," Whitman writes, "have a fine appearance, have good faces, and the air military. Altogether it is a significant show, and brings up some 'abolition' thoughts" (*PW,* II:589). It's as if these impressive black soldiers are calling Whitman back to earlier times, to nearly forgotten attitudes, to "'abolition' thoughts."

It may be significant that Whitman concludes his description of these troops by evoking what initially seems an unrelated detail: he leaves the black troops and walks to a solitary place on the "banks of the island" where he watches as "a water snake wriggles down the bank, disturb'd, into the water" (*PW*, II:589). We think back to his notes for his "Lucifer" passage, when Whitman decides to "lend" the "negro" "my own tongue": "I dart like a snake from your mouth." Here, now, late in his life, the snake of dangerous and rebellious expression is wriggling away, disturbed, as Whitman's words of regard for African Americans fade into the past and give way to his far more muted and distanced expressions, no longer speaking *as* the black man, or even *to* him but rather only *about* him.

Another of Whitman's final published recollections records a walk with an Englishman who, upon seeing "a squad of laughing young black girls" and "two copper-color'd boys . . . running after," comments on "What *gay creatures* they all appear to be." The Englishman goes on to note that among the "cultivated" class ("the literary and fashionable folks"), he had "never yet come across what I should call a really GAY-HEARTED MAN."

Whitman calls it "a terrible criticism—cut into me like a surgeon's lance. Made me silent the whole walk home" (*PW*, II:680). In the emerging United States of the final years of the century, Whitman was perhaps beginning to see, even if only reluctantly and tentatively, that the curtsying, assertive, animated black woman—with the Ethiopian flag on her head and the American flag in her eyes—might in fact bring a spirit and a past and a needed difference to a reconstructed American culture.

NOTES

I am grateful to the University of Iowa's Obermann Center for Advanced Studies and its director, Jay Semel, for invaluable support during the writing of this essay.

1. In 1955, Leadie M. Clark devoted an entire book to the debunking of Whitman as "the unqualified lover of all mankind," doggedly tracking Whitman's racialist beliefs and racist statements, concluding that "Whitman disliked the Negro, could not or would not believe in his ability to progress, and saw no place for him in America or the America to come." See *Walt Whitman's Concept of the American Common Man* (New York: Philosophical Library, 1955), 162, 71. Clark's book can be read as an eruption of disillusionment: "Whitman wanted to be a divine literatus . . . But he could offer only a partial dream" (170). Just two years earlier, African-American poet Langston Hughes, who had been taken to task for praising Whitman when he should have condemned him for his racism, offered a much more forgiving response "concerning Walt Whitman's American weaknesses in regard to race." Calling *Leaves of Grass* "a very great book," Hughes acknowledged that Whitman "sometimes contradicted his own highest ideals," but "it is the best of him that we choose to keep and cherish, not his worst." See Hughes, "Like Whitman, Great Artists Are Not Always Good People," *Chicago Defender* (Aug. 1, 1953): 11.

2. There have been two important recent books on Whitman and race: Martin Klammer, *Whitman, Slavery, and the Emergence of "Leaves of Grass"* (University Park: Pennsylvania State University Press, 1995); and Luke Mancuso, *The Strange Sad War Revolving: Walt Whitman, Reconstruction, and the Emergence of Black Citizenship, 1865–1876* (Columbia, S.C.: Camden House, 1997). Both Klammer and

Mancuso were students of mine, and their books are revisions of doctoral dissertations that they wrote under my direction. I want to acknowledge here my high regard for their work and my thanks to both these scholars for their friendship and for what I have learned from their work. Some of the most important other recent works dealing with Whitman and race include Christopher Beach, *The Politics of Distinction: Whitman and the Discourses of Nineteenth-century America* (Athens: University of Georgia Press, 1996), esp. chap. 2, "The Invisible Discourse: Slavery and Subjectivity in *Leaves of Grass*," 55–101; David S. Reynolds, *Walt Whitman's America: A Cultural Biography* (New York: Knopf, 1995), esp. 47–51, 468–80; Karen Sánchez-Eppler, *Touching Liberty: Abolition, Feminism, and the Politics of the Body* (Berkeley: University of California Press, 1993), esp. chapt. 2, "To Stand Between: Walt Whitman's Poetics of Merger and Embodiment," 50–82; and Dana Phillips, "Nineteenth-century Racial Thought and Whitman's 'Democratic Ethnology of the Future,'" *Nineteenth-century Literature* 49 (Dec. 1994): 289–320.

3. This manuscript is located in the Humanities Research Center at the University of Texas in Austin. See Ed Folsom, "Walt Whitman's Working Notes for the First Edition of *Leaves of Grass*," *Walt Whitman Quarterly Review* 16 (Fall 1998): 90–95.

4. These definitions and etymologies are from Noah Webster, *An American Dictionary of the English Language* (Springfield, Mass.: G. & C. Merriam, 1876); similar definitions began appearing in dictionaries of the 1840s.

5. See Joel Myerson, ed., *The Walt Whitman Archive* (New York: Garland, 1993), II:644.

6. See *NYD*, 108–14.

7. It is notable that, just after Lucifer disappeared in Whitman's poetry, *Lucifer, the Light Bearer* surfaced in 1883 as the new name of Moses Harman's Liberal League radical periodical (it had been the *Kansas Liberal*), which gained national notoriety during the 1880s. Whether Whitman's figure of Lucifer stood behind the new name is unclear (Whitman himself was sometimes invoked in defense of the *Lucifer* radicals whose individualist anarchism, "free language" policy, and battle against the "sex slavery" of women often got them in legal trouble), but the name clearly suggested the same kind of angry defiance against authority that Whitman's Lucifer so effectively expressed. The radical publisher Benjamin Tucker, responding

to the renaming of the journal, wrote of *Lucifer* that it was "quite the best name we know of, after Liberty!" Whitman's Lucifer was an effective model for the *Lucifer* freethinkers, who espoused rejection of all authority and freedom from any restriction based on race or gender, and who were not afraid to turn to violence to secure their rights. See Hal D. Sears, *The Sex Radicals: Free Love in High Victorian America* (Lawrence: Regents Press of Kansas, 1977), 53–64, 109.

8. See, for example, Gay Wilson Allen, *The New Walt Whitman Handbook* (New York: New York University Press, 1975), 240; and J. R. LeMaster, "Some Traditional Poems from *Leaves of Grass,*" *Walt Whitman Review* 13 (June 1967): 45–49. Earlier commentary on the poem is sparse but sometimes surprisingly positive: Franklin Benjamin Sanborn in 1876 asked, "How could the whole connection of slavery with the civil war and its results be better summed up than in this strong poem?" (In "Walt Whitman: A Visit to the Good Gray Poet," in Joel Myerson, ed., *Whitman in His Own Time* [Detroit: Omnigraphics, 1991], 12).

9. See Allen, *Handbook,* 240; LeMaster, "Some Traditional Poems," 45–49; John E. Schwiebert, *The Frailest Leaves: Whitman's Poetic Technique in the Short Poem* (New York: Peter Lang, 1992), 86–87; Vaughan Hudson, "Melville's *Battle-Pieces* and Whitman's *Drum-Taps:* A Comparison," *Walt Whitman Review* 19 (Sept. 1973): 81–92; and Betsy Erkkila, *Whitman: The Political Poet* (New York: Oxford University Press, 1989), 241–42.

10. Schwiebert suggests "Ethiopia" represents "a regression by Whitman into the strained mannerisms of his juvenilia: *(Frailest Leaves,* 87), something quite different from the sustaining retreat to form I am suggesting here. Vivian R. Pollak finds Whitman's use of rhyme and meter to be somehow suggestive of his desire to make the slave woman subservient: "In naturalizing an African-born, female figure's sexual and racial subservience, Whitman reverts, appropriately enough, to the traditional, full end-rhyme closure, internal rhyme, and stanzaic regularity of his pre–*Leaves* verse" (In "In Loftiest Spheres': Whitman's Visionary Feminism," in Betsy Erkkila and Jay Grossman, eds., *Breaking Bounds: Whitman and American Cultural Studies* [New York: Oxford University Press, 1996], 95–96).

11. W. T. Bandy, "An Unknown 'Washington Letter' by Walt Whitman," *Walt Whitman Quarterly Review* 2 (Winter 1984): 25.

12. See James M. McPherson, *Battle Cry of Freedom: The Civil War*

Era (New York: Oxford University Press, 1988), 840. Mancuso in *Strange Sad War Revolving* offers a detailed account of how the congressional debates over Reconstruction and the civil rights amendments were important to Whitman as he structured the 1867 and 1871 editions of *Leaves* and as he wrote *Democratic Vistas.* While I disagree with some aspects of Mancuso's assessment of Whitman's racial politics, I find his suggestions about the importance of the congressional debates and the push for federalism compelling.

13. See Blumenbach, *Elements of Physiology,* trans. Charles Caldwell (Philadelphia: Thomas Dobson, 1795).

14. W. Winwood Reade, *Savage Africa: Being the Narrative of a Tour . . .* (New York: Harper & Brothers, 1864); see esp. chap. 4, "The Paradise of the Blacks," 25–33, with its exploration of "Ethiopic character."

15. Reprinted in Ali Mazrui, *The Africans* (Boston: Little, Brown, 1985), 102.

16. Shakespeare used the term in just such a generic way: Claudio in *Much Ado about Nothing,* V.iv, avows that he will marry a woman he has never seen, even "were she an Ethiop"; see also *Midsummer Night's Dream,* III.ii, and *As You Like It,* IV.iii. The *OED* cites fourteenth- and fifteenth-century uses of "Ethiop" as a generic term for "a person with a black skin." The eighteenth-century black American poet Phillis Wheatley, in her poetry, refers to herself as "an Ethiop" (see John C. Shields, ed., *Collected Works of Phillis Wheatley* [New York: Oxford University Press, 1988], 16).

17. *UPP,* I:238.

18. See Joseph J. Rubin, *The Historic Whitman* (University Park: Pennsylvania State University Press, 1973), 132; and Reynolds, *Walt Whitman's America,* 180. "Ethiopian serenader," defined by the *OED* as "a 'nigger' minstrel, a musical performer with face blackened to imitate a negro," had, by the 1860s, become a generic term for black minstrels.

19. See LeMaster, "Some Traditional Poems," 46.

20. One case I've found of such usage is George Templeton Strong's description of a regiment of black soldiers (the Twentieth USCT) marching in New York in March 1864: "Ethiopia marching down Broadway, armed, drilled, truculent, and elate" (see Allan Nevins and Milton Halsey Thomas, eds., *Diary of George Templeton Strong* [New York: Macmillan, 1952], 411–12). This is an interesting de-

scription, evoking the black troops as a whole country or continent overtaking New York, and it relates to Whitman's own descriptions of armed blacks in Washington. My thanks to Dan Lewis for pointing out this passage to me. Another case is Sarah E. Shuften's 1865 poem, "Ethiopia's Dead," which appeared in *Colored American;* the poem is a tribute to fallen black Union soldiers: "Each valley, where battle is poured / It's purple swelling tide, / Beheld brave Ethiopia's sword / With slaughter deeply dyed" (In Paula Bernat Bennett, ed., *Nineteenth-century American Women Poets* [Malden, Mass.: Blackwell, 1998], 443).

21. *NYD,* 31.

22. In "Poem of Salutation" in the same year, Ethiopia is one of the ancient fertile places Whitman imagines himself traveling to: "I see the highlands of Abyssinia, . . . / And see fields of teff-wheat and places of verdure and gold" *(LGC,* 143). Up to the final year of his life, Whitman was still evoking Ethiopia as the home of the "ancient song, . . . *the elder ballads,* . . Ever so far back, preluding thee, America, / Old chants, Egyptian priests, and those of Ethiopia" *(LGC,* 547); Ethiopia here furnishes the first entry in the catalog of human song that evolved into America. For other Whitman notations on Ethiopia as a source of culture and religion, see *NUPM,* IV: 1401, 1566; and *DN,* III: 764.

23. William L. Andrews, ed., *The Oxford Frederick Douglass Reader* (New York: Oxford University Press, 1996), 129.

24. *The Survival of Ethiopian Independence* (London: Heinemann, 1976), 1.

25. In addition to Rubenson's work cited above, the following books have been helpful in piecing together the relevant history I trace out here: Rubenson, *King of Kings: Tewodros of Ethiopia* (Addis Ababa: Haile Sellassie I University, 1966); Richard Greenfield, *Ethiopia: A New Political History* (London: Pall Mall, 1965); Jean Doresse, *Ethiopia* (New York: G. P. Putnam's Sons, 1959); Edward Ullendorff, *The Ethiopians* (London: Oxford University Press, 1960); and E. A. Wallis Budge, *A History of Ethiopia* (1928; rpt., Oosterhout, Netherlands: Anthropological Publications, 1966).

26. See John Livingston Lowes, *The Road to Xanadu* (1927; rpt., Boston: Houghton Mifflin, 1964), 338–43.

27. Whitman occasionally distinguished Ethiopia from Abyssinia (though for most people in the nineteenth century, the names were

synonymous): he associated the Ethiopia of his own time with the "inland" and Abyssinia with the Red Sea coast: *"Abyssinians,* a large fine formed race of Abyssinia, black, athletic, fine heads" *(NUPM,* V:1972).

28. *The American Annual Cyclopaedia and Register of Important Events of the Year 1866* (New York: D. Appleton, 1867), 1; and *The American Annual Cyclopaedia . . . 1868* (New York: D. Appleton, 1869), 2. Further references are abbreviated as the *American Cyclopaedia* and are indicated simply by year and page number.

29. Charles I. Glicksberg, ed., *Walt Whitman and the Civil War: A Collection of Original Articles and Manuscripts* (Philadelphia: University of Pennsylvania Press, 1933), 33. Vivian Pollak sees the slave woman in "Ethiopia" as "a grotesquely aged Mammy who is explicitly described as 'hardly human'" ("Loftiest Spheres," 95); as we will see, Ethiopia is related to the "Mammy," but she suggests something far more than the reductive stereotype that Pollak detects.

30. Robert Penn Warren, ed., *Selected Poems of Herman Melville* (New York: Random House, 1970), 142.

31. Vedder, *The Digressions of V.* (Boston: Houghton Mifflin, 1910), 236.

32. It is worth noting that Phillis Wheatley, in her "To the Right Honourable William, Earl of Darmouth," offers a description of her own "snatching" from Africa that invites comparison to Ethiopia's account in Whitman's poem: "I, young in life, by seeming cruel fate / Was snatch'd from *Afric's* fancy'd happy seat: / What pangs excruciating must molest, / What sorrows labour in my parent's breast?" *(Collected Works,* 74). Wheatley, too, talks of being sundered from her parents, but her speech is elevated, and she speaks from the position of an "I," even though that I is portrayed as the victim of "cruel fate," a companion phrase to Whitman's "cruel slavers." There is no evidence that Whitman knew by Wheatley's work, though it is possible that he did (her work was occasionally discussed in the nineteenth-century histories and handbooks of American literature that also dealt with Whitman's work, and Whitman was inclined to keep close tabs on all the critical works that mentioned him).

33. Joseph Glatthaar, *The March to the Sea and Beyond: Sherman's Troops in the Savannah and Carolinas Campaign* (New York: New York University Press, 1985), 79.

34. Whitman respected General Sherman, who, in 1887, would

be one of the distinguished guests at Whitman's Lincoln lecture. Soon after seeing Sherman at that lecture, Whitman noted, "the Norse make-up of the man—the hauteur—noble, yet democratic," and he admired Sherman's "seamy, sinewy" style.

> The best of Sherman was best in the war but has not been destroyed in peace—though peace brought with it military reviews, banquets, bouquets, women, flirtations, flattery. I can see Sherman now, at the head of the line, on Pennsylvania Avenue, the day the army filed before Lincoln—the silent Sherman riding beyond his aides. Yes, Sherman is all very well: I respect him. *(WWC,* I:257)

Yet Whitman also could shudder at the thought of the man he called "cold-blooded Sherman" *(WWC,* I:406), who knew only one way that war could teach a lesson.

35. See Benjamin Quarles, *The Negro in the Civil War* (1953; rpt., New York: Da Capo, 1989), 314.

36. Corydon Edward Foote, *With Sherman to the Sea: A Drummer's Story of the Civil War,* as related to Olive Deane Hormel (New York: John Day, 1960), 215–16. There are numerous eyewitness accounts of old black slaves greeting the troops and the troops reacting with some confusion. One soldier on Sherman's march recalled slave women reacting as the troops came by: "Two Negro women clap their hands. Jump up and down, and shot 'God bless you,' as we march along"; this soldier particularly recalls "an old Negro over one hundred years of age" (In Loren J. Morse, ed., *Civil War Diaries and Letters of Bliss Morse* [Tahlequah, Okla.: Heritage Printing, 1985], 183–84. Another soldier recalls an old slave woman finding her long-lost daughter, at which point the soldiers had to process the situation before realizing they should react with some emotion: "The soldiers, hard as they seemed to be, were wonderfully moved when they knew what it all meant" (John Potter, *Reminiscences of the Civil War in the United States* [Oskaloosa, Iowa: Globe Presses, 1897], 110).

37. See, for one recent example, Nathanial Mackey, "Phrenological Whitman," *Conjunctions* 29 (1998): 249. Other readers recognize that a fictional narrator speaks, but they still assume that somehow Whitman fully identifies with or controls the narrator. Pollak, for example, says the slave woman "asks only to be accepted as human, though it is not clear that the speaker, depicted as a member of Sher-

man's army . . . , accepts her as such" ("Loftiest Spheres," 96). I am arguing that that is precisely Whitman's point—that he is portraying the irony of a liberating army that is blind to the significance of its actions.

38. Margaret Brobst Roth, ed., *Well Mary: Civil War Letters of a Wisconsin Volunteer* (Madison: University of Wisconsin Press, 1960), 113.

39. M. A. DeWolfe Howe, ed., *Marching with Sherman: Passages from the Letters and Campaign Diaries of Henry Hitchcock* (New Haven, Conn.: Yale University Press, 1927), 251.

40. *The Lunar Light of Whitman's Poetry* (Cambridge, Mass.: Harvard University Press, 1987), 254.

41. While some critics have claimed that Whitman never mentions the issue of slavery in the original *Drum-Taps* (see Clark, *Walt Whitman's Concept,* 64), he does in fact knowledge it. But he does so in two poems that he later removes from the cluster: "Pioneers! O Pioneers!" and "Chanting the Square Deific" (which originally appeared in *Sequel to Drum-Taps).* In "Pioneers," "all the masters with their slaves" become one example of "all the workmen at their work," part of the "Western movement beat" of the pioneers. At best, the reference is ambiguous; at worst, it is an acceptance of slavery as one acceptable form of labor in an expanding America. In "Chanting," Satan, the defiant transgressive force that continually denies authority and redefines limits, calls himself "Comrade of criminals, brother of slaves, . . . With sudra face and worn brow, black, but in the depths of my heart, proud as any" *(LGC,* 444). This aspect of Satan hints of slave revolt and seems related to the Lucifer passage of "The Sleepers," but, as we have seen, Whitman excised that passage after Reconstruction ended; it disappeared from his 1881 edition, by which point he had thoroughly altered the quasi-abolitionist rhetoric of his poetry. Like many antislavery writers, Whitman's radical identification with blacks diminished when slavery ended and when the much more difficult era of assimilation and equal rights began. "With the exception of the 'hardly human' black woman in 'Ethiopia Saluting the Colors,'" writes Erkkila, "black people are absent from his poetry of the postwar years, and in his letters and journals of the time, blacks remain on the periphery of his vision as sources of dread and emblems of retribution" *(Political Poet,* 240).

42. *ISit,* 90. For a fuller contextualization of Whitman's comments in this editorial, see Jerome Loving, *Walt Whitman: The Song of Himself* (Berkeley: University of California Press, 1999), 230–32.

43. Abraham Lincoln, *Speeches and Writings, 1859–1865* (New York: Library of America, 1989), 32.

44. *The Black Image in the White Mind: The Debate on Afro-American Character and Destiny, 1817–1914* (Middletown, Conn.: Wesleyan University Press, 1971), 165.

45. Thomas Carlyle, *Critical and Miscellaneous Essays* (London: Chapman and Hall, 1899), IV:348.

46. Mancuso hears Whitman's tone in this passage as "satiric" and believes that Whitman "neutralizes" Carlyle's "racism through satire"; he also suggests that Whitman's later deletion of the passage simply indicates that he found the whole argument "anachronistic because of the successful ratification of the Fifteenth Amendment in 1870" *(Strange Sad War Revolving, 74–75).*

47. Kenneth M. Price, "Whitman's Solutions to 'The Problem of the Blacks,'" *Resources for American Literary Study* 15 (Autumn 1985): 205–8.

48. Geoffrey Sill, "Whitman on 'The Black Question': A New Manuscript," *Walt Whitman Quarterly Review* 8 (Fall 1990): 69–75.

49. Such momentary clarity, however, is inevitably undercut by the return of Whitman's ambivalence. In his "Small Memoranda," published in *November Boughs* (1888), he once again puts in print for the first time some of his Civil War–era notes. Observing in August 1865 the procession of southerners seeking formal "special pardons" from the government; Whitman seems approving that every pardon is granted "with the condition that the grantee shall respect the abolition of slavery, and never make an attempt to restore it." At the same time, Whitman endorses President Johnson's refusal to "countenance at all the demand of the extreme Philo-African element of the North, to make the right of negro voting at elections a condition and *sine qua non* of the reconstruction of the United States south, and of their resumption of co-equality in the Union" *(PW,* II:611). Here, again, Whitman underscores what are his most common positions: for the abolition of slavery, against equal rights for the freed slaves.

50. Eric Foner, *Reconstruction: America's Unfinished Revolution, 1863–1877* (New York: Harper & Row, 1988), 62.

51. Whitman was, after the war, increasingly cognizant of the contributions of African Americans to the Union cause; in *Specimen Days,* he approvingly cites James A. Garfield's 1879 comments in the House of Representatives, in which the future president (whom Whitman knew personally) reminded Americans of the diversity of those who fought for the Union: "Do they remember that 186,000 color'd men fought under our flag against the rebellion and for the Union, and that of that number 90,000 were from the States which went into rebellion?" (*PW,* I:63).

The Political Roots of *Leaves of Grass*

Jerome Loving

Late in life in working-class Camden, New Jersey, Walt Whitman was surrounded by an array of liberal thinkers and literary progressives. Visitors to 328 Mickle Street included the prairie naturalist and future author of *Main-Traveled Roads*, Hamlin Garland; the future author of *Dracula*, Bram Stoker; the future wife of art critic Bernard Berenson, Mary Smith Costolloe; the future (first) wife of philosopher Bertrand Russell, Mary's sister Alys; the painter Thomas Eakins; and Julian Hawthorne, the son of Whitman's main literary model when he was writing fiction in the 1840s. For most of them (even Eakins, whose realistic, sometimes stark paintings were then considered untutored), the operative word was "future." Certainly, it was the shibboleth for such socialists and activists as the poet's biographer Horace Traubel, editor of the *Conservator,* who corresponded at length with radicals like Emma Goldman and Eugene Debs, and the silver-tongued agnostic and attorney Robert G. Ingersoll, whose pamphlet publications included "Crimes Against Criminals." Whitman had kept the same kind of company in Brooklyn in the 1850s, when he was encircled by abolitionists, Free-Soilers, protofeminists, and neo–Transcendentalists. Today, we tend to see the poet as politically "conservative" in his old age, but the contrast between his moderate political views and his radical friends at the close of his life points up a lifelong contradiction that is probably best summed up in these lines from "Song of Myself":

> Do I contradict myself?
> Very well then I contradict myself,
> (I am large, I contain multitudes.)

One subject that came up repeatedly in those Mickle Street conversations recorded in Traubel's *With Walt Whitman in Camden* (1906–96) was Henry George's then-popular idea of the "Single Tax." In 1855, the same year as the first *Leaves of Grass*, George, as a cabin boy, had sailed to Australia and India and was appalled by the extremes of poverty and wealth, which he also later observed in the American West and eastern cities. Later, as a journalist and economic philosopher, he observed in *Progress and Poverty* (1879) that while the economy was turning out new millionaires by the hundreds, the ranks of the impoverished appeared to be expanding exponentially. The culprit, he said, was private property, which limited interest and wages to marginal gains while its owners, or landlords, who were essentially nonproducers, reaped all the economic and social benefits. Since labor, not capital, increased the value of unused land through population increase and the corresponding development of the economy, its profit should be taxed as a "community-created value." His "single tax" would have shifted the tax burden from buildings to unused land, mostly owned by the rich (e.g., railroads) who would now pay taxes for the rest. Whether, as Traubel notes, Whitman possessed "any understanding of the peculiar base of the theory," the poet in spite of his vision in *Leaves of Grass*—indeed because of it—never put his unchecked faith in social panaceas.

"I would not put a straw in the way of the Anarchists, Socialists, Communists, Henry George men," he said, objecting in general to the idea of social cure-alls. "Is that not the attitude of every special reformer? Look at Wendell Phillips—great and grand as he was. . . . He was one-eyed, saw nothing, absolutely nothing, but that single blot of slavery. And if Phillips of old, others today." His "contention" for reform, he said, echoing Ralph

Waldo Emerson's American Scholar Address of 1837, was "for the whole man—the whole corpus—not one member—not a leg, an arm, a belly alone, but the entire corpus. . . . I know it is argued for this that [the "Single Tax"] will bring about great changes in the social system. . . . But I don't believe it—don't believe it at all."[1]

Emerson spoke out relatively early in the abolitionist campaign against slavery, if not as vigorously as Phillips, but he, like Whitman, never saw abolition as a social panacea.[2] Also flanked by reformers (including his second wife Lidian) most of his life, Emerson was never a fully committed social reformer himself. Both poets believed that social progress had to begin at home, with the individual. Yet at their literary heights, or at least immediately before or after, both Emerson and Whitman became involved with specific reform movements. Emerson spoke out against slavery long before the Fugitive Slave Law of 1850, beginning with his 1844 Address on the Tenth Anniversary of Emancipation in the West Indies. Whitman as well was preoccupied with the good of the group in his journalistic heyday, the long decade leading up to the first *Leaves of Grass*, as he edited and wrote for various newspapers, including the *Brooklyn Daily Eagle*.

Whitman's adult journalist career began with the founding of his own newspaper, the *Long-Islander*, in 1838. After teaching briefly, around 1840, he began writing for literary magazines; he edited at least one paper, the *Aurora*, for a month in 1842; and he freelanced for a number of others, including the *Evening Tattler*, the *New York Sun*, the *New York Mirror*, and the *Brooklyn Evening Star*. For almost two years, from 1846 to 1848, he was the editor of the *Eagle*. The issues he championed there in editorials, as well as in poems and short fiction, included opposition to the death penalty, improved schools, fairer wages for sewing women, personal hygiene, and temperance. Unfortunately, Whitman's journalism—where many of his political beliefs were either formed or developed—is the one area not altogether edited for scholarly consumption in the New York University Press edition of Whitman's *Collected Writings*.

Although Whitman's tenure on the *Eagle* has now been examined by Thomas L. Brasher, and many of his newspaper editorials have been edited in different collections,[3] not everything from the *Eagle* that Whitman wrote has been recovered and reprinted. Generally, what has been unearthed suggests a political moderate who asked for a fair chance for his own class but nothing more. Perhaps he believed that their "average" status was what made the working classes politically "divine," their lack of political and social power involuntarily distancing them from the materialism that blinded their capitalist "landlords." The first *Leaves*, as I have argued in my biography of the poet, came largely from Whitman's immediate blue-collar experiences, from the Ryerson Street neighborhoods of mechanics and Brooklyn shipyard workers on the eastern edge of expanding Brooklyn, where he finished the book in May 1855.[4] What we find in the first *Leaves of Grass* is not the suffering and oppression of his class but its stamina and diversity as human beings, as fathers and mothers, sisters and brothers, butchers and "counter jumpers," lawyers and firemen—in a sense, the old neighborhood as representative of the new world of Jacksonian democracy. In what was later entitled "To Think of Time," he describes a stage driver who died—not particularly "young" for the time—at age forty-one. Neither socially oppressed nor absolutely impoverished, he succumbed mainly to his voracious love of life.

He was a good fellow,
Freemouthed, quicktempered, not badlooking, able to take his own part,
Witty, sensitive to a slight, ready with life or death for a friend,
Fond of women . . . played some . . eat ["et"] hardy and drank hearty
Had known what it was to be flush . . grew lowspirited toward the last . . sickened, was helped by a contribution.

In another poem of the first edition, later called "I Sing the Body Electric," it is not, as most modern readings suggest, merely the body of sexual desire or that of a slave at auction that is prominent but the daily and enduring experience of the "common farmer," the "father of five sons," whose person is something of a neighborhood miracle—in the transcendentalist sense that life itself is always a miracle.

This man was of wonderful vigor and calmness and beauty of person,
The shape of his head, the richness and breadth of his manners, the pale yellow and white of his hair and beard, the immeasurable meaning of his black eyes,
These I used to go and visit him to see . . . . He was wise also,
He was six feet tall . . . . he was over eighty years old . . . his sons were massive clean bearded tanfaced and handsome,
They and his daughters loved him . . . all who saw him loved him . . . they did not love him by allowance . . . they loved him with personal love;
He drank water only . . . . the blood showed like scarlet through the clear brown skin of his face;

....

You would wish long and long to be with him . . . . you would wish to sit by him in a boat that you and he might touch each other.[5]

The most important poem of the first edition was, like the eleven others, initially untitled. Between 1860 and 1881, "Song of Myself" was called "Walt Whitman" because it evoked Emerson's representative poet at the center of the neighborhood, the poet who speaks for the rest—"what I assume you shall assume." The Brooklyn neighborhood in turn served Whitman as a microcosm for American democracy, just as nature serves as an emblem and microcosm of the Creator. Here we have the long catalog of such artisans and laborers: the carpenter dressing his plank, the "married and unmarried children" riding home to Thanksgiving dinner, the harbor pilot, the ship's mate, deacons, spinning girls, farmers (Whitman's grandfather, Cornelius Van Velsor), and even a lunatic (modeled perhaps after the poet's youngest sibling, Edward, possibly the victim of Down's syndrome).

By the time he wrote "Song of Myself," Whitman had exorcised whatever demons he had absorbed from the unstable economic and perhaps alcoholic turmoil in his family, as well as the shame of having to attend a poverty school in Brooklyn. The three influences most often credited for Whitman's transformation from journalist to poet are Emerson, the Italian opera, and the New Testament. From the first, he got his vision of the born-again individualist; through the second, this self-reliant vision was dramatized and heightened through the sound of the human voice on the operatic stage; and from the third, he absorbed the altruistic spirit of the Bible's central character, Jesus Christ. But we must add to this trinity (as Whitman added evil to the Holy Trinity in "Chanting the Square Deific") the turbulence of the times over the question of slavery, which led to the Civil War and Whitman's Christ-like mission in the military hospitals in Washington. His early poetry was generally maudlin and conventional, but the Compromise of 1850, which postponed the southern "rebellion" a decade by putting new teeth into the existing Fugitive Slave Law, gave him an original topic as well as his free-verse rhythm, which echoed, perhaps, the fiery speeches of that particular political period. Newspapers of the day reprinted many of the debates and speeches about the slavery issue, utterances full of American vernacular and the colloquial diction of its angry sarcasm.

Agitation for the compromise began in late January 1850 with a speech in favor of it by Henry Clay; this was followed by Daniel Webster's notorious "Seventh of March" speech in which the chief political spokesperson for New England abolitionists capitulated to slaveholding interests. Whitman, bitter from the recent defeat of the Wilmot Proviso, or Free-Soil campaign, which would have banned slavery outright from the western territories, entered the political fray with four antislavery poems. In a little over ninety days that winter and spring, between March 2 and June 14, he published two apiece in William Cullen Bryant's *New York Evening Post* and Horace Greeley's *New York Tribune*. "Song for Certain Congressmen" (later "Dough-Face Song") called Congress faceless as well as spineless for caving in to slavocracy interests. It appeared in the *Post* on March 2, as did "Blood-Money" on April 30, castigating Webster, naming him Judas.

("Blood-Money" is Whitman's first free-verse poem.) These were followed by two poems in the *Tribune* of June 14 and 21: "House of Friends" and "Resurgemus" (later "Europe").

Like Henry David Thoreau in "Resistance to Civil Government" (the Concord Saunterer would soon become an admirer of *Leaves of Grass*), Whitman thought the main obstacle to abolition was not southern slaveholders but the political representatives of northern merchants who profited from cheap slave labor.

> Virginia, mother of greatness,
> Blush not for being also mother of slaves.
> You might have borne deeper slaves—

Instead (and Whitman's fondness for the South, based on his three-month visit to New Orleans in 1848, should be noted), the true culprits were the hypocrites of the North.

> Doughfaces, Crawlers, Lice of Humanity—
> Terrific screamers of Freedom
> Who roar and bawl, and get hot i' the face, . . .
>
> ....
>
> Muck-worms, creeping flat to the ground,
> A dollar dearer to them than Christ's blessing. ("The House of Friends")

Congress, controlled by northern Democrats, who defeated the Free-Soil efforts in the 1840s, was "The House of Friends" (Whitman's title here), which would threaten the "good cause" of democracy from within.

One and all, Whitman's antislavery poems castigated the powerful for their betrayal of the poor and the principles of democracy, which were supposed to have protected them. Later, around 1854, he began to compose a political screed entitled "The Eighteenth Presidency!" that also assailed efforts to move slavery into the western territories and future states. The same year, he penned "A Boston Ballad" in reaction to the Anthony Burns incident in which the newly strengthened Fugitive Slave Law was tested in the national press and on the streets of Boston. The fugitive slave's forced return in chains to Virginia was so well publicized that Whitman felt he could write a poem about it without making any direct reference to the actual incident (confusing readers without a historical note today). Yet, aside from "The Eighteenth Presidency!" (which he never published) and "A Boston Ballad," which became another of the untitled poems in the first edition of *Leaves of Grass*, Whitman fell silent poetically until 1855. And, aside from the slave auction catalog in "I Sing the Body Electric," whose working title in a manuscript note to the 1855 edition was "Slaves,"[6] Whitman never again took up the question of slavery directly in his poetry.

As noted earlier, Whitman's journalism is known for its moderation, as well as its empathy with the working poor. This Whitman got from the Jacksonian spirit of his father, who was born on the eve of the French Revolution in 1789. The senior Walt, or Walter, admired radicals such as Fanny Wright and Thomas Paine, but the working-class perspective that he passed along to his son kept this radicalism tempered with reason and practicality. The future poet in the 1840s wrote mostly to improve on local matters of importance to the working middle class: better ventilated schools, music as part of the curriculum, no corporal punishment, regular visits to the neighborhood public baths, temperance, crime abatement, affordable housing, proper conduct for apprentices, and so on.

The main mission of newspapers in antebellum America, aside from being mouthpieces for this or that political view, was to promote the improvement of manners in a society whose democracy sometimes encouraged frontier behavior in an urban setting. Whitman came to his editorial posts as a teacher-journalist. Shortly before leaving his last teaching post on Long Island for New York City in the spring of 1841, he had authored a series of essays under the general heading "Sun-Down Papers from the Desk of a Schoolmaster." These editorials contained advice to "Our young men" regarding the hazards of smoking too many cigars, their envy of the rich, their dress and activities as apprentices, as well as more philosophical musings on personal ambition and the battle of the sexes.[7]

He continued this kind of journalistic preaching through his editorship on the *Eagle*, which he assumed on or around March 5, 1846. Six months into the job, he noted that the age of European chivalry had passed away: "Knights go forth no more, clad in the brazen armor, to redress the wrongs or the injury of the weak. . . . The time of the fluttering of pennants in the breeze, while, 'ladies faire' look down upon a sort of feudal boxing match, is also departed." Though this democrat admired Queen Victoria personally and came to love the British for their early acceptance of *Leaves of Grass*, Whitman hated England's aristocratic ways and wanted none of those artificial distinctions in America. "At this hour in some part of the earth," Whitman prophesied—as Karl Marx was already writing the early drafts of *Das Kapital*—"it may be, that the delicate scraping of a pen over paper, like the nibbling of little mice, is at work which shall show its results sooner or later in the convulsion of the social or political world. Amid penury and destitution, unknown and unnoticed, a man may be toiling on to the completion of a book destined to gain acclamations, reiterated again and again, from admiring America and astonished Europe!"[8]

Possibly, Whitman may have been entertaining the idea of writing such a book, and, in "Sun-Down Papers No. 7," he threatens to write one: "And who shall say that it might not be a very pretty book? Who knows but that I might do something very respectable?"[9] *Leaves of Grass* in 1845 would more than likely have been a long, leftist-leaning speech, a political version of the 1855 preface about the state of American literature. The point here is that Whitman in the 1840s was undergoing a shift in politics or, at least, a sea change as to how to implement his argument for his own kind. (Near the end of the decade, he found himself in transition from a single political point of view to the one in *Leaves of Grass,* which embraces all points of view: "I am large, I contain multitudes").

In this, he was undoubtedly influenced by the political conversation of the time, largely orchestrated by Horace Greeley's *Tribune,* to which Marx contributed. At the beginning of the 1840s, the *Tribune* popularized the writings of French socialist philosopher Charles Fourier, who had died in 1837. This was the year of

America's first major economic depression, which led to disillusionment about capitalism and a decade of reform movements the way the disenchantment over the Vietnam War of the 1960s and 1970s sparked reforms still simmering today. In the 1840s, the social consensus was challenged by the creation of utopian communities, the embryonic abolition movement, and the first women's rights convention in 1848. Emerson, who watched Amos Bronson Alcott quickly succumb to nature's reality in his utopian experiment at Harvard, Massachusetts ("Fruitlands"), did not join the utopian community of Brook Farm, which eventually became Fourieristic under the leadership of Greeley's associate Alfred Brisbane. Emerson cataloged Whitmanesquely in "New England Reformers" the "projects for the salvation of the world."

> One apostle thought all men should go to farming, and another that no man should buy or sell, that the use of money was the cardinal evil; another that the mischief was in our diet, that we eat and drink damnation. These [Mrs. Alcott among them at "Fruitlands"] made unleavened bread, and were foes to the death to fermentation. . . . Others attacked the system of agriculture, the use of animal manures in farming, and the tyranny of men over brute nature; these abuses polluted his food. The ox must be taken from the plough and the horse from the cart, the hundred acres of the farm must be spaded, and the man must walk, wherever boats and locomotives will not carry him. Even the insect world was to be defended. . . . Others assailed particular vocations, as that of the lawyer, that of the merchant, or the manufacturer, of the clergyman, of the scholar. Others attacked the institution of marriage as the fountain of social evils. Others devoted themselves to the worrying of churches and meetings for public worship; and the fertile forms of antinomianism among the elder puritans seemed to have their match in the plenty of the new harvest of reform.[10]

Surely one of the leading advocates of the social upheaval Emerson satirized was Horace Greeley. By 1846, as the national memory of the depression of 1837 began to fade, absorbed by the

new sense of nationalism begot by President James Polk's expansionist program leading to the Mexican War (1846–48), Greeley, found himself increasingly denounced for his quasi-socialist ideas regarding labor reform. This criticism was fueled by the famous "Socialistic Discussion," a debate between Greeley of the *Tribune* and Henry Raymond, a former *Tribune* employee and soon to become the founder of its most serious competitor, the *New York Times*. The debate took place in the pages of the *Tribune* and the *New York Courier and Enquirer* between November 20, 1846, and May 20, 1847.

As his *Recollections of a Busy Life* (1868) details, Greeley grew up as land-poor as those Henry George later envisioned as the proper beneficiaries of his "Single Tax." Greeley was the son of an unsuccessful tenant farmer in the rocky soil of New Hampshire. After spending his youth helping his father clear and farm unproductive land, he became a printer and later a journalist. His journalistic success was due to hard work and the genius of seizing the undeveloped issues of the day, which led him through several journalistic stints culminating in the founding of the *Tribune* in 1842. As a Universalist, he believed that man was naturally good and deserving of an equal share of not only eternal salvation but temporal prosperity.[11] Raymond was a Presbyterian who believed in the inherent evil or laziness of man, which the capitalistic system discouraged. According to Greeley's first biographer, his contemporary James Parton, the catalyst for the debate was a challenge in the *Tribune* by Brisbane upon his return from a politically troubled Europe, proposing certain social questions and inviting responses.[12]

In his opening argument on November 20, Greeley became probably the first public advocate of what we know today as welfare, or the eventual relocation of the source of charity from private hands to the public sector, or government, by the middle of the twentieth century. He certainly anticipated George's proposal for the "Single Tax" by calling for a redistribution of the world's bounty. Not necessarily opposing society's landlords, he nevertheless insisted upon "man's natural right to use any portion of the Earth's surface not actually in use by another." Yet by law, he said, "the landless have no inherent right to stand on a single square of the State of New York, except in the highways." The landless condition of the essentially homeless often led to joblessness, and yet there was no provision for such "Pauperism" other than the misery of the almshouses. "Society exercises no paternal guardianship over the poor man, until he has surrendered to despair. He may spend a whole year and his little all in vainly seeking employment, and all this when his last dollar is exhausted, and his capacities very probably prostrated by the intoxicating draughts to which he is driven to escape the horrors of reflection." Society required a radical change in order to guarantee full employment, and the change was to be found in Association.

Greeley defined Association as the merging of capital and labor under one, quasi-socialist umbrella to produce a better life for everyone, capitalist and laborer alike. He argued that "Civilization" must become "Association," in which the wealth is redistributed more equally. "Under the present system," he said, "Capital is everything, Man nothing, except as a means of accumulating capital." Raymond countered that such a system, which applied one standard to everyone without regard to talent or industry, would severely restrict individual freedom and social progress. It was also impractical to think that an association of previously "indolent or covetous persons" would improve without "*the moral transformation of its members*." And moral reconstruction had to begin with the individual, not society: "individual reform must precede any attempt at social reform." At that point, Greeley argued that the system itself created the poor, while Raymond insisted that indolence was the culprit. It is "not the Social System which abuses the bounty of the benevolent, "he concluded," it is simply the dishonesty and indolence of individuals, and they would do the same under any system, and especially in Association."

Greeley's point—that the capitalistic system and not the individual was responsible—had been discussed before in the press. In fact, about a year before the Greeley-Raymond exchange began, Whitman himself had sounded a similar if not identical note in "A Dialogue," published in the *Brooklyn Evening Star*. He argued against capital punishment mainly because the condemned were usually the victims of unavoidable poverty. In this piece, also published in the *Democratic Review*, society and a death-row inmate debate the merits and demerits of a social system predicated on capitalism. The convicted murderer asks whether society itself has committed any crimes, and the reply is: "None which the law can touch." Then, Whitman goes on in the same vein as Greeley, effectively blaming society and capitalism for crime.

> True, one of us had a mother [society says], a weak-souled creature, that pined away month after month, and at last died, because her dear son was intemperate, and treated her ill. Another, who is the owner of many houses thrusts a sick family into the street because they did not pay their rent, whereof came the deaths of two little children. And another—that particularly well dressed man—effected the ruin of a young girl, a silly thing who afterward became demented, and drowned herself in the river. One has gained much wealth by cheating his neighbors—but cheating so as not to come within the clutches of any statute.[13]

This sounds like Greeley in his attempt to blame crime on society instead of on the individual, though Whitman later in the piece seems to indicate that crime ought to be punished—though not with death, which only God should dictate. (He was similarly stubborn in "The Eighteenth Presidency!" in which he opposed slavery but still insisted that the fugitive slaves must be returned to their owners as long as the Constitution did not forbid slavery.)[14] Yet, in the beginning of "A Dialogue," he suggests that the root of crime is with the society and not the individual.[15]

While the Greeley-Raymond debate was still in progress, Whitman, as editor of the *Brooklyn Daily Eagle,* published two poems that allude to the general state of the worker in a capitalist society. It is at least remotely possible that Whitman is their author, for they employ iambic trimeter and tetrameter, Whitman's early, pre–*Leaves of Grass* choice for his conventionally metered poems. Whether they are from the poet's pen is quite beside the point, however, because they were no doubt selected by Whitman in his role as editor.

The first, published January 7, 1847, is entitled "There Must Be Something Wrong." It alternates between iambic trimeter and tetrameter and also employs an alternating rhyme.

When earth produces, free and fair,
  The golden waving corn;
When fragrant fruits perfume the air;
  And fleecy flocks are shorn;
When thousands move with aching head
  And sing this ceaseless song—
"We starve, we die, o, give us bread."
When wealth is wrought as reasons roll,
  From off the fruitful soil;
When luxury from pole to pole
  Reaps fruit of human toil,
When from a thousand, one alone,
  In plenty rolls along;
The others only gnaw the bone,
  There must be something wrong.

And when production never ends,
  The earth is yielding ever;
A copious harvest oft begins,
  But distribution—never!
When toiling millions work to fill
  The wealthy coffers strong;
When hands are crushed that work and till,
  There must be something wrong.

When poor men's tables waste away,
  To barrenness and drought;
There must be something in the way,
  That's worth the finding out;
With surfeits our great table bends,
  While numbers move along;
While scarce a crust their board extends,
  There must be something wrong.

Then let the law give equal right
To wealthy and to poor;
Let freedom crush the arm of might,
We ask for nothing more;
Until this system is begun,
The burden of our song
Must, and can be, only one—
There must be something wrong.

The poem, in ballad measure, resembles the Chartist verse of working-class English between 1837 and 1848 (when Parliament, nervous about the European revolutions of 1848, rejected the "People's Charter"). It appears to lend direct support to Greeley's point in his opening argument in the debate with Raymond about greedy capitalists taking most of the profit out of the land and certainly supports Henry George's point in arguing for the "Single Tax." "When wealth is wrought" while "others only gnaw the bone," the poem argues, it is time for redistribution according to social needs over personal talents. Nature, this poet observes, is "yielding ever," but "distribution—never!" The answer is to give "equal right to wealthy and to poor." No social progress can be made here unless "this system" (Association) is begun.

Whitman usually went with the little people, but he also held them mainly responsible for their failures, as the following poem suggests. "The Laborer," published in the *Eagle* of February 5, 1847, urges a self-respect based on a rather pragmatic reading of Transcendentalism and Emerson's idea of self-reliance. Though more open in form than the first and of a different tempo, it also alternates rhyme but employs—roughly—iambic tetrameter. It also exhibits enjambment, common to his early poems but almost entirely absent from *Leaves of Grass*.

Stand—erect! Thou hast the form
and likeness of thy God!—who more?
A soul as dauntless 'mid the storm
Of daily life, as warm
And pure as breast e're wore.

What then? thou art true a MAN
As moves the human mass along,
As much a part of the Great Plan
That with creation's dawn began,
As any of the throng.

Who is thine enemy?—the high
In station, or in wealth the chief?
The great, who coldly pass thee by,
With proud step and averted eye?
Nay! nurse not such belief.

If true unto thyself though wast,
What were the proud one's scorn to thee?
A feather, which though mightest cast
Aside, as idle as the blast
The light leaf from the tree.

No: uncurb'd passions—low desires—
Absence of noble self-respect—
Death in the breast's consuming fires,
To that high nature which aspires
For ever, till thus checked.

These are thine enemies—thy worst;
They chain thee to thy lowly lot—
Thy labour and thy life accurst,
Oh, stand thou free, and from them burst!
And longer suffer not!

Thou art thyself thine enemy!
The great! what better they than thou?
As theirs, is not thy will as free?
Has God with equal favours thee
Neglected to endow?

True, wealth thou hast not; 'tis but dust!
Nor place: uncertain as the wind!
But that thou hast, which, with thy crust
And water, may despise the lust
of both—a noble mind.

With this, and passions under ban,
True faith, and holy trust in God,
Thou are the peer of any man.
Look up then—that thy little span
Of life may be well trod!

Although the title of this poem promises an echo of the ideology in "There Must Be Something Wrong," it is actually an antidote to Greeley's pleas for the unworking poor and a reiteration of Raymond's Christian positivism. The themes of both poems reappear as opposite poles of Whitman's blend of social compassion and Emersonian individuality in the first edition of *Leaves of Grass*.

The 1855 preface signals Whitman's intention to celebrate America poetically rather than criticize it politically as he does in his antislavery poems and "The Eighteenth Presidency!" Here, the United States is "essentially the greatest poem," and its leaders are no longer "dough-face" congressmen but ideally "American poets," who "are to enclose old and new." "Presidents shall not be [this poetical people's] common referee so much as their poets." Now their greatest poet (enter Walt Whitman) "hardly knows [the] pettiness or triviality" of politics. In *Leaves of Grass,* liberty is threatened more by historical amnesia than slavery: "when the memories of old martyrs are faded utterly away." Hence, "A Boston Ballad," one of the two overtly political poems in the first *Leaves of Grass*, focuses not upon the current event of Anthony Burns's forced return to slavery (the details of which are missing from the poem) but, instead, examines the way this event manifests a betrayal of the grand movers and shakers of the Revolution. "What troubles you, Yankee phantoms?" the narrator asks of the ghosts of the founders. "What is all this chattering of bare gums?" With the sad state of liberty in 1854, Americans might as well "dig out King George's coffin . . . unwrap him quick from the graveclothes . . . box up his bones for a journey" and bring him back to "Boston bay." For with the Fugitive Slave Act alive and kicking in the Cradle of Liberty, George III might as well be ruling again over the colonies.[16]

The other political poem in the first *Leaves of Grass* was originally entitled "Resurgemus" in 1850 and had, of course, no title in 1855. Finally entitled "Europe, the 72d and 73d Years of These States," it recounts the failure of the European revolutions of 1848. Readers have wondered why this 1850 poem became a part of a book about the Transcendentalist present, but it serves the same purpose as "A Boston Ballad" and the political parts of the preface: to remind us of the former journalist now to be absorbed into the poetical present. The fact that the poem immediately precedes "A Boston Ballad" suggests a historical cause-and-effect of a democracy without ethical leadership. First it is lost abroad, then at home. The other ten poems of the book (perhaps originally one poem) generally follow the route of Emerson's American Scholar, for whom action, while important to his or her education, is inferior to nature and books that inspire. "Apart from the pulling and hauling stands what I am," Whitman proclaims in his most Emersonian poem, "Song of Myself." "Backward I see in my own days where I sweated through fog with linguists and contenders, / [Now] I have no mockings or arguments . . . I witness and wait."[17]

In his repeated attempts to promote himself and his book, especially after the war, Whitman cultivated the myth of having emerged with his poetical vision after traveling the country for two years. Whitman had seen a good part of the United States (as it was then constituted) when he traveled to and from New Orleans by way of the Ohio and Mississippi rivers and the Great Lakes. But the actual journey behind *Leaves of Grass* had been political, as his journalism and antislavery writings—including his editorship of the *Freeman*, a Free-Soil and abolitionist newspaper, in 1848 and 1849—suggest.

Whitman had taken quite a beating as editor of the *Freeman*. After producing his first (and only extant) issue on September 9, 1848, a conflagration—set possibly by proslavery interests—destroyed several blocks of the Brooklyn neighborhood that housed his newspaper. By the time he got the operation going again in the spring of 1849, the pro–Wilmot forces that had financed the *Freeman* had begun to weaken, and ultimately they gave in to the demands of the local and national Democrats, who now clearly opposed Wilmot. Whitman left in a huff on September 11, 1849, announcing, "I withdraw utterly from the Brooklyn *Daily Freeman.* To those who have been my friends, I take occasion to proffer the warmest thanks of a grateful heart. My enemies—and old Hunkers [conservative Democrats] generally—I disdain and defy the same as ever."[18] This experience and its anger (intensified perhaps by frequent unemployment in the 1850s) led to the antislavery poems full of expletives as in, for example, "The House of Friends" ("Doughfaces, Crawlers, Lice of Humanity").

Beginning in 1855, however, Whitman became an observer of life, the "witness" who *waits.*[19] Having exhausted his journalistic opportunities and having given up (no doubt because of the pitiful congressional debate over the Compromise of 1850) fleeting notions of becoming an orator, he combined his journalistic talent with the oratorical impulse to reinvent American poetry. Ever afterward, he determined that his efforts in life would be almost exclusively poetical and devoted to *Leaves of Grass.* "It seems to me quite clear and determined," he told himself as he prepared his second (1856) edition, "that I should concentrate my powers [on] 'Leaves of Grass'—not diverting any of my means, strength, interest to the construction of anything else."[20] Politics, that consuming interest that had brought forth the poetry, lay in the wake of his "bookmaking" during the second half of his life. Written immediately before, during, and after the central political event of the American nineteenth century, *Leaves of Grass* became his lens, through which everything was filtered. "My book and the war are one," he could even say in "To Thee Old Cause" (1871). Practically every experience got filtered into *Leaves of Grass* or its companion volume in 1876, *Two Rivulets,* which first collected the prose that was sorted out and arranged in *Specimen Days and Collect* in 1883.

Through this filter, politics became history—or poetry that celebrates (and laments) the human condition. "My book and I," Whitman exulted in the only prose he did not ultimately exclude from *Leaves of Grass,* "A Backward Glance o'er Travel'd Roads," "what a period we have presumed to span! those thirty years from 1850 to '80—and America in them!"[21] While cataloging its grittier conditions along with the sublime, he sees his "neighborhood" fellows, or humankind, as timeless extensions of nature (and thus God). The connection is poignantly made in Whitman's poems about death. In "Whispers of Heavenly Death," for example, death is the ultimate connection to life, nature, and God.

Whispers of heavenly death murmur'd I hear,
Labial gossip of night, sibilant chorals,
Footsteps gently ascending, mystical breezes wafted soft and low,
Ripples of unseen rivers, tides of a current flowing, forever flowing,
(Or it is the plashing of tears? the measureless waters of human
  tears?) (*LGC,* 442 [n.21])

A reader after the war of the Stoic philosophers, he often quoted Epictetus's statement that "what is good for thee, O nature, is good for me!"[22] To the end of his life, Whitman saw the continuity. In "A Voice from Death," written after the Johnstown flood of 1889, he finds the same link with nature and God.

A voice from Death, solemn and strange, in all his sweep and power,
With sudden, indescribable blow—towns drown'd—humanity by
  thousands slain.
The vaunted work of thrift, goods, dwellings, forge, street, iron
  bridge,
Dash'd pell-mell by the blow—yet usher'd life continuing on,
(Amid the rest, amid the rushing, whirling, wild debris,
A suffering woman saved—a baby safely born!)[23]

By the time of this poem, Whitman was near death himself, indeed had flirted seriously with it through a series of strokes and other ailments since 1888. The Johnstown flood happened on the poet's seventieth birthday. Six months later, he penned "To the Sun-Set Breeze" in which he speaks of hearing the same whisper of heavenly death—and life.

Ah, whispering, something again, unseen,
Where late this heated day thou enterest at my window, door,
Thou, laving, tempering all, cool-freshing, gently vitalizing,
Me, old, alone, sick, weak-down, melted-worn with sweat;

Thou, nestling, folding close and firm yet soft, companion better than talk, book, art,

....

(Distances balk'd—occult medicines penetrating me from head to foot,)
I feel the sky, the prairies vast—I feel the mighty northern lakes,
I feel the ocean and the forest—somehow I feel the globe itself swift-swimming in space;
Thou blown from lips so loved, now gone—haply from endless store, God-sent.[24]

Whitman was "part and parcel" with nature, just as Emerson had described himself in *Nature* (1836). In *Leaves of Grass,* as Emerson's representative poet, Whitman became everyone and everything. Through his book, he absorbed the political poisons along with the vast diversity of democratic life, as America grappled with issues of geographic expansion, slavery, the Mexican War, and the dispute with Great Britain over the Oregon Territory. He went from being a sixth-grade dropout from a Brooklyn poverty school to a political dropout in 1855. At the same time, he dropped out of the school of conventional poetry, which rhymed "blisses" with "kisses" and painted life without libidos and occupations. "Take my leaves America!" Whitman later said in "Starting from Paumanok."

Make welcome for them everywhere, for they are your own offspring;
Surround them, East and West, for they would surround you.[25]

Called "Proto-Leaf" in the 1860 edition, the poem recounts in more linear fashion than the more poetical proto-leaf ("Song of Myself") how this political poet became a full-fledged poet. Whitman made American life whole again, not only as the Poet of Democracy but as the poet of demography, who embraced existence at all levels, from the prostitute to the president. He would later say, "I sit and look out," but he did so only after immersing himself in the multitude of life he later celebrated: Americans of every persuasion and occupation, male and female, black and white. These were the political (and poetical) roots of *Leaves of Grass*.

NOTES

1. *WWC*, V:275.

2. Len Gougeon, *Virtue's Hero: Emerson, Antislavery, and Reform* (Athens: University of Georgia Press, 1990).

3. *BDE; NYA; GF;* and vol. 1 of *Walt Whitman: The Journalism*, ed. Herbert Bergman, Douglas A. Noverr, and Edward J. Recchia (New York: Peter Lang, 1998).

4. Jerome Loving, *Walt Whitman: The Song of Himself* (Berkeley: University of California Press, 1999). For a slightly different view of this evolution, see M. Wynn Thomas, *The Lunar Light of Whitman's Poetry* (Cambridge, Mass.: Harvard University Press, 1987).

5. Quotes from "To Think of Time" and "I Sing the Body Electric" are taken from *Walt Whitman's "Leaves of Grass": The First (1855) Edition*, ed. Malcolm Cowley (New York: Penguin, 1959), 100, 118. Asterisks are used here in place of italics to distinguish the editorial break from Whitman's use of dots as a sign of oratorical pause.

6. Loving, *Walt Whitman: The Song of Himself*, 198.

7. Previously reprinted in remote and scattered publications, all known installments of "Sun-Down Papers" are now presented in Bergman et al., eds., *Walt Whitman: The Journalism*, I:13–30.

8. *GF*, II:245–47.

9. *UPP*, I:37.

10. "New England Reformers," in *Essays: Second Series* (Boston: Houghton Mifflin, 1891), 240–41.

11. Marvin Olasky, *The Tragedy of American Compassion* (Washington, D.C.: Regnery, 1992), 50.

12. Charles Sotheran, *Horace Greeley and Other Pioneers of American Socialism* (New York: Mitchell Kennerley, 1915), 199–218, where the debate is summarized. The entire text, consisting of twenty-four "letters," was published by Harper's a few years after the debate in a now-rare pamphlet of eighty-three pages. Sotheran's view is socialist, his book one of a number of left-leaning studies published by Kennerley, also the publishers in 1914 and 1915 of Horace Traubel's *WWC*.

13. *UPP*, I:98, "A Dialogue" was first published in the *Brooklyn*

Evening Star of November 28–29, 1845, then in the *Democratic Review* 27 (Nov. 1845): 360–64.

14. "Must runaway slaves be delivered back? They must"; see *"The Eighteenth Presidency!" A Critical Text,* ed. Edward F. Grier (Lawrence: University of Kansas Press, 1956), 37.

15. "What would be thought of a man who, having an ill humor in his blood, should strive to cure himself by only cutting off the festers, the outward signs of it, as they appeared upon the surface? Put criminals for festers and society for the diseased man, and you may get the spirit of that part of our laws which expects to abolish wrong-doing by sheer terror—by cutting off the wicked, and taking no heed of the causes of wickedness" *(UPP,* I:97).

16. *Leaves of Grass: The First (1855) Edition,* 135–36. Quotations from the 1855 preface to *Leaves of Grass* are taken from *LGC,* 709–29. For the American Revolution and its heroes as one important source of the first *Leaves of Grass,* see Jerome Loving, *Emerson, Whitman, and the American Muse* (Chapel Hill: University of North Carolina Press, 1982), 70–82; and Betsy Erkkila, *Whitman: The Political Poet* (New York: Oxford University Press, 1989), 13–24, 69.

17. *Leaves of Grass: The First (1855) Edition,* 28.

18. *UPP,* Iliii, n. 2.

19. As I argue in *Walt Whitman: The Song of Himself,* 227–32, there is scant evidence that Whitman was more than a freelance writer for the *Brooklyn Daily Times* (and not editor); therefore, it is unlikely that Whitman wrote most of the editorials attributed to him in *ISit.*

20. *NYD,* 9–10.

21. *LGC,* 565.

22. *WWC,* IV:452.

23. *LGC,* 551.

24. *LGC,* 546.

25. *LGC,* 17.

Whitman and the Gay American Ethos

M. Jimmie Killingsworth

Historical critics have gradually come to see that Walt Whitman's striking images of the "body electric"—the human body charged with sexual energy, open to entreaties of companions male and female, driven by consuming desire, containing the sources of psychological, as well as political, power—were not exclusively the product and property of an inspired individual but were "socially constructed." During Whitman's time, the sexualized body became an increasing source of both anxiety and fascination, fully acknowledged and explicitly voiced in medical writings, social purity pamphlets, self-help books, and popular science, as well as pulp fiction, pornography, and underground confessional literature. Only a literary history focused entirely on the literature of parlors, schoolrooms, and highbrow literary journals could view Whitman's "poetry of the body" as unalloyed in its originality.

Yet, while Whitman was not alone in treating sex as transcendental ("sex contains all") and fundamental to human experience ("the life below the life"), *Leaves of Grass* remains distinctive not only in the wildness and enduring power of its style of celebrating the body but also in recording the emergence of a special character, or ethos, of modern life, which Michel Foucault has called the "homosexual species." Whitman's life history antedates the appearance of gay consciousness in modern life; before his time, there was homosexual experience but no sociopolitical category of consciousness, no gay "lifestyle," no discourse of homosexuality. Nineteenth-century, texts dealing explicitly with homosexuality are very rare, even among medical and legal writings. The very word "homosexuality" did not appear until the end of the nineteenth century, when it was coined by Havelock Ellis and John Addington Symonds for use in their ground-breaking study, *Sexual Inversion*. The word "gay" may have been used in Whitman's day as an underground code term, as Charley Shively suggests, but no solid evidence exists for this early dating, and the usage certainly had no public currency.[1]

Nevertheless, when students and younger readers today, schooled by the mass media in interpreting the signs of gay sensibility, ask the inevitable question—"Was Whitman gay?"—their eyes do not deceive them. Like others for whom gay life has become a historical reality—from late nineteenth-century admirers, like Symonds, Edward Carpenter, and Oscar Wilde, to current gay critics—readers today are justified in seeing Whitman, who said he contained "multitudes," as a gay writer, perhaps the earliest exemplar of this ethos in American literature. "Gayness" is, in this sense, a matter of discourse, a way of situating oneself historically in relation to other discourses, "not a name for a preexistent thing," as Harold Beaver says of homosexuality, "but part of a network of developing language."[2] Before such a phenomenon becomes a recognized set of rhetorical strategies and linguistic conventions, it exists only as a set of vague trends emerging on the fringes of social awareness. In this stage, we can say that it is "prehistoric." Whitman participated in bringing gayness into history by developing a rhetoric with the resonant power of an established discursive formation.

In other words, Whitman helped to invent gayness. My aim in this essay is to trace the process of invention by analyzing several movements in Whitman's rhetoric through the first three editions of *Leaves of Grass*, which culminated in the publication of the now-infamous "Calamus" poems. With the inclusion of the two groups of poems devoted to erotic attraction, "Calamus" and its heterosexual counterpart, "Children of Adam," beginning in the third (1860) edition, four such trends become clearly distinguishable in the poems devoted exclusively to male-male love: the movement from strong appeals to nature (metaphoric identifications) toward weak appeals to nature (metonymic associations), the movement from appeals to natural history (evolution) toward appeals to social history (distinction), the movement from rejecting existing literary conventions toward appropriating and subverting such conventions, and the movement away from claims of full disclosure (to go "undisguised and naked") toward a complex interplay of revealing and concealing a "secret" at the center of identity. This reading supplements the already extensive literature (and controversy) on the exact nature of Whitman's biographical status as gay or straight or something else entirely by attempting to treat the gayness of *Leaves of Grass* as a set of textual or formal imperatives, rooted not in the biographical or biological condition of sex and sexual preference but resulting from the emergence of a cultural phenomenon.[3] To set the stage for this reading, I begin with a brief account of the historical and social contexts and intertexts of the poems' treatment of sexuality and proceed from there to an explication of the four rhetorical movements that I argue constitute a kind of archaeological record of the first gay writing in American literary history.

The Body Electric in Context

The "poetry of the body" predominates in the first three editions of *Leaves of Grass*. Sexual themes figure prominently in all of the major poems—"Song of Myself," "The Sleepers," "Crossing Brooklyn Ferry," and "Out of the Cradle Endlessly Rocking"—and form the basis for two major groupings of poems that appear in all editions after 1860: "Children of Adam," dedicated to heterosexual attraction and "procreation," and "Calamus," dedicated to "the love of comrades" or "manly love."[4] In "Song of Myself," the first poem in the first edition of 1855 and a key text in every edition, the poet vows to bring forth "many long dumb" and "forbidden voices": "Voices of sexes and lusts, voices veil'd and I remove the veil, / Voices indecent by me clarified and transfigur'd" (*WCP*, 211). For Whitman, life is rooted in sex, which connects human experience to previous generations, to future generations, and to the natural order of the world with its evolutionary forces.

Urge and urge and urge,
Always the procreant urge of the world.

Out of the dimness opposite equals advance, always substance and increase, always sex,
Always a knit of identity, always distinction, always a breed of life. (*WCP*, 190)

The characters of the early poems—the woman hidden behind the blinds, longingly watching the young men bathing by the shore in section 11 of "Song of Myself"; the restless dreamers of "The Sleepers"; the young man seized by the impulse to masturbate in "Spontaneous Me"; the Adamic hero in "From Pent-up Aching Rivers"; the lonely sufferer of unrequited love or the eager friend in the "Calamus" poems—all seek the comfort of human sympathy and the satisfaction of strong desires. In celebrating the conditions of desire and in urging men and women toward the frank recognition and resolution of their desires, Whitman offers a utopian vision of the completed human individual and expresses faith that a race of such beings could create the world anew, giving birth to yet "greater heroes and bards . . . sons and daughters fit for these States . . . perfect men and women" (*WCP*, 259–60).

"Sex contains all," the poet proclaims in "A Woman Waits for Me" (*WCP*, 258), one of the central poems in "Children of Adam," controversially titled "Poem of Procreation" when it first appeared in the 1856 *Leaves*. On the grounds that sexual themes were central to the overall plan of *Leaves of Grass*, Whitman refused to remove this and other poems from his ever-growing volume, even on the advice of Ralph Waldo Emerson, whom he once called "Master." And though he ceased to celebrate sex with the same intensity in poems written after the Civil War and revised old poems for later editions to de-emphasize the frankly physical element, he continued to insist that sexual themes were essential to his poetic project and that sexual experience was both transcendental and fundamental in human life. In old age, he told his friend and biographer Horace Traubel that "the eager physical hunger, the wish of that which we will not allow to be freely spoken of is still the basis of all that makes life worthwhile . . . Sex: Sex: Sex." In an organic metaphor suggestive of the place of sex in the whole scheme of his *Leaves*, he called it "the root of roots: the life below the life" (*WWC*, III:452–53).

The historical significance of Whitman's concern with sexuality is deepened by his association of physical life with democratic politics. The poem "I Sing the Body Electric," the first version of which appeared in the 1855 *Leaves*, provides a kind of manifesto on the political power of sex. In twin sections on "a man's body at auction" and "a woman's body at auction," the poet associates the evil of both slavery and prostitution with the dualistic thinking that favors the soul over the body. A society that allows the body to be treated as "corrupt" ends up by "corrupting" itself, treating abstractions like social class, education, and money as more important than material life and human health. As the strongest foundation for the equal treatment of all moral beings, Whitman restores the body to a position equal to, even identical with the soul. At the end of a long catalog praising the parts of the body, he proclaims, "O I say these are not the parts and the poems of the body only, but of the soul, / O I say now these are the soul" (*WCP*, 190). The aesthetic significance of Whitman's democratic sexual politics, suggested in his identification of the "parts" of the body as "poems" in and of themselves, is fully developed in the famous lines of "Spontaneous Me," which shockingly identify the poem with the penis.

The real poems, (what we call poems being merely pictures,)
The poems of the privacy of the night, and of men like me,
This poem drooping shy and unseen that I always carry, and that all
 men carry,
(Know once for all, avow'd on purpose, wherever are men like me,
 are our lusty lurking masculine poems) (*WCP*, 260)

The centrality of sex in *Leaves of Grass* and Whitman's experimentation in language, above all his free verse (almost as unnerving as free-love to many readers) and his audacity in exploring metaphors and other tropes, earned him the contempt of many reviewers in his own time but also made him a hero among less conventional contemporaries and among later critics. An 1856 review in Boston's *Christian Examiner* argues, "In point of style, the book is an impertinence toward the English language; and in point of sentiment, an affront upon the recognized morality of respectable people. Both its language and thought seem to have just broken out of Bedlam. It sets off upon a sort of distracted philosophy, and openly deifies the bodily organs, senses, and appetites." A British reviewer of the same year calls Whitman "rough, uncouth, and vulgar" and predicts, "The depth of his indecencies will be the grave of his fame."[5] By contrast, and typical of twentieth-century criticism in the modernist vein, F. O. Matthiessen's highly influential *American Renaissance* (1941) understands sex to be the focal point of Whitman's largely successful "fusion of form and content." In Matthiessen's view, Whitman is unique even among the great artists of the mid–nineteenth century precisely because he believed that poetic expression was rooted deeply in the experiences of the physical body. This faith allowed Whitman to create a poetry more powerful and "earthy" than that of other nineteenth-century poets: "Whitman's language is more earthy because he was aware, in a way that distinguished him from every other writer of the day, of the power of sex."[6] The earthiness also proved attractive to many readers in Whitman's own day, even some whose own writing steered clear of sex and who may have had personal qualms about the intensity of Whitman's treatment. In a famous private letter, which Whitman made public in a notorious act of self-promotion, Emerson praised the "free and brave thought" of the 1855 edition, though in an equally famous exchange, he urged Whitman to omit several of the "Children of Adam" poems because they would hurt sales.[7] Henry David Thoreau, with his own blend of mental ruggedness and personal prudery, confided to a friend his impression of the 1855 *Leaves*.

> There are two or three pieces in the book which are disagreeable, to say the least: simply sensual. He does not celebrate love at all. It is as if the beasts spoke. I think that men have not been ashamed of themselves without reason. No doubt there have always been dens where such deeds were unblushingly recited, and it is no merit to compete with their inhabitants. But even on this side he has shown more truth than any American or Modern that I know. I found his poem exhilarating, encouraging. As for its sensuality,—and it may turn out to be less sensual than it appears,—I do not so much wish that those parts were not written, as that men and women were so pure that they could read them without harm, that is, without understanding them.[8]

The general reception of *Leaves of Grass* in the nineteenth century was surprisingly mixed. Banned in Boston in the 1880s, the book was still read and admired by many ladies and gentlemen in Victorian England.[9]

In the face of old stereotypes about the prudery of Victorian culture, historical scholarship in the 1980s and 1990s has demonstrated that Whitman's book was not unique in dealing with sex in a forthright and even celebratory manner. Whitman was a journalist before he was a poet, and in this capacity, he encountered all manner of speakers and writers hawking self-help and social reform, everything from sex education and hydrotherapy to women's rights and free-love. He was particularly attracted to alternative medical practitioners, including the phrenologists, who, in locating aspects of character in physical attributes and in proclaiming the need to dispense with the "conspiracy of silence" surrounding bodily functions and sexual acts, influenced the poet deeply and permanently. In addition, biographical critics have demonstrated Whitman's familiarity with pulp fictions and perhaps harder forms of pornography. His own early experiments in fiction, his magazine stories and his temperance novel, *Franklin Evans,* reveal scenes and characters that could have been lifted directly from this literary rough trade. The temperance movement itself emphasized bodily purification but also did its part to heighten public awareness of the body and contributed to emerging discourses of the social purity cause with its twin peaks of anti-prostitution and abolition, with Whitman builds into the structure of "I Sing the Body Electric." All of these early nineteenth-century discourses served to foreground the human body and confound the distinction between public and private, a distinction likewise undermined in the best of Whitman's poems, notably "Song of Myself" and "The Sleepers."[10]

Whitman's achievement consists partly in bringing these discourses into "dialogue" with the poetic tradition, expanding the vocabulary as well as the typical subject matter of the poetic canon. In a famous witticism, Emerson said *Leaves of Grass* blended the *New York Tribune* with the *Bhagavad Gita*, a remark that globalizes the regional assessment of an early review by Charles Eliot Norton, who called the poems a "mixture of Yankee transcendentalism and New York rowdyism."[11] Both David Reynolds and Christopher Beach use M. M. Bakhtin's theory of novelization to explain Whitman's stylistic and formal innovations, his unique blending of multiple "voices" from the "sociolect" of his times to create an artistic "idiolect," in the terms Beach appropriates from French theorist Roland Barthes.[12]

Even with his Bakhtinian "heteroglossia," however, his shifting from conventional poetic or biblical language to technical jargon borrowed from the sciences and then to street talk, Whitman is not altogether unique in his historical context. His favorite medical writers often "defamiliarized" the language of science and social purity with odd concepts and metaphors. Using a term that applies equally well to Whitman's style, historians have referred to these medical writers as "eclectic" in training, philosophy, and discourse.[13] One of the strange concepts they developed, which Whitman borrowed directly, was the idea that sexual attraction was literally electric. The notion appears throughout the writings of Orson Fowler and Lorenzo Fowler, founders of the phrenological firm Fowler and Wells, which employed the journalist Whitman to write for its magazine, *Life Illustrated,* and which assisted in promoting and distributing the 1855 and 1856 editions of *Leaves of Grass*. Dr. Edward H. Dixon, whose name and address appear in a Whitman notebook of 1856, was the author of a book entitled *The Organic Law of the Sexes: Positive and Negative Electricity and the Abnormal Conditions That Impair Vitality* (1861). In an earlier book, *Woman and Her Diseases*, the sixth edition of which Whitman reviewed in 1847, Dixon appropriates a metaphor from the history of photography, another fascination of the poet's. The soul, or moral nature, of a parent, Dixon explains in a discussion of heredity, is "daguerreotyped upon the brain or nervous system of his offspring."[14] The admixture of metaphysical, medical, and technological discourses in these writings reemerges in poems like "I Sing the Body Electric".

I sing the body electric,
The armies of those I love engirth me and I engirth them,
They will not let me off till I go with them, respond to them,
And discorrupt them, and charge them full with the charge of the
soul. (*WCP*, 250)

It is safe to say that the poet outdid his sources in the power and variety of his tropes and the intensity of his tone, as Christopher Beach demonstrates in his reading of "I Sing the Body Electric": "In his aggressive mixing of technical or medical diction with a level of more intimate and personal observation . . . , Whitman rhetorically elides the difference between social and personal forms of discourse, making possible a further synthesis . . . of poetic language (rhythmically varied, imagistically dense, linguistically creative) and the precision of scientific or anatomical discourse."[15]

But Whitman did not only merge diverse discourses on sexuality into a newly powerful poetic whole: he laid the groundwork for a new discourse of sexual consciousness that went well beyond the existing discourses of his own time. Homosexuality had no public discourse in mid–nineteenth-century America. Even legal writings on the topic were evasive. Blackstone's famous *Commentaries on the Laws of England*, for example, referred to sodomy (itself a vague biblical reference to "unnatural" sex acts) as "a crime not fit to be named among Christians," "the very mention of which is a disgrace to human nature."[16] The Latin version of Blackstone's phrase appeared in one of the earliest reviews of *Leaves of Grass*. In the *New York Criterion* of November 10, 1855, Rufus Griswold writes of Whitman's book that it is "impossible to convey . . . even the most faint idea of its style and contents, and of our disgust and detestation of them, without employing language that cannot be pleasing to ears polite." At the risk of offending his audience, however, Griswold undertakes a "stern duty": "The records of crime show that many monsters have gone on in impunity, because the exposure of their vileness was attended with too great delicacy. *Peccatum illud horrible, inter Christianos non nominandum.*"[17]

Griswold's remarks and his invocation of the Latin formula are highly significant. Mid-century references to Whitman's project on male-male love are practically nonexistent. By his old age, Whitman was regularly attracting the interest of younger homosexual intellectuals, especially Englishmen, who were quick to claim Whitman as a pioneer in developing a public discourse that comprehended gay life. But his poems on "manly love" were all but ignored in the 1850s and 1860s whereas his poems that celebrated "procreation" and heterosexual attraction, such as "A Woman Waits for Me," were regularly and heartily condemned and discussed widely in public and private writings. Griswold's rhetoric suggests that while careful readers could discern a special erotic intensity toward other men in Whitman's poems, they may have been afraid or "too delicate" to broach the topic.

Interestingly, Griswold's censure, based on an apparent perception of homoerotic tendencies, applies not to the "Calamus" poems, which did not appear until 1860, but to the 1855 poems. As Robert K. Martin suggests, poems like "Song of Myself" and "The Sleepers" provide plenty of pre–"Calamus" passages in the mode of homosexual dreams and visions. Moreover, as Byrne Fone and Michael Moon have demonstrated, the early fiction shows us that Whitman was working with homoerotic themes years before he wrote the first line of *Leaves of Grass*. Still, as the rest of this chapter demonstrates, the "Calamus" poems remain rhetorically distinct from the earlier poems and stories. Even though homosexual acts and fantasies appear to inform the scenes of the early fiction and provide subject matter and inspiration for the defamiliarizing tropes of the 1855 and 1856 *Leaves*, the 1860 introduction of "Calamus" signals the opening of a new discourse frontier, the poetic province of the first gay American.

From Nature as a Site of Metaphoric Identity to Nature as a Place of Alienated Association

"Calamus" embodies a special set of rhetorical strategies that results from its isolation of male-male love from other types of friendship and erotic attraction. "Children of Adam" attempts a similar kind of isolation with heterosexual love but may itself be seen as a rhetorical result of the placement of "Calamus" in *Leaves of Grass*. Mainly a dumping ground for previously composed poems, "Children of Adam" was probably an afterthought, a record of the poet's effort to balance the intensity of "Calamus" when it first appeared in 1860. The balancing strategy fits nicely with Whitman's understanding of the difference between male-female love and male-male love, an understanding based on two terms he borrowed from phrenology: "amativeness" and "adhesiveness." In a famous notebook entry of 1870 (ten years after the first publication of "Calamus"), he warns himself to suppress a "diseased, feverish disproportionate adhesiveness," apparently his term for homoerotic attraction.[18] The balancing act of his personal life—phrenology was a science of balance, of keeping all psychological faculties from developing to excess—is reflected in the rhetorical balancing of the two sections in the 1860 *Leaves*. At least one of the poems, "Once I Pass'd through a Populous City," could be placed in "Children of Adam" only after Whitman changed the gender of the speaker's lover, "a woman I casually met there who detain'd me for love of me" (*WCP*, 266). The woman was a man in the manuscript version. The 1860 "Calamus" is more tightly unified than "Children of Adam" ever was and was yet the more closely unified in manuscript. The manuscript version seems comparable to an Elizabethan sonnet cycle in using a series of short lyrics to narrate a story of personal love. No wonder that, with the study of the manuscripts, biographical scholars discarded the old speculation that Whitman had a heated heterosexual love affair when he lived briefly in New Orleans in 1848—the "populous city" of the altered poem?—and began instead to consider seriously the possibility that he had a homosexual affair that broke off in the late 1850s, an affair that inspired "Calamus" and that would account for the tonal darkness of the third (1860) edition of *Leaves of Grass*, when "Calamus" first appeared.

The dark tone is partly a function of the sense of alienation that creeps among the genial expressions of optimism and seems to qualify the "barbaric yawps" of the "friendly and flowing savage," who was the speaker and dominant character of the longest poems in the 1855 and 1856 editions. In many ways, the speaker of the "Calamus" poems seems more like the characters to whom the 1855 speaker ("Walt Whitman, a kosmos") offers encouragement and aid: the twenty-ninth bather, the sleeper troubled by erotic desire, the sufferer of unrequited love.

The rhetoric of 1855 and 1856 suggests a full sympathy between the confident speaker and his fellow human beings, as well as a deep identification with nature. We have already seen how the speaker of "Spontaneous Me" identifies "real poems" with the male genitalia—"This poem drooping shy and unseen that I always carry, and that all men carry" (*WCP*, 260)—in one sweep identifying writing with the natural act of regeneration and identifying the poet with "all men." The opening lines of the poem metaphorically associate natural objects with the sexualized body of the poet, creating a distinctively phallic landscape.

Spontaneous Me, Nature
The loving day, the mounting sun, the friend I am happy with,
The arm of my friend hanging over my shoulder,
The hillside whitened with blossoms of the mountain ash . . .
The rich coverlet of the grass, animals and birds, the private
  untrimm'd bank, the primitive apples, the pebble stones,
Beautiful dripping fragments, the negligent list of one after another
  as I happen to call them to me or think of them,
The real poems. (*WCP*, 260)

The "friend I am happy with" mentioned in the second line is of unnamed gender, but the context suggests male even though the poem, first written in 1856, was always part of "Children of Adam" after 1860. The placement of the poem is thematically effective and rhetorically consistent, however, for whenever Whitman treats sexuality either as a general form of attraction or as heterosexual (or "procreative"), he metaphorizes freely in all directions, finding analogs of the experience of his own body in all of nature. In "Children of Adam" and in longer lyrics such as "Song of Myself" and "The Sleepers," the implication is that the speaker's own libido is justified by the presence of analogs in nature; it is "natural." In "Song of Myself," for example, he completes a vision of identity with God, humanity, and nature again with a series of images locating the traits of the sexualized body in the natural landscape.

And I know that the hand of God is the promise of my own,
And I know that the spirit of God is the brother of my own,
And that all men ever born are also my brothers, and the women
my sisters and lovers,
And that a kelson the creation is love,
And limitless are leaves stiff or drooping in the fields,
And brown ants in the little wells beneath them,
And mossy scabs of worm fence, heap'd stones, elder, mullein and
poke-weed. (*WCP*, 192)

In this heroic mode, the speaker takes the very earth as his lover.

Press close bare-bosom'd night—press close magnetic nourishing
night!
Night of south winds—night of the large few stars!
Still nodding night—mad naked summer night.

Smile O voluptuous cool-breath'd earth!
Earth of the slumbering and liquid trees!

....

Far-swooping elbow'd earth—rich apple-blossom'd earth!
Smile for your lover comes. (*WCP*, 208)

The body and the earth become nearly indistinguishable in some passages; the terms that apply to one apply equally well to the other, and each is equally worthy of the poet's "worship."

If I worship one thing more than another it shall be the spread of my
  own body, or any part of it,
Translucent mould of me it shall be you!
Shaded ledges and rests it shall be you!
Firm masculine colter it shall be you!

....

Root of wash'd sweet-flag! timorous pond snipe! nest of guarded
  duplicate eggs! it shall be you!
Mix'd tussled hay of head, beard, brawn, it shall be you!
Trickling sap of maple, fibre of manly wheat, it shall be you!
Sun so generous it shall be you!
Vapors lighting and shading my face it shall be you!
You sweaty brooks and dews it shall be you!
Winds whose soft-tickling genitals rub against me it shall be you!
Broad muscular fields, branches of live oak, loving lounger in my
winding paths, it shall be you.

....

Something I cannot see puts upward libidinous prongs,
Seas of bright juice suffuse heaven. (*WCP,* 211–13)

The reference to the phallic "branches of live oak" in this passage from "Song of Myself" is interesting in light of the very different significance of the live oak in "Calamus." The "Calamus" poem "I Saw in Louisiana a Live-Oak Growing," which may have been the first poem of the group, called "Live Oak, with Moss" in the manuscript version,[19] suggests that the confident link of the poet with the natural world has been broken. The manly branch of the tree hung with moss still reminds the poet of his own body, but he cannot honestly complete the heroic identification.

I saw in Louisiana a live-oak growing,
All alone stood it and the moss hung down from the branches,

Without any companion it grew there uttering joyous leaves of
dark green,
And its look, rude, unbending, lusty, made me think of myself,
But I wonder'd how it could utter joyous leaves standing all alone
there without its friends near, for I knew I could not. (*WCP*, 279)

The poem details the process by which the poet switches from a metaphoric to a metonymic or associational rhetoric. He no longer identifies himself with the object of nature but keeps a twig of the tree twined with moss as a "curious token" that helps him think of "manly love." Rather than being deeply connected with nature, as heterosexual love is because of its functional relation to procreation, homosexual or "manly" love bears a more complex and subtle relation to nature, which includes a recognition of difference—difference from the heterosexual social norm, from the procreative standard. The "kosmos" poet of "Song of Myself" could proclaim, "These are really the thoughts of all men in all ages and lands" (*WCP*, 204), but the "Calamus" poet has lost the connection and the confidence. In a poem ultimately omitted from *Leaves of Grass* but included in 1860 as "Calamus 9," he laments:

Sullen and suffering hours! (I am ashamed—but it is useless—I am
what I am;)
Hours of my torment—I wonder if other men ever have the like,
out of the like feelings?
Is there even one other like me—distracted—his friend, his lover, lost
to him? (*LGC*, 596)

The association of erotic love with the outdoor world remains present in "Calamus." The forlorn speaker of "Calamus 9" still "withdraw[s] to a lonely and unfrequented spot"; the speaker of the opening "Calamus" poem, "In Paths Untrodden," takes as his setting "the growth by the margins of pond-waters, / Escaped from the life that exhibits itself" (*WCP*, 268); the waters of the ocean whisper "to congratulate" the speaker on the approach of his lover in "When I Heard at the Close of the Day" (*WCP*, 277); and the central image of the group, the calamus plant, is itself a phallic symbol. But the free-flowing metaphorical transformation of the world into what James E. Miller, Jr., has called an "omnisexual vision" is gone.[20] Nature has become an environment, something that surrounds and suggests, rather than a bank of justifying identifications. It whispers rather than shouts approval.

Some twentieth-century critics, drawing on a clinical (and, from a gay perspective, homophobic) model of homosexuality, have suggested that "Calamus" expresses emotions of guilt, anxiety, and regret resulting from the poet's growing recognition of his exclusive homosexual preference, of his having fallen into an "unnatural" state of affection, hence the sense of alienation from nature and society.[21] While an element of anxiety may well be present—witness the notebook entry on adhesiveness—there is more to the story than that. The alienation in poems like "We Two Boys Together Clinging" and "When I Heard at the Close of the Day," for example, is a recognition of difference colored not by guilt or angst but by pride and joy. The intermingling in "Calamus" of many emotions associated with difference, the bright as well as the dark, is a key to the realism of the poems and to their success as a representation of gay consciousness.

From Natural History to Social History

The complexity of the "Calamus" emotions is matched by the subtlety of its rhetorical appeals. We have seen how Whitman first had to abandon the strong appeal to nature implied in metaphoric identification. Along with this appeal, he had to discard for the most part the discourse of romantic abandon to the instinctual drives of procreation, such as we find in the "Children of Adam" poems. The poem "From Pent-up Aching Rivers" offers a typical case.

From my own voice resonant, singing the phallus,
Singing the song of procreation,
Singing the need of superb children and therein superb grown
  people,

Singing the muscular urge and the blending,
Singing the bedfellow's song, . . .

....

From the hungry gnaw that eats me night and day,

....

Singing the true song of the soul fitful at random,
Renascent with grossest Nature or among animals,
Of that, of them and what goes with them my poems informing,
Of the smell of apples and lemons, of the pairing of birds,
Of the wet of woods, of the lapping of waves,
Of the mad pushes of waves upon the land . . .

....

The female form approaching, I pensive, love-flesh tremulously
aching,

....

The mystic deliria, the madness amorous, the utter abandonment,

....

I love you, O you entirely possess me. (*WCP*, 248–49)

A correlative to this discourse was that of natural history, including work in the biological and geological sciences, which were flourishing in the nineteenth century, along with the pre-genetics philosophies of heredity and human descent. Whitman took an avid interest in popular books and lectures on these sciences and incorporated many of their ideas into his work, using appeals to science to bolster his appeals to nature. The happiest result of this influence was the diversification of his poetic language and his nourishing of pre–Darwinian theories of evolution, such as we find in "Song of Myself".

I find I incorporate gneiss, coal, long-threaded moss, fruits, grains,
esculent roots,
And am stucco'd with quadrupeds and birds all over,

And have distanced what is behind me for good reasons,
But call any thing back again when I desire it. (*WCP,* 217)

In addition to serving as an implied justification for the celebration of his omnisexual vision, the evolutionary themes and appeals to science serve a political purpose. In "I Sing the Body Electric," for example, Whitman combines the appeal to nature with the appeal to natural history to chastise the exponents of slavery. Regarding the "wonder" of a slave's body at auction, he writes:

Whatever the bids of the bidders they cannot be high enough for it,
For it the globe lay preparing quintillions of years without one
  animal or plant,
For it the revolving cycles truly and steadily roll'd. (*WCP,* 255)

In certain poems, however, the commitment to evolutionary schemes drifts toward eugenics and Social Darwinism, outlooks that conflict with the broadly democratic themes of *Leaves of Grass*. In many of the "Children of Adam" poems, notably the controversial "A Woman Waits for Me," an aggressive hereditarian doctrine drives the poet toward a reduction of his female characters to the muscular function of motherhood and toward an association with the darker side of the eugenic and human perfectibility movements, the relatively innocent advocates of which in mid–nineteenth-century America unwittingly provided support for white supremacy and anti-immigration groups and paved the way for radical exclusionists like the German Nazis in the twentieth century. It is understandable that a contemporary critic, reading "A Woman Waits for Me" out of context, could say that Whitman had the moral sensibility of a "stock breeder."[22]

In this sense, the movement of "Calamus" away from appeals centered on procreation, evolution, and other themes of natural history could only improve the impression that *Leaves of Grass* as a whole makes upon its readers. In "Calamus," appeals tend to be based on the poet's claim to distinction within the realm of social rather than natural history. The key poem on this theme is "Recorders Ages Hence."

Recorders ages hence,
Come, I will take you down underneath this impassive exterior, I
will tell you what to say of me,
Publish my name and hang up my picture as that of the tenderest
lover,
The friend the lover's portrait, of whom his friend his lover was
fondest,
Who was not proud of his songs, but of the measureless ocean of
love within him, and freely pour'd it forth,
Who often walk'd lonesome walks thinking of his dear friends, his
lovers,
Who pensive away from the one he lov'd often lay sleepless and dissatisfied at night,
Who knew too well the sick, sick dread lest the one he lov'd might
secretly be indifferent to him,
Whose happiest days were far away through fields, in woods, on
hills, he and another wandering hand in hand, they twain apart
from other men,
Who oft as he saunter'd the streets curv'd with his arm the shoulder
of his friend, while the arm of his friend rested upon him also.
(*WCP*, 275–76)

This poem, quoted in full here, is a reprise of all the main "Calamus" themes, showing the range of emotion and the depth of Whitman's changes in self-concept. The theme of alienation takes a prominent place, appearing as a melancholic sense of difference ("the sick, sick dread"), as joy over the lovers' isolation ("they twain apart from other men"), and as a sense of distinction based on historical uniqueness: the speaker is not just a tender lover but is the very model of tenderness, the "tenderest" of all.

Significantly, the poem suggests that Whitman may also have been alienated from his previous accomplishments, his "songs." The "tenderest lover," he says, "was not proud of his songs." A similar hint appears in other "Calamus" poems. In "When I Heard at the Close of the Day," the poet who had worked so hard to bring his name before the public claims, "When I heard at the close of the day how my name had been received with plaudits in the capital, still it was not a happy night for me that follow'd, / And . . . when my plans were accomplish'd, still I was not happy." What brings happiness instead is the thought that "my dear friend my lover was on his way coming" (*WCP*, 276). In "Calamus 8" of 1860 ("Long I Thought that Knowledge Alone Would Suffice"), a poem later omitted from *Leaves of Grass*, the alienation from his "songs" takes on a darker hue.

For I can be your singer of songs no longer—One who loves me is jealous of me, and withdraws me from all but love,
With the rest I dispense . . . it is now empty and tasteless to me,
I heed knowledge, and the grandeur of The States, and the example of heroes, no more,
I am indifferent to my own songs—I will go with him I love. (*LGC*, 596)

The pervasive feeling of alienation also encompasses the poet's attitude toward his readers. The welcoming persona of the "songs," the sympathetic hero and spiritual healer, now warns the "new person drawn toward me."

Do you suppose you will find in me your ideal?

....

Do you suppose yourself advancing on real ground toward a real heroic man?
Have you no thought O dreamer that it may be all maya, illusion? (*WCP*, 277)

This dramatic leave-taking from his former work, from his former themes, and from his former attitudes toward the reader reveals Whitman's own consciousness of his rhetorical shift in "Calamus," his sense that he was breaking new ground, setting off, as he says in the poem that introduces "Calamus," on "paths untrodden." In one sense, we can understand the alienation themes as a function of his frustration and disappointment over the reception of the early editions of *Leaves of Grass*. He felt rejected by the public. As a result, the poems both express his disappointment and explore a new avenue into the hearts of potential readers. In another sense, the one I want to emphasize, the poems represent alienation as a way of life, the sense of difference that a gay man in a predominantly heterosexual society must live with. It leads to depression at the worst of times, but in the best of times, it fuels the pride of distinction, of having contributed to a discourse and a life model that others will recognize and claim as their own.

From Rejecting to Appropriating Literary Conventions

As Beach has shown, cultural distinction was Whitman's great goal, and he pursued distinction in the 1855 and 1856 *Leaves* with a powerful independence. "The greatest poet," Whitman says in the 1855 preface, "is not one of the chorus . . . . he does not stop for regulation . . . he is the president of regulation" (*WCP*, 10; punctuation as per original). He dismisses "poems distilled from other poems": "The swarms of polished deprecating and reflectors and the polite float off and leave no remembrance" (*WCP*, 26). The greatest poet, in this view, takes not the poetic tradition but nature as a model. As "Song of Myself" puts it:

Creeds and schools in abeyance,
Retiring back a while sufficed at what they are, but never forgotten,
I harbor for good or bad, I permit to speak at every hazard,
Nature without check with original energy. (*WCP*, 188)

In many ways, "Calamus" heads in the same direction. The opening poem of the section claims to depart from "standards hitherto publish'd" and from "pleasures, profits, conformities," but now the poet identifies what he is departing from not only as traditional poetry but also his own previous writing—that which "too long I was offering to feed my soul."

In paths untrodden,
In the growth by margins of pond-waters,

Escaped from the life that exhibits itself,
From all the standards hitherto publish'd, from the pleasures, profits, conformities,
Which too long I was offering to feed my soul,
Clear to me now standards not yet publish'd, clear to me now that my soul,
That the soul of the man I speak for rejoices in comrades. . . .
(*WCP*, 268)

It is not "nature," "original energy" channeled through his soul, that he voices but rather a deep personal commitment, the realization of how deep is his love for comrades.

The very emphasis of "In Paths Untrodden" upon the uniqueness of the "Calamus" poems—their distinction from both the poetic tradition and Whitman's previous work—is paradoxical in some ways because the poems draw deeply upon the Romantic tradition of lyrical love poetry and what Michael Lynch calls "the friendship tradition" of Anglo-American verse, especially in its elegiac mode, a tradition that Byron and others had already used as a screen for homoeroticism, a strategy that may also have operated in the women's epistolary tradition described by Carroll Smith-Rosenberg.[23] To take but one example, the "Calamus" poet shares with these traditions the use of elegiac themes to intensify the portrayal of love. Love and death intermingle suggestively in poems like "Scented Herbage of My Breast."

Scented herbage of my breast,
Leaves from you I glean, I write, to be perused best afterwards,
Tomb-leaves, body-leaves growing up above me above death,

....

O I do not know whether many passing by will discover you or in hale your faint odor, but I believe a few will,
O slender leaves! O blossoms of my blood! I permit you to tell in your own way of the heart that is under you,
O I do not know what you mean there underneath yourselves, you are not happiness,
You are often more bitter than I can bear, you burn and sting me,

Yet you are beautiful to me you faint tinged roots, you make me think of death,
Death is beautiful from you, (what indeed is finally beautiful except death and love?) (*WCP*, 268–69)

The dead body of the poet sacrificed to love and death, the poems pushing forth above death from the entombed dead heart, these would be familiar themes to the nineteenth-century reader (though the lines also have a distinctively Whitmanian touch: the image of chest hair giving way to blades of grass pushing up from the grave). In the American tradition, Edgar Allan Poe was exploring these same themes and asserting in his essays that the death of a beautiful woman is the only theme fit for modern poetry.

Of course, Whitman's poem is not about the death and the love of women but rather about the death and the love of comrades, as he makes clear later in the poem, discarding his symbolic framework.

Emblematic and capricious blades I leave you, now you serve me not,
I will say what I have to say by itself,
I will sound myself and comrades only, I will never again utter a call, only their call,
I will raise it with immortal reverberations through the States,
I will give an example to lovers to take permanent shape and will through the States,
Through me shall the words be said to make death exhilarating. (*WCP*, 269)

Some readers in Whitman's day balked at the substitution of male for female in such poems. The poet and critic Thomas Wentworth Higginson—a steadfast enemy of Whitman's known best for his correspondence with Emily Dickinson, the poet who, like Whitman, took sentimental death themes to new lengths and heights—said of Whitman's poems, "There is the same curious deficiency shown in him, almost alone among poets, of anything like personal and romantic love. Whenever we come upon anything that suggests a glimpse of it, the object always turns out to be a man and not a woman."[24]

Higginson's telling phrase "almost alone among poets" and his recognition of Whitman's inversion of the sentimental tradition indicate that Whitman had found a new way in "Calamus" to achieve distinction. Now, instead of a poetics based on nature, he sought to redefine traditional forms of expressing love, appropriating conventions primarily associated with heterosexual and what is usually known (somewhat inappropriately) as "platonic" love for a deeply intensified portrayal of comradely affection. That he was thinking of sex as part of these relations can hardly be doubted, despite his refusal to "come out" and acknowledge this intention in his old age, when he was hounded by English writer John Addington Symonds. The language of "In Paths Untrodden" gives the game away to sensitive readers.

Here by myself away from the clank of the world,
Tallying and talk'd to here by tongues aromatic,
No longer abash'd, (for in this secluded spot I can respond as I
would not dare elsewhere,)
Strong upon me the life that does not exhibit itself, yet contains all
the rest,

....

I proceed for all who are or have been young men,
To tell the secret of my nights and days,
To celebrate the need of comrades. (*WCP*, 268)

The phrase "the life that does not exhibit itself, yet contains all the rest" recalls Whitman's formula for sex as it appears elsewhere—in the claim of "A Woman Waits for Me" that "sex contains all" (*WCP*, 258), for example, and in the statement to Traubel already quoted above: "that which we will not allow to be freely spoken of is still the basis of all that makes life worthwhile . . . Sex: Sex: Sex. . . . the life below the life" (*WWC*, III:452–53).

The heavy coding of this theme, however, especially as it

compares to the forthright treatment of sex in "Children of Adam" suggests the poet's intention not only to appropriate and subvert the literary conventions of the friendship tradition but also to wear those conventions as a disguise. The same strategy occurs in *Drum-Taps* (1865), first appended to the fourth edition of *Leaves of Grass* in 1867. The poems of comradely suffering and death allow the poet to give voice to the elegiac mode first fitted-out in "Calamus."[25] In *Drum-Taps*, though, the expression of homoeroticism sinks almost unnoticed because the intensification of the emotions is fully warranted by the context of war, whereas in "Calamus," the presence of death surprises the reader and urges a closer reading, a hunting for signs. Such encouragements led Alan Helms to say that Whitman "cruises the reader."[26] The giving and interpreting of specially coded signs, a key activity in the gay community, as in all underground or marginal social groups, thus figures prominently in the proto-gay discourse of "Calamus."

From the Naked Truth to the Secret

In one of the "Calamus" poems, Whitman tries out the figure of identification that had served him so well in "Song of Myself" but that he had all but abandoned in "I Saw in Louisiana a Live-Oak Growing." Titled "Earth, My Likeness," the poem plays with the idea of surfaces and hidden depths, significantly switching to something closer to simile than metaphor (the import being "I am like nature" rather than "I am nature").

Earth, my likeness,
Though you look so impassive, ample and spheric there,
I now suspect that is not all;
I now suspect there is something fierce in you eligible to burst forth,
For an athlete is enamour'd of me, and I of him,
But toward him there is something fierce and terrible in me eligible
to burst forth,
I dare not tell it in words, not even in these songs. (*WCP*, 284)

Here the earth figures much differently from the earth of "Song of Myself," of which the poet boasts, "The press of my foot to the earth springs a hundred affections" (*WCP*, 200), and cries out to his "lover," the "voluptuous cool-breath'd earth": "Prodigal, you have given me love—therefore I to you give love!" (*WCP*, 208). By contrast, in "Earth, My Likeness," the "Calamus" poet suspects that his knowledge of the earth is not complete, that hidden beneath a welcoming surface is a depth unknown, perhaps threatening and volcanic. In himself, there is the same, and, despite his promise of "In Paths Untrodden" to "tell the secret of my nights and days" (*WCP*, 268), here he stops short of disclosing the whole story about his love for the "athlete" of whom he is "enamour'd": "I dare not tell it in words, not even in these songs."

The tension that Whitman creates between promising to tell a secret and then withdrawing from full candor is an effect that comes to the fore in the 1860 *Leaves*, especially in "Calamus." In the 1855 preface, Whitman had claimed, "The great poets are also to be known by the absence in them of tricks and by the justification of perfect personal candor. . . . How beautiful is candor! All faults may be forgiven of him who has perfect candor" (*WCP*, 19). Even in the 1855 preface, in the interplay of the great poet's traits of "sympathy" (the tendency to merge with others) and "prudence" (the tendency to caution, the tendency to self-protection and assertion), we find the seeds of the trend that reaches fruition in "Calamus." But sympathy, honesty, and the drive to confession and self-display rule the day in 1855 and 1856. "I will go to the bank by the wood and become undisguised and naked," says the speaker of "Song of Myself" in a characteristic moment.

In "Calamus," confession does not flow but is painful and dangerous, yet it is equally transformative, like a ritual bloodletting, as we see in "Trickle Drops".

From my breast, from within where I was conceal'd, press forth red
drops, confession drops,
Stain every page, stain every song I sing, every word I say, bloody
drops,

Let them know your scarlet heat, let them glisten,
Saturate them with yourself all ashamed and wet,
Glow upon all I have written or shall write, bleeding drops,
Let it all be seen in your light, blushing drops. (*WCP*, 278)

Nor can confession be complete, for the poet is uncertain not only of his connection with nature but also of his relation to other men. The feelings expressed in "Calamus 9" of 1860 ("Hours Continuing Long") are those of the closeted gay, who sends out sensitive feelers in an attempt to connect with others of his kind.

Hours of my torment—I wonder if other men ever have the like, out of the like feelings?
Is there even one like me—distracted—his friend, his lover, lost to him?
Is he too as I am now? Does he still rise in the morning, dejected,
thinking who is lost to him? and at night, awaking, think who is lost?
Does he harbor his friendship silent and endless? harbor his anguish and passion?
Does some stray reminder, or the casual mention of a name, bring
the fit back upon him, taciturn and deprest? (*LGC*, 596)

Finally, even this level of confession was too much for Whitman. He excluded this poem as well as "Calamus 8" ("Long I Thought that Knowledge Alone Would Suffice") from later editions of *Leaves of Grass*. In biography as well as bibliography, he replicated the form of alternately revealing and concealing the depths of his heart. It remains unclear how "far he went" with the young men he courted throughout his life with his sentimental language and adoring attentions. And, as Gary Schmidgall has shown in great detail, he taunted Traubel with the promise to tell a "secret" that would explain himself better than any other. He never fulfilled the promise. Yet we do not need this confession to finish our sketch of the gay ethos as it emerged in "Calamus." The movement between confession and concealment completes the picture as far as the discourse analyst is concerned. Whitman's contribution to gay literature and gay rhetoric—his crafting of strategies, his modeling of linguistic behaviors, his attraction of sympathetic readers—is unparalleled in American literary history. We "recorders ages hence" need not revive the corpse of the old man and force his confession. The record bespeaks him and has become him: "Camerado, this is no book, / Who touches this touches a man" (*WCP*, 611).

NOTES

1. See Havelock Ellis and John Addington Symonds, *Sexual Inversion* (1897; rpt., New York: Arno, 1975); Michel Foucault, *The History of Sexuality*, vol. 1, *An Introduction*, trans. Robert Hurley (New York: Pantheon, 1978), 43; M. Jimmie Killingsworth, *Whitman's Poetry of the Body: Sexuality, Politics, and the Text* (Chapel Hill: University of North Carolina Press, 1989), 97–101; Michael Lynch, "'Here Is Adhesiveness': From Friendship to Homosexuality," *Victorian Studies* 29 (1985): 67–96; Robert K. Martin, *The Homosexual Tradition in American Poetry* (Austin: University of Texas Press, 1979), 51; and Charley Shively, ed., *Calamus Lovers: Walt Whitman's Working-class Camerados* (San Francisco: Gay Sunshine, 1987), 110. The *Oxford English Dictionary* gives mid–nineteenth-century references for the use of "gay" as an adjective for (female) prostitutes, but the first reference for the usage applied to homosexual males does not appear until 1935.

2. Beaver, "Homosexual Signs," *Critical Inquiry* 8 (Autumn 1981): 101.

3. This is hardly the first time such a reading has been attempted. My own earlier studies were already built upon the fine work of others, notably Joseph Cady's "*Drum-Taps* and Nineteenth-century Male Homosexual Literature," in *Walt Whitman: Here and Now*, ed. Joann P. Krieg (Westport, Conn.: Greenwood, 1985), 49–59; Alan Helms, "Hints . . . Faint Clews and Indirections': Whitman's Homosexual Disguises," in Krieg, ed., *Here and Now*, 61–67; Lynch's "'Here Is Adhesiveness'"; and, especially, Robert K. Martin's pioneering Whitman chapter in *The Homosexual Tradition in American Poetry*. More recent readings that effectively identify formal and rhetorical effects suggestive of gay consciousness and emerging culture include Byrne Fone's *Masculine Landscapes: Walt Whitman and the Homoerotic Text* (Carbondale: Southern Illinois University Press, 1992); Michael Moon's *Disseminating Whitman: Revision and Corporeality in*

"Leaves of Grass" (Cambridge, Mass.: Harvard University Press, 1991); many of the essays collected in *The Continuing Presence of Walt Whitman: The Life after the Life,* ed. Robert K. Martin (Iowa City: University of Iowa Press, 1992); and *Breaking Bounds: Whitman and American Culture Studies,* ed. Betsy Erkkila and Jay Grossman (New York: Oxford University Press, 1996). Building upon previous work, I try to consolidate in this chapter a reading that offers a new focus based on the concept of rhetorical appeals. For gay revisionist work in Whitman biography, see Charley Shively's *Calamus Lovers* and his *Drum Beats: Walt Whitman's Civil War Boy Lovers* (San Francisco: Gay Sunshine, 1989); and Gary Schmidgall's *Walt Whitman: A Gay Life* (New York: Dutton, 1997). On the continuing controversy on biographical questions surrounding Whitman's own sexual preferences, see David Reynold's comments on the evidence (or lack thereof) in chapter 7 of *Walt Whitman's America: A Cultural Biography* (New York: Knopf, 1995); and Schmidgall's treatment of "civilian" (that is, non-gay) biographers (including Reynolds) in chapter 2 of *A Gay Life.* The controversy is an old one. Even in the 1950s, Whitman's two major biographers disagreed on the question. Roger Asselineau insisted on Whitman's homosexual preference in his 1954 *L'Evolution de Walt Whitman* (translated as *The Evolution of Walt Whitman,* 2 vols., Cambridge, Mass.: Harvard University Press, 1960, 1962); but Gay Wilson Allen stopped short of agreeing, assenting only to the poet's "homoeroticism" in what was for years the standard biography, *The Solitary Singer* (New York: Macmillan, 1955); rev. ed., Chicago: University of Chicago Press, 1985).

4. For a full analysis of the evolution of Whitman's treatment of sexuality and particularly sexual politics in the various editions of *Leaves,* see my *Whitman's Poetry of the Body;* Moon's *Disseminating Whitman;* and Christopher Beach's excellent chapter "Figuring the Boy in *Leaves:* Whitman and the Discourse of Corporeality," in his *The Politics of Distinction: Whitman and the Discourses of Nineteenth-century America* (Athens: University of Georgia Press, 1996), 152–84.

5. *CH,* 62, 56–57.

6. Matthiessen, *American Renaissance: Art and Expression in the Age of Emerson and Whitman* (London: Oxford University Press, 1941), vii, 523.

7. See Reynolds, *Walt Whitman's America,* 341–43; also Jerome Loving, *Emerson, Whitman, and the American Muse* (Chapel Hill: Uni-

versity of North Carolina Press, 1982), 105–6. The full text of Emerson's letter appears in *CH,* 21–22.

8. Thoreau, in *CH,* 67–68.

9. On the critical history of *Leaves of Grass,* see my book *The Growth of "Leaves of Grass": The Organic Tradition in Whitman Studies* (Columbia, S.C.: Camden House, 1993).

10. On Whitman's use of medical and social purity discourses, see Harold Aspiz, *Walt Whitman and the Body Beautiful* (Urbana: University of Illinois Press, 1980); Beach, *Politics of Distinction;* and Killingsworth, *Whitman's Poetry of the Body.* On sensational themes in Whitman's early fiction and the possible influence of contemporary pulp literature, see Fone, *Masculine Landscapes; Moon,* Disseminating Whitman; David Reynolds, *Beneath the American Renaissance: The Subversive Imagination in the Age of Emerson and Melville* (New York: Knopf, 1988); and Michael Warner, "Whitman Drunk," in Erkkila and Grossman, eds., *Breaking Bounds,* 30–43.

11. Emerson quoted in Paul Zweig, *Walt Whitman: The Making of a Poet* (New York: Basic, 1984), 8; Norton quoted in *CH,* 51.

12. Reynolds, *Beneath the American Renaissance;* Beach, *Politics of Distinction;* Bakhtin, *The Dialogic Imagination: Four Essays,* ed. Michael Holquist, trans. Caryl Emerson and Michael Holquist (Austin: University of Texas Press, 1981); Roland Barthes, *Elements of Semiology,* trans. A. Lavers and C. Smith (New York: Hill and Wang, 1977).

13. John S. Haller and Robin M. Haller, *The Physician and Sexuality in Victorian America* (New York: Norton, 1974).

14. On Dixon, the Fowlers, and the general influence of the eclectic medical writers on Whitman, see Killingsworth, *Whitman's Poetry of the Body,* chap. 2.

15. Beach, *Politics of Distinction,* 178.

16. William Blackstone, *Commentaries on the Laws of England,* ed. John Frederick Archbold (London: William Reed, 1811), IV:215.

17. In *CH,* 33.

18. In Schmidgall, *A Gay Life,* 192–93; see also Lynch; "'Here Is Adhesiveness'"; and Killingsworth, *Whitman's Poetry of the Body,* 11–26.

19. See Hershel Parker, "The Real 'Live Oak, with Moss': Straight Talk about Whitman's 'Gay Manifesto,'" *Nineteenth-century Literature* 51 (1996): 145–60.

20. James E. Miller, Jr., "Whitman's Omnisexual Vision," in *The*

Chief Glory of Every People: Essays on Classic American Writers, ed. Matthew J. Bruccoli (Carbondale: Southern Illinois University Press, 1973), 253–59.

21. See Stephen A. Black, *Whitman's Journey into Chaos: A Psychoanalytic Study of the Poetic Process* (Princeton: Princeton University Press, 1975); Clark Griffith, "Sex and Death: The Significance of Whitman's 'Calamus' Themes," *Philological Quarterly* 39 (1960): 18–38; Edwin Haviland Miller, *Walt Whitman's Poetry: A Psychological Journal* (New York: New York University Press, 1968).

22. See Killingsworth, *Whitman's Poetry of the Body,* 71–72.

23. Lynch, "Here Is Adhesiveness'"; Carroll Smith-Rosenberg, "The Female World of Love and Ritual: Relations between Women in Nineteenth-century America," *Signs* 1 (1975): 1–29.

24. T. W. Higginson, "Recent Poetry," *Nation* 55 (1892): 12. For more on Whitman's inversion of the sentimental tradition, see Killingsworth, *Whitman's Poetry of the Body,* 97–111.

25. See Cady, "*Drum-Taps* and Nineteenth-century Male Homosexual Literature"; also Killingsworth, *Whitman's Poetry of the Body,* 136–40.

26. Helms, "'Hints,'" 65; see also Beaver, "Homosexual Signs," 104–5.

Whitman and the Visual Arts

Roberta K. Tarbell

Walt Whitman and his writings were shaped by the architecture, art, and artists of his time. Some of the most exciting new insights into Whitman have arisen from recent analyses of his connectedness to international perspectives in the fine arts. During the 1990s, scholars have discerned and published far more about the interrelationships between Whitman and the visual arts than they had in the first hundred years after his death.[1] During his years as a journalist in New York City, Whitman was directly involved in the arts: he attended countless operatic, theatrical, and musical performances, frequented art galleries, befriended many artists, understood the global perspectives they represented, and critiqued them in his newspaper columns. During those years, Whitman was immersed in the form and content of colloquialisms, popular fiction, and mass media used in the service of democracy. During his late years, artists came to Camden, New Jersey, to pay homage to the aging bard and often returned to create a portrait of him. Whitman's writings continue to authenticate creative urges upwelling in writers and artists and to give them courage to break free from whatever fetters bind their originality. His faith in America and American art is as important today as when he first expressed it.

The aesthetic ideals Whitman probed, beginning with the 1855

Leaves of Grass, define avant-garde art and architecture in Europe and America thereafter. What role did the fine arts play in Whitman's transition from a competent newspaper critic and eclectic writer during his formative years to the poet who, in 1855, transformed poetry and who, thereafter, assumed the role of the patriarchal hero of modernism to writers and artists?

Whitman's Early Experiences with Art and Architecture

The only works of art specifically mentioned in Whitman's will were "the portraits of my father and mother and one old large Dutch portrait," undistinguished oil paintings that he had known since childhood and that hung in his Mickle Street house.[2] A decade after Whitman's death, Willis Steel, in his attempt to separate the myth of the poet from the real person, interviewed people still living on Long Island who recalled Whitman and his family.[3] Firsthand witnesses from West Hills, Long Island, remembered that the poet's father, Walter Whitman, was a woodcutter and a carpenter, trades at which the younger Walt worked for a while during the 1840s and which he celebrated in his verse contemporary to Jean-François Millet's painted depictions of similar workingmen. Both Millet and Whitman nostalgically used icons of workers in rural settings to bring attention to the increasing numbers of people who had left their farms to work in the new urban centers. They marked a passing era for France, America, and, in particular, the Whitman family. The elder Walter Whitman had moved from rural West Hills to Brooklyn because of the promise of a steady income funded by the building boom in progress there in 1823. Steel also learned that Whitman's lifelong fascination with ferries began when the Whitman family moved to Brooklyn, near the ferry. From an early age, then, Whitman began crossing the East River on a ferry boat. At some point in his life, on these frequent ferry rides, he learned how to disengage himself from mindful, everyday language in order to tap another, more fertile level of his consciousness. His thoughts were framed by the cadence and pitch of multivalent conversations and by the formal arrangement of the buildings on the opposite shore, which grew increasingly hard-edged as each new structure rose and broke through the skyline.

In 1831, when the twelve-year-old Whitman worked for his first newspaper, the *Long Island Patriot*, he learned about one of the macabre duties of professional sculptors: placing wet plaster on a dead person's face until it hardened, creating a concave mold from which a plaster death mask could be cast. Samuel E. Clements, editor of the *Patriot*, and John Browere, who had in his "Gallery of Busts" in Manhattan a collection of life-mask portraits he had made, went to a Jericho, Long Island, graveyard, dug up the corpse of the recently deceased Quaker preacher Elias Hicks, and molded a death mask of his head and face in order to record Hicks's likeness. Whitman, who had accompanied his parents to hear Hicks preach, later owned one of the several portrait busts that resulted from this grave robbery, wrote a newspaper article about the incident in the *Brooklyn Daily Times* in 1857, included both prose and pictorial portraits of Hicks in *November Boughs*, and perhaps reworked his adolescent, gruesome experience in the surreal poem "The Sleepers."

A shroud I see and I am the shroud, I wrap a body and lie in the
  coffin,
It is dark here under ground, it is not evil or pain here, it is blank
  here, for reasons.
(It seems to me that every thing in the light and air ought to be happy,
Whoever is not in his coffin and the dark grave let him know he has
  enough.)[4]

Sixty years after exhuming Hicks, Whitman was the subject of a death mask that was molded by realist painter Thomas Eakins (1844–1916) and his student Samuel M. Murray, a sculptor who spent almost every day with Eakins during the last thirty years of the Philadelphia painter's life. Using the mask as a guide, Murray modeled a prize-winning portrait bust of Whitman that, in 1892, was cast in plaster and bronze and exhibited in 1893 at the World's Columbian Exposition in Chicago.[5] The importance of obtaining a "real" likeness of a famous person was indelibly imprinted on the youthful Whitman. Later, he made sure that his own famous countenance was photographed and published frequently as adjuncts to the self-portraits he created in his publications.

Beginning in the spring of 1835, Whitman spent one year living and working in Manhattan, an extraordinary, mind-expanding experience for a sixteen-year-old youth, not only because printing was undergoing new technology at an astounding rate, but also because of the cultural milieu into which he was thrust.[6]

During his stay he could not have missed the dramatic Egyptian Revival structure that English-born architect John Haviland (1792–1852) designed for the Halls of Justice, known as "the Tombs," which was constructed in New York in 1835 and 1836. How exotic the monumental open-lotus-bud columns, battered walls, and winged sun disks must have appeared to Whitman![7] Haviland had selected a castellated Gothic style for a slightly earlier prison, Eastern State Penitentiary, nearing completion in Philadelphia.[8] Yet another style, Greek, was chosen for two other monumental structures recently completed or rising in New York during 1835. One, LaGrange Terrace (1833; see p. 238), also known as Colonnade Row, was a residential building with twenty-eight two-story Corinthian columns forming a rhythmic pattern along tree-lined Lafayette Place (now Lafayette Street) between Fourth Street and Astor Place. LaGrange Terrace had been designed by the influential architects Ithiel Town, Alexander Jackson Davis, and James Dakin as townhouses for the Astor, Delano, and Vanderbilt families, making it the most elegant residential district before the Civil War. Whitman later wrote:

> Among the elder buildings, only the Astor House, in its massive and simple elegance, stands as yet unsurpassed as a specimen of exquisite design and perfect proportion. It is thoroughly modern in its uses and appropriateness to its purpose, but classic and severe as a Greek temple.[9]

Whitman marks himself as a "modern" because his criteria for quality in architecture are function and abstract form. On those same criteria, Whitman mocks the Customs House (later, the

Sub-Treasury Building; now the Federal Hall National Memorial) on Wall Street, also designed by Town and Davis.

> The Savings Bank in Bleeker [*sic*] street just east of Broadway is Grecian, of the most ornamental and florid order. It is a wonderful and lovely edifice. But the *surroundings*, (the Greeks always had a reference to these,) are enough to spoil it—let alone the discordant idea of a Greek temple, (very likely to Venus) for a modern Savings Bank!
>
> Such considerations as these make one laugh at the architecture of the New York Custom House, with its white sides and its mighty fluted pillars. In the original some twenty-three or five hundred years ago, when Socrates wandered the streets of Athens talking with young men, . . . there stood the original, the temple of the ideal goddess, the learned, brave, and chaste Minerva. It was of immense extent, and was manly, a simple roof supported by columns. There were performed the rites—in that city and among that people, they and the building belonged. And to that the United States government has gone back and brought down (a miniature of it,) to modern America in Wall Street, amid these people these years, for a place to settle our finances and tariffs. How amusing![10]

Like the ancient Parthenon in Athens, the Customs House had a giant two-story portico of eight Doric fluted columns. The self-taught mason turned sculptor John Frazee (1790–1852), whom Henry Tuckerman dubbed "the artistically inclined stonecutter," supervised its sculptural decoration from 1834 to 1840.[11] Thus, Whitman expressed admiration for the "massive and simple elegance" of the classic severity of Town and Davis's Astor House and disdain for their Customs House. Such coexistence of opposites is typical of Whitman. Sometimes he invokes it unconsciously, and in other instances he calculates it. Despite his disdain for the appropriateness of its form, Whitman must have experienced—if not in these new buildings, then in others—the monumental massing and volumes of space found in architecture vast in proportion to human size. The feeling matches Whitman's ideas of the grandeur of America expressed so frequently in his writings.

The Egyptian Revival style that accounted for some of the remarkable structures under construction during Whitman's early decades was more important as a stylistic determinant in the United States—especially for cemeteries and prisons—than in France or Britain, part of the American Romantic fascination with the sublimity of places distant and times past. Whitman was well versed in Egyptian archaeology. In an article in the *Brooklyn Daily Eagle* (November 7, 1846), Whitman refers to the popularity of lectures by Egyptologist George R. Gliddon, which he probably attended, and, in 1854 and 1855, Whitman interspersed seeing Egyptian artifacts at the home of Dr. Henry Abbott in New York with extensive reading on the subject. Bucke reports that Whitman visited Abbott's Egyptian collection (of about 1,000 artifacts) many times.[12] References to Egyptian art, architecture, and culture are interspersed throughout Whitman's writings. In "Song of Myself," a child asks,"What is grass?" Among many answers, Whitman writes, "I guess it is a uniform hieroglyphic."[13] In "Song of the Exposition," Whitman describes American technological know-how and manufacturing abilities as the "great cathedral sacred industry," which he claims made "Silent the broken-lipp'd Sphynx in Egypt, silent all those century-baffling tombs" and which is "mightier than Egypt's tombs." A few verses later:

> (This, this and these, America shall be *your* pyramids and obelisks,
> Your Alexandrian Pharos, gardens of Babylon,
> Your temple at Olympia.)[14]

Whitman likened the tremendous power of America's mechanical and technical capabilities on view in the first international world's fair to the most enduring monuments of the millennia.

From 1863 to 1873, Whitman's Washington, D.C., years, he witnessed the erection of a white obelisk, Robert Mills's Washington Monument, which was completed in 1884. His poem "Washington's Monument, February, 1885" demonstrates that he understood how an Egyptian icon of "this marble, dead and cold, far from its base and shaft expanding" could symbolize the seminal power of freedom that contemporary America represented.[15] Mills described himself as the first native-born American purposefully trained for the profession of architecture. One of the hospital wards in which Whitman worked during the Civil War was located in Mills's Greek Revival Patent Office Building which now is the Smithsonian Institution's National Museum of American Art and National Portrait Gallery, two city blocks between Seventh and Ninth streets and F and G streets.[16] The spaces in this spectacular granite building, which has two exterior grand staircases leading up to giant, octastyle Doric porticos, are so capacious that the block-long gallery on the third floor was used in March 1865 for Lincoln's second inaugural ball. During the Civil War, hospital cots had filled the same space and also had been nestled among the glazed cases displaying inventions along the long F Street galleries of the U.S. Patent Office. Mills is significant not only because, as federal architect and engineer during the 1830s, he imposed the discipline of professional training and a stark abstract simplicity on his monumental Greek Revival buildings, but also because he was a writer whose aesthetic philosophy foreshadowed Whitman's. Mills advised American artists to "study your country's tastes and requirements, and make classic ground *here* for your art. Go not to the old world for your examples. We have entered a new era in the history of the world: it is our destiny to lead, not to be led."[17]

Whitman was aware that architects chose one style or another to express the purpose of the structure via values associated with the antique style selected. In his poems, Whitman is comfortable writing word pictures of ancient monuments, sculptures, and buildings that he had seen re-created in the United States in emulation of Egyptian, Greek, Roman, and Gothic prototypes. He never traveled to Europe. The eclecticism in the arts that Whitman exhibits marks him as a person of his own country and his own time. Architect Town commissioned Thomas Cole (1801–48), one of the founding fathers of the Hudson River school of American landscape painting, to create *The Architect's Dream* (1840) to present his aesthetic philosophy of architectural style. In the foreground, a miniature Town, surrounded by his architectural folios filled with engravings, plans, and elevations of historic buildings, reclines on top of a fluted, classical column and surveys the architectural landscape. On his left, he views a church in Gothic Revival, a style considered appropriate for churches because Christianity reached the apex of its influence during the medieval epoch. In like manner, Town views on his right Greek and Roman Revival civic buildings and, in the distance, a colossal Egyptian pyramid. Such attitudes assigning associative values to art and architecture were dominant in the United States during the first half of the nineteenth century. Not only did intellectuals consider certain styles sublime, beautiful, or picturesque, they also believed that correctly styled public buildings and sculptures could improve the morals of people who encountered them. A committee that was determining the appropriate style for a prison in 1829 wrote, "There is such a thing as architecture adapted to morals; that other things being equal, the prospect of improvement, in morals, depends in some degree upon the construction of the buildings."[18]

Whitman perceived the irrationality of this, but he was one of many intellectuals, architects, artists, and arbiters of taste who shared an enthusiasm for classical and Egyptian antiquities. Americans of all classes were exposed to such eclectic historicizing material culture, most without consciousness of the theory behind it. When Whitman designed his own tomb shortly before his death, he chose a simple, masculine, Greek temple silhouette, which he executed with massive granite walls that look more Egyptian than anything erected in Greece. Egyptian seemed right to him for a tomb, an attitude fostered by the Egyptian Revival architecture popular during the second quarter of the nineteenth century in the United States, which he had known since his adolescent years. Hudson River landscape paintings, *The Architect's Dream* and the moralizing iconography of many of Cole's other works, and the Egyptian and Greek Revival architecture by Town and Davis represent several of many manifestations of Romanticism that dominated arts and letters in the United States at the beginning of Whitman's career. Architectural style, form, and associative values were important aspects of Whitman's ambient culture.

Genre Painting

Whitman and contemporary painters, like Americans William Sidney Mount (1807–68) and Eastman Johnson (1824–1906) and Europeans Jean François Millet (1814–75) and Gustave Courbet (1819–77), shared subject matter, especially genre scenes set in rural Long Island, New York, or images of laborers as symbols of a new democratic society or of sociopolitical change. Whitman cited "the combination of my Long Island birth-spot, sea-shores, childhood's scenes, absorptions, with teeming Brooklyn and New York" as important factors in shaping his character.[19] Focusing on the years from 1830 to 1860, art historian Elizabeth Johns places Mount and other American painters who depicted local, everyday life in their works into the context of a rapidly changing social structure. In the time period covered and the textual sources uncovered, Johns's study parallels for American genre painting what David S. Reynolds discovers for American literature in *Beneath the American Renaissance* and for Whitman in *Walt Whitman's America*. Both authors look to contemporary mass media expressions and colloquialisms to help explain polarized cultural issues such as religion, reform, gender, class, race, sex, money, and politics to analyze painted and poetic works in various regions. Both consciously replace earlier consensus models with what Johns labels "the conflictual model that emphasizes citizens' differences and conflicts."[20] Neither Whitman nor Mount created sentimental or utopian interpretations of pre–Civil War American culture. Both were more willing than their colleagues to deal with controversial issues of their time, but often they used ambiguous "language" to decrease the intensity of factional reactions of others and to mask their own ambivalence and changing attitudes toward these tough issues.

Both Reynolds and Johns discuss Mount's *Farmers Nooning* (1836), but they reach different conclusions.[21] Johns deduces that, with this painting, Mount was criticizing the overzealous abolitionists who had raised tensions over slavery so high that people were afraid that economic and political chaos were imminent. Johns suggests that Mount had depicted the African American in *Farmers Nooning* as healthy and well-dressed in order to support the contention of slave owners that slaves did not need to be freed because they were well cared for by their paternalistic owners. In like manner, Mount's depiction of the black man as sensual and lazily asleep on a haycock in the sun seems to uphold racist stereotypes. The three white men in the painting range from industrious to idle and from neatly dressed to tattered and unkempt, but all of them can own land and vote, which the black man cannot. The tam-o'-shanter on the young boy symbolizes the Scottish and Presbyterian emancipation societies in the British Isles and the United States that were the major financial supporters of the abolitionists. The boy "tickles the ear" of the African American to symbolize a vernacular expression that meant filling someone's head with foolish ideas, in this case, the "impossible" dream of freedom. Mount created more images of African Americans in company with American citizens than any other contemporary artist and far more sympathetically than the stereotypes in popular culture. But, after decoding the symbolic language, it is clear that Mount wishes to communicate the complexities and contradictions of such apparent racial harmony, and, in *Farmers Nooning*, he is speaking as the anti-abolitionist New Yorker that he is. Reynolds writes that Whitman, like Mount, also

> had a divided history on the issues of race and slavery: a spirit of African-American participation in Brooklyn life, confirmed personally by his friendship with Mose, but also an animus against abolitionists—a feeling he would share not only with most Brooklynites but also most Northerners throughout the antebellum period.[22]

Yet, in another passage, Whitman describes "the picturesque giant" of a Negro who "holds firmly the reins of his four horses,"[23] which is as revolutionary an image as Mary Cassatt's Woman and Child Driving (1881). Rarely in nineteenth-century literature or art are disfranchised women or racial minorities depicted actively in charge and holding the reins of power. With these driving images, Whitman and Cassatt challenge the accepted social order and predict the future in a far more decisive manner than did Mount in Farmers Nooning.

Remarkable in its absence in the entire literature on Walt Whitman and the visual arts is any documented connection to, influence from, or impact on women artists. In the ten years since I heard Wanda Corn point this out, no new research has been published to fill this gap.[24]

Bryant, Brown, the American Art Union, and Whitman's Mission

William Cullen Bryant (1794–1878), a lawyer, Anglophile poet, and first associate editor (1826–29) and then editor (1829–78) of the *New York Evening Post,* was an important catalyst to the American nationalism that characterizes the sculpture of Henry Kirke Brown and Whitman's writings after 1855. When Whitman traveled from Camden to New York City to attend Bryant's funeral, he recalled that, beginning in 1845, Bryant would walk to Brooklyn and the two poets would ramble for miles and talk for hours: "On these occasions he gave me clear accounts of scenes in Europe—the cities, looks, architecture, art, especially Italy—where he had traveled a great deal."[25] Between 1849 and 1856, Bryant traveled to Cuba, Great Britain, Europe, and the Near East. Fifty-four of his letters from these travels were published in the *Evening Post,* which, presumably, Whitman read. Even if he had not, Bryant's articulate narratives during their walks together were an important source of information for Whitman. These dialogues, and countless others with artist friends in their studios,[26] filled in some gaps in Whitman's education and gave him courage to develop his convictions, which he published during the 1850s in numerous articles on the visual arts and, ultimately, in the first edition of *Leaves of Grass*. "Pictures," a long poem that was not published in Whitman's lifetime, can be read as a walk through the kind of large exhibition one encounters at world's fairs. His rambling, fragmentary descriptions of the seven wonders of the world, myriad sculptures, photographs, paintings, and the like were perhaps influenced by his recollections of Bryant's descriptions heard on their walks together or from the travelogues that Bryant published.[27]

On a trip to Boston in 1881, after he had called on Henry Wadsworth Longfellow, Whitman reflected on the essence of Longfellow, Emerson, Bryant, and Whittier, "the mighty four who stamp this first American century with its birth-marks of poetic literature." He found Bryant distinctive for

> pulsing the first interior verse-throbs of a mighty world—bard of the river and the wood, ever conveying a taste of open air, with scents as from hayfields, grapes, birch-borders—always lurkingly fond of threnodies—beginning and ending his long career with chants of death, with here and there through all, poems, or passages of poems, touching the highest universal truths, enthusiasms, duties—morals as grim and eternal, if not as stormy and fateful, as anything in Eschylus.[28]

Bryant fostered strong nationalist viewpoints in both Whitman and Brown and was a decisive mentoring force for both of them. Whitman told Traubel that, in Brooklyn, he

> fell in with Brown, the sculptor—was often in his studio, where he was always modelling something—always at work. There many bright fellows came—[John Quincy Adams] Ward among them: there we all met on the freest terms. . . . The Brown habitues were more to my taste [than the Longfellow literary circles]. . . . Young fellows . . . would tell us of students, studios, the teachers, they had just left in Paris, Rome, Florence. . . . There was Launt Thompson: you know him? He came to Brown's studio though not in my time. They were big, strong, days—our young days—days of preparation: the gathering of the forces.[29]

Henry Kirke Brown (1814–86), born in Leyden, Massachusetts, took the portrait busts he had modeled in Boston and Albany with him to Florence in 1842 to have Italian artisans replicate them in marble but decided, instead, to cut the stone versions himself. Disdaining classical subjects, Brown chose to create in Italy a marble sculpture of what he considered a typically American subject, *Indian Boy*. While Brown modeled the portrait of Bryant in his studio in Rome in 1845 (see p. 240), the poet persuaded Brown to return to the United States to establish his studio in New York City.[30]

Brown for a while in Italy had succumbed to European aesthetics, which accorded primacy to Roman and Renaissance idealized, classicizing, white marble sculpture characterized by hard, clear contour lines and subjects that would have baffled most Americans. By 1850, Brown and Whitman shared Bryant's conviction that artists in the United States should create works of art uniquely American in form and content. That year, Brown exhibited his white marble portrait of Bryant at the National Academy of Design, of which he was a member.

Brown sketched Native Americans and created many sculptures of them in a style that merged classicism with naturalism. Whitman likely read this early analysis of Brown's work written in February 1851 by a critic named N. Cleveland, which he echoed in March in his address to the Brooklyn Art Union:

> It was his ambition to become, not a European, but an American sculptor. If a school of art, with characteristics in any degree national, is ever to grow up among us, its work must be done mainly upon American ground, and amidst American influences. He felt that the artist's independence and originality might be endangered by too long a familiarity with the faultless models of antiquity. . . . to exert over his countrymen a powerful and wholesome influence, it [art] must be accomplished by the presentation of other subjects than the unclad beauties or the fabulous forms of ancient Greece.[31]

Like Whitman and Brown, John Quincy Adams Ward was earthy and unpretentious, emphasized direct observation and expression of life in his sculptures, and was determined to establish an indigenous American style and subject for his art. Both Ward and Whitman avoided European training. Ward, however, unlike Whitman, believed with traditional sculptors that the European canon should be followed. Ward wrote:

> Adhere to nature, by all means, but assist your intelligence and correct your taste by the study of the best Greek works.

> . . . Art means the selection and the perpetuation of the noble and beautiful and free—else we might as well have photography. In portraiture especially the best movements, forms, and expressions should be taken. The true significance of art lies in its improving upon nature.[32]

Whitman fought valiantly to record reality without trying to improve on it by means of classic poetic cadences. Ward, through his extensive teaching and by means of his energetic leadership of influential arts organizations in New York such as the National Academy of Design, the National Sculpture Society, the National Arts Club, and the Metropolitan Museum of Art, mentored hundreds of students and developed vastly increased patronage of American sculptors, especially for the creation of public monuments. In 1876, Ward ordered five copies of Whitman's "complete" works, demonstrating that the ideas of Bryant, Brown, and Whitman, with whom he had dialogued during his formative years, remained important to him throughout his career.[33]

Bryant, Brown, and Whitman shared a conviction that American arts and letters not only could survive independent of European arts and letters but had to do so. They shared an interest in the indigenous and extraordinary shared experiences of Americans. Brown and Whitman awakened an interest in art that celebrated the power of American natural and material icons. Whitman, as the first elected president of the short-lived Brooklyn Art Union, spoke in front of the group on March 31, 1851, and concluded the address with eighteen lines from his poem "Resurgemus." He argued that aesthetic appreciation was crucial for the human spirit in an increasingly materialistic age and that art could improve the quality of life of the working classes. The American Art Union, an egalitarian forum, had been initiated in 1838 as the Apollo Gallery in New York to provide exhibition space for artists. Through 1842, the works distributed through the annual lottery were European, but in 1843 Mount's *Farmers Nooning* was selected. Art unions were organized in cities throughout the United States, including the short-lived one in Brooklyn with which Whitman was associated. When the New York state legislature declared lotteries illegal in 1852, the art unions in Manhattan and Brooklyn folded.

Throughout his career, Whitman demonstrated his comprehensive knowledge of sculptural forms and the symbolic significance of their different stances and gestures in his word pictures. For example, he described America as a matriarchal goddess whose deification is signaled by enthronement: "A grand, sane, towering seated Mother, / Chair'd in the adamant of Time."[34] The "adamant of time" could refer to a heavy marble or granite sculpture of a personification of America. In the pictorial arts, America was not frequently depicted as a seated goddess until the centennial. Although Greenough had deified George Washington in tons of white marble (emulating the fifth-century B.C. enthroned effigy of Zeus at his temple at Olympia), and many monumental sculptures of an enthroned female personifying America were created later, Whitman's is an early use of the image. Colonists in the Americas had been slow to see themselves collectively in symbolic form. The standing image of the Indian princess, a young, partially nude, dark-skinned female dressed in feathers or tobacco leaves, was the icon most frequently used by Europeans during the seventeenth and eighteenth centuries. During the early federal period, classical personifications of such "American" virtues as justice, freedom, liberty, and independence accompany George Washington, an American eagle or flag, or female goddess-like images of Columbia or America; Whitman's America is attended by "Freedom, Law and Love."[35]

Photography

Whitman related to the new art of photography in several ways: as the natural media to service democratic ideals, as an apparently realistic form of art relatively free of traditional affectations that he could and did use as a model to construct his poems (a new way of seeing), and as the format he preferred for portraits of himself. He regarded photographs not as equal in importance to other pictorial works of art but as superior to them, because

American citizens could both understand their descriptive imagery and afford to commission or buy them. During the 1840s, he frequented New York's daguerreotype galleries. Ed Folsom has argued convincingly that Whitman responded strongly and positively to photography because this medium of art related to his ideas of the democratic foundations of America.[36]

> Photography, after all, was the merging of sight and chemistry, of eye and machine, of organism and mechanism, much as America was, and thus it took root more rapidly here than elsewhere, became the precise American instrument of seeing. Whitman knew that no culture was more in love with science and technology than America was, and the camera was the perfect emblem of the joining of the human senses to chemistry and physics via a machine.[37]

Just as some nineteenth-century writers used exhaustive lists of flora, fauna, and other miraculous aspects of nature as teleological arguments to prove the existence of God, so Whitman liked daguerreotypes and other photographic prints, especially in large group exhibitions, because collectively they enumerated the myriad aspects of democracy and the people in it. Photography was the art of the common folk, the accessible, informal, chaotic art of everyday democratic citizens. "A literary class in America always strikes me with a laugh or with nausea: it is a forced product—does not belong here. We should not have professional art in a republic: it seems anti to the people—a threat offered our dearest ideals."[38] Whitman observed that "the best plain men are always the best men, anyhow—if there is any better or best among men at all. The cultivated people, the well-mannered people, the well-dressed people, such people always seem a trifle overdone—spoiled in the finish."[39]

Whitman understood that in their idiosyncratic interpretations of city life, photographs were equivalent to his poems: both were images of reality to be regarded as works of art. He acknowledged that, as a newspaper reporter, he had assumed the role of an observer wandering through the modern city searching for extremes of public existence, that role of "flaneur" that art historians have identified as a crucial determinant of the form and content of realist paintings of nineteenth-century urban life.[40] Susan Sontag notes that a photographer's camera was the natural extension of the eye of the flaneur, "an armed version of the solitary walker reconnoitering, stalking, cruising the urban inferno, the voyeuristic stroller who discovers the city as a landscape of voluptuous extremes."[41] Instead of creating works of art in a studio using a traditional, academic, pictorial vocabulary, some photographers, painters, and writers immersed themselves in the phenomenal world of modern life and captured fragmentary glimpses of it in their works. Thus, both the form and the content changed. In order to express the staccato beat and fragmentation of modern life, Whitman cataloged what he saw in free verse, Manet depicted real objects in a compressed space, and photographers shot views cluttered with things haphazardly positioned. Whitman's democracy was a gestalt that was greater than the sum of millions of citizens added together. Writers and artists suggested that each work of art displayed one tiny fragment of modern life and that, in order to understand the whole, the viewer/reader had to add thousands of such particulars. Everyone who approached photographs would go away with very different visions in mind. When Whitman reviewed a daguerreotype exhibition, he wrote, "We infer many things, from the text they preach—to pursue the current of thoughts running riot about them."[42]

Whitman and his contemporaries were the first people able to trace gradual changes over time in their personal appearances and to retain "scientific" records of loved ones after they had died. Can you imagine the awe with which they regarded the documentation of their own aging process, imperceptible day by day but obvious when analyzing photographic prints taken over decades? Whitman treasured the daguerreotypes of his parents, Walter and Louisa Whitman. The "carpenter portrait"of the poet that Gabriel Harrison shot in 1854 was the basis of the engraving used as the frontispiece of the first edition of *Leaves of Grass*. Whitman was almost gleeful in his expressions of delight in the number and variation of the photographic portraits of him, especially because they were a permanent image of so many of the personae he had created for himself in his poetry. "No one has been photographed more than I have," he boasted to Horace Traubel.[43] The iconography of Whitman includes photographic records of him both young and old; clothed in shirt sleeves and open collar and in stiffer, more formal attire; sometimes robust and other times sickly and frail; usually alone but other times with friends. He loved the camera's ability to capture his likeness just as he was at one moment in time. On the other hand, Whitman was aware that he and the photographer could manipulate the medium to establish the premeditated identity he fancied that day or year. He chose to be photographed in certain ways just as he created certain attitudes toward himself and his writings through his letters to critics and his anonymous reviews of his own publications. The 1883 studio portrait of Whitman with a butterfly perched on his finger was contrived to suggest the poet's communion with nature: the butterfly was a paper cutout (found in 1995 in one of the four slender notebooks that had been lost in 1941, which turned up at Sotheby's auction house). He planned appropriate photographic icons for his relatively sophisticated marketing plan.

Before long, photographs were widely used to document everything from paintings to battlefields. We are surprised that Whitman, who expected that his avant-garde views on most subjects would offend many of his readers, objected to unedited selections of photographs for public viewing. Because gory views of mangled human bodies photographed on Civil War battlefields caused too much distress to civilians who saw them, Whitman decided to limit his verbal interpretations of his direct experiences with soldiers to softer, more positive observations. In reality, both the actual battle sites, which he witnessed when he visited the war front in December 1862 in search of his soldier/brother, George, as well as the pictorial interpretations of them overwhelmed the poet. He had a human—some say feminine—aversion to art or literature that delineated images of people in such painful distress.

Landscape Painting

Whitman's buoyant, panoramic, verbal views of the unique landscapes of the United States are paralleled in landscapes painted by artists. For 200 years, writers and painters theorized about the visual values in their works that they had in common. Did reading poetry train the artist's eye to select the most beautiful, sublime, or picturesque view? Or, did profound experiences with paintings enable poets to create painterly poems? In *Kindred Spirits* (1849), Asher B. Durand (1796–1866) immortalized painter Thomas Cole in transcendental communion with poet William Cullen Bryant as they stood together on a rocky promontory in the primordial forests of the Catskill Mountains in New York. At the same time, while Whitman was formulating his mature aesthetic philosophy, he saw this painting in which his poet/friend, Bryant, and the renowned painter stood in a natural paradise untouched by technology or the paraphernalia that then symbolized the European cultural tradition. Ironically, raw nature continued to symbolize the United States even after Europeans lauded American technology at the international fairs that began in 1851. Whitman must have identified with the partnership between artist and poet. *Kindred Spirits* illustrates some of Whitman's recurrent themes: the uniqueness and unparalleled beauty of the American landscape, the importance of celebrating what was American rather than feeling compelled to repeat European formulas, the importance of taking the time to get lost in nature, and the poetic lens. Whitman wrote in his poem "Give Me the Splendid Silent Sun," "Give me solitude, give me Nature, give me again O Nature your primal sanities."[44]

Although Hudson River school painters carefully observed and meticulously rendered detailed landscapes, they subjected the scenes to the sublime content and formulas for composition typical of European Baroque painters, especially Claude Lorrain (1600–1682). Durand, the archetypal Hudson River school painter, created landscape paintings like transcendental poems to convey the presence of God that he perceived as he painted. Collectively, Thomas Doughty (Whitman's favorite), Cole, Durand, and other landscape painters created an American Edenic iconography that was more sublime and spiritually uplifting than the delineators of American topography who had preceded them. Hudson River school paintings were regularly on view during the years that Whitman wrote art criticism, and he wrote, for example, that everything that Durand did was good and that Doughty was "the prince of landscapists."[45] Although the artists of this first school of American landscape painting subjected their compositions to European paradigms, for the most part they celebrated American subject matter. By the time Durand died in 1866, American painters of the first rank wanted to study in Europe, especially in France. In 1866, Winslow Homer (1836–1910) and Eakins, who depicted quintessentially American subjects, were in Paris studying. Other American painters in Paris that year included Elihu Vedder, William T. Richards, and expatriates Mary Cassatt and James A. McNeill Whistler. For the next eighty years, a tension between European and American influences and subjects marked the history of American art.

A painter who was Whitman's near contemporary, George Inness (1824-94), offers some interesting parallels with the poet. Both were born in rural New York state and moved with their families to a New York City borough, where they spent their childhoods and experienced their first professional successes during the 1840s; both lived in Brooklyn during the 1850s and moved to New Jersey during the 1870s. *Apple Blossom Time* (1883), *October* (1886), *Early Autumn, Montclair* (1891), *Home at Montclair* (1892), and *The Red Oaks* (1894), paintings by Inness that colorfully highlight different seasons and moods of nature are echoed in poems by Whitman and by many other writers. Whitman included "Colors—A Contrast," prose observations of two November days, in *Specimen Days*.

> Such a play of colors and lights, different seasons, different hours of the day—the lines of the far horizon where the faint-tinged edge of the landscape loses itself in the sky. As I slowly hobble up the lane toward day-close, an incomparable sunset shooting in molten sapphire and gold, shaft after shaft, through the ranks of the long-leaved corn, between me and the west.
>
> *Another Day.*—the rich dark green of the tulip-trees and the oaks, the gray of the swamp-willows, the dull hues of the

sycamores and black-walnuts, the emerald of the cedars (after rain,) and the light yellow of the beeches.[46]

Beech trees are a motif common to this Whitman passage and Durand's *The Beeches* (1845).

Whitman wrote, "Give me the splendid silent sun with all his beams full-dazzling."[47] In "Songs of Parting," Whitman penned a "Song of Sunset".

Splendor of ended day floating and filling me,
Hour prophetic, hour resuming the past,
Inflating my throat, you divine average,
You earth and life till the last ray gleams I sing.

....

O spirituality of things!
O strain musical flowing through ages and continents, now reaching
me and America!
I take your strong chords, intersperse them, and cheerfully pass
them forward.

I too carol the sun, usher'd or at noon, or as now setting,
I too throb to the brain and beauty of the earth and of all
the growths of the earth,
I too have felt the resistless call of myself.[48]

Both "Song of Sunset" and Whitman's "A Prairie Sunset" mark a national and personal time of transition and celebrate the technicolor power of nature—and especially of the setting sun.

Shot gold, maroon and violet, dazzling silver, emerald, fawn,
The earth's whole amplitude and Nature's multiform power
consign'd for once to colors;
The Light, the general air possess'd by them—colors till now
unknown,
No limit, confine—not the Western sky alone—the high meridian—
North, South all,
Pure luminous color fighting the silent shadows to the last.[49]

Sunsets, which occur at twilight, are symbolic of dualism, a dividing line between opposites, ambivalence, transformation, all concepts easily interpreted for the history of the United States at mid-century. On the eve of the development of scientifically based theories of light and color, which led directly to Impressionism, sunsets had special meaning to mid–nineteenth-century poets and painters internationally. John Wilmerding's treatise and exhibition, *American Light: The Luminist Movement (1850–1875)* brought together a group of painters who were fascinated by and attempted to capture the effects of radiant light on various landscapes.[50] Sunset paintings as different as John Frederick Kensett's *Sunset, Camel's Hump, Vermont* (c. 1851), Frederick Edwin Church's *Twilight in the Wilderness* (1860), Sanford Robinson Gifford's *Sunset* (1863), and George Inness's *The Close of Day* (1863) further document the parallels and aesthetic philosophies shared by Whitman and American painters.

In 1855, the first president of the new Delaware, Lackawanna and Western Railroad commissioned Inness to paint the roundhouse (a circular shed for storing, switching, and repairing locomotives) near Scranton, Pennsylvania, in the valley of the Lackawanna River. Inness regarded the work, originally entitled *The First Roundhouse of the D.L. & W.R.R.*, as commercial advertising rather than poetic expression. Ironically, the painter traveled by stagecoach rather than train to make sketches of the train and its housing. Later, Inness recognized "the considerable power" of *The Lackawanna Valley*, as it came to be known.[51] The impending industrial rape of the American Edenic landscape is indicated by tree stumps in the foreground, the smoke-belching train in the middle ground, and the roundhouse in the distance. The machine, the symbol of the new industrial age and of America, here coexists with the garden but spawns new forms of art. The train, here still a relatively innocuous intruder in the natural landscape, will loom larger and larger in war, peace, art, and life in the United States. For example, the North won the Civil War in part because it controlled 88 percent of the existing railroads. American transportation, communication, unification, and self-image were transformed when the transcontinental railroad was completed on May 10, 1869, with a golden spike driven into the ground at Promontory Point, Utah. Although Whitman's attitudes toward railroads and technology in general changed over time, his single poem dedicated exclusively to the train, "To a Locomotive in Winter" (1876; rev. 1881), is an enthusiastic endorsement of this "modern—emblem of motion and power," this "pulse of the continent," which Whitman describes as a "Fierce-throated beauty!"[52] More than anything else, the train represented hope for the unification of the nation after a divisive Civil War.

Whitman wrote the poem "Death's Valley" and an additional stanza "to accompany a picture; by request." In it, he described death as something that all of the people of the great civilizations of the past had entered and suggested that he and Inness, whose painting *Valley of the Shadow of Death* (1867) was published along with the poem in *Harper's Magazine* in April 1892, would go peacefully through the dark valley. Both Whitman and Inness had remained independent of the mainstream of poetry and painting in the United States throughout their careers. They shared a fierce nationalism and a belief in their idiosyncratic visions of art.

Two French Social Realist Painters: Millet and Courbet

Whitman was enthusiastic about the contemporary painter he regarded as his kindred spirit: "Millet is my painter: he belongs to me: I have written Walt Whitman all over him. . . . Or, is it the other way around? Has he written Millet all over me?"[53] Traubel reported that Whitman "welcomes every allusion to Millet—every anecdote, every criticism."[54] Whitman claimed that Millet was a "whole religion in himself: the best of democracy, the best of all well-bottomed faith is in his pictures. The *Leaves* are really only Millet in another form—they are the Millet that Walt Whitman has succeeded in putting into words."[55]

Because of the tantalizing coincidence of realist style and social realist content among three innovative contemporaries—Whitman, Millet, and Courbet—scholars have been searching for links between Whitman and either of the French painters. Meixner dealt only with the post–Civil War epoch, and Reynolds found no evidence that Whitman had been aware of either Millet or Courbet before he produced the early editions of *Leaves of Grass*.[56] When asked "When did you first happen upon Millet?" Whitman answered, "I had often seen fugitive prints—counterfeits: bits about Millet in papers, magazines: it was in Boston that I first happened upon Millet originals."[57] Whitman visited the home of Quincy Adams Shaw near Boston in April 1881 and spent "two rapt hours" before his collection of Millet pictures. *The Sower* (1850) engaged his attention first.

> Never before have I been so penetrated by this kind of expression. . . . There is something in this that could hardly be caught again—a sublime murkiness and original pent fury. Besides this masterpiece there were many others, (I shall never forget the simple evening scene, "Watering the Cow,") all inimitable, all perfect as pictures, works of mere art; and then it seem'd to me, with that last impalpable ethic purpose from the artist (most likely unconscious to himself) which I am always looking for. To me all of them told the full story of what went before and necessitated the great French revolution—the long precedent crushing of the masses of a heroic people into the earth, in abject poverty, hunger—every right denied, humanity attempted to be put back for generations—yet Nature's force, titanic here, the stronger and hardier for that repression—waiting terribly to break forth revengeful—the pressure on the dykes, and the bursting at last—the storming of the Bastile [*sic*]—the execution of the king and queen—the tempest of massacres and blood. . . . Will America ever have such an artist out of her own gestation, body, soul?[58]

Whitman's interpretation is far more radical than the benign, sentimental view many Americans had of Millet's *Angelus* (1857–59) or *Gleaners* (1857), which can be read very differently, depending on one's point of view. *The Sower* represents nostalgic agrarianism to many viewers. Others believe he, like Whitman and Courbet, is speaking for the oppressed, landless working class. Whitman's reaction to Millet's paintings demonstrates the demands for basic human and civil rights that both were communicating. In 1887, Whitman said that he had been striving for thirty-five years to state, restate, repeat, and insist upon the kind of democracy that Victor Hugo and J. F. Millet presented. Each of them separately had proselytized for a government and arts that originated with the working people. Each had lobbied for political change through his creative works. In discovering so powerful a spokesperson for his own causes, Whitman felt that his often-misunderstood quest had been validated.

The excitement that Whitman displayed upon discovering Millet was matched by Albert Boime's when he discovered the political, philosophical, and aesthetic analogies between Courbet and Whitman. "The thematic and subjective affinities of Whitman and Courbet," Boime wrote, "are so striking that past failure to make a case for their relationship appears as an historical oddity."[59] No one, however, has documented any instance in which Whitman or Courbet saw the work or mentioned the name of the other. Boime convincingly demonstrates that the 1848 French Revolution mobilized both Courbet and Whitman to a heightened realization of social needs.

> It is in this period that both came to realize their road to success was bound up with the commonplace, and they located themselves squarely in the center of working-class institutions, family, customs, town and country. Not fortuitously, it was a period of counterrevolution in Europe, when the worker and peasant were courted by savvy governments in the wake of violent insurrection from below, while in the United States the crisis over slavery played out in connection with the newly annexed territories engendered a burgeoning of propaganda aimed at the working classes in the free states.[60]

In a dramatically worded editorial in the *Brooklyn Daily Eagle* that foreshadows *Leaves of Grass*, Whitman called upon the blue-collar, hard-working men

> to speak in a voice whose great reverberations shall tell all quarters that the *working-men* of the free United States, and their business, are not willing to be put on the level of negro

slaves, in territory which, if got at all, must be got by taxes sifted eventually through upon them, and by their hard work and blood.[61]

Traubel noted that Whitman owned framed photographic reproductions of the work of both Millet and Jean-Leon Gérôme, the latter left there by Eakins, who, from 1866 to 1869, had studied at the Ecole des Beaux-Arts in Gérôme's atelier. Whitman preferred Millet to Gérôme, saying, "The *grand* does not appeal to me: I dislike the simply *art* effect—art for art's sake, like literature for literature's sake, . . . because literature created on such a principle (and art as well) removes us from humanity, while only from humanity in mass can the light come."[62] As it was to Eakins and Whitman, the nude human form was central to the oeuvre of Gérôme, though, as the academic artist he was, Gérôme devised mythological or exotic settings to rationalize the inclusion of nude female figures in his compositions: Pygmalion and Galatea or a slave market in a north African country. Eakins, the sober scientific realist, also contrived settings to rationalize the inclusion of a nude figure: anatomical studies or William Rush's need for a nude model in order to carve his *Allegorical Figure of the Schuylkill River,* (1809) whom Eakins included in his painting *William Rush Carving His Allegorical Figure of the Schuykill River* (1877).

Thomas Eakins and Winslow Homer

In 1887, the Turkish-born Talcott Williams, writer for and managing and then associate editor of the *Philadelphia Press*, took Eakins to Camden to meet Whitman, and the poet and the painter remained friends for the rest of Whitman's life. Every Eakins scholar has written about their dynamic relationship and about the photographic and painted portraits Eakins executed of Whitman in Camden.[63] Eakins, Whitman, and Courbet have been celebrated in the twentieth century for the same qualities for which they were criticized in their own time and place: crude-ness, obscenity, and apparent lack of discipline in the construction of their purposefully unidealized works. Speaking about *Walt Whitman* (1887; see p. 249), the portrait that Eakins painted of him, the poet mused:

> It is about finished. Eakins asked me the other day: "Well, Mr. Whitman, what will you do with your half of it?" I asked him: "Which half is mine?" Eakins answered my question in this way: "Either half, . . . Somehow I feel as if the picture was half yours, so I'm going to let it be regarded in that light." Neither of us at present has anything to suggest as to its final disposition. The portrait is very strong—it contrasts in every way with Herbert Gilchrist's, which is the parlor Whitman. Eakins' picture grows on you. It is not all seen at once—it only dawns on you gradually. It was not at first a pleasant version to me, but the more I get to realize it the profounder seems its insight. I do not say it is the best portrait yet—I say it is among the best: I can safely say that. I know you boys object to its fleshiness; something is to be said on that score; if it is weak anywhere perhaps it is weak there—too much Rabelais instead of just enough. Still, give it a place: it deserves a big place.[64]

Part of Whitman's fascination with Eakins's likeness of him resulted from the painter's profound knowledge of human anatomy, which yields the real, architectonic core of the apparently freely drawn "fleshiness," and the loosely brushed impasto pigments in the portrait.

Eakins had studied anatomic draftsmanship at the Pennsylvania Academy of the Fine Arts and medical anatomy at Jefferson Medical College for many years during the 1860s and 1870s. His quest to understand the anatomical correctness of the human figure in motion prompted him to experiment with the stopped-action serial photography pioneered by English-born Eadweard Muybridge (1830–1904). By 1878, Muybridge had devised the zoopraxiscope which recorded motion on a rotating disk of film. Both Edward H. Coates, a trustee of the Pennsylvania Academy of the Fine Arts and a friend of Whitman's who commissioned *The*

Swimming Hole (1885; see p. 249) from the painter, and Eakins worked with Muybridge in Philadelphia. There, in 1884 and 1885, Muybridge photographed horses and humans with a series of cameras rapidly tripped in sequence, ground-breaking scientific experiments that contributed significantly to the history of art.[65] From this time forward, Eakins used photography, along with anatomy and mathematically based perspective schema, as an integral part of his developmental processes for his paintings. Coates, Williams (the learned cultural critic who had introduced Eakins to Whitman and who is the reclining figure in Eakins's *Swimming*), Traubel, and Whitman, who were members of the Contemporary Club founded in Philadelphia in 1886, were all knowledgeable about science and art.

Imagery of nude male figures and relaxed attitudes toward sexuality, which Eakins and Whitman shared, are pronounced in *Swimming,* one of Eakins's masterpieces. Section 11 of "Song of Myself," Whitman's ingenious parable of himself as a female poet/lover who is physically with the "twenty-eight men" who "bathe by the shore," almost certainly was in Eakins mind as he painted his allegory with his self-portrait as seer.[66] "Sexuality is without doubt crucial to *Swimming,*" writes Elizabeth Johns in her essay "*Swimming*: Thomas Eakins, the Twenty-ninth Bather," and she states that "the dilemma for contemporary interpretation is to decide whether the sexual atmosphere in the image alludes to specific sexual practices or to Eakins' more general absorption in the sensuality of the body."[67] Johns insightfully concludes that Eakins's sensuality as we find it in his personal papers and in his creative works "resembles that expressed in the poetry of his friend and older contemporary, Walt Whitman: it is a passionate devotion to the body and to the material manifestations of the spirit within it."[68] In another 1855 poem, later entitled "I Sing the Body Electric," Whitman in a few lines delineates experiences that we also find in Eakins's painting.

The swimmer naked in the swimming-bath, seen as he swims
through the salt transparent green-shine, or lies with his face up
and rolls silently to and fro in the heave of the water;

....

Such-like I love—I loosen myself, pass freely, am at the mother's
breast with the little child,
Swim with the swimmers, and wrestle with the wrestlers.[69]

Eakins and Whitman connected swimming with silent communion, freedom of movement of their own bodies, and spiritual and human connection. Especially for Whitman, ailing throughout his later years, swimming also was a rare time relatively free of physical pain; the buoyancy of the water was therapeutic because it supported and eased motion. Marc Simpson notes that, like Whitman's poetry, Eakins's painting is full of contradictions.

> One of the chief reasons that Thomas Eakins' *Swimming* compels admiration is its overwhelming quiet—a stillness not of lassitude or ease but of taut balance sustained on many levels. . . . On the surface the scene in *Swimming* pays clear homage to the natural life, featuring six men, swimming, sunning, naked, and at ease with themselves.[70]

Simpson points out that the serenity is countered by two active figures, one diving, something rarely found in the history of art, not even in Michelangelo's *Battle of Cascina,* which also depicted male bathers, and a man at the lower right (probably Eakins) treading water to keep his head above water.

Eakins chose scullers and rowers for another of his signature motifs, an image that Whitman also included in "I Sing the Body Electric": "The bending forward and backward of rowers in rowboats." Both were fascinated with reflections in water. "There is so much beauty in the reflections," Eakins conjectured, "that it is generally worthwhile to try to get them right," an effort he obviously devoted to the creation of glancing lights in *The Swimming Hole.*[71] Just one of many references to reflections on water in Whitman are these lines in "Crossing Brooklyn Ferry."

I too many and many a time cross'd the river of old,
Watched the Twelfth-month sea-gulls, saw them high in the air
floating with motionless wings, oscillating their bodies,

Saw how the glistening yellow lit up parts of their bodies and left
the rest in strong shadow,
Saw the slow-wheeling circles and the gradual edging toward the
south,
Saw the reflection of the summer sky in the water,
Had my eyes dazzled by the shimmering track of beams,
Look'd at the fine centrifugal spokes of light round the shape of my
head in the sunlit water.[72]

This interest in the perceptual phenomena of light and its reflections predicts (in Whitman's case) and echoes (in Eakins's) the interests of the French Impressionist painters.

Franklin Kelly writes, "The sea was never far from Homer's life, and its appearance in his art was regular from the earliest years of his career. Its presence could be assertively obvious. . . . Or, it might be visible only in the far distance."[73] If you substitute the word "river" for "sea," the statement is true for Whitman as well. The analogies between Winslow Homer and Whitman are paramount and have been most sensitively perceived by Nicolai Cikovsky, Jr., who interprets Homer's painting *The Veteran in a New Field* (1865) as the same expression of the dispersal of the volunteer army immediately following the Civil War that Whitman had voiced. "The peaceful and harmonious disbanding of the armies in the summer of 1865," Whitman wrote, was one of the "immortal proofs of democracy, unequall'd in all the history of the past."[74] The last poems of *Drum-Taps* bring to light the poignant, bittersweet anxieties and issues of veteran soldiers. In Homer's painting, the veteran is a Cincinnatus who had earlier put aside his plow to wield the sword and now puts down his weapon to reclaim his farm tools. The veteran is alone in his wheatfield, which has waited patiently for him to return from war. Like Millet's solitary figure planting winter wheat in *The Sower*, Homer's lone figure carries the weight of significant and bewildering social, political, economic, and geographic changes. Like Millet's *The Gleaners*, the people in the paintings suggest the biblical stories of Ruth and Boaz or Isaiah. The veteran, who has just returned from the war, has thrown down his army jacket and has picked up a scythe to harvest the bountiful field with the grim reality of the reaper of death. Just as each leaf of Whitman's grass and Millet's *The Sower* and *The Gleaners* have dialectical meaning, Homer's painting of stalks of grain suggests paradoxes. The North could harvest its bounty after the Civil War; the South could not. Harvest, usually a celebration of a community, is in *The Veteran in a New Field* a lonely occupation. Homer has created a momento mori, a lamentation, and a memorial to the dead. Yet the sun shines and brilliantly illuminates the veteran's white shirt. He has immersed himself in nature to glean its healing powers. Winslow Homer and Walt Whitman speak the same language.

Whitman and Technological Advances in Architecture

Impressed with the accomplishments of his engineer brothers, Jeff and George, and attuned to its increasing international importance, Whitman praised the technological revolution happening in the United States and predicted that the collective powers of engineers and inventors would transform the world.[75] In his landmark book, *Space, Time and Architecture,* Sigfried Giedion convincingly argues that the strong impact of the United States on Europe began with American displays of technology at the Great London Exhibition of 1851. Many European writers commented on the ingenious qualities of the American inventions and manufactured items on view in London in American pavilions.[76]

Whitman was fascinated by metal cage construction, the primary architectural invention of modern times. Because of the strength of a steel skeleton cantilevered from the center, massive stone walls no longer were necessary as load-bearing structural supports. Walls, often of glass, could be hung like curtains to defend against external elements and to enclose and separate interior spaces because they did not have to bear the weight of the structure. The New York Crystal Palace at the World's Fair of 1853 inspired the following lines in "Song of the Exposition."

Around a palace, loftier, fairer, ampler than any yet,
Earth's modern wonder, history's seven outstripping,
High rising tier on tier with glass and iron facades,
Gladdening the sun and sky, enhued in cheerfulest hues,
Bronze, lilac, robin's-egg, marine and crimson,
Over whose golden roof shall flaunt, beneath thy banner Freedom.[77]

Before British gardener Joseph Paxton designed and built this Crystal Palace, a prefabricated structure of standardized, mass-produced parts, he had built similar structures for the first international exposition, the London Exhibition of 1851. Glass and iron walls had also been used during the first half of the nineteenth century for greenhouses, winter gardens, and transportation structures. Whitman was convinced that "iron and glass are going to enter more largely into the composition of buildings. . . . So far iron used in large edifices is a perfect success."[78] On August 26, 1876, the same day he saw iron and glass buildings at the Centennial Exposition in Philadelphia, Whitman reacted to the rising pile of masonry forming the new City Hall on four acres of William Penn's Center Square. When completed in 1881, its tower, which reached a height of 548 feet, made it the tallest building in America. The architect, John McArthur, Jr., emulated the Second Empire style that H.-M. Lefuel had used for his addition (1852–57) to the Louvre in Paris. Although City Hall's mansard roof, massive weight, and dense surface encrustation, with sculptural and architectural ornamentation, sharply contrast with the simple, functional, prefabricated construction of the exposition buildings, Whitman's architectural and aesthetic lexicons were broad enough to encompass both.

> I got out to view better the new, three-fifths-built marble edifice, the City Hall, of magnificent proportions—a majestic and lovely show there in the moonlight—flooded all over, facades, myriad silver-white lines and carv'd heads and mouldings, with the soft dazzle—silent, weird, beautiful—well, I know that never when finish'd will that magnificent pile impress one as it impress'd me those fifteen minutes.[79]

In 1873, the Scottish-born, Paris-trained sculptor Alexander Milne Calder, the first of three generations of sculptors named Alexander Calder, had started to carve hundreds of figurative allegories, which project in relief from the building's surfaces. Calder did not finish his work at City Hall until 1894, when his 37-foot, 26-ton bronze portrait of William Penn was put in place.

Whitman usually was more modern than his literary cohorts, and he inspired nearly every avant-garde artist and architect in the decades after his death. But, when Louis Sullivan (1856–1924), the incomparable architect and theorist of the Chicago school of functional, steel-cage skyscrapers, wrote a paean to Whitman, the poet was unaware of his importance. Traubel recalled that Whitman said of Sullivan, "Whatever he does I'll bet he does big: he writes as if he reached way round things and encircled them. He's an architect or something."[80] Sullivan had presented two important papers at meetings of the Western Association of Architects in 1885 and 1886, but, because they were published in obscure journals they were not as influential as they might have been. Whitman had not read them. Sullivan's two most important aesthetic statements, "Ornament in Architecture" and "The Tall Office Building Artistically Considered," were published later, in 1892 and 1896. Like Whitman, Sullivan wrote about and used general principles of attitudes toward his art and an intellectual process of thinking, instead of easily mimicked designs for surface or structure. Sullivan claimed his buildings were poetic and Whitman drew analogies between his poetry and architecture. Sullivan wrote on February 3, 1887, just six days after excavation had begun for Adler and Sullivan's massive, blocky Auditorium Building, designed to be almost devoid of ornament, and about the time that H. H. Richardson's Marshall Field Wholesale Building was completed—two landmark commercial buildings of the Chicago school by three of its undisputed master architects. In 1887, when Sullivan wrote to Whitman about his reaction to *Leaves of Grass*, which he had read the year before, "You then and there entered my soul, have not departed, and never will depart."[81] Sullivan was impressed that Whitman had achieved Sullivan's goals, that is, the "subtle unison" of the creator/man "with nature and Humanity" and the harmonious blending of the soul with materials.[82] The powerful designs of Adler and Sullivan's most innovative skyscrapers, the Wainwright Building (1890–91, St. Louis) and the Guaranty Building (1894–95, Buffalo), which fulfilled the architect's goal of creating skyscrapers as "proud and soaring things," were informed with Whitman's spirit. Whitman had a far greater impact on American and international artists in the decades after his death than he did in his lifetime.

Impact on Twentieth-century Art and Artists

Walt Whitman's poetry and philosophy had an enormous impact on realist and avant-garde artists who emerged during the early twentieth century. In "Song of the Exposition," Whitman wrote:

> I raise a voice for far superber themes for poets and for art,
> To exalt the present and the real,
> To teach the average man the glory of his daily walk and trade.[83]

His eternal message of the inventiveness, vitality, and validity of America's down-to-earth people, material culture, and vast, natural landscape reached beyond Whitman's "present" to the ensuing generations of intellectual artists and writers who also were determined to create an American art of American people and places that was free of both traditional standards and European affectations. In his written and oral discourse, painter and teacher Robert Henri, for one, forged realist theory for American art based on Whitman's thinking, especially his ideals of individualism and creating art from life as it is experienced directly.

> Before a man tries to express anything to the world he must recognize in himself an individual, a new one, very distinct from others. Walt Whitman did this, and that is why I think his name so often comes to me. The one great cry of Whitman was for a man to find himself, to understand the fine thing he really is if liberated.[84]

Henri had been the mentor to four artist/reporters in Philadelphia during the 1890s: John Sloan, George Luks, Everett Shinn, and William Glackens, who immersed themselves in the life of Philadelphia until photomechanical technology rendered their news drawings obsolete. Eventually, all five moved to New York City. They knew and admired Whitman's writings, perhaps in part because he also had worked for newspapers for years. On the occasion of a large independent exhibition that Henri helped to organize in 1910, he again stated his Whitmanian convictions: "As I see it, there is only one reason for the development of art in America, and that is that the people of America learn the means of expressing themselves in their own time and in their own land."[85] When these five painters and three other progressive artists exhibited together in 1908 at the Macbeth Gallery in New York, they were dubbed "The Eight," referring to eight artists whose work was original and unacceptable to the juries of the National Academy of Design, and also as the "Ash-Can School," because they included in their paintings objects that were as mundane, ugly, and real as garbage cans.

When one of these realist painters, John Sloan (1871–1951), walked across the Brooklyn Bridge for the first time, he immediately thought of Whitman's poem "Crossing Brooklyn Ferry," and as he strolled around Brooklyn for a while that day, he recalled how well Whitman had known the town.[86] Two of Sloan's paintings of 1907, *The Wake of the Ferry, No. 1* and *The Wake of the Ferry, No. 2* portray a subject familiar and important to Whitman with the same duality of experience that the poet had expressed in "Crossing Brooklyn Ferry." In the beginning of the poem, Whitman exults and feels "refresh'd by the gladness of the river and the bright flow." But his mood darkens seemingly without cause in the middle, and he alludes to "dark patches," "evil," and "contrariety." He writes that he "had guile, anger, lust, hot wishes" and "was wayward, vain, greedy, shallow, sly, cowardly, malignant." He then recovers and once again rejoices, instructing the river to

Frolic on, crested and scallop-edg'd waves!
Gorgeous clouds of the sunset! drench with your splendor me, or
the men and women generations after me!

Cross from shore to shore, countless crowds of passengers!
Stand up, tall masts of Mannahatta! stand up, beautiful hills of
Brooklyn.[87]

Sloan must have felt that Whitman had written these lines for him, one of "the men and women generations after." Sloan wrote that both of his paintings of the wake of the ferry boat depicted a melancholy day, and another time he said that the paintings were morbid. If the lone figure, a woman, is staring at the ferry's wake, she is at the stern looking back. If she had felt optimistic, she would have stood in the bow of the boat to look forward to what lay ahead.[88] His other paintings, in general, depend on a wider spectrum of colors, brighter tones, and more hopeful themes.

Whitman's writings inspired the vanguard photographer, gallery proprietor, and publisher Alfred Stieglitz and the artists he led. John Marin, Arthur G. Dove, Marsden Hartley, Max Weber, Georgia O'Keeffe, and other artists in the Stieglitz circle issued no manifesto, but several tenets central to their aesthetic philosophies were straight from Whitman. They fervently believed in artistic individuality and integrity, in being open to new ideas, and in distinctly American subject matter, all of which they combined with European modernist formal solutions, which included Cubism, Expressionism, Abstraction, and Futurism. Kaplan entitled one chapter of his biography of Whitman "Phalanxes," because the young poet had urged artists to unite in a "close phalanx, ardent, radical, and progressive" in order to be able to create a vernacular and independent national art.[89] The artists who exhibited at Stieglitz's Little Gallery of the Photo Secession, known as "291" because of its location at 291 Fifth Avenue, were just such a phalanx. They manifested their inspiration from Whitman's message in their personal and published writings, notably in Stieglitz's publication *Camera Work*, in their optimism, and in the exuberant spirit of their cutting-edge works of art. One example will suffice to document this important connection. In Paris, Abraham Walkowitz was thunderstruck when he saw a performance of the modern improvisational dancer Isadora Duncan, whom he had just met when Max Weber took him to meet French master sculptor Auguste Rodin in his studio. "She was a Muse. She had no laws," Walkowitz said, looking back on the moment that catalyzed him to create 5,000 gestural drawings of the fluidity of Duncan's spontaneous, abstract motion. "She didn't dance according to rules. She created. Her body was music. It was a body electric, like Walt Whitman."[90] Walkowitz suggests that, for him, Whitman's celebration of human sexuality and his equation of the natural body with its soul empowered him to exult in a gifted dancer who also defied traditions and expressed the same erotic power.

When European and American Dada artists and some of the realist painters founded the Society of Independent Artists in the fall of 1916, they did so in the name of Walt Whitman. This New York organization, modeled on the Parisian Société des Artistes Indépendants (founded in 1884), disallowed jury selection and prizes so that all artists, for a modest fee, could show their works in widely publicized annual exhibitions.[91] Like the art unions founded during the mid–nineteenth century, the New York SIA and many similar societies of independent artists founded subsequently in the United States dramatically democratized art. At Marcel Duchamp's suggestion, some of the organizers celebrated the first day of the first exhibition of the Independents (April 10, 1917) with the publication of the *Blindman* (the title refers to reactionary art critics). They summoned the ghost of Whitman because they shared with him a fervent desire to foster an art that was uniquely American: "May the spirit of Walt Whitman guide the Indeps. Long live his memory, and long live the Indeps!"[92] In a similar fashion, in 1917, the *Seven Arts*, like many other avant-garde journals, first paid homage to Whitman as its spiritual father in its support of American art: "The Spirit of Walt Whitman stands behind the *Seven Arts*. What we are seeking is what he sought."[93]

Many artists who had earlier found their inspiration in Parisian modernism wanted to celebrate indigenous American qualities after World War I. On May 31, 1919, Americans and Parisians in Paris enthusiastically celebrated the centennial of the birth of the poet who personified to both nationalities the American spirit. One vanguard American sculptor, John Storrs (1885–1956), had been trying since he had studied sculpture with Charles Grafly at the Pennsylvania Academy of the Fine Arts in 1910 to have a monumental public sculpture of his design erected in Whitman's memory. Marguerite Chabrol, the French journalist whom he had married, reported that Storrs had gathered in his sculpture new forces—the persistent forces that had built Chicago, Boston, Philadelphia, and New York—which had given him the motivation to conceive the most modern designs in sculpture.[94] Storrs was one of the first American sculptors to create a consistent body of geometric abstract sculptures, columnar multimedia works inspired by the skyscrapers pioneered in his native city of Chicago. Storrs had written to Horace Traubel in August 1917 that a Whitman monument would express the greatness and the soul of the nation.

> Aside from a few of our designers of bridges, grain elevators, steel mills, etc., Walt Whitman stands practically alone as one who has discovered a national soul and has given it expression in a form that can be called beautiful—that can be called art.[95]

Storrs's ideas predict the discoveries of American functional and industrial vernacular architecture by the Swiss architect LeCorbusier, which he published in *Vers un Architecture* (1923) and which determined his seminal modern style.

In two essays published in 1918, before the end of the war, the Harvard-trained literary and cultural critic Van Wyck Brooks lamented the absence of a uniquely American culture, and he agitated, as Whitman and Brown had done sixty years earlier, for vital, new, distinctly national forms of art.[96] Over the course of the twentieth century, whenever American nationalism and icons of American art and literature are discussed, Whitman has almost always been at the center of the dialogue. John Dewey, the American philosopher and educator with whom Storrs had studied in Chicago during the 1890s, answered Brooks's challenge and stated that a strong and developed American culture had already been manifested in myriad local expressions and that artists would continue to find "universal truth and expression" as they observed "the localities of America as they are."[97]

Precisionist artists and writers adapted science-oriented methods of visual perception to redefine reality, assumed Objectivist aesthetics, and shared Whitman's celebration of "place" in their works. As he took endless ferry rides and walks around the burgeoning towns of America, Whitman jotted down chroniclers' lists of staccato phrases that somehow evoked the sense of being in those places more than prose descriptions. Like the later Imagist and Objectivist poets whom he inspired, Whitman, in his persona as a solitary insightful observer, described concrete images of many local genres and the feelings they evoked in him. In 1917, poet, critic, and essayist William Carlos Williams wrote in "America, Whitman, and the Art of Poetry" that a successful work of art had to exhibit a "a common interlocking quality" of form and place, that artists had to gain contact with their own localities and had to self-consciously use all phases of their environment: the physical, spiritual, mental, and moral aspects of America.[98] As they believed Whitman had done, the Precisionists approached American objects and places without preconceived associations engendered by Europeans or by traditional artists and writers. In this way, and again like Whitman, the Precisionists hoped to create a fresh, modern view of their own surroundings. For Williams, Whitman, and the major exponent of Precisionism for painting, Charles Sheeler, the aesthetics and objectivity of photography were important in the formation of their mature styles. In 1921, Williams asserted that painters in America could avail themselves of the lessons of modern art that Europe had to offer as long as they derived their own works from immediate, intelligent, and informed contacts with their own localities.[99] Sheeler fulfilled Whitman's and Williams's call for contact with familiar places in a series of paintings of the barns that had fascinated him during the years he had lived in Bucks County, Pennsylvania. He loved their simple, functional, no-nonsense designs and the richness of the local materials of which they were built. They were timeless abstract icons of American Whitmanian qualities.

Whitman inspired Paul Strand and Charles Sheeler to record with striking architectonic geometry the skyscrapers, trains, steamships, and bridges of lower Manhattan in photographic prints that they assembled in a short, pioneering film, *Manahatta*.

This six-minute documentary, subtitled with quotations from Whitman's poem of the same name, was shown under the title *New York the Magnificent* at the Rialto Theater in New York in July 1921. Both European and American critics realized its importance. The hard edges, right angularity, steep parallax, dramatic lighting, abstraction, and directness of its images had never before been seen in a film. In 1941, Whitman's poetry was again coupled with vanguard photography when the Limited Editions Club of New York commissioned Edward Weston to create photographs to illustrate a new edition of Whitman's *Leaves of Grass*. Weston spent ten months traveling 25,000 miles to record the Americanness of America. He recorded industrial and rural aspects of the nation in panoramic and in close-up, sharply focused views of people, places, flora, and fauna. How appropriate that Walt Whitman, who had been mesmerized by the first exhibitions of photography during the 1840s, should have his *Leaves of Grass* illustrated a hundred years later by a master photographer who set about his task as if the poet himself were there instructing him how to do it.

Max Kozloff, in his essay "Walt Whitman and American Art," focuses on Whitman's "autocratic imagination," which, welded to his "egalitarian social conscience," produced a "psychic ruckus" that has stirred American artists ever since. From the statements of recent American artists, Kozloff distills a list of their central themes, which coincides with Whitman's.

> the quest for some naked, unequivocal internal identity;
> the need to overcome, either by compensation or exaltation, a feeling of solitude;
> a nostalgia for some future harmony of understanding in which the individual creator is accepted by the mass of his compatriots as a peer;
> anxiety and insecurity about the function of art in a democratic society;
> metaphoric overextensions of potency and will, caprice and style, as a means of self-assertion;
> mistrust of collective structures and intellectual traditions as enemies of impulse;
> macaronic confusions between "high" and "low" art;

mixed sensations of urban and rural experience and messianic aspirations toward a public statement;
finally and conversely, a dedication to artistic effort as labor in which the artist views himself as a blue-collar worker.[100]

Kozloff convincingly connects these themes, and thus the spirit of Whitman, to Eakins, Inness, Marin, Barnett Newman, Adolph Gottlieb, Clyfford Still, Robert Motherwell, Jackson Pollock, David Smith, Claes Oldenburg, Robert Smithson, Sullivan, and Frank Lloyd Wright. Kozloff's discussion again underscores Whitman's vital and direct connection with most major modern developments in American art throughout the twentieth century.

Whitman understood the modern idea of continual progress, the urgency shared by nineteenth- and twentieth-century innovators in art and music to invent what had never been known when he declared that *Leaves of Grass* "must drive on, drive on, no matter how rough, how dangerous, the road may be."[101] He hoped to be—and he was—the point of catharsis for receptive minds who read what he wrote, just as Emerson's and Bryant's words had been for him. To the present day, his words inspire the creators of our monuments. Iranian-American sculptor Siah Armajani chose a passage from "Song of the Exposition" to execute in large copper letters, which he installed on the 145-foot-long steel balustrade positioned to greet the estimated 16 million passengers who arrive annually at the new North Terminal of the National Airport in Washington, D.C.

Around a palace, loftier, fairer, ampler than any yet,
Earth's modern wonder, history's seven outstripping,
High rising tier on tier with glass and iron facades,
Gladdening the sun and sky, enhued in cheerfulest hues,
Bronze, lilac, robin's-egg, marine and crimson,
Over whose golden roof shall flaunt, beneath thy banner Freedom,
The banners of the States and flags of every land,
A brood of lofty, fair, but lesser palaces shall cluster.
Somewhere within their walls shall all that forwards perfect human life be started,
Tried, taught, advanced, visibly exhibited.[102]

Whitman had written these lines to celebrate two crystal palaces that Joseph Paxton had built for two world's fairs, 1851 and 1853, on two continents, buildings that foreshadowed the methods and materials of the future of modern architecture. Armajani's tribute to Whitman and international travelers is revealed by the light from a fifty-four-foot-high glass window in the building designed by architect Cesar Pelli, which opened on July 27, 1997. Thus, as travelers enter Washington, D.C., they are inspired by Whitman's tribute to architecture and by a vista of the city where Whitman lived for ten years. As much as the fine arts influenced the symbolism and form of Whitman's best writings, his words, in turn, continue to inspire artists and architects today.

NOTES

1. Some of the most important recent publications are Jessica Haigney, *Walt Whitman and the French Impressionists* (Lewiston, N.Y.: Edwin Mellen, 1990); Geoffrey M. Sill and Roberta K. Tarbell, eds., *Walt Whitman and the Visual Arts* (New Brunswick, N.J.: Rutgers University Press, 1992); Denise Bethel, "'Clean and Bright Mirror': Whitman, New York and the Daguerreotype," *Seaport: New York's History Magazine* 26 (Spring 1992); Ed Folsom, "WW and the Visual Democracy of Photography," in *Walt Whitman of Mickle Street: A Centennial Collection,* ed. Geoffrey M. Sill (Knoxville: University of Tennessee Press, 1994), 80–93; and David S. Reynolds, *Walt Whitman's America: A Cultural Biography* (New York: Knopf, 1995), esp. chap. 9, "Toward a Popular Aesthetic: The Visual Arts." I extend my appreciation to Milan R. Hughston, chief librarian, and Rick Stewart, director, Amon Carter Museum for sharing with me their considerable research files on the subject. Earlier publications that have informed my analyses include F. O. Matthiessen, *American Renaissance* (London: Oxford University Press, 1941); Max Kozloff, "Walt Whitman and American Art," in *The Artistic Legacy of Walt Whitman: A Tribute to Gay Wilson Allen,* ed. Edwin Haviland Miller (New York: New York University Press, 1970); Justin Kaplan, *Walt Whitman: A Life* (New York: Simon and Schuster, 1980); and David S. Reynolds, *Beneath the American Renaissance: The Subversive Imagination in the Age of Emerson and Melville* (Cambridge: Knopf, 1988).

2. In May 1998, Richard Wolbers, paintings conservator, Win-

terthur Museum, Winterthur, Del., examined this painting, still in the Whitman House in Camden. Based on the canvas-maker's stamp, the construction of the stretchers, and the composition of the pigments, he determined that it was an eighteenth-century copy of a seventeenth-century Dutch portrait. The copyist painted the date "1617," which had been inscribed on the original painting.

3. Willis Steel "Walt Whitman's Early Life on Long Island," *Munsey's Magazine* 40 (Jan. 1909, 497–502; rpt., n.p.: Norwood Eds., 1977).

4. *LGC,* 427–28; for an illustration of Hicks's portrait by Henry Inman and Whitman's essay on Hicks, see *WCP,* 1220–44. For Browere, see Wayne Craven, *Sculpture in America* (New York: Cornwall Books; Newark, Del.: University of Delaware Press, 1984), 87–97; Charles H. Hart, *Browere's Life Masks of Great Americans* (New York: Doubleday and McClure, 1899).

5. Plaster and bronze casts of the poet's portrait are two of the forty-five sculptures by Murray in the collection of the Hirshhorn Museum and Sculpture Garden. See Michael W. Panhorst, *Samuel Murray: The Hirshhorn Museum and Sculpture Garden Collection, Smithsonian Institution* (Washington, D.C.: Smithsonian Institution Press, 1982), p. 7 and catalog nos. 2 and 3, and "Samuel Murray, Sculptor," M.A. thesis, University of Delaware, 1982. In 1886, Murray studied painting at the Art Students' League of Philadelphia with Eakins, and thereafter shared a studio on Chestnut Street with him until 1900. From 1890 until 1941, Murray taught anatomy and sculpture at the Philadelphia School of Design for Women (now Moore College of Art). When Eakins visited Whitman in Camden, beginning in 1887, Murray often accompanied him.

6. We have no documented accounts of his involvement with art and music during that impressionable year, but the American Academy of the Fine Arts, founded in 1802 by merchants, owned and displayed a collection of plaster casts of ancient sculptural masterpieces such as the *Appolo Belevedere,* the *Laocoon,* and the *Dying Gladiator* and organized exhibitions of art from 1816 until 1839, when a fire destroyed its building. Meanwhile, artists had initiated a rival organization, the National Academy of Design, founded in 1825 as the Society for the Improvement of Drawing, which established the Antique School in 1826 and also held annual exhibitions comprised mostly of paintings by its members.

7. Egyptian style had been revived after Emperor Napoleon

Bonaparte's victories in Egypt in 1798 and 1799 and the British campaign of 1801, when artifacts, including the Rosetta Stone, were taken to the British Museum. See Richard G. Carrott, *The Egyptian Revival: Its Sources, Monuments and Meaning, 1808–1858* (Berkeley: University of California Press, 1978).

8. Whitman criticized the English Gothic style of James Renwick, Jr.'s Grace Protestant Episcopal Church, built in 1846 at Broadway and Tenth Street. Renwick was an engineer who designed St. Patrick's Cathedral (1858–79) in New York and the original castellated Smithsonian Institution building in Washington, D.C. Whitman found the architecture of Grace Church more "showy" than beautiful: "The stainless marble, the columns, and curiously carved tracery, are so attractive that the unsophisticated ones of the congregation may well be pardoned if they pay more attention to the workmanship about them than to the preaching." *The Gathering of Forces,* vol. 2, ed. Cleveland Rodgers and John Black (New York: G. P. Putnam's Sons, 1920), pp. 91–92.

9. *ISit,* p. 128.

10. Ibid., 128–29.

11. Henry Tuckerman, *Book of the Artists* (New York: G. P. Putnam & Son, 1867). For a recent comprehensive survey, see Wayne Craven, *American Art: History and Culture* (Madison, Wis.: Brown and Benchmark, 1994).

12. Richard Maurice Bucke, *Walt Whitman* (Philadelphia: David McKay, 1883), 21. Abbott brought the collection to New York in 1853 and returned to Cairo in 1855; after he died there in 1859, his Egyptian artifacts were purchased by the New-York Historical Society. See Floyd Stovall, *The Foreground of "Leaves of Grass"* (Charlottesville: University Press of Virginia, 1974), 161–65; and Kaplan, *A Life,* 170–71.

13. *LGC,* 33–34.

14. *WCP,* 344–46.

15. *WCP,* 622–23. In this poem, Whitman's description of "the round zones, encircling" sounds more like the Washington Monument in Baltimore (1814–29), also designed by Robert Mills, which had been cut in the shape of a colossal Doric column recalling Trajan's Column in Rome, the Vendome Column in Paris, and the Nelson Column in London. Whitman, however, was more familiar with the Mills designs for the District of Columbia Monument during his

years there than he was with the monument as it was completed in 1884. The finished project did not include the classic, circular colonnade found in earlier plans. See H. M. Pierce Gallagher, *Robert Mills, Architect of the Washington Monument* (New York: Columbia University Press, 1935).

16. Between 1836 and 1841, Mills erected the F Street South Gallery from the exterior plans designed by Ithiel Town and William Parker Elliot. Mills, in collaboration with Thomas Ustick Walter, built, between 1849 and 1852, the East (7th Street) Wing, which enclosed the long gallery in which Whitman nursed soldiers and, later, Lincoln danced at his second inaugural ball. Walter erected the West Wing between 1852 and 1856, at the same time that he began enlarging the U.S. Capitol—the classic, soaring cast-iron dome was completed in 1865, about the time that Whitman returned to Washington, D.C.

17. Quoted in David P. Handlin, *American Architecture* (London: Thames and Hudson, 1985), 54.

18. The Boston Prison Discipline Society, quoted in R[ichard] W[ebster] "John Haviland: Eastern State Penitentiary," in Philadelphia Museum of Art, *Philadelphia: Three Centuries of American Art, Bicentennial Exhibition* (Philadelphia: Philadelphia Museum of Art), 257–58.

19. "Sources of Character—Results—1860," *WCP*, 705–6.

20. Johns, *American Genre Painting: The Politics of Everyday Life* (New Haven: Yale University Press, 1991), 205, n. 1.

21. Ibid., 33–38; pl. 4; Reynolds, *Walt Whitman's America*, 292–94. For my discussion of Mount and Whitman, I am indebted to these two sources.

22. Reynolds, *Walt Whitman's America*, 49.

23. "Song of Myself," *LGC*, 39–40.

24. See Wanda Corn, "Postscript: Walt Whitman and the Visual Arts," in Sill and Tarbell, eds., *Walt Whitman and the Visual Arts* 172–73.

25. *WCP*, 819.

26. That Whitman introduced his sister Hannah to painter Charles Heyde suggests to me both that he was close to a circle of people whose livelihood was art and that he considered the profession worthy. Hannah and Charles were married in 1852 and moved to Vermont, eventually settling in Burlington. Neither their marriage nor Heyde's art amounted to very much.

27. *LGC*, 642–49.

28. *WCP*, 902–3.

29. *WWC*, II:502–3.

30. I am indebted to Wayne Craven for bringing to my attention "Henry Kirke Brown: The Father of American Sculpture," several volumes of unpublished letters and journals in the Manuscript Division of the Library of Congress. See also Craven, "Henry Kirke Brown in Italy," *American Art Journal* 1 (Spring 1969): 65–77.

31. "Henry Kirke Brown," *Sartrain's Magazine of Literature and Art* 8 (Feb. 1851): 137, quoted in Wayne Craven, "Henry Kirke Brown: His Search for an American Art in the 1840s," *American Art Journal* 4 (Nov. 1972): 44–45.

32. G. W. Sheldon, "An American Sculptor," *Harper's New Monthly Magazine* 57 (June 1878): 63, 66; quoted in Lewis I. Sharp, *John Quincy Adams Ward: Dean of American Sculpture, with a Catalogue Raisonné* (Newark, Del.: University of Delaware Press, 1985). 20–21.

33. *WWC*, II:278–79.

34. *WCP*, 616.

35. See E. McClung Fleming, "From Indian Princess to Greek Goddess: The American Image, 1783–1815," *Winterthur Portfolio* 3 (1967): 37–66, and "The American Image as Indian Princess," *Winterthur Portfolio* 2 (1965): 65–81; and Joshua C. Taylor, "America as Symbol," in *America as Art* (Washington, D.C.: National Collection of Fine Arts, 1976), 1–35.

36. Folsom, "Walt Whitman and the Visual Democracy of Photography," 80–93.

37. Ibid., 82.

38. *WWC*, II:107.

39. *WWC*, I:71.

40. Folsom, "Walt Whitman and the Visual Democracy of Photography," 87. For the importance of the flaneur in shaping modern art and literature in the second half of the nineteenth century, see Walter Benjamin, "The Flaneur," in *Charles Baudelaire: Lyric Poet in the Era of High Capitalism*, tr. H. Zohn (London: New Left, 1973); T. J. Clark, *The Painting of Modern Life: Paris in the Art of Manet and His Followers* (Princeton, N.J.: Princeton University Press, 1984); and Griselda Pollock, *Vision and Difference: Femininity, Feminism and the Histories of Art* (London: Routledge, 1988), 50–90, abridged as "Modernity and the Spaces of Femininity," in *The Expanding Dis-*

course: Feminism and Art History, ed. Norma Broude and Mary D. Garrard (New York: Icon Editions, Harper Collins, 1992). Pollock established the flaneur as an exclusively male role: women were not allowed the privilege of wandering alone, day or night, to observe the public spaces of modern life.

41. Sontag, *On Photography* (New York: Delta, 1978), 55.

42. *GF,* II:116–17.

43. *WWC,* II:45.

44. *WCP,* 446.

45. *Brooklyn Daily Eagle,* April 14, 1847, on Durand, and *Brooklyn Daily Eagle,* November 18, 1847, on Doughty. Durand's nine "Letters on Landscape Painting," published in the *Crayon* in 1855, could be considered the manifesto of the Hudson River school. Durand's writings deserve a close reading and comparison to Whitman's 1855 *Leaves of Grass.*

46. *WCP,* 794.

47. *WCP,* 446.

48. *WCP,* 602–3.

49. *WCP,* 632.

50. See, especially, Wilmerding's essay on "Luminism and Literature," in the chapter "The Luminist Movement: Some Reflections," in his *American Light* (Washington, D.C.: National Gallery of Art, 1980).

51. Inness is quoted in Alfred Werner, *Inness Landscapes* (New York: Watson-Guptill, 1973), 24. See also George Inness, Jr., *Life, Art, and Letters of George Inness* (New York: Plenum, 1917), and Nicolai Cikovsky, Jr., *George Inness* (New York: Praeger, 1971).

52. *LGC,* 470–72.

53. *WWC,* I:62–63.

54. *WWC,* I:72.

55. *WWC,* I:7.

56. Meixner, "The Best of Democracy," in Sill and Tarbell, eds., *Walt Whitman and the Visual Arts;* and Reynolds, *Walt Whitman's America,* 298. Meixner's comparative study of Whitman and Millet is a full and reasoned account of many areas of common ground, including agrarian nostalgia, peasant and labor imagery, attitudes toward democracy and revolution, national land policies, and reception of their poetry and art.

57. *WWC,* III:88.

58. *WCP,* 903–4.

59. Boime, "*Leaves of Grass* and Real Allegory," in Sill and Tarbell, eds., *Walt Whitman and the Visual Arts,* 53. Boime acknowledges in n. 1 many scholars who have linked Whitman and Courbet. His is the most informed and complete analysis to date. In n. 35, he broaches the idea of a direct relationship based on the extent of the reputations of Whitman in France and Courbet in the United States and the familiarity of both artists with a wide range of cultural news and issues.

60. Ibid., 68–69.

61. *GF,* I:210–11.

62. *WWC,* I:72.

63. The Eakins monographs that I find most useful are Lloyd Goodrich, *Thomas Eakins,* 2 vols. (Cambridge, Mass.: Harvard University Press, for the National Gallery of Art, 1982); William Innes Holmer, *Thomas Eakins: His Life and Art* (New York: Abbeville, 1992); and Elizabeth Johns, *Thomas Eakins: The Heroism of Modern Life* (Princeton, N.J.: Princeton University Press, 1983).

64. *WWC,* I:39.

65. Traubel, Whitman, and Eakins were friends with Coates and his wife, Florence E. Coates. See *WWC,* II:112, 156, 215, 235, 237, 321, 336–37, 341–42, 348; and *WWC,* III:11, 482. See *TC,* IV:204, for Whitman-Coates correspondence. William Dennis Marks, Harrison Allen and Francis X. Dercum, *Animal Locomotion: The Muybridge Work at the University of Pennsylvania* (Philadelphia: J. B. Lippincott 1888), includes contributions by Eakins, who, in 1884, had been appointed to the Muybridge commission at the University of Pennsylvania. See also Fairman Rogers, "The Zootrope," *Art Interchange* 3 (July 9, 1879), and *Muybridge's Complete Human and Animal Locomotion: All 781 Plates from the 1887 Animal Locomotion by Eadweard Muybridge,* 3 vols. (New York: Dover Publications, 1979).

66. *LGC,* 38–39.

67. Doreen Bolger and Sarah Cash, eds. *Thomas Eakins and the Swimming Picture* (Fort Worth, Tex.: Amon Carter Museum, 1996), 69. This volume documents the commission, provenance, and multivalent meanings of the painting. In *Walt Whitman Quarterly Review* 15 (Summer 1997): 27–35, see Joann P. Krieg, "Percy Ives, Thomas Eakins, and Whitman"; William Innes Homer, "Whitman, Eakins, and the Naked Truth"; and Ed Folsom, "Whitman Naked? A Response." Also offering many new insights are Betsy Erkkila and Jay

Grossman, eds., *Breaking Bounds: Whitman and American Cultural Studies* (New York: Oxford University Press, 1996); Michael Moon, *Disseminating Whitman: Revision and Corporeality in "Leaves of Grass"* (Cambridge, Mass.: Harvard University Press, 1991); and Susan Danly and Cheryl Liebold, eds., *Eakins and the Photograph* (Washington, D.C.: Smithsonian Institution Press, 1994).

68. Johns, *Thomas Eakins,* 69.

69. *LGC,* 94–95.

70. Simpson, "Swimming through Time: An Introduction," in Bolger and Cash, eds., *Thomas Eakins and the Swimming Picture,* 1.

71. Eakins, "Reflections in the Water," part of his manuscript on linear perspective, c. 1884, Philadelphia Museum of Art, quoted in Kathleen A. Foster, "The Making and Meaning of *Swimming,*" in Bolger and Cash, eds., *Thomas Eakins and the Swimming Picture,* 25.

72. *WCP,* 309.

73. Kelly, "Time and Narrative Erased," in Kelly and Nicolai Cikovsky, Jr., *Winslow Homer* (Washington, D.C.: National Gallery of Art; New Haven and London: Yale University Press, 1995), 301.

74. Quoted in Cikovsky, "A Harvest of Death: *The Veteran in a New Field,*" in Marc Simpson, *Winslow Homer: Paintings of the Civil War* (San Francisco: Fine Arts Museums of San Francisco, 1988), 94, from *WCP,* 929–93.

75. For Whitman's attitudes toward technology, see Reynolds, *Walt Whitman's America,* 495–506, 522–25, 532, 557–58, and 562.

76. Giedion, "American Development," in his *Space, Time and Architecture: The Growth of a New Tradition* (Cambridge, Mass.: Harvard University Press, 1967), 335–428. This influential book, which developed out of Giedion's presentation of the Charles Eliot Norton Lectures for 1938–39, was first published in 1941 and revised and enlarged through the fifth edition in 1967.

77. *WCP,* 344–45.

78. *ISit,* 129. Whitman predicted that modern architecture would be as long lasting as the Egyptian monuments that had so impressed him during his youth: "If iron architecture comes in vogue, as it seems to be coming, words are wanted to stand for all about iron architecture . . . —those blocks of buildings, seven stories high, with light strong facades, and girders that will not crumble a mite in a thousand years." In Horace Traubel, ed., *An American Primer* (Boston: Small, Maynard, 1904), 8.

79. *WCP,* 849.

80. *WWC,* III:26–27. Traubel published Sullivan's letter and Whitman's response. See Hugh Morrison, *Louis Sullivan: Prophet of Modern Architecture* (New York: W. W. Norton, 1935, 1962); Narcisco Menocal, *Architecture as Nature: The Transcendentalist Idea of Louis Sullivan* (Madison: University of Wisconsin Press, 1981); and Robert Twombly, *Louis Sullivan: His Life and Work* (New York: Viking, 1887), and Weingarden. "Louis Sullivan's Emersonian Reading of Walt Whitman," in Sill and Tarbell, eds., *Walt Whitman and the Visual Arts,* 99–120.

81. *WWC* III:26.

82. Ibid.

83. *WCP,* 347.

84. Henri, "Progress in Our National Art Must Spring from the Development of Individuality of Ideas and Freedom of Expression: A Suggestion for a New Art School," *Craftsman* 15 (Jan. 1909): 387–401.

85. Henri, "The New York Exhibition of Independent Artists," *Craftsman* 18 (May 1910): 161.

86. Entry for May 31, 1910, in *John Sloan's New York Scene from the Diaries, Notes, and Correspondence, 1906–1913,* ed. Bruce St. John (New York: Harper & Row, 1965), 428. That evening, Sloan and his wife, Dolly, sat with Traubel at the Whitman Fellowship Dinner at the Brevoort Hotel. Sloan met Traubel after he subscribed to Traubel's *Conservator,* beginning in 1909. When he visited New York, William Butler Yeats, the noted Irish poet and playwright, borrowed from his good friend, Sloan, two volumes of Whitman's writings (432).

87. *WCP,* 312

88. Rowland Elzea, *John Sloan's Oil Paintings: A Catalogue Raisonné,* (Newark: University of Delaware Press and London: Associated University Presses, 1991) I:74 and 77, nos. 78 and 83.

89. In The *New York Evening Post* (Feb. 1, 1851), Whitman challenged American artists to band together in "a close phalanx, ardent, radical, and progressive" to create a "grand and true" art worthy of both their country and their progressive times.

90. Abram Lerner and Bartlett Cowdrey, "A Tape-recorded Interview with Abraham Walkowitz," *Journal of the Archives of American Art* 9 (Jan. 1969): 15. See William Innes Homes, *Alfred Stieglitz and the American Avant-Garde* (Boston: New York Graphic Society, 1977), esp. 83, 107, 140, 142, 149, 163, 175, and 202. As Homer established in that

book and Baigell in "Walt Whitman and Early Twentieth Century Art; in Sill and Tarbell; eds., *Walt Whitman and the Visual Arts,* many of the ideas that early twentieth-century American artists celebrated in Whitman could also be found in earlier writings by Emerson. The artists, however, felt more passionate about the poetry and the new paradigm of the more flamboyant Whitman than they did about Emerson's publications.

91. H. P. Roché, "The Blindman," *Blindman,* no. 1 (Apr. 10, 1917): 3–4.

92. Ibid., 6.

93. *Seven Arts* (May 1917): vii. Robert Coady, founding editor of the *Soul* is another good example. For many references to Whitman's vital role in the development of modernism in American art and literature, see Dickran Tashjian, *Skyscraper Primitives: Dada and the American Avant-Garde, 1910–1925* (Middletown, Conn.: Wesleyan University Press, 1975).

94. Paraphrased and translated from the statement (in French) by Marguerite Chabrol Storrs in *John Storrs* (New York: Folsom Galleries, 1920), quoted in Henry McBride, "John Storrs Making First Appearance in the Folsom Galleries," *New York Herald Tribune,* Dec. 19, 1920. This section on Storrs is adapted from my more complete statement, "John Storrs and the Spirit of Walt Whitman," in Sill and Tarbell, eds., *Walt Whitman and the Visual Arts,* viii–xi. On the day that Storrs completed a small model of the monument, Feb. 17, 1919, he wrote that he wanted to create "an arrangement in pure form . . . a study in weight and balance of masses." See the Storrs Papers, Archives of American Art, Smithsonian Institution, microfilm 1548, frame 324.

95. Draft of a letter from Storrs to Traubel, n.d., with a letter from Louise Bryant to Storrs, postmarked Aug. 15, 1917, saying that she and Jack Reed had intervened on Storrs's behalf to promote the project with their friend Horace Traubel. Storrs Papers (mf1551, frames 1090–1103). See also Louise Bryant, "John Storrs," *The Masses* 9 (Oct. 1917): 21.

96. Brooks, "War's Heritage to Youth," *Dial* 64 (Jan. 17, 1918): 47–50, and "On Creating a Useable Past," *Dial* 64 (Apr. 11, 1918): 337–41. In a series of seminal books, Brooks documented the evolution of America's literary identity. In *America's Coming-of-Age* (New York: B.W. Huebsch, 1924), he determined that the American prefer-

ence for material over intellectual and artistic endeavors had emerged from Puritan ethics and had stymied the full flowering of American genius. In 1947, he celebrated the creativity of Whitman in *The Times of Melville and Whitman* (New York: Dutton, 1947), the third in his series called *Makers and Finders.*

97. Dewey, "Americanism and Localism," *Dial* 68 (June 1920): 684–88. This article catalyzed William Carlos Williams and Robert McAlmon to found the little magazine *Contact,* which promoted Dewey's theories of the importance of "localism." These ideas are fully developed in "An Awakening Sense of Place, chap. 1 of Patrick L. Stewart's Ph.D. diss., "Charles Sheeler, William Carlos Williams, and the Development of the Precisionist Aesthetic, 1917–1931," University of Delaware, 1981. For the importance and development of *Contact,* see Gorham B. Munson, *Destinations: A Canvass of American Literature since 1900* (New York: Boni and Liveright, 1928).

98. Williams, "America, Whitman, and the Art of Poetry," *Poetry Journal* 8 (Nov,. 1917): 27–36. For the section on Precisionism, I have depended on Steward, "Development of the Precisionist Aesthetic." See also the Objectivist anthology in *Poetry* magazine (1931).

99. Williams, "Sample Critical Statement," *Contact* 4 (Spring 1921): 5–8. Ideas from this influential essay were echoed in Paul Rosenfeld, "American Painting," *Dial* 71 (Dec. 1921): 649–70, and Matthew Josephson, "The Great American Bill-Poster," *Broom* 3 (Nov. 1922): 305.

100. Kozloff, "Walt Whitman and American Art," 30.

101. *WWC,* II:107.

102. *WCP,* 344–45. Siah Armajani's sculpture was brought to my attention by Sherwood Smith of the Washington Friends of Walt Whitman with his note, "Whitman Saluted in Airport Artwork," *Walt Whitman Quarterly Review* 15 (Summer 1997): 59.

Whitman the Democrat

Kenneth Cmiel

Walt Whitman is America's democrat. For the last 150 years, writers have pointed to the poet, quoted from *Leaves of Grass*, and announced, "This is the best America can do!" Progressive reformers early in the century, New Dealers and communists in the 1930s, and gay rights' activists in our own day have all found Whitman friendly to their cause. Yet turning the poet into an icon can create its own problems. What *sort* of democrat was Whitman? What did he believe in? The poet has been tagged in many ways: radical democrat, socialist, liberal democrat, plebeian democrat, Jacobin, republican, artisanal republican. Which are accurate? What were Whitman's politics?

One way to orient ourselves to Whitman's political ideas is to remember his background. Whitman grew up in Brooklyn, New York, in a working-class family. He was active in Democratic party politics in his twenties, particularly close to its working-class wing. Whitman earned his living sometimes as a carpenter, sometimes as a newspaper editor. Yet he grew disenchanted with party politics around 1850, appalled by the unwillingness of either major party to confront slavery. At the same time, he became increasingly interested in the ideas of early nineteenth-century literary romantics. Whitman's political ideas became a mesh of his working-class background and literary aspirations.

Another way to orient ourselves to Whitman's political sensibilities is to compare his thinking to other sorts of political imagination. Today, a distinction is often made between "liberals" and "radical democrats." Liberals, like Harvard political philosopher John Rawls, see liberty and protection of basic rights as the most important political values. Care for these first, all else follows.[1] Democrats, on the other hand, see collective rule or the common good as central. Rights might or might not be helpful, radical democrats argue (strong property rights are always suspect); what is crucial is the ability of people to take control of their own lives.[2] Such a stark distinction between liberals and democrats blurs the subtleties of each position. Differences tend to be over priorities; debates arise over implications of particular issues. Is the perusal of pornography a right protected under the First Amendment, for example, as liberal Nadine Strossen of the American Civil Liberties Union argues? Or is it abusive toward women, inhibiting their ability to be democratic actors, as claimed by legal scholars like Catherine MacKinnon and Cass Sunstein?[3]

Historians have traced debates between liberals and democrats to the late eighteenth and early nineteenth century. To grasp what Whitman was about, we need to understand his relation to these battles of the formative period. The result, I believe, will be a Whitman a bit less radical than is often portrayed. Nevertheless, it will be a Whitman more in touch with the contradictions of his era.[4] Whitman's politics reflect his participation in a characteristically American form of artisanal democracy, one that included a strong distrust of the state. Whitman was a liberal, if by that we mean putting liberty first. But he was also a liberal of quite a different type than those more measured political actors and theorists who were the best-known liberals of the time. Such men argued that liberty had to take priority over collective rule. Whitman would not choose one or the other. He was a blend: a liberal defender of freedom and a radical democrat.

Whitman's political ideas can be traced from a rather standard artisanal position in the 1840s, to the rather stunning mix of liberalism and democracy evident in *Leaves of Grass*, first published in 1855, and to an increasingly stale and out-of-touch version of that same position in the early 1870s. Through it all, however, Whitman maintained that liberty and democracy did not have to be in tension, that the two might live together in a happy and equal union. His was always a balancing act on the razor's edge of liberal democracy.

Against Democracy: Liberalism as a Governing Doctrine

Before we look at Whitman's political thinking, it is necessary to step back and briefly outline the most important set of political ideas to emerge in the early nineteenth century. This cluster of ideas is now known as "liberalism," "classical liberalism," or "liberal democracy." At the time, it was commonly referred to as "representative government." Whatever the label, it was a set of ideas in tension with more radical versions of democracy.[5]

Especially since we, at the end of the twentieth century, take the idea of democracy for granted and use the word so casually, it is worth reminding ourselves just how scary the term remained even in the early 1800s. Reticence was common. The troubling violence of the French Revolution in the 1790s had convinced important influentials that pure democracy was the rule of the mob, a destructive force. The specter of revolutionary radicals drenching the streets in blood, indiscriminately marching their opponents to the guillotine while crowds cheered the heads dropping from torsos to baskets—such was the stuff of countless cautionary tales in those decades, not unlike stories of communist oppression in our recent past. While the U.S. revolution did not suffer the dramatic sort of violence that erupted in France, those continental images nevertheless did the same work in America. Even many who favored the basic drift of events still worried that "the people" could not always be trusted.

Between 1815 and 1840, a string of political theorists appeared who had no use for the undiluted rule of kings but still resisted the rule of the people. The Swiss political theorist Simonde de Sismondi and the important French historian and politician François Guizot rejected the very notion of the sovereignty of the people. Such an idea led to despotism, they thought, to regimes fickle and unchecked. Instead, they argued, true sovereignty rested in "reason" and "justice."[6] Other liberals, like the French political theorist Benjamin Constant in the 1810s or the American legal scholar Joseph Story two decades later, maintained their commitment to popular sovereignty but also argued that it had to be checked by the rule of reason.[7]

In the context of Euro-American political thinking, reason and justice were lodged between more radical and reactionary ideals. Defenders of the more radical moments of the French Revolution in France, or Chartist working-class reformers in England, continued to argue that "the people" should rule. On the other side, reactionaries still sang the praises of a monarchy. The call in those decades for a sovereignty based on reason and justice was a position of the political center.

Most Americans thought that some form of popular sovereignty was an inevitability. Liberals could still argue, however, that it had to be checked in some way. This was the view of Alexis de Tocqueville, whose towering *Democracy in America* was published in two volumes in 1835 and 1840 and stands as one of the most important statements of early nineteenth-century liberalism. Tocqueville derived his political sympathies from men like Guizot and Constant. By the 1830s, he had moved somewhat to the left of Guizot politically. Theoretically, he was convinced that rule by the people was an inexorable force in the world. The same was also true for American writers such as Story, whose three-volume *Commentaries on the Constitution* (1833) explored various ways to hedge in more radical democracy while still remaining committed to some basic form of popular sovereignty.

A number of ideas were used to check popular rule. One was the concept of the "rule of law". This is an ancient idea in Western thought, going back to Aristotle. Rule of law implied that citizens were governed by laws instead of arbitrary whim and that no person was above the law. Should you be subject to whatever some local lord decided that day, or to laws applied to all citizens equally? Should Bill Clinton, the president himself, face a sexual harassment suit while serving in office? The affirmative answer to that question, rendered by the Supreme Court in 1998, reaffirmed the ancient rule-of-law principle that no one is above the law. For early nineteenth-century liberals, the rule of law meant that popularly elected officials could not act arbitrarily. This often was tied to another idea of the time, "constitutionalism." Constitutionalism, or the need for a written constitution, meant that there were basic rules that temporary majorities could not easily change. For someone like Benjamin Constant, constitutionalism and the rule of law meant that no Jacobin crowd might take the law into its own hands.[8] This was aptly expressed by American editor Horace Greeley, who remarked that one of the great principles of the Whig party was "the supremacy of Law over Will or Force or Numbers." The age of democracy was one of "incessant Agrarian upheaval and radical convulsion," Greeley thought. The country needed "something which holds fast, something which opposes a steady resistance to the fierce spirit of Change and Disruption." Law, he argued, was that something.[9]

Another central pillar of liberal thinking was the principle of representation. Guizot, building on a long-standing republican tradition, placed the locus of discussion inside the representative chamber. Sismondi, in his *Studies on the Constitutions of Free Peoples* (1836), thought that having elected representatives discuss affairs of state was one of the preeminent privileges of a free nation.[10] This was tied to liberalism's fear of popular passions. Instead of freewheeling debate that might happen in the streets and get rowdy, senators and representatives would have calm and rational civic discussion. It was an important idea in European political thinking throughout the 1800s, somewhat less important in the United States. It depended upon a faith that legislative assemblies adequately "represented" the nation. As we shall see, this was being roundly criticized by the 1850s. Yet this did not trouble the original theorists of liberal democracy. For them, representation was another way to rein in public opinion, to replace "wildness" with "reason."

Finally, as with their contemporary heirs, liberals made liberty the central political value. Liberty, first of all, implied freedom from the coercive powers of government. The fear that an active state was an abusive state was a constant theme among nineteenth-century liberals. Kings and presidents, aristocrats and bureaucrats, must all be kept in check. Popular sovereignty had only limited sway, Constant thought, because there was "a part of human existence which by necessity remains individual and . . . which is, by right, outside any social competence."[11] This freedom from the state also implied, often but not always, the right to pursue your economic advantage. *Enrichessez-vous!* ("Get rich!") was one of Guizot's slogans, the one most often cited against him by his critics to the left. The importance of the concept of freedom as a strain of thinking opening up capitalism in the nineteenth century cannot be underestimated. Liberty was often a code word for letting the market rule. But while the term implied economic freedom, it also implied personal discipline. The two, in fact, were the flip sides of the same coin, for you needed discipline to pursue the capitalist project. Nothing was more common among liberals than distinguishing "liberty" from "license." Freedom was *not* about doing whatever you wanted. It was the measured ability to pursue your own course in life. Democracy, liberals thought, unchecked by tradition or religion or the laws of nature, led to the savage and licentious behavior witnessed periodically wherever crowds managed to run wild.[12]

Walt Whitman's Artisanal Democracy: The 1840s

This cluster of ideas emerged throughout the Western world in the early nineteenth century. Yet, while certainly important in the United States, such ideas were not without their critics. In crucial arenas their dominance was not yet secured. Local criminal courts in Philadelphia still resolved disputes informally, without feeling constrained by lawyers and their doctrines. If you had a complaint against someone in your neighborhood, you told your story to the local justice of the peace, someone who was not a lawyer and singularly untroubled by any need to follow formal law. Local common sense ruled. It took a concerted political push after 1850 to establish the rule of law in such settings.[13] Similarly, in cities and towns throughout the nation, the power of the crowd to inject itself into all sorts of political fights was common. "Out-of-doors" action in places like New York and San Francisco during the 1830s and 1840s was often quite rowdy. A crowd protesting the price of bread in New York in 1837 began their protest with the cry "Again to the Park—To the Park. The People are Sovereign."[14] Such action mocked the theories of calm deliberation found in writers like Guizot or Sismondi. Throughout the nation, labor activists could occasionally be heard to attack "the law" itself, arguing that "the people" should govern instead of some arcane set of rules.[15] The nation, even in the middle of the century, was engaged in a protracted struggle between the liberal rule of law and more assertive forms of democracy.

One pivotal force for this democratic pressure came from the artisan community of the day. Artisans, those who worked with skills, such as shoemakers, or bricklayers, stood socially above day laborers, who had to rely completely upon their brawn for a living. Politically, in the United States, artisans were the principal expositors of more radical visions of democracy. This was the culture Walt Whitman came from. His father was a carpenter, and early in life, Whitman alternately worked as a printer and carpenter.

As was still common in the early nineteenth century, Whitman moved from being a printer to a writer. He worked on various newspapers, all of which sold to a basically working-class audience. From March 1846 to January 1848, Whitman edited the *Brooklyn Eagle*, a Democratic party daily. He also wrote, reviewing books, discussing politics, exploring manners and mores, and commenting on the city. His writing is a good window to his political sensibilities, a good place to judge his relationship in the 1840s to the liberalism of his time.

Whitman, like the proponents of liberal democracy, loved liberty. It was a central term in his political vocabulary. Unlike the "old and moth-eaten systems of Europe," he wrote on July 28, 1846, in the United States "we have planted the standard of freedom." Such a sentiment included, as it did for liberals, a strong distrust of the state. Whitman believed in what twentieth-century political theorists have come to call "negative" liberty. A steady theme of his editorials was the need to guard against "meddlesome laws." He was adamant that government not regulate business. People should be "masters unto themselves," Whitman thought, for in "this wide and naturally rich country, the best government indeed is 'that which governs least.'" We needed to carefully guard our personal rights, Whitman argued, for "man is the sovereign of his individual self."[16]

If such thoughts sound suspiciously like the antigovernment sentiments of liberals, they were also common in many American artisanal circles. American artisans often drew on the legacy of Thomas Jefferson and Thomas Paine, both figures who combined faith in popular rule with a keen distrust of government. They stood in distinction to a French radical tradition that drew on eighteenth-century philosopher Jean-Jacques Rousseau and that associated liberty with collective rule. In this sense of liberty, often now called "positive" liberty, you were free if you helped make civic decisions. Controlling politics was associated with controlling your destiny. And while there were artisans in the United States who were developing a more radical analysis of the American political economy, Whitman was not among them.[17] Unlike labor radicals, who were trying to experiment with a workingman's political party, Whitman remained connected to the Democrats, albeit to their left edge. He spoke in the 1840s to a still popular sentiment among artisans that combined distrust of the state with celebration of collective rule.[18]

If Whitman's idea of freedom sounds in some ways like that of his era's liberals, it still differed in important ways. Whitman, in fact, pressed the idea of liberty much further than men like Tocqueville, Guizot, or Story. Whereas liberty was an important public value for them, they also felt that successful representative government needed widespread personal probity in the population. To flourish, the regime of liberty needed disciplined souls. Distrust of mass instincts often led liberals to defend laws meant to keep the population in order. Guizot and Sismondi still defended property restrictions on voting. France did not allow divorce at this time. Tocqueville had a profoundly conservative vision of the family and woman's role. Only if women kept the family together, he thought, would democracy not turn wild. This was simply a matter of natural law to Tocqueville.

In the United States, laws against the sale of alcohol, pornography, the seduction of women, and the operation of businesses on Sunday were all experimented with during the 1840s. Whitman, however, vehemently attacked such laws, using the same antigovernment rhetoric that he used to condemn efforts to regulate business.[19] It was not that Whitman was antithetical to all discipline. By the end of the decade, he had lent support to a nascent movement to stamp out masturbation, recoiled against certain forms of popular rioting, and routinely spoke of "rational" freedom, implying that there was some "irrational" freedom of which he did not approve. Still, Whitman was not like the liberals. He did not distrust the basic instincts of the citizenry, nor did he think that all rowdiness was dangerous. He was suspicious of any effort to use the state to discipline the population. Whitman refused to distinguish between liberty as a political or economic value and liberty as a personal value. All ran up against his deep distrust of a powerful government. Whitman was more libertarian than the liberals

On the other end of the political spectrum, Whitman's love of liberty pushed him further than numerous artisans and important segments of the Democratic party. One of the great fights in the mid–nineteenth century was to reform the law so that women could control their own property. Until that time, fathers and husbands automatically had legal ownership of a daughter's or wife's property (including any wages she might earn). The reform efforts were principally organized by Whigs or activists coming from Whig families. Democrats did not pay a lot of attention to women's issues. As early as 1847, however, Whitman was editorializing against this system, again using the language of personal liberty. Husbands should not "own" their wives' wages, he argued, because marriage should not "destroy woman's individuality." She should enjoy "every right which is naturally hers."[20]

Something similar might be said about Whitman and slavery. While consistently abusive toward abolitionists (the "dangerous fanatical insanity of Abolitionism," he wrote) and certainly not above racist views of his own, Whitman nevertheless thought slavery was an evil whose extension to new states had to be stopped. The whole system had to eventually disappear, and he criticized his own Democratic party for evading the issue: *"We must plant ourselves firmly on the side of freedom, and openly espouse it."*[21]

In still one more way, Whitman overlapped with mainstream liberals. In the mid-1840s, he sang the praises of representative government. He did not mind losing elections, because the system was fair. We owed great respect to our elected officials, he thought. His faith in progress buoyed him. In the long run, things would work out for the best. Like Tocqueville, Guizot, and John Stuart Mill, Whitman was friendly to rule by elected officials.

Yet, here too, Whitman agreed with a difference. Unlike Tocqueville, Mill, or Guizot, Whitman did not believe that personal freedom was in tension with democracy. This stance gave Whitman's prose a strikingly different tone. He gloried in those he variously called "the people," the "common people," the "masses," or the "workingman." He was simply without any fear of the majority. Instead, he spoke of the "youthful Genius of the people," of the "great things" we might expect from a "radical, true, far-scoped [and] thorough-going Democracy."[22]

It should not be surprising, then, that Whitman praised the raucous democracy of the streets, exactly the sort of crowd behavior so troubling to more moderate liberal democrats like Guizot or Story. The "destructiveness" of democracy was "beautiful" to Whitman. All "that is good and grand in any political organization" came from "turbulence and destructiveness." Whitman did want crowds who were guided by "common sense," but he was sure that was usual in popular assemblies. He certainly did not want to center debate inside the legislative chamber. All the "noisy tempestuous scenes of politics" were "*good* to behold," he wrote. "They evince that the *people act*."[23]

Nor should it be surprising that there were no odes to the rule of law in Whitman's 1840s editorials. There were laws he liked and disliked, but his main thrust was to fight the increasing reliance on law. Adding mountains of new statutes only confused the people, he argued. Far more important than baskets of laws were a few clear principles to guide the political system. Those who thought that "every thing is to be *regulated by laws*" earned his contempt.[24]

Whitman in the 1840s was a liberal with a twist. His principal political value was liberty, but he was actually more libertarian than many of the so-called "liberals" of his own time. And, unlike more moderate liberals, he was untroubled by the crowd. His was a particularly populist form of liberal democracy.

There were gaps in the *Brooklyn Eagle* political essays. Whitman never addressed how liberty and democracy would be reconciled. Unlike mainstream liberals, he simply assumed that they harmonized. Nor did Whitman have anything to say about poverty. By the 1840s, there were more radical artisan voices questioning the sort of economic liberty that Whitman still took for granted. Also, Whitman might have supported civil rights for women (now) and African Americans (eventually!), but he said nothing about their political rights. Should women vote? Were freed slaves to take part in crowd action? Finally, Whitman never really explained who "the people" he championed actually were. Indeed, this was a common practice in early nineteenth-century artisanal rhetoric. Yet it was not unquestioned. Tocqueville and the authors of the Seneca Falls Declaration of Women's Rights were among those noting the term's ambiguities. The same year that Whitman was writing in the *Brooklyn Eagle*, Karl Marx was observing that the "word 'proletariat' is now used as an empty word, as is the word 'people' by the democrats."[25] Whitman, though, was untroubled.

Today, a variety of political theorists point out the incoherence of claims made in the name of "the people."[26] And historians make the point in their own way. If some artisan-based radicals of the early nineteenth century were already attacking the idea that legislators adequately represented the people, it is easy today to see how those artisans at their best did not adequately represent women or people of color and all too often actively suppressed them.[27] Populist calls to "the people," in other words, were often enmeshed in their own mystifications.

Transcendental Democracy in the 1850s: The First Edition of "Leaves of Grass"

Whitman lost his job at the *Brooklyn Daily Eagle* in January 1848. He had swung too far to the left of the paper's owner, a more moderate Democrat. In the next years, Whitman wrote some articles for publication and worked on his poetry, but he mostly earned his living building houses. In the early 1850s, he grew increasingly disenchanted with mainstream politicians, especially for their evasion of the slavery issue. By the time he published *Leaves of Grass* in 1855, Whitman was no longer actively engaged in party politics. But, removed from the partisan fray, he developed a much richer sense of what democracy might be. It is the expansive vision in *Leaves of Grass* that makes Whitman's position secure, a key figure in our cultural heritage.

In *Leaves of Grass*, Whitman did his best to distance himself from elected representatives, quite a shift from 1847. "Great is Justice," he wrote in the last poem of the book, but justice was "in the soul" not "settled by legislators and laws." The people were a remarkable thing, he thought, but they would not be found in a president's message or a report from the treasury. Whitman was adamant. The rule of law should not check the rule of the people: "All doctrines, all politics and civilization exurge from you."[28]

An uncharacteristically bitter poem in the first edition of *Leaves of Grass* highlights Whitman's distance from representative institutions. The poem was an attack on the Fugitive Slave Act, which was passed by Congress in 1850 and mandated that northern states had to return escaped slaves to the South. The act outraged even moderates in the North as it seemed to suggest that they had to participate actively in the perpetuation of the slave system. The poem in *Leaves of Grass* is a meditation on one of the most notorious instances of the act in practice, the 1854 removal of Anthony Burns from Boston back to captivity, an event that took the active intervention of 1,000 federal troops to accomplish. Whitman was unsparing in his portrait, and his distaste for elected politicians was evident. He mentions three times in the poem that the marshal was "the President's marshal." Yankee phantoms from 1776 were groaning in their graves, Whitman wrote. Those departed friends of liberty had to watch from six feet under as their descendants propped up bondage. Whitman played heavily on sepulchral and gothic imagery. Maybe the mayor (another elected official) could go dig out King George's coffin, find a "swift Yankee clipper" and "steer straight towards Boston bay." Then there could be another procession, this too managed by the "President's marshal" and "government cannon." While we were at it, we might "fetch home the roarers from Congress" as well. Unpack King George's bones, Whitman wrote, "and set up the regal ribs and glue those that will not stay." Then, with his skull clapped "on top of the ribs" and "a crown on top of the skull," we could have a triumphant return of George through the streets of Boston. "You have got your revenge old buster! . . . . The crown is come to its own and more than its own."[29]

Despite the criticisms of elected officials, the tone of *Leaves of Grass* is overwhelmingly optimistic. The "people," the "common people" were great, Whitman thought. Yet Whitman had also, in important ways, moved beyond the artisanal political vocabulary so prominent in his 1840s editorials. While he continued to sing of the glories of "the people" or the "common people," he expanded his discussion beyond such abstractions. And he did this by infusing plebeian literary forms into his poetry.

At several points in *Leaves of Grass,* Whitman resorts to listing social types he finds admirable. He identifies each "type" and, in a phrase or two, gestures to its activity: "The machinist rolls up his sleeves. . . . the policeman travels his beat . . . the gatekeeper marks who pass." These lists, in certain places, can go on for pages. They are one of the most characteristic and well-known dimensions of Whitman's poetry, contributing mightily to its chantlike quality. In one such catalog, Whitman serially names the pure contralto, carpenter, married and unmarried children, pilot, mate, duck shooter, deacon, spinning girl, farmer, lunatic, printer, quadroon girl, drunkard, machinist, policeman, gatekeeper, young fellow, half-breed, marksman, newly come immigrants, overseers, gentlemen, dancers, youth, the reformer, "darkey," squaw, connoisseur, deckhands, young sister, elder sister, wife, Yankee girl, pavingman, canal boy, conductor, child, drover, "pedlar," bride, opium eater, prostitute, crowd, president, matrons, Missourian, fare collector, floormen, tinners, masons, pikefisher, squatter, flatboatmen, coon seekers, Indian patriarchs, the old husband, the young husband, and more.[30]

These passages are odes, celebrations of those they notice. Their cumulative message is the phenomenal diversity of humanity, the sheer multiplicity of our social roles and personality types. At the level of each individual mention, such passages imply that the work of all of us, no matter how lowly, deserves dignity. So many people in the world and the democratic poet sings of them all!

Such lists moved Whitman far beyond the rhetorical abstraction of "the people" by identifying "the people" in its varied particularity. All sorts of peoples not usually included in the artisanal political imagination could now be drawn into Whitman's expansive vision of democracy. For just as much as Americans,

> The barbarians of Africa and Asia are not nothing,
> The common people of Europe are not nothing . . . the American aborigines are not nothing,
> A zambo or a foreheadless Crowfoot or a Camanche is not nothing.[31]

Such sentiments became even more prominent in poems later added to *Leaves of Grass*, particularly "Salut au Monde!" (first published in 1856). Here Whitman hails everyone, the "Australians pursuing the wild horse," the "Arab muezzin calling from the top of the mosque," the "Hebrew reading his records and psalms." Around the globe Whitman moved, praising nomadic tribes of Asia, Brazilian vaquero, the men and women in the world's great cities, and tribespeople and peasants of Asian villages.

> I see ranks, colors, barbarisms, civilizations, I go among them, I mix indiscriminately,
> And I salute all the inhabitants of the earth.[32]

This remarkable capaciousness, Whitman's drive to name everyone, to give each and all their due, was certainly rare in his own day. It is the part of Whitman that allows late twentieth-century writers to press him, whatever his other limitations, into the contemporary multicultural project. It is certainly an important part of what makes *Leaves of Grass* a compelling read today.

This said, however, it is still important not to confuse Whitman with someone of the late twentieth century. Whitman in the late 1850s said contradictory things about the place of women in public life.[33] He held racist views of African Americans, despite his desire for their freedom. He also differed from many late twentieth-century progressives in having a deep faith in the idea of progress, making him cavalier about the imperial push of Western nations over the globe. His version of liberalism was not the one suggested by Judith Shklar, that of making cruelty the worst vice of them all.[34] He looked not to end cruelty now but to an ever-better future. Whitman was placid about the turmoil that shook the world and crushed some peoples because he was convinced that things would get better for everyone in the long run.

Whitman was caught in a classic tension of populist thinking. To celebrate the people, even the lowliest or those with the least amount of power, certainly contributes to democratic respect. In 1855, even more than today, it was important to say, "The wife—and she is not one jot less than the husband, / The daughter—and she is just as good as the son." But if such praise dignifies, it also leaves conventions standing where they are. Whitman might have been able to sing of "The female soothing a child . . . the farmer's daughter in the garden or cowyard." He even had the courage to announce that "the prostitute is not nothing." In the end, however, this still left women only being mothers, daughters, and prostitutes. Praising women for what they did ignored what they were not allowed to do. What of the fact that women were not stockbrokers or lawyers or ministers or even artisans? The portrait of women in *Leaves of Grass* is limited, not by any misogyny on Whitman's part, but by the populist conundrum that celebrating the people as they are also freezes the people where they are.[35]

Where did Whitman's capacious and generous lists come from? As David Reynolds has noted, such techniques were drawn from the popular literature of the day. The bizarre, the unusual, the great panoply of human actors (especially in the city) were all common themes of what Reynolds has called the "subversive" literature of the mid–nineteenth century.[36] Also during the 1840s, a whole literature on social "types" emerged throughout the Western world: "physiologies," books that painted portraits of social types, such as the Englishman in Paris, the drunkard, the salesgirl, the stevedore. Such collections of stereotypes were one way people learned to navigate cities like New York, which were rapidly filling up with strangers.[37]

Whitman was well acquainted with such literature even during the 1840s. Yet the conventions of the time largely segregated plebeian literary production, with its interest in the multiplicity of social types, from artisan political rhetoric, with its steady invocation of "the people." In his *Brooklyn Eagle* editorials, Whitman followed the convention. Eight years later, however, in *Leaves of Grass*, Whitman married the two. Whereas popular subversive literature often ended by dwelling on the weird (akin to the more refined writing of Edgar Allan Poe), Whitman combined the preoccupation with honest crooks, sexuality, and the manifold diversity of the world with the artisanal celebration of "the people." To better understand the book, it helps to underscore the obvious: *Leaves of Grass* is poetry, not a political tract. Whitman's distance from daily partisan politics opened up the imaginative space that made his remarkable vision of democracy possible.

Yet *Leaves of Grass* drew on more than plebeian literary conventions. Whitman also borrowed from Romantic aesthetics. After he left partisan politics, he started to take seriously the Romantic notion that poets were the true legislators of the world. The power that he thought the poet had—the power to chant a new form of life into being—was built on this assumption. This emphasis on the poet's creative powers also encouraged him to dream of new ways of expressing his democratic sympathies. Whitman's more explicit commitment to Romantic ideas, ideas that encouraged him to stand outside the immediate political frays of the time, were deeply important for his expansion and elaboration of "the people."

In another way contemporary literary sensibilities fed into the politics of *Leaves of Grass*. The book opens with one of the most evocative portraits of a protean self in modern literature. What we now call "Song of Myself" (none of the poems were titled in the original version) is a dramatic paean to a self inventing itself. The unique individuality of each of us is a central theme in the book.

Preoccupation with self-invention appeared in numerous

places in American culture, but it was not ubiquitous. Such ideas, for example, were not always evident in plebeian literature (with its interest in social "types") nor was it a routine part of mid–nineteenth-century populist thinking. Whitman, though, urged us to celebrate ourselves. He said nothing negative about this robust, even cosmic, egoism. Yet there was more to Whitman's rumination than simple self-interest. The self is always in motion, he thought, constantly in the process of making itself. Every person and thing we have contact with contributes to the ongoing formation of our personality: "I fly the flight of the fluid and swallowing soul." The egoism described in "Song of Myself" is not narcissistic, not contained within itself or stemming from an inability to connect with others. Whitman's egoism looks resolutely outward, roaming the world, the whole universe for that matter, soaking it all in. Nothing is alien; everything contributes—science, the wind, another human being's touch, listening to whatever sounds are around us, sex, "the gigantic beauty of a stallion," people of all kinds, with all quirks, a blade of grass, the farthest star. Since the universe itself is limitless, there can be no end to this journey. We can not learn this from others, Whitman thought: "Logic and sermons never convince." Experience the world and be receptive to it, Whitman says. The ideal soul that Whitman describes is truly both "fluid" and "swallowing."[38]

The mainstream liberal self was built on self-denial: you conquered the world by disciplining your passions. Nothing could be more distant from the democratic personality of *Leaves of Grass*. Whitman presents himself as a "loafer," available to every fleeting sensation. His flaneur-like persona wanders the city, nation, and globe, dazzled by the manifold diversity of existence. It is a personality not shaped into a disciplined character but emerging through an embrace of all Being.

Whitman's fluid self is another of his ideas very attractive in the late twentieth century. On the one hand, this is a corporeal, sensuous self. In Whitman, the soul is never removed from the body. And in our postmodern age of decentered selves and multiple identities, Whitman's call for us to make ourselves again and again as we go on, to joyously embrace our contradictions, remains a source of inspiration.[39]

In *Leaves of Grass*, Whitman moved even further from mainstream liberals than he was in the 1840s. He now had little good to say about representative institutions. He argued for continual self-invention instead of a disciplined self. He had no reservations about the rule of the people. Whitman presented a populist democracy that put individual liberty at its center. At the same time, however, Whitman had moved at least some distance from his artisanal roots. The book's protean self, its spiritual expansiveness and receptivity toward the whole world were not the usual fare in artisanal political rhetoric. *Leaves of Grass* differed tonally and in content. It is not surprising that it was not a bestseller. Whitman had imagined a democratic life far more encompassing than either the popular or liberal politics of the time.

While Whitman's elaboration of the people filled one hole in his 1840s editorials, *Leaves of Grass* still left unaddressed the issue that had given rise to theories of representative government: the tension between liberty and democracy. Whitman continued to assume their compatibility. Any tensions in the world would ultimately be resolved by the cosmic law that governed us all, according to Whitman. Whitman did no better with poverty. He was so hospitable to the long view and so preoccupied with slavery that any arguments about the imbalance of the market, such an important strain of more radical artisan voices, never surfaced in the first edition of *Leaves of Grass*.

Still, the book dramatically expanded Whitman's 1840s marriage of liberty and democracy. He now not only celebrated the people but celebrated them in all their magnificent diversity. He not only praised the individual, he sang of how the individual made him- or herself. And the *manner* in which we each make ourselves is the crucial link between the individual and the crowd. The democratic soul invents itself not by discipline, as the liberals hoped. Nor is it given to simple selfishness or sensuality. Instead, the democratic soul is born through a wondrous receptivity to other people and things. Democratic egoism happens by respecting the whole universe. It is an enormously attractive vision, generous, inquisitive, respectful. One we can still learn from.

Hollowness at Heart: Evaluating Liberalism in the 1870s

By 1840, the basic principles of nineteenth-century liberal theory were well known. The next four decades was a time of assessment. Political theorists spent considerable energy evaluating liberal democracy to see if it lived up to its promise. Marx attacked modern civil liberties as a cover for bourgeois rule. Mill argued that earlier ideas about representation were simplistic, earlier ideas about liberty timid. Women's rights activists and African Americans similarly questioned how "representative" representative government really was. Whitman's 1855 *Leaves of Grass*, with its distrust of elected officials and its sense that the heart of democracy was in people not institutions was a part of this same wave of evaluation. In the years following the Civil War, Whitman became even more disenchanted with mainstream politics. In the late 1860s, he wrote a series of political essays that were published in 1871 under the title *Democratic Vistas*.

In that book, Whitman remembered the war heroically. For him, it was a time when the people themselves fought for the principles of democracy. He remembered Abraham Lincoln similarly, as the captain who guided the ship through its worst storm. For Whitman, however, the next years were bleak. Practically every imaginable elite—literary, legal, commercial, and political—came in for abuse. "The best class we show, is but a mob of fashionably dress'd speculators and vulgarians." But now even broader doubts about his beloved "people" occasionally surfaced.[40]

The central problem was rampant materialism. It was not that riches were bad, but there had to be more. There had to be some idealism driving the country to greatness. The nation needed a spiritual purpose. Instead, however, it was descending into sordid money grubbing. The "moral conscience," it seemed to Whitman, was either "entirely lacking, or seriously enfeebled or ungrown." "Never," he wrote, "was there . . . more hollowness at heart than at present, and here in the United States."[41]

The country was filled with selfishness. Too many were out for their own gain. Whitman was finally recognizing a tension between individual freedom and the collective good, but he hardly addressed this in the way liberal defenders of representative government had. Whitman did not want democracy checked by liberty. He worried about a false liberty rampant. Individualism had become too materialistic, too self-satisfied. It was destroying any possibility of solidarity.[42]

Complaints about selfishness were common in post–Civil War America. But they most often came from those well-educated men and women of the professional classes who were also the most articulate defenders of liberalism. Unlike Whitman, they often responded to this perceived selfishness with a reaffirmation of those principles of representative government worked out in the early years of the century. Like Whitman, E. L. Godkin, editor of the *Nation*, the country's leading journal of opinion, thought after the war that Americans were becoming too self-indulgent. Yet, for Godkin, one important source of this self-indulgence were those labor activists who were, in his mind, agitating to get something for nothing. Godkin, who voiced the opinions of much of America's cultural elite, responded to the postwar mood by reaffirming the importance of a free market in economics and self-discipline in personal deportment.[43]

Whitman, conversely, continued to support popular rule. But now the country as a whole seemed less interested. Now it was not just the politicians who were suspect. Whitman in *Leaves of Grass* had envisioned the marriage of the spiritual and material, soul and body. Now he saw only body, a mean-spirited, crabbed world, a nakedly self-centered nation. Whitman also continued to register his faith in individuality and freedom. Government should not merely keep order but help develop all "aspiration for independence" in the citizenry.[44]

Whitman's older commitments were evident in the solutions he offered. The country needed a renewed feel for the spiritual force that ran through literally every particle of the universe. Remembering this would change the way we looked at the world, turn instrumentality into wonder, selfishness into receptivity. Through active contact with "the fresh, eternal qualities of Being," Whitman wrote, we might "vitalize our country and our days." The "core" of democracy was "the religious element," he argued elsewhere in the book. One of the most insistent themes in *Democratic Vistas* was the need to shape a more spiritual personality. Whitman came back to it again and again. The individual, he said at one point, needs to learn how to commune with the unutterable. The answer to the problems of materialism, in other words, was to create the sort of democratic personality he envisioned in *Leaves of Grass*.[45]

Moreover, as in *Leaves of Grass*, Whitman continued to argue that literature was the key conduit for this new personality. We need three or four great bards, Whitman thought, who might teach a more noble character. We need literatures that express democracy and the modern, literatures that might reveal some "prophetic vision" for the nation.[46] Whitman attacked the literary classes of the day for their genteel remoteness from the masses, for their unwillingness to pursue democracy. He hated culture with a capital *C*, the sort of culture supported by men and women like Godkin. Yet, just as much as the more conservative critics, Whitman's solution to the crisis was a cultural one.

His response to selfishness continued to be framed in terms of Romantic aesthetics. The nation would be saved by having poets sing of the affinity between a democratic people and the great laws that ruled the cosmos. What mattered was the cultivation of democratic—meaning expansive—personalities, just the sort of individuality he had sketched in *Leaves of Grass*.

Yet *Democratic Vistas* was stale compared to *Leaves of Grass*. "Song of Myself" is an ode to a personality that is remaking itself with each encounter. It is constantly changing, wandering through the world and evolving at every step. In *Democratic Vistas*, though, Whitman let his worries about materialism get the best of him. While he opened the book talking about the variety of character types and the "numberless" directions that human nature took, such language quickly disappeared. Whitman wanted so much to get the right sort of personality that his language became far more static. Literature should picture "a typical personality," he wrote at one point; we need an "American stock-personality" at another. Our literature must create "a single image-making work," he now argued. Whitman's prose tended less to ongoing wonder and self-invention, more to a fixed point of reference.[47]

Moreover, the artisanal sympathies so prominent in his *Brooklyn Eagle* days and the first edition of *Leaves of Grass* were now less evident. Whitman worked as a clerk in the Department of Interior in the years after the war. He was less intimately tied to either working-class life or the culture of the street than he had been in New York during the 1840s and 1850s. It is striking that the word "workingman," so prominent in Whitman's vocabulary prior to the war, does not appear anywhere in *Democratic Vistas*. To be sure, Whitman continued to praise the idea of popular democracy. "The People," he claimed, remained "essentially sensible and good." Yet he also felt that he could no longer "gloss over the appalling dangers of universal suffrage" and would now admit to seeing "the crude, defective streaks in all the strata of the common people." Humanity as a whole had become more flawed for Whitman. He still had faith in democracy, but increasingly he relied more upon the redemptive power of history than on working people themselves. It would all work out in the long run, Whitman thought—with, of course, the help of a prophetic literature.[48]

Whitman retreated on both the individual and democratic sides of his project. And not only was his prose becoming stale. His solution was largely irrelevant. By the 1870s, aggressive businessmen were reshaping the marketplace; the era of big business was dawning in America. Workers were becoming increasingly militant, and large-scale industrialization was throwing the nation into turmoil. To respond to all this by calling for a literature that would instill a renewed respect for the wonders of Being can, to be generous, only be described as limited.

It is not that I find spirituality a bad quality. In other contexts, I would argue that more respect for some force in the universe larger than ourselves would be healthy. Yet, however important to us as human beings, it cannot be the complete sum of a political project. Politics requires more mundane considerations.

To understand how limited Whitman's 1870s assessment of liberal democracy was, how close he remained to the liberal democratic tradition, it is worth comparing him to others who were taking stock of the project. At the same time Whitman was writing his editorials for the *Brooklyn Eagle* celebrating the marriage of liberty and democracy, Marx was already arguing that modern liberty was a cover for the rule of the bourgeoisie, that the theory of representative government was incoherent, and that the marriage of freedom and democracy of the kind that Whitman dreamt of would only emerge in the wake of a violent revolution that would overthrow capitalism. None of this was ever a part of Whitman's thinking. In the 1870s, he continued to call on working people to assert themselves, yet he never developed a structural critique of the economy. He never thought there had to be a revolution for the marriage of liberty and democracy to take place. While Whitman attacked selfish businessmen in *Democratic Vistas*, he attacked *everyone* in that book. Far from being a protosocialist, Whitman praised the "true gravitation hold of liberalism in the United States," which he described as "a more universal ownership of property, general homestead, general comfort—a vast intertwining reticulation of wealth." While he might decry the "yawning gulf" that was the "labor question," Whitman still "hailed with joy" the "business materialism of the current age." If it could only be spiritualized, all would be well.[49]

Nor did Whitman get to even more modest types of institutional reform. Already in 1848, some French republicans were arguing that the state should guarantee employment for the people. Radical republicans like Alexandre Ledru-Rollin attacked the "empty sovereignty" of representative democracy. These early appeals for social democracy (opposed at the time by liberals like Tocqueville and Guizot) set the stage for the emergence of the welfare state in the twentieth century.[50] Eventually, this theory would directly confront the tensions between liberty and democracy with theorists claiming that solidarity had trumped liberty.[51] Nothing remotely resembling this was in Whitman's thinking. Whitman continued to fear that the state was potentially a danger.

Whitman also did not consider structural reforms to the representative system. He attacked politicians while he contradictorily praised the electoral process. Yet, at just about the same time, John Stuart Mill was making a more concrete suggestion. In his *Considerations on Representative Government* (1862), Mill argued that no legislature could adequately represent the nation if it was made up of only winners of elections. Guizot, in other words, had been wrong. In a winner-take-all system (as in today's United States), candidates who get 49 percent of the vote will not get to the assembly. The goal of proportional representation, now widely used in other parts of the world, is to make sure that minorities—and minority vote getters—have some role in legislative assemblies. First presented by Mill in 1862, this idea is now an important part of the representative system in many countries outside the United States. Whitman, however, at the same time, was responding to the failure of public life with calls for a new literature.

While people like Marx, Ledru-Rollin, and Mill were all influenced by Romanticism, none were defined by it. Neither was Whitman in the original *Leaves of Grass*, with its faith in the inventiveness and diversity of common people. But as Whitman became less satisfied with artisanal democracy, he simply lapsed into a foggy rapture about what a democratic literature could do for the spiritual imagination of the people. Communism, social democracy, proportional representation all addressed the same issues and, for better or worse, with a harder institutional edge to them. Whitman, in *Democratic Vistas*, helped assess the success and failure of nineteenth-century liberal democracy, but he contributed nothing in that book to a rethinking of either liberalism or democracy.

Whitman in the 1840s evoked a populist version of liberal democracy, one in which the primacy of liberty did not entail any checks on popular sovereignty. And personal freedom, moreover, was not built by repression of instinct. In the 1850s, Whitman expanded this vision in his remarkable *Leaves of Grass*. In the late 1860s, as Whitman became a bit more skeptical about popular passions, it might at first glance seem that he moved closer to mainstream liberal democrats, with their clear ranking of liberty, first, and democracy, second. Indeed, Whitman's claim that the purpose of democracy was to train free individuals might suggest this. So, too, might his praise of wealth making or his reticence to attack the system of capitalism. Yet that would be misreading. Whitman, in *Democratic Vistas*, did not want to limit democracy. Instead, he vaguely held out the hope for a spiritual rebirth that might solve the "paradox" that had opened up inside it. Whitman, unlike mainstream liberal democrats, did not see the tension between personal freedom and the common good as built into the nature of things. In the end, he had no doubt, individualism and patriotism would merge "and will mutually profit and brace each other."[52]

By 1871, Whitman had freed himself from the classic paradox of populist thinking: how to praise the people without accepting whatever they might do. He now knew the "masses" were not always right. But coming to this realization did not lead Whitman to embrace the liberal tension, that which posited constant strain between individual freedom and popular rule. Nor did Whitman's imagination lead him to spin out theories of revolution or even any sort of protosocial democracy. Whitman's democratic sympathies did not flag after the Civil War. Rather, he was losing any way to see them being put into practice. What was failing was his imagination.

Whitman tried to sketch out a radical liberalism, if by "liberal" we mean that the value of personal freedom is central. He unabashedly defended negative liberty, and, with the great exception of the war to end slavery itself, he was suspicious of handing power over to the state. Yet Whitman was not a perfect liberal. By the 1850s, he was not sold on the practice of representative government. And, while he always praised the Constitution (even in *Democratic Vistas*), he was not enamored of the principle of the rule of law. Nor did he fear that individuality and democracy were in tension.

What remains attractive today about Whitman's political vision is his proto-multiculturalism and his sense of a fluid self. It is here that contemporaries find the poet most appealing, especially now that the dreams of Marxism have faded for progressive intellectuals and activists. Yet, such commentators rarely mention Whitman's commitment to freedom. The hope that we—both singly and collectively—could invent our own lives was a strong and persistent part of Whitman's political vision. Recently, political theorist Wendy Brown has asked why radical democrats and progressives do not spend energy defending the value of freedom and expanding its practice in the world. She worries about "the turn toward law and other elements of the state for resolution of antidemocratic injury."[53] If sentiments may be as rare today on the left as Brown suggests this suggests that ours is *not* a Whitmanesque moment, for Brown's suggestions echo back to the poet. Whitman was a radical democrat who always put freedom center stage.

NOTES

1. John Rawls, *Political Liberalism* (New York: Columbia University Press, 1993).

2. Chantal Mouffe, *The Return of the Political* (London: Verso, 1993).

3. Strossen, *Defending Pornography: Free Speech, Sex, and the Fight for Women's Rights* (New York: Scribner, 1995); MacKinnon, *Only Words* (Cambridge, Mass.: Harvard University Press, 1993); and Sunstein, *Democracy and the Problem of Free Speech* (New York: Free Press, 1995).

4. For examples of a more radical Whitman, see Betsy Erkkila, *Whitman: The Political Poet* (New York: Oxford University Press, 1989); and Betsy Erkkila and Jay Grossman, eds., *Breaking Bounds: Whitman & American Cultural Studies* (New York: Oxford University Press, 1996).

5. For some literature on these political ideas, see Gordon Wood, *The Radicalism of the American Revolution* (New York: Vintage Books, 1991); Pierre Manent, *An Intellectual History of Liberalism* (Princeton: Princeton University Press, 1994); and Carl Schmitt, *The Crisis of Parliamentary Democracy* (Cambridge, Mass.: MIT Press, 1985).

6. J. C. L. Simonde de Sismondi, *Études sur les constitutions des peuples libres* (Bruxelles: H. Dumont, 1836), 18, 39, 216–18; and Guizot, *History of the Origin of Representative Government in Europe* (London: Henry G. Bohn, 1861), 55–75.

7. Constant, "Principles of Politics Applicable to All Representative Governments" (1818), in Constant, *Political Writings* (Cambridge, England: Cambridge University Press, 1988), 169–83; and Story, *Commentaries on the Constitution of the United States* (Boston: Hilliard, Gray, and Co.; 1833), I:304.

8. Constant, "Principles of Politics," 171; also see Story, *Commentaries*, III:759–60.

9. Greeley quoted in John Ashworth, *"Agrarians" and "Aristocrats": Party Political Ideology in the United States, 1837–1846* (Cambridge, England: Cambridge University Press, 1983), 155.

10. Guizot, *History of Representative Government*, 78–81; Sismondi, Études, 260.

11. Constant, "Principles of Politics," 177.

12. For an insightful discussion of Tocqueville's argument that liberal democracy needed religion and a conservative nuclear family, see Pierre Manent, *Tocqueville et al nature de la democratie* (Paris: Julliard, 1982), 117–49.

13. Allen Steinberg, *The Transformation of Criminal Justice: Philadelphia, 1800–1880* (Chapel Hill: University of North Carolina Press, 1989).

14. Mary Ryan, *Civic Wars: Democracy and Public Life in the American City during the Nineteenth Century* (Berkeley: University of California Press, 1997), 131.

15. Christopher Tomlins, *Law, Labor, and Ideology in the Early American Republic* (Cambridge, England: Cambridge University Press, 1993).

16. *GF*, I:10–11, 61, 64, 52, 70.

17. See Sean Wilentz, *Chants Democratic: New York City and the Rise of the American Working Class, 1788–1850* (New York: Oxford University Press, 1984).

18. On the connection of workingmen to the Democratic party and the ideological implications of this see, Ashworth, *"Agrarians" and "Aristocrats"*, 87–111; Ryan, *Civic Wars*, 109–13; and David Montgomery, *Citizen Worker* (Cambridge, England: Cambridge University Press, 1993), 5–8, 137–39.

19. *GF*, I:62–73.

20. *GF*, I:73–74.

21. *GF*, I:194, 201–2, 206, 222.

22. *GF*, I:4, 24; II:180–83; I:26.

23. *GF*, II:13; I:3; II:36; I:4.

24. *GF*, I:24.

25. Quoted in R. Nicolaievsky, "Toward a History of the Communist League, 1847–1852," *International Review of Social History* 1 (1956): 249.

26. Jacques Derrida, "Declarations of Independence," *New Political Science* 15 (Summer 1986): 7–15; Bonnie Honig, "Declarations of

Independence: Arendt and Derrida on the Problem of Founding a Republic," *American Political Science Review* 85 (Mar. 1991): 97–113; and Pierre Rosanvallon, *Le peuple introuvable: Histoire de la représentation démocratique en France* (Paris: Gallimard, 1998).

27. For some examples of this widespread historiographical tendency, see Anna Clark, *The Struggle for the Breeches: Gender and the Making of the British Working Class* (Berkeley: University of California Press, 1995), 220–47; Christine Stansel, *City of Women: Sex and Class in New York, 1789–1860* (Urbana and Chicago: University of Illinois Press, 1987), 130–54; and David Roediger, *The Wages of Whiteness: Race and the Making of the American Working Class* (New York: Verso, 1991).

28. *WCP*, 144, 92–93.

29. *WCP*, 135–37.

30. *WCP*, 39–42. For other examples of these lists, see 84, 90–91, 100–101, 104–5, 114–16, 118–19.

31. *WCP*, 105.

32. *WCP*, 287–97. Quotes are from 288, 294.

33. On the one hand, in 1858 he described a group of women's rights activists as "amiable lunatics," on the other hand he wrote just a few years earlier that he looked forward to the time when women will take part in mass public democratic gatherings alongside men. Compare *Isit*, 45–46, and Walt Whitman, *An American Primer* (Stevens Point, Wis.: Holy Cow Press, 1987), 13.

34. See Judith N. Shklar, *Ordinary Vices* (Cambridge, Mass.: Harvard University Press, 1984).

35. *WCP*, 91, 119, 105.

36. David S. Reynolds, *Beneath the American Renaissance: The Subversive Imagination in the Age of Emerson and Melville* (New York: Knopf, 1988).

37. On the physiologies, see Robert Ray, "Snapshots: The Beginning of Photography," in *The Image in Dispute: Art and Cinema in the Age of Photography*, ed. Dudley Andrew (Austin: University of Texas Press, 1997): 293–307.

38. *WCP*, 27–88. Quotes are from 63, 56.

39. See, for example, Michael Moon, *Disseminating Whitman: Revision and Corporeality in Leaves of Grass* (Cambridge, Mass.: Harvard University Pres, 1991); George Kateb, *The Inner Ocean: Individualism and Democratic Culture* (Ithaca, N.Y.: Cornell University Press, 1992).

My own reading of Whitman's sense of individuality in this essay borrowed heavily from Kateb.

40. *WCP*, 937–38, 930, 946, 948.

41. *WCP*, 937. On the need for idealism, see, especially, the note on 951.

42. On the tension between individualism and democracy, see *WCP*, 940–41.

43. On the liberalism of Godkin and cultural elites, see David Montgomery, *Beyond Equality: Labor and Radical Republicans, 1862–1872* (Urbana: University of Illinois Press, 1967), esp. 379–86; on the cultural conservatism, see Kenneth Cmiel, *Democratic Eloquence: The Fight over Popular Speech in Nineteenth-century America* (New York: William Morrow, 1990), 123–47.

44. *WCP*, 947.

45. *WCP*, 969, 949, 965.

46. *WCP*, 931, 957.

47. *WCP*, 929, 962, 936, 955.

48. *WCP*, 948, 930, 946.

49. *WCP*, 950, 990, 986.

50. Jacques Donzelot, *L'invention du social: Essai sur le déclin des passions politiques* (Paris: Fayard, 1984), 17–72.

51. See, for example, Herbert Croly, *The Promise of American Life* (New York: Macmillan, 1909), 207–08. Nor was this only an American sentiment. Croly crowned his argument for solidarity over liberty with a quote from the French progressive legal scholar, Emile Faguet.

52. *WCP*, 941.

53. Wendy Brown, *States of Injury: Power and Freedom in Late Modernity* (Princeton: Princeton University Press, 1995), 3–29. Quote is on 28.

ILLUSTRATED CHRONOLOGY

Whitman's Life	Historical Events
1819: Walter Whitman born (May 31) in West Hills, New York, the second child of Walter Whitman and Louisa Van Velsor Whitman.	**1819:** First major economic panic sweeps America. Missouri applies for statehood, provoking national discussion of whether the western territories should be slave or free.
1823: The senior Walter Whitman takes his family to live in Brooklyn.	**1820:** Missouri Compromise prohibits slavery in new territories above latitude 36° 30'.
1825–c. 1830: Whitman attends District School No. 1 in Brooklyn.	**1825:** The Marquis de Lafayette makes triumphant tour of American cities, including Brooklyn. Opening of the Erie Canal.
1829: Is deeply stirred by sermon delivered in Brooklyn by Quaker leader Elias Hicks.	**1827:** Slavery abolished in New York state.
1830–31: Works as office boy for lawyers James B. and Edward Clarke.	**1829–37:** Andrew Jackson serves two terms as U.S. president.
1831–32: Works as printer's apprentice on the *Long Island Patriot.*	**1830:** Steam-powered railroad train exhibited in Baltimore. Rubber overshoes and brimstone matches introduced. Indian Removal Act passed by Congress, forcing Native Americans to move west of the Mississippi.
1832–35: Compositor for Alden Spooner's *Long-Island Star.*	**1831:** Street railway introduced. In Virginia, Nat Turner leads slave revolt, killing more than 57 whites.
1835: Works as compositor in Manhattan. Leaves after printing district is destroyed by fire. Moves back to Long Island.	**1832:** Nullification crisis occurs when South Carolina declares two national tariffs illegal and threatens to secede from Union.
1836–38: Teaches school in Long Island villages of Norwich, West Babylon, Long Swamp, and Smithtown.	
1838: Founds, edits, and distributes a Huntington newspaper, the *Long-Islander.* Unsuccessfully seeks printing job in Manhattan. Writes articles for *Long Island Democrat* (Jamaica). Teaches at Jamaica Academy.	

(Left) The poet's father, Walter Whitman. Library of Congress. (Right) The poet's mother, Louisa Van Velsor Whitman. Library of Congress.

Walt Whitman's birthplace, West Hills, New York. Library of Congress.

1839–41: Teaches school at Little Bayside, Trimming Square, Woodbury, and Whitestone. Writes for various Long Island newspapers.

1841: Moves to New York City (May). Works for *New World* and writes stories for *Democratic Review* and other periodicals. From 1841 to 1854, writes 24 pieces of fiction, 19 poems, and countless journalistic pieces. From 1841 through 1844, lives in various Manhattan boardinghouses.

1842: Edits two Manhattan newspapers, the *Aurora* (spring) and the *Evening Tattler* (summer). Writes for the *Daily Plebian.* Publishes a popular temperance novel, *Franklin Evans,* and several poems and short stories.

1835: Steam press for newspapers introduced. Huge fire destroys Manhattan printing district.

1836: Launching of world's first large advertising campaign, for Brandreth's Vegetable Universal Pills. In battle over Texas, 183 Americans die at the Alamo, and 412 are massacred at Goliad.

1837: Phineas T. Barnum hoodwinks public with exhibition of a black woman, Joice Heth, purportedly 161 years old. Economic depression results in five years of hard times.

1839: The icebox and daguerreotype introduced.

LaGrange Terrace, also known as Colonnade Row, 428–34 Lafayette St. between Fourth St. and Astor Place, New York City (1832–33). Illustrates the classical revival froms that dominated art and architecture in America during Whitman's formative years. Photograph by Wayne Andrews.

1843: Edits a semiweekly Democratic paper, the *Statesman*. Reports on police station and coroner's office for Moses Beach's famous penny paper, the *New York Sun*.

1844: Writes for the *New York Mirror*. Briefly edits the *Democrat*. Writes tales for a magazine, the *Aristidean*.

1845: Returns to Brooklyn and writes for the *Brooklyn Evening Star.*

1846–48: Edits *Brooklyn Daily Eagle,* the Democratic party organ of Kings County. Writes many articles, including several opposing the extension of slavery into western territories. Begins to write notebook jottings in free verse.

1848: Travels south with brother Jeff and works for *New Orleans Daily Crescent* (Feb.–May). Attends Buffalo Free-Soil Convention (Aug.) Founds the short-lived *Brooklyn Freeman,* a Free-Soil paper.

1849: Phrenologist Lorenzo N. Fowler reads his bumps (July). Runs small store and print shop in Brooklyn. Publishes articles in local papers.

1850: Publishes four political poems, three of which protest the Compromise of 1850 and one of which ("Resurgemus," about the failed European revolutions) will later be included in *Leaves of Grass*.

1840: Cyrus McCormick invents mechanical reaper.

1840–41: "Log Cabin" campaign results in election of Whig William Henry Harrison, who dies shortly after inauguration and is succeeded by John Tyler. Emerson's *Essays: First Series* published (1841).

1840–45: Washingtonian temperance movement sweeps America, gaining some 500,000 members.

1842: Croton Aqueduct opens in Manhattan, improving city's water and sanitation.

1843: Popular singing family from New Hampshire, the Hutchinsons, makes first Manhattan appearance. The nation's first minstrel troupe, the Virginia Minstrels, makes its appearance. Wagon trains begin rolling west to Oregon Country.

Ralph Waldo Emerson. Library of Congress.

1851: Addresses Brooklyn Art Union on "the gospel of beauty."

1852: Writes supportive letter to Senator John P. Hale, the Free Democratic party presidential candidate. Runs house-building business in Brooklyn.

1853: Writes the poem "Pictures" and notebook fragments anticipating *Leaves of Grass*. Goes almost daily to Crystal Palace exposition in Manhattan.

1854: Writes "A Boston Ballad," an ironic poem criticizing the rendition of fugitive slave Anthony Burns.

1855: Files copyright for *Leaves of Grass* (May 15), which he publishes himself in early July. Father dies July 11. Sales of his volume are slow, reviews are mixed, but the book receives some high praise, notably in a glowing letter from Emerson (July 21).

Whitman as portrayed in the frontispiece to the 1855 edition of Leaves of Grass. *Ed Folsom Collection.*

Henry Kirke Brown's portrait bust, William Cullen Bryant *(1845–46). National Portrait Gallery, Smithsonian Institution.*

1844: Samuel F. B. Morse introduces electric telegraph. Completion of Long Island Railroad, the only rail route from Brooklyn to Boston. Emerson's *Essays: Second Series* published.

1845: President James Polk takes office. Editor John L. O'Sullivan coins the phrase "manifest destiny." First clipper ship is launched.

1846: Mexican War begins. Congressman David Wilmot makes proposal to ban slavery from western territories newly acquired in the war.

1847: Rotary steam press introduced. Stephen Foster's song "Oh! Susanna" becomes popular.

View of Manhattan street life, 1855. Library of Congress.

Examples of working-class types Whitman extolled in his poetry. (Left) Stone cutter holding mallet and chisel. Library of Congress. (Right) Woman at sewing machine. Library of Congress.

1856: Publishes second edition of *Leaves of Grass*, which contains 32 poems and a public letter from Whitman to Emerson. Writes unpublished political tract "The Eighteenth Presidency!" Is visited in Brooklyn by Henry David Thoreau and Amos Bronson Alcott.

1857–59: Edits *Brooklyn Daily Times.* Is disappointed by lukewarm reception of *Leaves of Grass* but continues to write poetry and plans "the great construction of the new Bible."

1860: Mixes with bohemian crowd at Charles Pfaff's underground restaurant on Broadway. Spends three months in Boston to supervise printing of third edition of *Leaves of Grass*, published by Thayer and Eldridge. Walks in Boston with Emerson, who asks him to delete some sexual passages from "Children of Adam." He refuses.

1861–62: Writes articles on miscellaneous topics for *Brooklyn Daily Standard* and other newspapers. Visits the sick and wounded at New-York Hospital. Learns his brother George has been wounded and goes to army camp in Virginia (Dec. 1862).

1863–64: Settles in Washington, D.C. Works as part-time clerk in army paymaster's office. Visits war hospitals on almost daily basis to give comfort and material aid to injured and dying soldiers. Takes sick leave in Brooklyn (June 1864).

1848: Mexican cession gives California and New Mexico to U.S. Popular revolutions arise in Europe. Zachary Taylor elected president. First women's rights convention takes place in Seneca Falls, N.Y. "Spirit rappings" in Hydesville, N.Y., fuels spiritualism movement.

1849: California gold rush. Asiatic cholera sweeps American cities. 22 people are killed in riot accompanying appearance of British actor Charles Macready at the Astor Place Opera House in Manhattan.

1850: In congressional compromise over slavery, a harsh new fugitive slave act is passed. Zachary Taylor dies in office and is succeeded by Millard Fillmore. Swedish singer Jenny Lind begins her American tour. Hawthorne's *The Scarlet Letter* and Emerson's *Representative Men* are published.

1851: Melville's *Moby-Dick* is published.

1852: Franklin Pierce elected president. Italian contralto Marietta Alboni gives concerts in Manhattan. Stowe's *Uncle Tom's Cabin* is published.

1853: World art and industry exposition opens at New York's Crystal Palace.

1865: Works as clerk in Department of Interior in Washington; is fired by Secretary James Harlan, reportedly because of his authorship of *Leaves of Grass,* and is transferred to post in attorney general's office. After assassination of Lincoln, writes "O Captain! My Captain!" and "When Lilacs Last in the Dooryard Bloom'd." Publishes *Drum-Taps* and *Sequel*. Meets Irish streetcar conductor Peter Doyle.

1866: A Washington friend, William Douglas O'Connor, writes *The Good Gray Poet,* a pamphlet attacking Harlan and defending Whitman.

1867: Fourth edition of *Leaves of Grass*. Receives ardent praise in William Michael Rossetti's article "Walt Whitman's Poems" in the London *Chronicle* and in John Burroughs's book *Notes on Walt Whitman as Poet and Person.*

Elihu Vedder's painting Jane Jackson *(1865). Possibly the model for the emancipated woman slave in "Ethiopia Saluting the Colors." National Academy of Design, New York City.*

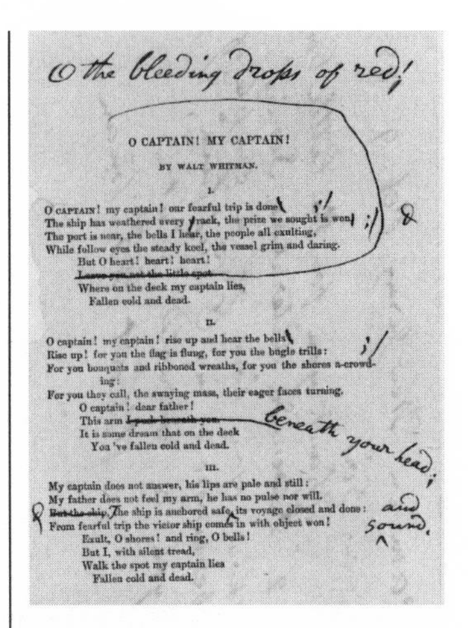

O the bleeding drops of red!

O CAPTAIN! MY CAPTAIN!

BY WALT WHITMAN.

I.

O CAPTAIN! my captain! our fearful trip is done;
The ship has weathered every rack, the prize we sought is won;
The port is near, the bells I hear, the people all exulting,
While follow eyes the steady keel, the vessel grim and daring.
But O heart! heart! heart!
~~Leave you not the little spot~~
Where on the deck my captain lies,
Fallen cold and dead.

II.

O captain! my captain! rise up and hear the bells;
Rise up! for you the flag is flung, for you the bugle trills:
For you bouquets and ribboned wreaths, for you the shores a-crowding:
For you they call, the swaying mass, their eager faces turning.
O captain! dear father!
This arm ~~I push beneath you~~ beneath your head;
It is some dream that on the deck
You 've fallen cold and dead.

III.

My captain does not answer, his lips are pale and still:
My father does not feel my arm, he has no pulse nor will.
~~But the ship,~~ The ship is anchored safe and sound, its voyage closed and done:
From fearful trip the victor ship comes in with object won!
Exult, O shores! and ring, O bells!
But I, with silent tread,
Walk the spot my captain lies
Fallen cold and dead.

Whitman's handwritten revisions of "O Captain! My Captain!" Library of Congress.

William Douglas O'Connor, Whitman's fervent champion. Library of Congress.

Patients in Armory Square Hospital, one of the military hospitals in Washington D.C., that Whitman frequented during the Civil War. Library of Congress.

1868: Rossetti's expurgated *Poems of Walt Whitman* appears in London.

1870: Prints fifth edition of *Leaves of Grass* as well as *Passage to India* and prose treatise *Democratic Vistas,* all dated 1871. Anne Gilchrist, who had fallen in love with Whitman from a distance, publishes "An Englishwoman's Estimate of Walt Whitman" in the *Boston Radical*.

1871: Swinburne writes him a poetic tribute, and Tennyson sends a friendly letter. Gilchrist declares her love to him. He reads "After All, Not to Create Only" at American Institute Exhibition in Manhattan.

1854: Passage of Kansas-Nebraska Act opens western territories to slavery. Fugitive slave Anthony Burns is captured in Boston and returned south. Thoreau's *Walden* is published.

1855: Brooklyn's population has soared to 500,000, making it the nation's third largest city.

1856: In Kansas, battles between proslavery and antislavery forces cause over 200 deaths. Massachusetts senator Charles Sumner is beaten senseless on Senate floor by Preston L. Brooks of South Carolina. James Buchanan is elected president.

Civil War corpses by a fence near a road. Library of Congress.

1872: Suffers heat prostration and becomes ill. Has major quarrel with O'Connor that leads to long-term estrangement.

1873: Suffers paralytic stroke (Jan.). Goes to Camden, N. J. to see his ailing mother, who dies three days later (May). Stays on in Camden, living with his brother George.

1874–75: Publishes several poems, including "Prayer of Columbus," in magazines.

1857: Dred Scott decision denies citizenship to blacks and declares Missouri Compromise unconstitutional.

1858: Abraham Lincoln and Stephen Douglas debate slavery issue in Illinois.

1859: Abolitionist John Brown takes over federal arsenal at Harpers Ferry, Va., to incite slave revolt; is captured, convicted of murder and treason, and hanged. Nation's first oil strike is made in Titusville, Pa.

Whitman in the late 1860s. Ed Folsom Collection.

1876: Publishes Centennial Edition of *Leaves of Grass* (a reprint of the 1871 edition) as well as *Two Rivulets, Memoranda during the War,* and "Walt Whitman's Actual American Position," an anonymously published article that provokes international controversy. Frequently visits the Stafford family farm in nearby Timber Creek; becomes intimate with young Harry Stafford.

1877: Gives Stafford a ring, takes it back, then gives it to him again. With Stafford, visits family of Burroughs in upstate New York.

1878: Henry Wadsworth Longfellow visits him in Camden.

1860–61: After election of Lincoln as president, 11 southern states secede from Union, forming Confederate States of America. Shelling of Fort Sumter, S.C. begins Civil War. Battle of Bull Run on July 21, a Union defeat, is first major battle of the war. Nation's first income tax is passed.

1862: Battle between ironclad ships *Merrimack* and *Monitor*. Battles of Antietam, Shiloh, Vicksburg, and Fredericksburg. Congress passes Homestead Act, giving 160 acres of land to anyone who farms it for five years.

1863: Lincoln's Emancipation Proclamation, freeing slaves in states disloyal to the Union, is issued. Passage of northern draft law prompts riots in cities; the worst is in Manhattan, where at least 74 people are killed. Battles of Chancellorsville, Cemetery Ridge, Gettysburg. Lincoln's Gettysburg Address.

1864: Union generals Grant, Sheridan, and Sherman launch "total war" on South. Sherman captures Atlanta and marches through Georgia to the sea. Lincoln defeats McClellan in presidential election.

1879: Travels west to Colorado. Becomes ill and stays with brother Jeff in St. Louis.

1880: Travels in Canada.

1881: Visits childhood haunts on Long Island. Goes to Boston to oversee new edition of *Leaves of Grass,* which is published by James R. Osgood and Co. Pays visit to Emerson in Concord.

1882: Visited by Oscar Wilde in Camden. Boston district attorney charges that *Leaves of Grass* is "obscene literature," and Osgood withdraws the edition, which is reprinted by Rees Welsh and Co. (later David McKay) in Philadelphia.

1884: Moves into humble house at 328 Mickle Street, which he purchases for $1,750.

1885: A large group of well-wishers, including Mark Twain and John Greenleaf Whittier, donates a horse and buggy that enable him to travel locally.

1887: His lecture on Lincoln at Manhattan's Madison Square Theatre (Apr. 14) is huge success and nets him $600. Is visited in Camden by artist Thomas Eakins, writer Edmund Gosse, and others.

1865: Thirteenth Amendment, banning slavery, is passed. Richmond falls on Apr. 2. Lee surrenders on Apr. 9. Lincoln assassinated on Apr. 14. Andrew Johnson takes office. Freedmen's Bureau created to provide food, jobs, and education for former slaves. Salvation Army founded.

1866: Underwater transatlantic telegraph cable links U.S. and England.

1867: Fourteenth Amendment, granting citizenship to all persons born in the U.S., is passed. Reconstruction Act is passed over President Johnson's veto.

1868: Senate's effort to impeach Johnson fails by one vote. Typewriter is perfected.

1869: Transcontinental railroad is completed at Promontory Point, Utah.

1870: Fifteenth Amendment, forbidding states from denying African-American men the vote, is ratified.

1872: Montgomery Ward issues the first mail-order catalog.

1873: Banking house of Jay Cooke collapses, beginning a long economic depression; businesses fail, unemployment soars.

Whitman in 1891, the year before his death. Ed Folsom Collection.

1888: Publishes 32 poems and several prose pieces in the popular *New York Herald*. Is struck by another paralytic stroke (June) and severe illness. Publishes *November Boughs and Complete Poems and Prose.*

1890: Signs contract for construction of large granite tomb in Camden's Harleigh Cemetery.

1891: Publishes *Good-Bye My Fancy* and "Deathbed" Edition of *Leaves of Grass.*

1892: Dies (Mar. 26) in Mickle Street home; is buried (Mar. 30) in Harleigh Cemetery.

1874: Electric streetcar introduced.

1875: Mary Baker Eddy's *Science and Health with Key to the Scriptures* is published.

1876: End of Reconstruction. Centennial Exhibition held in Philadelphia. Alexander Graham Bell exhibits the telephone. Colonel George A. Custer is defeated at battle of Little Big Horn. The National League is created, the beginning of modern professional baseball.

1877: Phonograph introduced by Thomas Edison. Steel sodbusting plow is marketed. Widespread railway strikes.

1878: Milking machine invented.

1879: Edison demonstrates the first electric light bulb. Cash register invented.

1881: Helen Hunt Jackson publishes *A Century of Dishonor*, about maltreatment of Native Americans.

1882: John D. Rockefeller forms the Standard Oil Trust. Edison builds the first electric power plant in New York City. Congress passes Chinese Exclusion Act.

1883: Buffalo Bill opens his popular Wild West show in Omaha, Nebr.

1884: Fountain pen introduced.

Thomsn Eakins's portrait, Walt Whitman (*1887*). *Pennsylvania Academy of the Fine Arts.*

1885: Transcontinental railroad completed in Canada. Twain's *Adventures of Huckleberry Finn* published. Sheet music for home use introduced.

1886: American Federation of Labor is founded. Statue of Liberty unveiled in New York harbor. F. W. Woolworth founds the first 5 and 10 cents store.

1887: Automatic air brake invented. Electric streetcar introduced. Thomas Edison introduces a phonograph using cylindrical wax records.

1888: Adding machine invented. The lightweight Kodak camera is perfected. Labor unrest causes Haymarket Riot in Chicago.

Thomas Eakins, The Swimmimg Hole *(1885). Amon Carter Museum.*

Horace Traubel, who visited Whitman almost daily from 1888 to 1892 and made voluminous records of the poet's conversations. Library of Congress.

John Flanagan's relief medallion of Walt Whitman.

1889: Jane Addams founds Hull-House.

1890: U.S. census announces that the nation no longer has a frontier and that one out of three Americans is a city dweller. Slaughter of nearly 300 Native Americans at Wounded Knee Creek, in present-day South Dakota, marks end of Indian wars.

1891: Farmers and labor unions form the Populist party. Basketball invented.

1892: Andrew Carnegie forms the Carnegie Steel Company. Ellis Island becomes first stopping place for immigrants to U.S.

Bibliographical Essay

David S. Reynolds

Editions of Whitman's Writings

Six editions and several reprints of Whitman's poetry collection *Leaves of Grass* appeared in the poet's lifetime. The first edition (1855), containing twelve untitled poems and a prose preface, was printed privately by Whitman. The second edition (1856) contained thirty-two poems, all titled, along with an appendix that included reviews and Emerson's letter praising Whitman. In the third edition (1860), published in Boston by Thayer and Eldridge, the number of poems had risen to 166, of which 134 were new. For the first time, the poems were arranged in "clusters," or meaningful arrangements on topics such as society and politics ("Chants Democratic"), love between the sexes ("Enfans d'Adam"), and same-sex love ("Calamus").

His poems about the Civil War and Lincoln appeared in *Drum-Taps* and its *Sequel* (1865) and then were incorporated into the fourth edition (1867) of *Leaves of Grass*. The fifth edition (1870–71) arranged the poems into twenty-two groups, sixteen of them titled. It featured forty new poems in three annexes: *Passage to India, After All, Not to Create Only*, and *As a Strong Bird on Pinions Free*. This edition was reprinted in 1876 as the so-called Centennial Edition, along with a companion volume, *Two Rivulets*, which contained the prose pieces *Democratic Vistas* and *Memoranda during the War* and assorted poems. Seventeen new poems appeared in the sixth edition (1881), published by James R. Osgood and Co. After Osgood dropped the volume in response to charges of obscenity, Rees Welsh (later David McKay) reprinted this edition in Philadelphia. A later reissue of this edition came in 1888 and included the autobiographical prose works *November Boughs* and *Specimen Days*. The so-called Deathbed Edition (1891–92) was another reprint of the Osgood edition, with an annex of recent poems titled "Good-Bye My Fancy."

The definitive, though still incomplete, modern edition of Whitman is *The Collected Writings of Walt Whitman*, published by New York University Press. Besides including virtually all of the published poetry and prose, this wonderful edition contains notebooks, correspondence, unpublished prose manuscripts, and early poetry and fiction that are useful in placing Whitman in his times. Missing are manuscript versions of the poems, some of which can be found in Joel Myerson's *Walt Whitman Archive*.

Also missing from the *Collected Writings* is Whitman's voluminous journalism. Until recently scholars had to rely on the samples of the journalism reprinted in the volumes edited by Rubin and Brown, Holloway and Schwartz, and Rodgers and Black. In 1998 there appeared a comprehensive collection of the newspaper writings, edited by Herbert Bergman, Douglas A. Hovers, and Edward J. Recchia. Ten important Whitman notebooks, missing from the Library of Congress since World War II, were rediscovered in 1995, scanned digitally, and are available on the World Wide Web (http://lcweb.loc.gov). An informative and lively contemporary source is the multivolume *With Walt Whitman in Camden*, a transcript of the poet's conversations made late in his life by his friend Horace Traubel.

There are a number of fine anthologies of Whitman's writings. One of the best is the Norton Critical Edition, edited by Bradley and Blodgett, which reproduces the Deathbed Edition of *Leaves of Grass* along with many important uncollected poems and representative prose works. Also excellent is Justin Kaplan's edition of the *Complete Poetry and Collected Prose*, which contains the Deathbed Edition, the original 1855 edition, and a broad sampling of the prose.

Biographies and Critical Works on Whitman

Some fifteen biographies of Walt Whitman have been published. The narrative of his life has been most thoroughly told in the biographies by Gay Wilson Allen, Jerome Loving, and myself. Allen's 1955 book, *The Solitary Singer,* consolidated all then-known information about the poet and rendered it in judicious, fluid fashion. Loving, in *Walt Whitman: The Song of Himself,* separates fact from legend in the life story, ridding it of many accumulated myths and hypotheses. My *Walt Whitman's America: A Cultural Biography* places the poet's life and writings against the backdrop of politics, the slavery debate, religion, philosophy, science, sex and gender issues, music and theater, oratory, the visual arts, the Civil War, and Reconstruction. Also useful are the biographies by Justin Kaplan, who writes with economy and verve, and by Paul Zweig and Joseph Jay Rubin, who focus on short periods of the life. There is also a rich tradition of psychoanalytic commentary on Whitman, extending from Jean Catel through Roger Asselineau to Stephen Black, Edwin Haviland Miller, and David Cavitch.

Whitman's life intersected in so many ways with contemporary society and culture that it has been ripe for historical analysis. My *Beneath the American Renaissance* probes Whitman's ambiguous relationship with the fertile and often raucous and bizarre popular culture of his time. Other scholars have explored the relationship between Whitman and a variety of historical currents. The influence of baseball, photography, and American Indian culture on the poet are featured in Ed Folsom's *Walt Whitman's Native Representations*. Recent books have explored Whitman's religious attitudes (Chari, Kuebrich, Hutchinson), his politics (Erkkila, Pease, Thomas), his debts to literary tradition (Price) and contemporary journalism (Fishkin), his modes of seeing (Dougherty), his views on race and slavery (Klammer, Mancuso), his place in the publishing world (Greenspan), his connections with science and medicine (Aspiz, Davis), and his ideas about language and poetic voice (Warren, Nathanson, Beach).

An ongoing point of discussion has been Whitman's sexual orientation. For years, the poet's homosexuality was either minimized (Holloway) or dismissed as a "peculiar" tendency (Arvin).

More recently, scholars such as Moon, Shively, Fone, Martin, and Schmidgall have portrayed him as actively homosexual. Although he had fleeting affairs with women, both his homoerotic poetry and his romantic relationships with young men indicate that he was gay. Whether his homosexuality was ever consummated sexually may never be known for certain. Still, recent scholars have used his homosexuality to illuminate his poetry and his life.

Comparative studies have been made between Whitman and many others. His debt to Emerson has been discussed at length by Loving (*American Muse*), Bloom, and Stovall. Links between him and Jean Toomer, Alfred Stieglitz, and Isadora Duncan have been drawn (Hutchinson, "The Whitman Legacy"; Dougherty; Bohan). A fascinating sampling of appreciations of Whitman by creative writers from his day to ours is provided in the collection edited by Perlman, Folsom, and Campion. Ronald Wallace discovers in Whitman slapstick jokes and backwoods humor, while C. Carroll Hollis finds traces of journalism and oratory. Sophisticated analyses of Whitman's language and diction have been contributed by Nathanson, Warren, Bauerlein, and Thurin. Nearly every one of Whitman's poems and prose pieces are explicated by a host of scholars in *The Walt Whitman Encyclopedia* (LeMaster and Kummings). A number of fine collections of essays on the poet have recently appeared, including those edited by Folsom, Erkkila and Grossman, Greenspan, and Martin.

None of the members of Whitman's immediate family has been the subject of a biography, though collections of letters by his brothers Thomas Jefferson Whitman (Berthold and Price) and George Whitman (Loving) have been published, as has a collection by his sister-in-law Mattie (Waldron).

A useful overview of the recent criticism is M. Jimmie Killingsworth's *The Growth of "Leaves of Grass": The Organic Tradition in Whitman Studies*, which argues that historical interpretations of Whitman must be complemented by recognition of the authority of the poet and the poetic text. Ed Folsom's chapter on Whitman in Richard Kopley's *Prospects for the Study of American Literature* provides a concise summary of current critical approaches. Joel Myerson's descriptive bibliography of Whitman gives a wonderfully detailed account of the publishing history and physical features of the various editions of *Leaves of Grass*.

Modern Collections of Whitman

Whitman, Walt. *Complete Poetry and Collected Prose.* Ed. Justin Kaplan. New York: Library of America, 1982.
———. *The Correspondence.* Ed. Edwin Haviland Miller. 6 vols. New York: New York University Press, 1961–77.
———. *Daybooks and Notebooks.* Ed. William H. White. 3 vols. New York: New York University Press, 1978.
———. *The Early Poems and the Fiction.* Ed. Thomas L. Brasher. New York: New York University Press, 1963.
———. *The Gathering of the Forces.* Ed. Cleveland Rodgers and John Black. 2 vols. New York: G. P. Putnam's Sons, 1920.
———. *I Sit and Look Out: Editorials from the Brooklyn Daily Times.* Ed. Emory Holloway and Vernolian Schwartz. New York: AMS Press, 1966.
———. *Leaves of Grass.* Ed. Sculley Bradley and Harold W. Blodgett. New York: Norton, 1973.
———. *"Leaves of Grass": Comprehensive Reader's Edition.* Ed. Harold Blodgett and Sculley Bradley. New York: New York University Press, 1965.
———. *"Leaves of Grass": A Textual Variorum of the Printed Poems.* Ed. Sculley Bradley et al. 3 vols. New York: New York University Press, 1980.
———. *Notebooks and Unpublished Prose Manuscripts.* Ed. Edward Grier. 6 vols. New York: New York University Press, 1984.
———. *Prose Works, 1892.* Ed. Floyd Stovall. 2 vols. New York: New York University Press, 1963–64.
———. *Walt Whitman of the New York Aurora.* Ed. Joseph J. Rubin and Charles H. Brown. State college, Pa.: Bald Eagle Press, 1950.
———. *Walt Whitman: The Journalism.* Ed. Herbert Bergman, Douglas A. Noverr, and Edward J. Recchia. New York: Peter Lang, 1998.

Secondary Works

Allen, Gay Wilson. *The Solitary Singer: A Critical Biography of Walt Whitman.* Rev. Ed. Chicago: University of Chicago Press, 1985.
Arvin, Newton. *Whitman.* New York: Macmillan, 1938.

Aspiz, Harold. *Walt Whitman and the Body Beautiful.* Urbana: University of Illinois Press, 1980.

Asselineau, Roger. *The Evolution of Walt Whitman: The Creation of a Poet.* Cambridge, Mass.: Harvard University Press, 1960.

———. *The Evolution of Walt Whitman: The Creation of a Book.* Cambridge, Mass.: Harvard University Press, 1962.

Bauerlein, Mark. *Whitman and the American Idiom.* Baton Rouge: Louisiana State University Press, 1991.

Beach, Christopher. *The Politics of Distinction: Whitman and the Discourses of Nineteenth-century America.* Athens: University of Georgia Press, 1996.

Berthold, Dennis, and Kenneth Price. *Dear Brother Walt: The Letters of Thomas Jefferson Whitman.* Kent, Ohio: Kent State University Press, 1984.

Black, Stephen A. *Walt Whitman's Journey into Chaos.* Princeton: Princeton University Press, 1975.

Bloom, Harold. *Poetry and Repression.* New Haven, Conn.: Yale University Press, 1976.

Bohan, Ruth L. "'I Sing the Body Electric': Isadora Duncan, Whitman, and the Dance." In Greenspan, ed., *Cambridge Companion,* 166–93.

Catel, Jean. *Walt Whitman: La naissance du poète.* Paris: Rieder, 1929.

Cavitch, David. *My Soul and I: The Inner Life of Walt Whitman.* Boston: Beacon, 1985.

Chari, V. K. Walt *Whitman in the Light of Vedantic Mysticism: An Interpretation.* Lincoln: University of Nebraska Press, 1965.

Clarke, Graham. *Walt Whitman: The Poem as Private History.* London: Vision / St. Mark's, 1991.

Davis, Robert Leigh. *Whitman and the Romance of Medicine.* Berkeley: University of California Press, 1997.

Dougherty, James. *Walt Whitman and the Citizen's Eye.* Baton Rouge: Louisiana State University Press, 1993.

Erkkila, Betsy. *Walt Whitman among the French.* Princeton, N.J.: Princeton University Press, 1980.

———. *Whitman: The Political Poet.* New York: Oxford University Press, 1989.

Erkkila, Betsy, and Jay Grossman, eds. *Breaking Bounds: Whitman and American Cultural Studies.* New York: Oxford University Press, 1996.

Fishkin, Shelley Fisher. *From Fact to Fiction: Journalism and Imaginative Writing in America.* Baltimore: Johns Hopkins University Press, 1985.

Folsom, Ed., *Walt Whitman's Native Representations.* New York: Cambridge University Press, 1994.

———, ed. *Walt Whitman: The Centennial Essays.* Iowa City: University of Iowa Press, 1994.

Fone, Byrne. *Masculine Landscapes: Walt Whitman and the Homoerotic Text.* Carbondale: Southern Illinois University Press, 1992.

Greenspan, Ezra. *Walt Whitman and the American Reader.* New York: Cambridge University Press, 1991.

———, ed. *The Cambridge Companion to Walt Whitman.* New York: Cambridge University Press, 1995.

Hollis, C. Carroll. *Language and Style in "Leaves of Grass."* Baton Rouge: Louisiana State University Press, 1983.

Holloway, Emory. *Whitman: An Interpretation in Narrative.* New York: Knopf, 1926.

Hutchinson, George. *The Ecstatic Whitman.* Columbus: Ohio State University Press, 1985.

———. "The Whitman Legacy and the Harlem Renaissance." In Folsom, *Centennial Essays,* 201–16.

Kaplan, Justin. *Walt Whitman: A Life.* New York: Simon and Schuster, 1980.

Killingsworth, M. Jimmie. *The Growth of "Leaves of Grass": The Organic Tradition in Whitman Studies.* Columbia, S.C.: Camden House, 1993.

———. *Whitman's Poetry of the Body: Sexuality, Politics, and the Text.* Chapel Hill: University of North Carolina Press, 1989.

Klammer, Martin. *Whitman, Slavery, and the Emergence of "Leaves of Grass."* University Park: Pennsylvania State University Press, 1995.

Kuebrich, David. *Minor Prophecy: Walt Whitman's New American Religion.* Bloomington: Indiana University Press, 1989.

Kummings, Donald D., ed. *Approaches to Teaching Whitman's "Leaves of Grass."* New York: Modern Language Association, 1990.

———. *Walt Whitman, 1940–1975: A Reference Guide.* Boston: G. K. Hall, 1982.

LeMaster, J. R., and Donald D. Kummings, eds. *Walt Whitman: An Encyclopedia.* New York: Garland, 1998.

Loving, Jerome, ed. *Civil War Letters of George Washington Whitman.* Durham, N.C.: Duke University Press, 1975.
———. *Emerson, Whitman, and the American Muse.* Chapel Hill: University of North Carolina Press, 1982.
———. *Walt Whitman: The Song of Himself.* Berkeley: University of California Press, 1999.
Mancuso, Luke. *The Strange Sad War Revolving: Walt Whitman, Reconstruction, and the Emergence of Black Citizenship, 1865–1876.* Columbia, S.C.: Camden House, 1997.
Martin, Robert K. *The Homosexual Tradition in American Poetry.* Austin: University of Texas Press, 1979.
———, ed. *The Continuing Presence of Walt Whitman: The Life after the Life.* Iowa City: University of Iowa Press, 1992.
Miller, Edwin Haviland. *Walt Whitman's Poetry: A Psychological Journey.* New York: New York University Press, 1968.
Moon, Michael. *Disseminating Whitman: Revision and Corporeality in "Leaves of Grass."* Cambridge, Mass.: Harvard University Press, 1991.
Myerson, Joel. *The Walt Whitman Archive.* 3 vols. New York: Garland, 1993.
———. *Walt Whitman: A Descriptive Bibliography.* Pittsburgh, Pa.: University of Pittsburgh Press, 1993.
Nathanson, Tenney. *Whitman's Presence: Body, Voice, and Writing in "Leaves of Grass."* New York: New York University Press, 1992.
Pease, Donald. *Visionary Compacts: American Renaissance Writings in Cultural Context.* Madison: University of Wisconsin Press, 1987.
Perlman, Jim, Ed Folsom, and Dan Campion, eds. *Walt Whitman: The Measure of His Song.* Minneapolis: Holy Cow! Press, 1981.
Price, Kenneth M. *Whitman and Tradition: The Poet in His Century.* New Haven, Conn.: Yale University Press, 1990.
Reynolds, David S. *Beneath the American Renaissance.* New York: Knopf, 1988.
———. *Walt Whitman's America: A Cultural Biography.* New York: Knopf, 1995.
Rubin, Joseph. *The Historic Whitman.* University Park: Pennsylvania State University Press, 1973.
Schmidgall, Gary. *Walt Whitman: A Gay Life.* New York: Dutton, 1997.
Shively, Charley, ed. *Calamus Lovers: Walt Whitman's Working-class Camerados.* San Francisco: Gay Sunshine, 1987.

———, ed. *Drum Beats: Walt Whitman's Civil War Boy Lovers.* San Francisco: Gay Sunshine, 1989.

Stovall, Floyd. *The Foreground of "Leaves of Grass."* Charlottesville: University Press of Virginia, 1974.

Thomas, M. Wynn. *The Lunar Light of Whitman's Poetry.* Cambridge, Mass.: Harvard University Press, 1987.

Traubel, Horace. *With Walt Whitman in Camden.* 7 vols. (Vols. 1–3, New York: Rowman and Littlefield, 1961; Vols. 4–7, Carbondale, Ill.: Southern Illinois University Press, 1959–92).

Waldron, Randall H., ed. *Mattie: The Letters of Martha Mitchell Whitman.* New York: New York University Press, 1977.

Wallace, Ronald. *God Be with the Clown: Humor in American Poetry.* Columbia: University of Missouri Press, 1984.

Warren, James Perrin. *Walt Whitman's Language Experiment.* University Park: Pennsylvania State University Press, 1987.

Zweig, Paul. *Walt Whitman: The Making of the Poet.* New York: Basic, 1984.

Contributors

KENNETH CMIEL is Professor of History at the University of Iowa. He is the author of *Democratic Eloquence: The Fight over Popular Speech in Nineteenth-Century America* and *A Home of Another Kind: One Chicago Orphanage and the Tangle of Child Welfare.* He is particularly interested in political thought and has published a number of essays on nineteenth- and twentieth-century U.S. history.

ED FOLSOM is F. Wendell Miller Distinguished Professor of English at the University of Iowa and has edited the *Walt Whitman Quarterly Review* since 1983. He is the author of *Walt Whitman's Native Representations* and editor or coeditor of *Walt Whitman: The Centennial Essays, Walt Whitman: The Measure of His Song, Walt Whitman and the World, Major Authors on CD-ROM: Walt Whitman,* and a volume of selections from W. S. Merwin entitled *Regions of Memory: Uncollected Prose, 1949–82.* Currently he is coediting (with Kenneth M. Price) *Major Authors Online: Walt Whitman* and the *Walt Whitman Hypertext Archive,* both Web-based research and teaching tools. His essays on Whitman and other American poets have appeared in numerous journals and collections.

M. JIMMIE KILLINGSWORTH is Professor of English at Texas A & M University. A specialist in nineteenth-century American literature, he is the author of numerous books and articles in the field. His Whitman-related books include *Whitman's Poetry of the Body: Sexuality, Politics, and the Text,* a study of the poet's sexual images in the context of nineteenth-century sexual rhetoric and mores, and *The Growth of Leaves of Grass: The Organic Tradition in Whitman Studies,* an overview of critical approaches to the poet's oeuvre. Killingsworth is also an authority in composition and technical writing whose other books include *Information in Action: A Guide to Technical Communication* and, with Jacqueline S. Palmer, *Ecospeak: Rhetoric and Environmental Politics in America.*

JEROME LOVING is Professor of English at Texas A & M University. He is the author of *Walt Whitman: The Song of Himself,* a critical biography. His other books include *Lost in the Customhouse: Authorship in the American Renaissance, Emily Dickinson: The Poet on the Second Story, Emerson, Whitman, and the American Muse,* and *Walt Whitman's Champion: William Douglas O'Connor.* He is also the editor of Walt Whitman's *Leaves of Grass, Civil War Letters of George Washington Whitman,* and Frank Norris's *McTeague.* Currently he is at work on a critical biography of Theodore Dreiser. He has published numerous articles on Whitman, Dickinson, Poe, Hawthorne, Warton, Whittier, and other writers.

DAVID S. REYNOLDS is University Distinguished Professor of English and American Studies at Baruch College and the Graduate Center of the City University of New York. He is the author of *Walt Whitman's America: A Cultural Biography,* winner of the Bancroft Prize and the Ambassador Book Award and finalist for the National Book Critics Circle Award. His other books include *Beneath the American Renaissance: The Subversive Imagination in the Age of Emerson and Melville* (winner of the Christian Gauss Award and Honorable Mention for the John Hope Franklin Prize), *George Lippard,* and *Faith in Fiction: The Emergence of Religious Literature in America.* He is the editor of *George Lippard, Prophet of Protest: Writings of an American Radical* and the coeditor of *The Serpent in the Cup: Temperance in American Literature* and of a new edition of three works by the popular nineteeenth-century novelist George Thompson.

ROBERTA K. TARBELL is Associate Professor of Art History and Museum Studies at Rutgers, the State University of New Jersey at Camden. She has been an adjunct Associate Professor in the Winterthur Museum/University of Delaware Art Conservation Programs, for which she helped develop a Ph.D. in Art Conservation. Previously she taught art history at the University of Delaware at Newark. She is the author or coauthor of book-length catalogs for such museums as the National Museum of American Art, Smithsonian Institution (*Marguerite Zorach, Peggy Bacon,* and *Hugo Robus*); the Whitney Museum of American Art (*The Figurative Tradition*); and Rutgers University Art Gallery (*Vanguard American Sculpture*). She contributed two essays to and coedited, with Geoffrey Sill, *Walt Whitman and the Visual Arts.*

Index

Page numbers in *italics* indicate illustrations.

running right through the centre of it. The sky, the elegant bridges, the river banks, the buildings on the banks, their shimmering second selves standing on their heads in their reflections.

Team, Keith said in the dark. Thank you all for being here. Water is history. Water is mystery. Water is nature. Water is life. Water is archaeology. Water is civilisation. Water is where we live. Water is here and water is now. Get the message. Get it in a bottle. Water in a bottle makes two billion pounds a year in the UK alone. Water in a bottle costs the consumer roughly ten thousand times the amount that the same measure of tapwater costs him. Water is everything we imagine at Pure. The Pure imagination. That's my theme today. So here's my question. How, precisely, do we bottle the imagination?

One of the shaveys shifted in his chair as if to answer. Keith held a hand up to quieten him.

Ten years ago, Keith said, there were twenty-eight countries in the world with not enough water. In less than twenty years' time, the number of countries which don't have enough water will have doubled. In less than twenty years' time, over eight hundred million people – that's right, eight hundred million people, people very much, in their way, exactly like you or me – will be living without access to enough water. Lights, please. Thanks.

The picture of our town on the screen paled. Keith was sitting up on the desk at the end of the room with his legs crossed like a Buddha. He looked down at us all. Though I'd only been working here for half a week I'd heard rumours about these meetings. Becky on Reception had told me about them. The phones had to be muted for them. One of the High School girls had mentioned them, how weird it was when the Tuesday Creative Lecture was over and everybody came out as if hypnotised, or wounded. That's what she called it, the Tuesday Creative Lecture. Keith, she'd told me, flew over for these meetings specially. He flew in every Monday, then out again after every Tuesday Creative Lecture.

I felt suddenly sick. I'd been late for the Tuesday Creative Lecture. Maybe the boss of bosses would be late for his outward flight because of me.

That's why Pure's here, Keith was saying. That's why Pure is branching into water subsidiary, that's why Pure is investing such a wealth of international finance and promise into such a small locality. Team, fresh water. The world is running out of it. Forty per cent of all the world's freshwater rivers and streams are now too polluted for human use or consumption. Think about what that really means.

He drew himself up, his back straight, suddenly silent. Everyone in the room sat forward, pencils and Palm Pilots at the ready. I felt myself sitting forward too. I didn't know why. He held his hands up in the air for a moment, as if to stop time. Then he spoke.

What it means is that water is the perfect commodity. Because water is running out. There will never, ever, ever again, not be an urgent need for water. So how will we do it? Question one. How will we bottle our Highland oil? Question two. What will we call it? Question three. What shape will its bottles be? Question four. What will it say on the labels on the bottles? And finally, question five. Will it say anything on the lids of the bottles? Answers, team! Answers!

All round me there was frantic scribbling down, there were little clickings of buttons. Keith got down off the desk. He began to walk back and fore at the top of the room.

What you come up with, he said, will need to indicate that water really matters to us. It will need to let us know that human beings aren't ruled by nature, that on the contrary, they ARE nature. That's good. They ARE nature. It will need to be about mindset. It will need not just to open minds to our product, but to suggest that our product is the most open-minded on the market. We can't use Purely. The Alaskans use Purely. We can't use Clearly. The Canadians use Clearly. We can't use Highland. Our biggest rivals use Highland. But our name will need to imply all three. So come on, people. Throw me a name. I need a name. We need a name for our water. Come on. Ideas. I need to hear them. Purely. Clearly. Highland. Nature. Power. Ideas. Now. Concepts. Now.

Keith snapped his fingers as he said each single word.

Fluidity, a nice shavey called out next to me. Recycling. How water is smart, how water is graceful, how water, since it can change shape and form, can make us versatile –

Good, Keith said, good, good! Keep it coming –

– and how we're all actually about seventy-five per cent water. We need to suggest that water IS us. We need to suggest that water can unite us. No matter what our political or national differences.

That's very, very good, Keith said. Well done, Paul. Run with it.

The whole room turned and bristled with jealousy at Paul.

Of the first water, the one who was maybe called Brian said. Still waters run deep, a shavey called Dominic shouted from across the room. Soon the room was running pretty deep in thesaurus clichés. In deep water. Won't hold water. Get into hot water. Head above water. Throw cold water.

Water is about well-being, Midge said. About being well.

Nobody heard her.

It's all about well-being, an unfamiliar Creative said on the other side of the room.

I like that, Keith said. Very good point, Norm.

I saw Midge look down, disheartened, and in that moment I saw what it was that was different about my sister now. I saw it in the turn of her head and the movement of her too-thin wrist. How had I not seen it? She was far too thin. She was really thin.

And product package will dwell on how water makes you healthy, keeps you healthy, Dominic said.

Maybe marketed with health-conscious products or a healthy make-yourself-over or let-yourself-relax package specifically aimed at women stroke families, Norm said. Water keeps your kids healthy.

Good point, Norm, Keith said.

I'd had enough.

You could call it Och Well, I said.

Call it – ? Keith said.

He stared at me.

The whole room turned and stared at me.

I'm dead, I thought. Och well.

You could call it Affluent, I said. That pretty much sums it up. Or maybe that sounds too like Effluent. I know. You could call it Main Stream. On the lid it could say You're Always Safer Sticking With The Main Stream.

The whole room was silent, and not in a good way.

You could call it Scottish Tap, I said into the hush. That'd be good and honest. Whatever good means.

Keith raised his eyebrows. He jutted out his chin.

Transparency, Midge said quick. It's not a bad route, Keith. It could be a really, really good route, no?

A we-won't-mess-with-you route, Paul said nodding. It's mindset all right. And it combines honesty and nationality in the same throw. Honest Scottishness. Honest-to-goodness goodness in a bottle.

It takes and makes a stand, Midge said. Doesn't it? And that's half the bottle, I mean battle.

Where you stand lets you know what really matters. If we suggest our bottled water takes and makes a stand, it'll become bottled idealism, Paul said.

Bottled identity, Midge said.

Bottled politics, Paul said.

I went to stand by the window where the water cooler was. I pressed the button and water bubbled out of the big plastic container into the little plastic cup. It tasted of plastic. I'm dead, I thought. That's that. It was a relief. The only thing I was sorry about was troubling Midge. She had been sweet there, trying to save me.

I watched a tiny bird fling itself through the air off the guttering above the Boardroom window and land on its feet on a branch of the tree over the huge Pure corporation sign at the front gate of the building. The bird's casual expertise pleased me. I wondered if that group of people outside, gathered at the front gate under the Pure sign, had seen it land.

They were standing there as if they were watching a play. Some were laughing. Some were gesticulating.

It was a lad, dressed for a wedding. He was up a ladder doing some kind of maintenance on the sign. The work experience girls from the school were watching him. So was Becky from Reception, some people who looked like passers-by, and one or two other people I recognised, people Midge had introduced me to, from Pure Press and Pure Personnel.

The nice shavey called Paul was standing beside me now at the water cooler. He nodded to me, apologetic, as he took a plastic cone and held it under the plastic tap. He looked grave. I was clearly going to be shot at dawn. Then he looked out of the window.

Something unorthodox seems to be happening at the Pure sign, he said.

When everybody in the Boardroom was round the window I slipped off to get my coat. I switched my computer off. I'd not yet put anything in the drawers of my desk so there was very little to take with me. I went past the empty reception, all the lights flashing like mad on the phones, and ran down the stairs and out into the sun.

It was a beautiful day.

The boy up the ladder at the gate was in a kilt and sporran. The kilt was a bright red tartan; the boy was black-waistcoated and had frilly cuffs, I could see the frills at his wrists as I came closer. I could see the glint of the knife in his sock. I could see the glint of the little diamond spangles on the waistcoat and the glint that came off the chain that held the sporran on. He had long dark hair winged with ringlets, like Johnny Depp in Pirates of the Caribbean, but cleaner. He was spray-painting, in beautiful red calligraphy, right under the Pure insignia, these words:

DON'T BE STUPID. WATER IS A HUMAN RIGHT. SELLING IT IN ANY WAY IS MORALLY WRO

The work experience girls were applauding and laughing. One of them was singing. Let the wind blow high, let the wind blow low. Through the streets in my kilt I'll go. All the lassies say hello. They saw me and waved at me. I waved back. A Press person was on a mobile. The rest of Press and Personnel were crowded round looking concerned. Two security men stood listlessly at the foot of the ladder. One of them pointed towards the building; I looked up, but its windows, including the window I had myself been staring through a minute ago, were the kind you can't see into.

I wondered if my sister was watching me from up there. I had an urge to wave.

NG., the boy wrote.

The security men shook their heads at each other.

Becky from Reception winked at me then nodded, serious-faced, at the security men. We watched the long-limbed boy sign off, with a series of arrogant and expert slants and curlicues, the final word at the bottom of his handiwork:

IPHISOL.

He shook the paintcan, listened to the rattle it made, thought about whether to keep it or to chuck it away, then tucked it into the pocket of his waistcoat. He took hold of the sides of the ladder, lifted his feet off the rung in one move, put them on the outsides of the downstruts and slid himself neatly to the ground. He landed on his feet and he turned round.

My head, something happened to its insides. It was

as if a storm at sea happened, but only for a moment, and only on the inside of my head. My ribcage, something definitely happened there. It was as if it unknotted itself from itself, like the hull of a ship hitting rock, giving way, and the ship that I was opened wide inside me and in came the ocean.

He was the most beautiful boy I had ever seen in my life.

But he looked really like a girl.

She was the most beautiful boy I had ever seen in my life.

you

(Oh my God my sister is A GAY.)

(I am not upset. I am not upset. I am not upset. I am not upset.)

I am putting on my Stella McCartney Adidas track-suit bottoms. I am lacing up my Nike runners. I am zipping up my Stella McCartney Adidas tracksuit top. I am going out the front door like I am a (normal) person just going out of a (normal) front door on a (normal) early summer day in the month of May and I am going for a run which is the kind of (normal) thing (normal) people do all the time.

There. I'm running. That feels better. I can feel the road beneath my feet. There. There. There.

(It is our mother's fault for splitting up with our father.)

(But if that's true then I might also be a gay.)

(Well obviously that's not true then, that's not true at all.)

(I am definitely, definitely not a gay.)

(I definitely like men.)

(But so does she. So did she. She had that boyfriend, Dave, that she went out with for ages. She had that other boyfriend, Stuart. She had that one called Andrew and that weird English boyfriend, Miles or Giles who lived on Mull, and that boy Sammy, and there was one called Tony, and Nicholas, because she always had boyfriends, she had boyfriends from about the age of twelve, long before I did.)

I am crossing at the lights. I am going to run as far as I can. I am going to run along the river, through the Islands, round by the sports tracks, past the cemetery and up towards the canal

(is that the right way to say it, a gay? Is there a correct word for it?)

(How do you know if you are it?)

(Does our mother know about Anthea being it?)

(Does our father know?)

(It is completely natural to be a gay or a homosexual or whatever. It is totally okay in this day and age.)

(Gay people are just the same as heterosexual people, except for the being gay, of course.)

(They were holding hands at the front door.)

(I should have known. She always was weird. She always was different. She always was contrary. She always did what she knew she shouldn't.)

(It is the fault of the Spice Girls.)

(She chose the video of Spiceworld with Sporty Spice on the limited edition tin.)

(She was always a bit too feminist.)

(She was always playing that George Michael cd.)

(She always votes for the girls on Big Brother and she voted for that transsexual the year he was on, or she, or whatever it is you're supposed to say.)

(She liked the Eurovision Song Contest.)

(She still likes the Eurovision Song Contest.)

(She liked Buffy the Vampire Slayer.)

(But so did I. I liked it too. And it had those girls in it who were both female homosexuals and they were portrayed as very sweet, and it was okay because it was Willow, and she was clever, and we knew to like her and everything, and her friend Tara was very sweet, and I remember one episode where they kissed and their feet came off the ground and they levitated because of the kiss, and I remember that the thing to do when we talked about it at school the next day was to make sick noises.)

Four texts on my phone. Dominic.

WOT U UP 2?

COMIN 2 PUB?

GET HERE NOW.

U R REQD HERE.

(I hate text language. It is so demeaning.)

(I will text him when I get back from my run. I will say I left my mobile at home and didn't get the message till later.)

I am down to just over seven stone.

I am doing well.

We are really revolutionising the bottled water market in Scotland.

Eau Caledonia. They love it as a tag. I got a raise.

I get paid thirty-five thousand before tax.

I can't believe I'm earning that much money. Me!

I am clearly doing the right thing. There is good money in water.

(She is still insisting on calling them shaveys or whatever, and it is unfair of her to lump them all together. It is just fashion. Boys are worse followers of fashion than girls. I mean, men than women. She is wrong to do that. She is wrong)

(they were holding hands at the front door, where any neighbour could see, and then I saw Robin Goodman lean my sister gently into the hedge, back against the branches of it, she was so gentle, and)

(and kiss her.)

(I should have known when she always liked songs that had I and you in them, instead of he and I, or he and she, we always knew, we used to say at college that that was the giveaway, when people preferred those songs that had the word you instead of a man or a woman, like that classic old Tracy Chapman album our mother left behind her that she was always playing before she went.)

(I will never leave my children when I have fallen in love and am married and have had them. I will have them young, not when I am old, like the selfish generation. I would rather give up any career than not have them. I would rather give myself up. I would rather give up everything including any stupid political principle than leave children that belonged to me. Look how it ends. Thank God that feministy time of selfishness is over and we now have everything we will ever need, including a much more responsible set of values.)

It is a lovely day to go for a run. It is not raining. It doesn't even look like it will rain later.

(My sister is a gay.)

(I am not upset.) (I am fine.)

(It'd be okay, I mean I wouldn't mind so much, if it was someone else's sister.)

(It is okay. Lots of people are it. Just none that I have known personally, that's all.)

I am running along the riverside. I am so lucky to live here at this time in history, in the Capital of the Highlands, which is exceptionally buoyant right now, the fastest-developing city in the whole of the UK at the moment thanks to tourism and retirement, and soon also thanks to the growing water economy, of which I am a central part, and which will make history.

We speak the purest English here in the whole country. It is because of the vowel sounds and what happened to them when Gaelic speakers were made to speak English after the 1745 rebellion and the 1746 defeat when Gaelic was stamped out and punishable by death, and then all the local girls married the incoming English-speaking soldiers.

If I can remember the exact, correct words to all the songs on that awful Tracy Chapman album, which I can't have heard for years, it must be at least ten years, I'll be able to run for at least three more miles.

It is good to be goal-orientated. It makes all the other things go out of your mind.

I could go via the canal and past the locks and up over towards the Beauly road and then round by

(but dear God my sister has been hanging around for weeks with a person who is a criminal and against whom the company I work for is pressing charges, and not just that but a person whom I remember from school, and a person, I also remember, we all always called that word behind her back at school, and now this person has turned my sister into one of them, I mean One of Them. And I mean, how did we know to call Robin Goodman that word at school? Adolescent instinct? Well, I didn't know, I never really knew. I thought it was because she had a boy's name instead of a girl's name. That's what I used to think, or maybe because she came in on the bus from Beauly, with the Beauly kids, from somewhere else, and because she had a boy's name, that's what I thought. And because she was a bit different, and didn't people used to say that her mother was black, Robin Goodman, and her father was white, or was it the other way round, and was that even true? I don't remember there being any black people living in Beauly, we'd surely have known, we'd all have known, if there was.)

(I can't bring myself to say the word.)

(Dear God. It is worse than the word cancer.)

(My little sister is going to grow up into a dissatisfied older predatory totally dried-up abnormal woman like Judi Dench in that film Notes on a Scandal.)

(Judi Dench plays that sort of person so well, is what I thought when I saw it, but that was when I didn't think my sister was going to maybe be one of them and have such a terrible life with no real love in it.)

(My little sister is going to have a terrible sad life.)

(But I saw Robin Goodman lean my sister into the hedge with such gentleness, there is no other word for it, and kiss her, and then I saw, not so gently, Robin Goodman shift one of her own legs in between my sister's legs while she kissed her, and I saw my sister, it wasn't just one-sided, she was kissing Robin Goodman back, and then they were both laughing.)

(They were laughing with outrageous happiness.)

(Neighbours must have seen. It was broad daylight.)

(I might have to move house.)

(Well, that's all right. That's all right. If I have to move house I have enough money to.)

Thirty-five thousand, very good money for my age, and for me being a girl, our dad says, which is a bit sexist of him, because gender is nothing to do with whether you are good at a job or not. It is nothing to do with me being a woman or not, the fact that I am the only woman on the Highland Pure Creative board of ten of us – it is because I am good at what I do.

Actually, I think Keith might ask me to go to the States, maybe for training with the in-house Creatives at Base Camp. I think Base Camp is in LA!

He seems very pleased with the Eau Caledonia tag.

He thinks it will corner not just the English-speaking market but a good chunk of the French market, which is crucial, the French market being so water-sales-established worldwide. Scottish, yet French. Well done, he said. They'd like you at Base Camp. You'd like it there.

Me! Los Angeles!

He seemed to be intimating it. He intimated it last Tuesday. He said I'd like it there, that's what he said last week, that I'd like it, that they'd like me.

I told Anthea he had intimated it. She said: Keith intubated you? Like on ER?

I said: you're being ridiculous, Anthea.

(There is also that gay woman doctor character on ER whose lovers always die in fires and so on.)

(Gay people are always dying all the time.)

Anthea is being ridiculous. I got her a good position and now she is at home doing nothing. She is really clever. She is wasting herself.

(I was sitting at home trying to think of a tag, I'd thought of MacAqua, but McDonald's would sue, I'd thought of Scotteau, I'd been saying the word Eau out loud, and Anthea walked past the table as I said it, and she added Caledonia, we're such a good team, we'd be a good team, we'd have been a good team, oh my God my sister is a)

Well, it is bloody lucky Keith intimates anything to

me at all after they did me that favour at Pure about Anthea. She is so naïve, she has no idea what an unusually good salary level she was started at, it is really lucky nobody has associated me with how rude she was that day and that thing happening to the Pure sign

(which is clearly where they met. Maybe I saw the oh so romantic moment they met, last month, I was watching out the window, and the weirdo vandal came down the ladder and she and Anthea were talking, before Security took her away to wait for the police. I saw the name on the forms Security made her fill out. I recognised it. I knew it, the name, from when we were girls. It's a small town. What else can you do, in a small town?)

(Unless they were in cahoots before that and had decided on it as a dual attack on Pure, which is possible, I mean, anything under the sun is possible now.)

(Everything has changed.)

(Nothing is the same.)

I've stopped. I'm not running. I'm just standing.

(I don't want to run anywhere. I can't think where to run to.)

(I better make it look like there is a reason for me to

be just standing. I'll go and stand by the pedestrian crossing.)

That word *intimated* is maybe something to do with the word intimate, since the word intimate is so much a part of, almost the whole of, the word intimated.

I am standing at the pedestrian crossing like a (normal) person waiting to cross the road. A bus goes past. It is full of (normal-looking) people.

(My sister is now one of the reasons the man who owns Stagecoach buses had that million-pound poster campaign all over Scotland where they had pictures of people saying things like 'I'm not a bigot but I don't want my children taught to be gay at school', that kind of thing.)

(They were laughing. Like they were actually happy. Or like being gay is okay, or really funny, or really good fun, or something.)

I am running on the spot so as not to lose momentum.

(It is the putting of that leg in between the other legs that I can't get out of my head. It is really kind of unforgettable.)

(It is so . . .

intimate.)

I stop running on the spot. I stand at the pedestrian crossing and look one way, then the other. Nothing is coming. The road is totally clear.

But I just stand.

(I don't know what's the matter with me. I can't get myself to cross from one side to the other.)

(My sister would be banned in schools if she was a book.)

(No, because the parliament lifted that legislation, didn't it?)

(Did it?)

(I can't remember. I can't remember either way. I didn't ever think that particular law was anything I'd ever have to remember, or consider.)

(Have I ever noticed or considered anything about it? Should I have?)

(I did. I have. I remember reading in the paper about how people all across the world, and not just people but governments, in Poland and in Russia, but also in Spain, and Italy, are getting more and more tough on people being it. I mean, you'd expect that in Russia and in Poland. But in Italy? In Spain? Those are places that are supposed to be like here.)

(It said in the paper this morning that teenagers who are it are six times more likely to commit suicide than teenagers who aren't it.)

(I don't know what to do with myself.)

I stand at the crossing with no cars coming in either direction and I still don't move to cross the road. I feel a little dizzy. I feel a little faint.

(Anyone looking at me will think I'm really weird.)

There's only Dominic and Norman in the pub.

Where've you been, you useless slag? Norman says.

Don't call me that, I say.

Can't take a joke? he says. Loosen up. Ha ha!

He goes to the bar and brings me a glass of white.

Norm, I said a Diet Coke, I say.

But I've bought it now, Norman says.

So I see, I say.

Do you want me to take it back and change it? Norman says.

No, it's okay, I'll drink it since it's here now, I say.

I texted you, Madge, Dominic says.

(My name's Imogen.)

Did you? I say.

I texted you four times, Dominic says.

Ah. Because I left my mobile at home, I say.

I can't believe you didn't have your mobile with you, when I'd told you I was going to text you, Dominic says.

He looks really offended.

No Paul or anybody? I say. I thought everybody was coming.

Just us, Norman says. Your lucky night. Bri's coming later. He's bringing Chantelle.

I'd bring Chantelle any day, Dominic says.

I'd do a lot more to Chantelle than just bring her, Norman says. Paul's gay, man. He won't come out on a Monday night because of University Challenge being on.

Paul isn't gay, I say in a small voice.

Paul's hoping there'll be questions on tonight about Uranus, Dominic says.

Paul isn't gay, I say again louder.

You talking from experience then? Norman says.

Scintillating conversation, I say.

I make my face look bored. I hope it will work.

Dominic doesn't say anything. He just stares at me. The way he's looking at me makes me look away. I pretend I'm going to the ladies. I slip into the other bar and phone Paul.

Come to the pub, I say. I try to sound bright.

Who's there? Paul asks.

Loads of us, I say.

Is it Dom and Norm? Paul says. I'm only asking because they left an abusive message on my answerphone.

Uh huh. And me, I say. I'm here.

No offence, Imogen. But I'm not coming out, Paul says. They're wankers. They think they're so funny, they act like some nasty double act off tv. I don't know what you're doing out with them.

Go on, Paul, please, I say. It'll be good fun.

Yeah, but the world now divides into people who think it's good fun looking up pictures on the net of women fucking horses and dogs, and people who don't, Paul says. If you need me to come and get you, call me later.

Paul is very uptight, I think when I press the button to hang up.

I don't see why he can't just pretend to find it funny like the rest of us have to.

(Maybe he *is* gay.)

So what about that other work experience girl, then? Norman is saying when I get back through. The one who's not Chantelle. What about work-experiencing her?

I've other things in mind, Dominic says looking at me.

I look above his eyes, at his forehead. I can't help noticing that both Dominic and Norman have the exact same haircut. Norman goes to the bar and comes back with a full wine bottle. He and Dominic are drinking Grolsch.

I can't drink all that, I say. I'm only out for one or two, I've got to get back.

Yes you can, Norman says. He fills the glass up past the little line, right to the very top, so that it's almost spilling over onto the table, so that to drink anything out of it at all I'm going to have to lean over and put my mouth to it there on the table, or pick it up with superhuman care so as not to spill it.

We're off for a curry in a minute, Dominic says. You're coming too. Drink it fast.

I can't, I say. It's Monday. There's work tomorrow.

Yes you can, Norman says. We work too, you know.

I drink four glasses filled to the top like this. It

makes them roar with laughter when I bend right down to drink it. Eventually I do it so that that's what it will do, make them laugh.

At the restaurant, where everything smells too strong, and where the walls seem to be coming away from their skirting boards, they talk about work as if I'm not there. They make several jokes about Muslim pilots. They tell a long complicated joke about a blind Jewish man and a prostitute. Then Brian texts Dominic to say he can't come. This causes a shouted dialogue with him down the phone about Chantelle, about Chantelle's greggy friend, and about whether Chantelle's greggy friend is there with Chantelle right now so that Brian can 'watch'. Meanwhile I sit in the swirling restaurant and wonder what the word greggy means. It's clearly a word they've made up. It makes them really laugh. It makes them laugh so much that people round us are looking offended, and so are the Indian people serving us. I can't help laughing too.

The word seems to mean, on the whole, that they don't think the other work experience girl wears enough make-up to work, regardless of the fact she's sixteen and should really know how to by now, as Norman says.

That she wears the wrong kinds of clothes. That she is a bit of a disappointment.

That she's a bit, you know, greg, Dominic says.

I think I'm beginning to understand, I say.

I mean, take you. You exercise, and everything. You've got a top job, and everything. But that doesn't make you a greg. That bike you've got. You can get away with it, Norman says.

So the fact that I look all right on a motorbike means I'm not a greg? I say.

They both burst out laughing.

So it means unfeminine? I say.

I'd like to see her gregging, Norman says looking at me. You and that good-looking little sister of yours.

They roar with laughter. I am beginning to find the laughter a bit like someone is sandpapering my skull. I look away from the people all looking at us. I look down at the tablecloth.

Aw. She doesn't like not knowing the politically correct terms for things, Dominic says.

Greggy greggy greggy. Use your head, Norman says. Come on. Free associate.

Dreggy? I say. Something to do with dregs?

Getting there, getting there, Norman says.

Go on, give her a clue, Dominic says.

Okay. Here's a great big clue. Like the man at the BBC, Norman says.

What man? I say.

The man who got the sack for Iraq, who used to run the BBC until he let people say what they shouldn't have, out loud, on the news, Norman says.

Um, I say.

Are you retarded? Greg Dyke. Remember? Dominic says.

You mean, the work experience girl is something to do with Greg Dyke? I say.

They both laugh.

You mean, she says things out loud that she shouldn't? I say.

She's, like, a thespian, Norman says.

A what? I say.

A lickian, Norman says. Well, she looks like one.

Like that freakshow who daubed the Pure sign that day, Dominic says. Fucking dyke.

(My whole body goes cold.)

Now there's one trial I can't wait to see come to

court. I hope we all get to come to it, Norman is saying.

We will, Dominic says. They'll need men for there to be any coming at a trial like that.

Just what I was telling Brian, Norman says. Be ready to step in, now, when the moment's right.

You know, I say, it said in the paper this morning that teenagers who are gay are six times more likely to kill themselves than teenagers who aren't.

Good. Ha ha! Norman says.

Dominic's eyes cloud. Human species, self-patrolling, he says.

They start talking as if I'm not there again, like they did when they were talking about work.

See, that's what I don't get, Dominic says shaking his head, serious. Because, there's no way they could do it, I mean, without one. So it's like, pointless.

Freud defined it, Norman says (Norman did psychology at Stirling), as a state of lack. A state of lacking something really, you know, fundamental.

Dominic nods, grave-faced.

Exactly, he says. Obviously.

Adolescent backwardness. Marked underdevelopment, Norman says.

Yeah, but a really heavy case of underdevelopment, Dominic says. I mean, never mind anything else. Never mind how weird it is. Like, what gets me is, there's nothing to do the job. Nothing to do the jiggery-pokery with. And that's why Queen Victoria didn't make rugmunch illegal.

How's that? Norman says.

It was on Channel Four. Apparently she said there was no such thing, like, it didn't exist. And she was right. I mean, when men do it, poofs, in sexual terms, I mean, it's fucking disgusting and it leads to queer paedophilia and everything, but at least it's real sex they have, eh? But women. It's, like, how can they? I just don't get it. It's a joke, Dominic says.

Yeah, but it's good, Norman says, if you're watching and they're both fuckable.

Yeah, but the real ones are really mostly pretty unfuckable, you have to admit, Dominic says.

(Oh my God my sister who is related to me is a greg, a lack, unfuckable, not properly developed, and not even worth making illegal.)

(There are so many words I don't know for what my little sister is.)

Dominic and Norman are somehow roaring with laughter again. They have their arms round each other.

I have to go now, I say.

No you don't, they say in unison and fill my glass with Cobra.

Yes, I do, I say.

I shake them off at the multi-storey. I dodge behind a car so they don't know where I've gone. I wait there until the legs I can see moving about have disappeared. I hear them go up the stairs and I watch them fumble at the exit ticket machine until finally whichever one of them is driving finds the ticket, works out how to put it into the machine the right way and their car goes under the lifted barrier.

I throw up under a tree at the side of the road on my way home. I look up. The tree I've just been sick under is in full white blossom.

(Adolescent backwardness.)

(I am fourteen. Myself and Denise MacCall are in a geography classroom. It is interval. We have somehow managed to stay in; maybe Denise said she was feeling sick or maybe I did; that was how you got to stay in over interval. We often said we felt sick if it was raining or cold.

There is a pile of homework jotters on the table. Denise is going through them, reading out people's names. We say out loud at each name whether we pass or fail the person, like the game Anthea and I play at home at the countdown of the chart on Top of the Pops. Hurray for someone we like. Boo for someone we don't.

Denise finds Robin Goodman's jotter.

For some reason Denise MacCall really dislikes Robin Goodman from Beauly, with her short curly dark hair thick on top of her head, her darkish skin, her long hands that the music teacher is always going on about when she plays her clarinet, her serious, studious, far-too-clever face. I dislike her too, though I hardly know her. She is in two or three of my classes, that's all I know about her, apart from that she plays the clarinet. But it makes me feel happy to dislike her right now, because this is proof that I am Denise's friend. Though I am not so sure that I like Denise all that much either, or that Denise wouldn't boo me if she got to a jotter with my name on it and I wasn't here in the room with her.

Denise and I write the letters L, E and Z, on the

front of Robin Goodman's jotter, with the black Pentel I have in my pencil case. Or, to be more exact, I write the letters and she draws the arrow pointing at them.

Then we slide the jotter back into the middle of the pile.

When geography class starts, and Horny Geog, which is what we call Miss Horne, the old lady teacher who teaches us it, gives out the jotters, we watch to see Robin Goodman's response. I am sitting a couple of rows behind her. I see her shoulders tense, then droop.

When I go past her at the end of the period and glance down at the book on her desk I can see that she's made Denise's arrow into the trunk of a tree and she's drawn hundreds of little flowerheads, all around the letters L, E and Z, like the letters are the branches of the tree and they've all just come into bloom.)

The same Robin Goodman, ten years later, with her long dark hair and her dark, serious, studious face, is

(oh my God)

right here in my house when I get home. She is sitting on the couch with a cup of tea in front of her.

She is reading a book. I am too drunk and dizzy to make out the cover of the book she is reading. I stand in the doorway and hold on to the doorframe.

Hi, she says.

(Oh my God and also my sister is a)

What have you done with my sister? I say.

Your sister's in the bath, she says.

I sit down. I lean my head back. I feel sick.

(I am sitting in the same room as a)

Robin Goodman leaves the room. When she comes back, she puts something into my hand. It's a glass. It's one of my glasses from the cupboard.

Drink that, she says, and I'll get you another one.

You haven't changed much, since school, I say. You look exactly the same.

So do you, she says. But some things have changed, thank God. We're not schoolgirls any more.

Apart from. Your hair. Got longer, I say.

Well, ten years, she says. Something's got to give.

I went away to unversity, I say. Did you go?

If you mean university, yes, I did, she says.

And you came back, I say.

Just like you, she says.

Do you still play the clarnet? I say.

No, she says.

There's a silence. I look down. There's a glass in my hand.

Drink it, she says.

I drink it. It tastes beautiful, of clearness.

That'll be better, she says.

She takes the empty glass and leaves the room. I hear her in my kitchen. I look down at myself and am surprised to see I'm still wearing the tracksuit I put on after work. I'm not completely sure where I've just been. I begin to wonder if I made up the whole evening, if I invented the pub, the curryhouse, the whole thing.

That's my kitchen you were just in, I say when she comes back through.

I know, she says and sits down in my sitting room.

This is my sitting room, I say.

Yep, she says.

(I am sitting in the same room as a)

She is the kind of person who does not really care what she is wearing or what it looks like. At least she is wearing normal clothes. At least she is not wearing that embarrassing Scottish get-up.

Not wearing your kilt tonight? I say.

Only for special occasions, she says.

My company that I work for, you know, Pure Incorported, is going to take you to court, I say.

They'll drop the charges, she says.

She doesn't even look up from her book. I have to look at my hand because it's covered in the water I've spilled on myself. I hold the glass up and look through it. I look at the room through the bit with water in it. Then I look at the same room through the bit with no water in it. Then I drink the water.

Eau Caledonia, I say.

Need another? she says.

(I am sitting in the same room as a)

A lass and a lack, I say.

This pun makes me laugh. It is unlike me to be witty. It is my sister who is the really witty one. I am the one who knows the correct words, the right words for things.

I lean forward.

Tell me what it is, I say.

It's water, Robin Goodman says.

No, I say. I mean, what's the correct word for it, I

mean, for you? I need to know it. I need to know the proper word.

She looks at me for a long time. I can feel her looking right through my drunkness. Then, when she speaks, it is as if the whole look of her speaks.

The proper word for me, Robin Goodman says, is me.

us

Because of us, things came together. Everything was possible.

I had not known, before us, that every vein in my body was capable of carrying light, like a river seen from a train makes a channel of sky etch itself deep into a landscape. I had not really known I could be so much more than myself. I had not known another body could do this to mine.

Now I'd become a walking fuse, like in that poem about the flower, and the force, and the green fuse the force drives through it; the force that blasts the roots of trees was blasting the roots of me, I was like a species that hadn't even realised it lived in a near-desert till one day its taproot hit water. Now I had taken a whole new shape. No, I had taken the shape I was always supposed to, the shape that let me hold my head high. Me, Anthea Gunn, head turned towards the sun.

Your name, Robin had said on our first underwater

night together deep in each other's arms. It means flowers, did you know that?

No it doesn't, I'd said. Gunn means war. The clan motto is Either Peace or War. Midge and I did a clan project at school when I was small.

No, I mean your first name, she said.

I was named after someone off the tv, I said.

It means flowers, or a coming-up of flowers, a blooming of flowers, she said. I looked you up.

She was behind me in the bed, she was speaking into my shoulder.

You, she was saying. You're a walking peace protest. You're the flower in the Gunn.

And what about you? I said. I tried looking you up too. I did it before we'd even met. What does the weird name mean?

What weird name? she said.

It isn't in the dictionary, I said. I looked. I Googled you. It doesn't mean anything.

Everything means something, she said.

Iphisol, I said.

Iff is sol? she said. Iffisol? I don't know. I've no idea. It sounds like aerosol. Or Anusol.

She was holding me loosely, her arms were round me and one leg over my legs keeping me warm, I could feel the smooth new skin of her from my shoulders down to my calves. Then the bed was shaking; she was laughing.

Not Iffisol. Eye fizz ol, she said. Iphis is said like eye fizz. And it's not ol, it's 07. Like, the name, Iphis, but with the year, the oh and the seven of two thousand and seven.

Oh. Iphis oh seven. Oh, I said.

I was laughing now too. I turned in her arms and put my head on her laughing collarbone.

Like double oh seven. Daniel Craig in Casino Royal, rising out of the water like that goddess on a shell, I said. Lo and behold.

Ursula Andress did it first, she said. I mean, after Venus herself, that is. In fact, Daniel Craig and Ursula Andress look remarkably alike, when you compare them. No, because last year I used Iphis06. The year before I was Iphis05. God knows what you'd have thought *they* said. Iffisog. Iffisos.

It had been exciting, first the not knowing what Robin was, then the finding out. The grey area, I'd discovered, had been misnamed: really the grey area was a whole other spectrum of colours new to the eye. She had the swagger of a girl. She blushed like a boy. She had a girl's toughness. She had a boy's gentleness. She was as meaty as a girl. She was as graceful as a boy. She was as brave and handsome and rough as a girl. She was as pretty and delicate and dainty as a boy. She turned boys' heads like a girl. She turned girls' heads like a boy. She made love like a boy. She made love like a girl. She was so boyish it was girlish, so girlish it was boyish, she made me want to rove the world writing our names on every tree. I had simply never found anyone so right. Sometimes this shocked me so much that I was unable to speak. Sometimes when I looked at her, I had to look away. Already she was like no one else to me. Already I was fearful she would go. I was used to people being snatched away. I was used to the changes that came out of the blue. The old blue, that is. The blue that belonged to the old spectrum.

My grandfather used to say that all the time, lo and behold, I told her. They're dead, my grandparents. They drowned. This used to be their house.

Tell me about them, she said.

You tell me about you first, I said. Come on. Story of your life.

I will, she said. Yours first.

If my life was a story, I said, it'd start like this: Before she left, my mother gave me a compass. But when I tried to use it, when I was really far out, lost at sea, the compass didn't work. So I tried the other compass, the one my father had given me before he left. But that compass was broken too.

So you looked out across the deep waters, Robin said. And you decided, by yourself, and with the help of a clear night and some stars, which way was north and which was south and which way was east and which was west. Yes?

Yes, I said.

Then I said it again. Yes.

Now do you want to know mine? she said.

I do, I said.

It begins one day when I come down a ladder off an interventionist act of art protest, and turn round and see the most beautiful person I've ever seen. From that moment on, I'm home. It's as if I've been struggling upstream, going against the grain, until that moment.

Then we get married, me and the person, and we live together happily ever after, which is impossible, both in story and in life, actually. But we get to. And that's the message. That's it. That's all.

What sort of story's that? I said.

A very fishy sort, she said.

It sounds a bit lightweight, as stories go, I said.

I can be heavy-handed if you want, she said. Fancy a bit of heavy-handing? Or would you prefer something lighter? You choose.

Then she held me tight.

Lo and be held, she said.

You're very artful, you, I said.

You're not so bad yourself, she said.

We woke up. It was light. It was half past two in the morning. We got up and opened the window; we leaned together on the sill and watched the world wake up, and as the birds fought to be heard above one another before all the usual noise of day set in to drown them out she told me the story of Iphis.

A long time ago on the island of Crete a woman was pregnant and when the time came close to her giving birth her husband, a good man, came to her and said, if it's a boy we'll keep him, but if it's a girl we can't. We can't afford a girl, she'll have to be put to death, I'm so sorry, but it's just the way things are. So the woman went to the temple and prayed to the goddess Isis, who miraculously appeared before her. You've been true to me so I'll be true to you, the goddess said. Bring the child up regardless of what it is and I promise you everything will be fine. So the child was born and it was a girl. The mother brought her up secretly as a boy, calling her Iphis, which was a name both boys and girls could be called. And Iphis went to school and was educated with her friend Ianthe, the beautiful daughter of a fine family, and Iphis and Ianthe grew up looking into each other's eyes. Love touched their innocent hearts simultaneously and wounded them both, and they were betrothed. As the wedding day approached and the whole of Crete prepared for the celebration, Iphis got more and more worried about how, being a girl like Ianthe, she would ever be able to please her bride, whom she so loved. She worried that she herself would never really enjoy her bride the way she longed to. She complained bitterly to the gods and goddesses about it. On the night before the wedding, Iphis's mother went back to the temple and asked the goddess to help. As she left the empty temple its walls shook, its doors trembled, Iphis's jaw lengthened, her stride lengthened, her ribcage widened and broadened, her chest flattened, and the next day, the wedding day, dawned bright and clear and there was rejoicing all over the island of Crete as the boy Iphis gained his own Ianthe.

Though actually, the telling of it went much more like this:

A long time ago, on the island of Crete, Robin said behind me, into my ear –

I've been there! We went there! I said. We had a holiday there when we were kids. We spent a lot of it at the hospital in Heraklion, actually, because our dad went to hire a motorbike to impress this woman in a motorbike hire shop, and before he'd hired one he rode it a few yards round a corner to get a feel for it, and fell off it and scraped the skin off half the side of his body.

A long time ago, Robin said, long before motorbike

hire, long before motors, long before bikes, long before you, long before me, back before the great tsunami that flattened most of northern Crete and drowned most of the Minoan cities, which, by the way, was probably the incident responsible for the creation of the myth about the lost city of Atlantis –

That's very interesting, I said.

It is, she said. There's pumice stone fifty feet up on dry land in parts of Crete, and cow-bones all mixed up with sea-creature remains, far too high for any other geological explanation –

No, I mean that thing about responsibility and creating a myth, I said.

Oh, she said. Well –

I mean, do myths spring fully formed from the imagination and the needs of a society, I said, as if they emerged from society's subconscious? Or are myths conscious creations by the various money-making forces? For instance, is advertising a new kind of myth-making? Do companies sell their water etc by telling us the right kind of persuasive myth? Is that why people who really don't need to buy something that's practically free still go out and buy bottles of it? Will they soon be thinking up a myth to sell us air? And do people, for instance, want to be thin because of a prevailing myth that thinness is more beautiful?

Anth, Robin said. Do you want to hear this story about the boy-girl or don't you?

I do, I said.

Right. Crete. Way back then, she said. Ready?

Uh huh, I said.

Sure? she said.

Yep, I said.

So there was this woman who was pregnant, and her husband came to her –

Which one was Iphis? I said.

Neither, she said. And her husband said –

What were their names? I said.

I can't remember their names. Anyway, the husband came to the wife –

Who was pregnant, I said.

Uh huh, and he said, listen, I'm really praying for two things, and one of them is that this baby gives you no pain in the giving birth.

Hmm, right, his wife said. That's likely, isn't it?

Ha ha! I said.

No, well, no she didn't, Robin said. I'm imposing far too modern a reading on it. No, she acted correctly for her time, thanked him for even considering, so graciously, from his man's world where women didn't really count, that there'd be any pain at all involved for her. And what's the other thing you're praying for? she asked. When she said this, the man, who was a good man, looked very sad. The woman was immediately suspicious. Her husband said, look, you know what I'm going to say. The thing is. When you give birth, if you have a boy, that'll be fine, we can keep it, of course, and that's what I'm praying for.

Uh huh? the woman said. And?

And if you have a girl, we can't, he said. We'll have to put it to death if it's a girl. A girl's a burden. You know it is. I can't afford a girl. You know I can't. A girl's no use to me. So that's that. I'm so sorry to have to say this, I wish it wasn't so, and I don't want to do this, but it's the way of the world.

The way of the world, I said. Great. Thank God we're modern.

Still the way of the world in lots of places all over

the world, Robin said, red ink for a girl, blue for a boy, on the bottom of doctors' certificates, letting parents know, in the places it's not legal to allow people just to abort girls, what to abort and what to keep. So. The woman went off to do some praying of her own. And as she knelt down in the temple, and prayed to the nothing that was there, the goddess Isis appeared right in front of her.

Like the Virgin Mary at Lourdes, I said.

Except much, much earlier, culturally and historically, than the Virgin Mary, Robin said, and also the woman wasn't sick, though certainly there was something pretty rotten in the state of Knossos, what with the whole kill-the-girl thing. And the goddess Isis had brought a lot of her god-friends and family with her, including that god whose head is like a jackal. What's his name? Damn. I really like – he's got, like, these jackal ears, and a long snout – a kind of dog-god – he guards the underworld –

I don't know. Is it a crucial part of the story? I said.

No. So Isis thanked the woman for the constant faith she had in things, and told her not to worry. Just give birth as per usual, and bring the child up, she said.

As per usual? I said. A goddess used the phrase *as per usual*?

The gods can be down-to-earth when they want, Robin said. And then she and all her god-friends disappeared, like they'd never been there, like the woman had just made them up. But the woman was very happy. She went and stood under the night sky and held her arms out open to the stars. And the time came for the baby to be born. And out it came.

You can't stay in the womb all your life, I said.

And it was a girl, Robin said.

Of course, I said.

So the woman called her Iphis, which was the child's grandfather's name –

I like that, I said.

– and was also, by chance, a name used both for girls and boys, which the woman thought was a good omen.

I like that too, I said.

And to keep her child safe she brought her up as a boy, Robin said. Lucky for Iphis, she looked rather good as a boy, though she'd also have looked very handsome as a girl. She was certainly every bit as handsome as her friend, Ianthe, the beautiful fair-haired daughter of one of the finest families on the island.

Aha, I said. I think I see where this is going.

And Iphis and Ianthe, since they were exactly the same age, went to school together, learned to read together, learned about the world together, grew up together, and as soon as they were both of marrying age their fathers did some bargaining, swapped some livestock, and the village got ready for the wedding. But not just that. The thing is, Iphis and Ianthe had actually, for real, very really, fallen in love.

Did their hearts hurt? I said. Did they think they were underwater all the time? Did they feel scoured by light? Did they wander about not knowing what to do with themselves?

Yes, Robin said. All of that. And more.

There's more? I said. Man!

So to speak, Robin said. And the wedding day was set. And the whole village was coming. Not just the village, but all the fine families of the island were coming. And some people off faraway other islands. And off the mainland. Several gods had been invited and many had actually said they'd come. And Iphis was in quite a bad way, because she couldn't imagine.

She couldn't imagine what? I said.

She couldn't imagine how she was going to do it, Robin said.

How do you mean? I said.

She stood in a field far enough away from the village so nobody would hear except maybe a few goats, a few cows, and she shouted at the sky, she shouted at nothing, at Isis, at all the gods. Why have you done this to me? You fuckers. You jokers. Look what's happened now. I mean, look at that cow there. What'd be the point in giving her a cow instead of a bull? I can't be a boy to my girl! I don't know how! I wish I'd never been born! You've made me wrong! I wish I'd been killed at birth! Nothing can help me!

But maybe her girl, what's her name, Ianthe, *wants* a girl, I said. Clearly Iphis is exactly the kind of boy-girl or girl-boy she loves.

Well, yes. I agree, Robin said. That's debatable. But it's not in the original story. In the original, Iphis stands there shouting at the gods. Even if Daedalus was here, Iphis shouted, and he's the greatest inventor in the world, who can fly across the sea like a bird though he's just a man! But even *he* wouldn't know what to invent to make this okay for Ianthe and me. I mean, you were kind, Isis, and you told my mother it'd be fine, but now what? Now I've got to get married, and it's tomorrow, and I'll be the laughing stock of the whole village, because of you. And Juno and Hymen are coming. We'll be the laughing stock of the heavens too. And how can I get married to my girl in front of them, in front of my father, in front of everyone? And not just that. Not just that. I'm never, ever, ever going to be able to please my girl. And she'll be mine, but never really mine. It'll be like standing right in the middle of a stream, dying of thirst, with my hand full of water, but I won't be able to drink it!

Why won't she be able to drink it? I said.

Robin shrugged.

It's just what she thinks at this point in the story, she said. She's young. She's scared. She doesn't know yet that it'll be okay. She's only about twelve. That was the marriageable age, then, twelve. I was terrified, too, when I was twelve and wanted to marry another girl. (Who did you want to marry? I said. Janice McLean, Robin said, who lived in Kinmylies. She was very glamorous. And she had a pony.) Twelve, or thirteen, terrified. It's easy to think it's a mistake, or you're a mistake. It's easy, when everything and everyone you know tells you you're the wrong shape, to believe you're the wrong shape. And also, don't forget, the story of Iphis was being made up by a man. Well, I say man, but Ovid's very fluid, as writers go, much more than most. He knows, more than most, that the imagination doesn't have a gender. He's really good. He honours all sorts of love. He honours all sorts of story. But with this story, well, he can't help being the Roman he is, he can't help fixating on what it is that girls don't have under their togas, and it's him who can't imagine what girls would ever do without one.

I had a quick look under the duvet.

Doesn't feel or look like anything's missing to me, I said.

Ah, I love Iphis, Robin said. I love her. Look at her. Dressed as a boy to save her life. Standing in a field, shouting at the way things are. She'd do anything for love. She'd risk changing everything she is.

What's going to happen? I said.

What do you think? Robin said.

Well, she's going to need some help. The father's not going to be any good, he doesn't even know his boy's a girl. Not very observant. And Ianthe thinks that's what a boy is, what Iphis is. Ianthe's just happy to be getting married. But she won't want a humiliation either, and they'd be the joke of the village. She's only twelve, too. So Iphis can't go and ask her for help. So. It's either the mother or the goddess.

Well-spotted, Robin said. Off the mother went to have a word with the goddess in her own way.

That's one of the reasons Midge is so resentful, I said.

The what who's so what? Robin said.

Imogen. She had to do all that mother stuff when ours left, I said. Maybe it's why she's so thin. Have you noticed how thin she is?

Yep, Robin said.

I never had to do anything, I said. I'm lucky. I was born mythless. I grew up mythless.

No you didn't. Nobody grows up mythless, Robin said. It's what we do with the myths we grow up with that matters.

I thought about our mother. I thought about what she'd said, that she had to be free of what people expected of her, otherwise she'd simply have died. I thought about our father, out in the garden in the first days after she went, hanging out the washing. I thought about Midge, seven years old, running downstairs to take over, to do it instead of him, because the neighbours were laughing to see a man at the washing line. Good girl, our father had said.

Keep telling the story, I said. Go on.

So the mother, then, Robin said, went to the temple, and she said into the thin air: look, come on. You told me it'd be okay. And now we've got this huge wedding happening tomorrow, and it's all going to go wrong. So could you just sort it out for me? Please.

And as she left the empty temple, the temple started to shake, and the doors of the temple trembled.

And lo and behold, I said.

Yep. Jaw lengthens, stride lengthens, absolutely everything lengthens. By the time she'd got home, the girl Iphis had become exactly the boy that she and her girl needed her to be. And the boy their two families needed. And everyone in the village needed. And all the people coming from all over the place who were very anxious to have a really good party needed. And the visiting gods needed. And the particular historic era with its own views on what was excitingly perverse in a love story needed. And the writer of Metamorphoses needed, who really, really needed a happy love story at the end of Book 9 to carry him through the several much more scurrilous stories about people who fall, unhappily and with terrible consequences, in love with their fathers, their brothers, various unsuitable animals, and the dead ghosts of their lovers, Robin said. Voilà. Sorted. No problemo. Metamorphoses is full of the gods being mean to people, raping people then turning them into cows or streams so they won't tell, hunting them till they change into plants or rivers, punishing them for their pride or their arrogance or their skill by changing them into mountains or insects. Happy stories are rare in it. But the next day dawned, and the whole world opened its eyes, it was the day of the wedding. Even Juno had come, and Hymen was there too, and all the families of Crete were gathered in their finery for the huge celebration all over the island, as the girl met her boy there at the altar.

Girl meets boy, I said. In so many more ways than one.

Old, old story, Robin said.

I'm glad it worked out, I said.

Good old story, Robin said.

Good old Ovid, giving it balls, I said.

Even though it didn't need them. Anubis! Robin said suddenly. The god with the jackal head. Anubis.

Anubis colony? I said.

Come on, Robin said. You and me. What do you say?

Bed, I said.

Off we went, back to bed.

We were tangled in each other's arms so that I wasn't sure whose hand that was by my head, was it hers or mine? I moved my hand. The hand by my head didn't move. She saw me looking at it.

It's yours, she said. I mean, it's on the end of my arm. But it's yours. So's the arm. So's the shoulder. So's everything else it's connected to.

Her hand opened me. Then her hand became a wing. Then everything about me became a wing, a single wing, and she was the other wing, we were a bird. We were a bird that could sing Mozart. It was a music I recognised, it was both deep and light. Then it changed into a music I'd never heard before, so new to me that it made me airborne, I was nothing but the notes she was playing, held in air. Then I saw her smile so close to my eyes that there was nothing to see but the smile, and the thought came into my head that I'd never been inside a smile before, who'd have thought being inside a smile would be so ancient and so modern both at once? Her beautiful head was down at my breast, she caught me between her teeth just once, she put the nip into nipple like the cub of a fox would, down we went, no wonder they call it an earth, it was loamy, it was good, it was what good meant, it was earthy, it was what earth meant, it was the underground of everything, the kind of soil that cleans things. Was that her tongue? Was that what they meant when they said flames had tongues? Was I melting? Would I melt? Was I gold? Was I magnesium? Was I briny, were my whole insides a piece of sea, was I nothing but salty water with a mind of its own, was I some kind of fountain, was I the force of water through stone? I was hard all right, and then I was sinew, I was a snake, I changed stone to snake in three simple moves, stoke stake snake, then I was a tree whose branches were all budded knots, and what were those felty buds, were they – antlers? were antlers really growing out of both of us? was my whole front furring over? and were we the same pelt? were our hands black shining hoofs? were we kicking? were we bitten? were our heads locked into each other to the death? till we broke open? I was a she was a he was a we were a girl and a girl and a boy and a boy, we were blades, were a knife that could cut through myth, were two knives thrown by a magician, were arrows fired by a god, we hit heart, we hit home, we were the tail of a fish were the reek of a cat were the beak of a bird were the feather that mastered gravity were high above every landscape then down deep in the purple haze of the heather were roamin in a gloamin in a brash unending Scottish piece of perfect jigging reeling reel can we really keep this up? this fast? this high? this happy? round again? another notch higher? heuch! the perfect jigsaw fit of one into the curve of another as if a hill top into sky, was that a thistle? was I nothing but grass, a patch of coarse grasses? was that incredible colour coming out of me? the shining heads of – what? butter-cups? because the scent of them, farmy and delicate, came into my head and out of my eyes, my ears, out of my mouth, out of my nose, I was scent that could see, I was eyes that could taste, I loved butter. I loved everything. Hold everything under my chin! I was all my open senses held together on the head of a pin, and was it an angel who knew how to use hands like that, as wings?

We were all that, in the space of about ten minutes. Phew. A bird, a song, the insides of a mouth, a fox, an earth, all the elements, minerals, a water feature, a stone, a snake, a tree, some thistles, several flowers, arrows, both genders, a whole new gender, no gender at all and God knows how many other things including a couple of fighting stags.

I got up to get us a drink of water and as I stood in the kitchen in the early morning light, running the water out of the tap, I looked out at the hills at the back of the town, at the trees on the hills, at the bushes in the garden, at the birds, at the brand new leaves on a branch, at a cat on a fence, at the bits of wood that made the fence, and I wondered if everything I saw, if maybe every landscape we casually glanced at, was the outcome of an ecstasy we didn't even know was happening, a love-act moving at a speed slow and steady enough for us to be deceived into thinking it was just everyday reality.

Then I wondered why on earth would anyone ever stand in the world as if standing in the cornucopic middle of the Hanging Gardens of Babylon but inside a tiny white-painted rectangle about the size of a single space in a car park, refusing to come out of it, and all round her or him the whole world, beautiful, various, waiting?

them

(It is really English down here in England.)

First class all the way. I was the only person in Carriage J when we set off. Me! A whole train carriage to myself! I am doing all right

(and that train getting more and more English the further south we came. The serving staff doing the coffee changed into English people at Newcastle. And the conductor's voice on the speakers changed into English at Newcastle too and then it was like being on a totally different train though I hadn't even moved in my seat, and the people getting on and sitting in the other seats round me all really Englishy and by the time we'd got to York it was like a different)

OUCH. Oh sorry!

(People in England just walk into you and they don't even apologise.)

(And there are so many, so many! People here go on and on for miles and miles and miles.)

(Where's my phone?)

Menu. Contacts. Select. Dad. Call.

(God, it is so busy here with the people and the noise and the traffic I can hardly hear the)

Answerphone.

(He never answers it when he sees my name come up.)

Hi Dad, it's me. It's Thursday, it's a quarter to five. Just leaving you another to tell you I'm not in first class on the train any more, I'm in that, eh, Leicester Square, God it's really sunny down here, it's a bit too warm, I've got half an hour between very important business meetings so was just calling to say hi. Eh, right, well, I'll give you a wee call when I'm out of my meetings, so bye for now. Bye now. Bye.

End call.

Menu. Contacts. Select. Paul. Call.

Answerphone.

(Damn.)

Oh hi Paul, it's just me, it's just eh Imogen. It's Thursday, it's about a quarter to five, and I was just wondering if you could check with secretarial for me, I eh can't get through, I've been trying and it's constantly engaged or maybe something's up with the signal or something, anyway sorry to be calling so late in the afternoon, but because I couldn't get through I thought what'll I do, oh I know, I can always phone Paul, he'll help me out, so if you'd just check with them for me that the market projection email and the colour print-outs went off to Keith down here and whether he'll have seen it all before I get over to the office? I should be there in about fifteen minutes. I'll wait for your call, Paul. Thanks, Paul. Bye for now. Bye now. Bye.

Menu. Contacts. Select. Anthea. Call.

Answerphone.

Hi. This is Anthea. Don't leave me a message on this phone because I'm actually trying not to use my mobile any longer since the production of mobiles involves slave labour on a huge scale and also since mobiles get in the way of us living fully and properly in the present moment and connecting properly, on a real level, with people and are just another way to sell us short. Come and see me instead and we'll talk properly. Thanks.

(For God's sake.)

Hi, it's me. It's Thursday, it's ten to five. Can you hear me? I can hardly hear myself, it's so noisy here, it's just ridiculous. Anyway I'm on my way to a meeting and I was walking through a kind of a park or square at the back of the Leicester Square, where I got the underground to, and there was this statue of William Shakespeare there in it, and the thought came into my head, Anthea'd like that, and then, like, you wouldn't believe it! About two seconds later I saw right across from it this statue of Charlie Chaplin! So I thought I'd just phone and tell you. I'm actually coming up to Trafalgar Square now, it's all, like, pedestrian now, you can walk right across it, the fountains are on, it's so warm down here that people are actually jumping about in the water, it can't be hygienic, loads of people are wearing shorts down here, nobody's got a coat on, I've actually had to take mine off, that's how warm it is, oh! and there's Nelson! but he's like so high up you can't really see him at all, I'm right under him now, anyway I was just phoning, because every time I come here and see the famous things it makes me think of us, you know, watching tv, when we were kids, and Nelson's Column and Big Ben and wondering if we'd ever in a million years get to see them really, for real, eh, well now I'm waiting for the green man at a pedestrian crossing right under Nelson's Column, you should hear all the different languages, all round me, it's very very interesting to hear so many different voices at once, oh well, now I'm on a road that's all official-looking buildings, well, just calling to say I'll see you when I get back, I'm back tomorrow, I'll have to have a wee look at my map now, I'll have to get it out of my bag, so, well, I'll stop now. Bye for now. Bye.

End call.

(Still no Paul.)

(She won't ever hear that message. That message'll just delete itself off Orange in a week's time.)

(But it was nice to be talking on my phone here, made me feel a bit safer, and though I was ostensibly just saying stuff for no reason it kind of felt good to.)

(Maybe it's easier to talk to someone who won't ever actually hear what you say.)

(What a funny thought. What a ridiculous thought.)

Is this Strand?

(She loves all that Shakespeare stuff, and she loved that film, so did I, where the posh people are unveiling the new white statue and they pull the cover off and lying fast asleep in its arms is Charlie Chaplin, and later the blind girl gets her sight back because he gets rich with a windfall and spends it all on her sight operation, but then he sees that now that she can see, he's clearly the wrong kind of person, and it's tragic, not a comedy at all.)

(Still no Paul.)

(I can't see a streetname. I think I might not be on the right road for)

(oh look at that, that's an interesting-looking one, right in the middle of the road, what is it, a memorial? It's a memorial with just, as if empty clothes are hanging all round it on hooks, like empty clothes, a lot of soldiers' and workers' clothes.)

(But they look strange. They look like they've got the shapes of bodies still in them. And though they're men's clothes, the way all their folds are falling looks like women's –)

(Oh, right, it's a statue to the women who fought in the war. Oh I get it. It's like the clothes they wore, which they just took off and hung up, like a minute ago, like someone else's clothes they just stepped into briefly. And the clothes have kept their shape so that you get the bodyshape of women but in dungarees and uniforms and clothes they wouldn't usually wear and so on.)

(London is all statues. Look at that one. Look at him up on his high horse. I wonder who he was. It says on the side. I can't make it out. I wonder if he actually looked like he looks there, when he was alive. The Chaplin one didn't look anything like Chaplin, not really. And the Shakespeare one, well, no way of knowing.)

(Still no Paul.)

(I wonder why they didn't get to be people, like him, with faces and bodies, those women, they just got to be gone, they just got to be empty clothes.)

(Was it because there were too many girls and it had to be symbolic of them all?)

(But no, because there are always faces on the soldiers on war memorials, I mean the soldiers on those memorials get to be actual people, with bodies, not just clothes.)

(I wonder if that's better, just clothes, I mean in terms of art and meaning and such like. Is it better, like more symbolic, *not* to be there?)

(Anthea would know.)

(I mean, what if Nelson was symbolised by just a hat and an empty jacket? Sometimes Chaplin is just a hat and boots and a walking stick or a hat and a moustache. But that's because he's so individual that you know who he is from those things.)

(Both our grandmothers were in that war. Those clothes on that memorial are the empty clothes of our grandmothers.)

(The faces of our grandmothers. We never even saw our mother's mother's face, well, only in photos we saw it. She was dead before we were born.)

(Still no Paul.)

That sign says Whitehall.

I'm on the wrong road.

(God, Imogen, can't you do anything right?)

I better go back.

My ambition, Keith says, is to make Pure oblivion possible.

Right! I say.

(I hope I say it brightly enough.)

What I want, he says, is to make it not just possible but natural for someone, from the point of rising in the morning to the point of going to sleep again at night, to spend his whole day, obliviously, in Pure hands.

So, when his wife turns on his tap to fill his coffee machine, the water that comes out of it is administered, tested and cleaned by Pure. When she puts his coffee in the filter and butters his toast, or chooses him an apple from the fruit bowl, each of these products will have been shipped by and bought at one of the outlets belonging to Pure. When he picks up the paper to read at the breakfast table, whether it's a tabloid or a Berliner or a broadsheet, it's one of the papers that belong to Pure. When he switches on his computer, the server he uses is Pure-owned, and the breakfast tv programme he's not really watching is going out on one of the channels the majority of whose shares is held by Pure. When his wife changes the baby's diaper, it's replaced with one bought and packed by Pure Pharmaceuticals, like the two ibuprofen she's just about to neck, and all the other drugs she needs to take in the course of the day, and when his baby eats, it eats bottled organic range Ooh Baby, made and distributed by Pure. When he slips the latest paperback into his briefcase, or when his wife thinks about what she'll be reading at her book group later that day, whatever it is has been published by one of the twelve imprints owned by Pure, and bought, in person or online, at one of the three chains now owned by Pure, and if it was bought online it may even have been delivered by a mail network operated by Pure. And should our man feel like watching some high-grade porn, – if you'll excuse me, ah, ah, for being so crude as to suggest it –

I nod.

(I smile like people suggest it to me all the time.)

– on his laptop or on his phonescreen on the way to work, while he keeps himself hydrated by drinking a bottle of Pure's Eau Caledonia, he can do so courtesy of one of the several leisure outlets owned, distributed and operated by Pure.

(But I am feeling a bit uneasy. I am feeling a bit disenchanted. Has Keith driven me all this way out of London in a specially-chauffeured car to this collection of prefab offices on the outskirts of a New Town just to give me a Creative lecture?)

And that's just breakfast, Keith is saying. Our Pure Man hasn't even reached work yet. That's just the opener. There's the whole rest of the day to come. And we've only touched on his wife, only skimmed the surface of his infant. We haven't even begun to consider his ten-year-old son, his teenage daughter. Because Pure Product is everywhere. Pure is massive throughout the global economy.

But most important, Pure is pure. And Pure must be perceived by the market as pure. It does what it says on the tin. You get me, ah, ah ?

Imogen, Keith, yes, Keith, I do, I say.

Keith is walking me from prefab to prefab, holding forth. There seems to be almost nobody else working here.

(Maybe they've all gone home. It's seven p.m., after all.)

(I wish there were at least one or two other people around. I wish that chauffeur bloke had stayed. But no, he pulled out of the car park as soon as he dropped me off.)

(The angle the sun is at is making it hard for me to do anything but squint at Keith.)

Right, Keith, I say

(even though he hasn't said anything else.)

(He isn't in the least bit interested in the print-outs. I've tried bringing them into the conversation twice.)

. . . trillion-dollar water market, he is saying.

(I know all this.)

. . . planned takeover of the Germans who own Thames Water, naturally, and we've just bought up a fine-looking concern in the Netherlands, and massive market opportunities coming up with the Chinese and Indian water business, he says.

(I know all this too.)

Which is why, ah, ah, he says.

Imogen, I say.

Which is why, Imogen, I've brought you down here to Base Camp, Keith says.

(*This* is Base Camp? Milton Keynes?)

. . . putting you in charge of Pure DND, Keith says.

(Me! In charge of something!)

(Oh my God!)

Thanks, Keith, I say. What's, uh – what exactly is – ?

With your natural tact, he is saying. With your way with words. With your natural instinctual caring talent for turning an argument on its head. With your understanding of the politics of locale. With your ability to deal with media issues head-on. Most of all, with your style. And I'm the first to admit that right now we need a woman's touch on the team, ah, ah. We need that more than anything, and at Pure we will reward more than anything your ability to look good, look right, say the right thing, on camera if necessary, under all pressures, and to take the flak like a man if anything goes pear-shaped.

(Keith thinks I'm overweight.)

We've stopped outside a prefab identical to all the others. Keith presses the code-buttons on a door and lets it swing open. He stands back, gestures to me to look inside.

There's a new desk, a new computer set-up, a new chair, a new phone, a new sofa, a shining pot plant.

Pure Dominant Narrative Department, he says. Welcome home.

Pure – ? I say.

Do I have to carry you over the threshold? he says. Go on! Take a seat at the desk! It's your seat! It was purchased for you! Go on!

I don't move from the door. Keith strides in, pulls the swivel chair out from behind the desk and sends it rolling towards me. I catch it.

Sit, he says.

I sit in it, in the doorway.

Keith comes over, takes the back of the chair, swivels it round and stands behind me

(which reminds me of what the boy used to do when we went to the shows at the Bught, on the waltzers, the boy who'd hold the back of the waltzer if there were girls in it then make us all laugh like lunatics by giving it an especially dizzying spin.)

Keith's head is by my head. He is speaking into my right ear.

Your first brief, Keith is saying, is a piece replying to the article in the British-based Independent newspaper this morning, which you'll have seen –

(I haven't. Oh God.)

– about how bottled water uses much less stringent testing than tap water. DDR, ah, ah.

DD . . .? I say.

Deny Disparage Rephrase, Keith says. Use your initiative. Your imagination. So many of those so-called regulated tests on tap water useless and some of them actually harmful. Science insists, and many scientists insist. Statistics say. *Our* independent findings versus *their* crackpot findings. You pen it, we place it.

(He wants me to do – what?)

Your second brief is a little tougher. But I know you'll meet it. Small body of irate ethnics in one of our Indian sub-interests factioning against our planned filter-dam two-thirds completed and soon to power four Pure labs in the area. *They say*: our dam blocks their access to fresh water and ruins their crops. *We say*: they're ethnic troublemakers who are trying to involve us in a despicable religious war. Use the word terrorism if necessary. Got it?

(Do what?)

(This chair feels unsafe. Its slight moving under Keith's arm is making me feel sick.)

Fifty-five and upwards per annum, Keith says, negotiable after the handling of these first two briefs.

(But it's – wrong.)

Our kind of person, Keith says.

(Keith's midriff is close to my eyes. I can see that his trousers are repressing an erection. More, I can see that he wants me to see it. He is actually showing me his hidden hard-on.)

. . . brightest star in the UK-based Pure-concern sky, he's saying, and I know you can do it, ah, ah, –

(I try to say my name. But I can't speak. My mouth's too dry.)

(It's possible that he came all the way out here to this prefab and set the height level of this chair at the exact height for me to see his erection properly.)

. . . only girl this high in management, he is saying.

(I can't say anything.)

(Then I remember the last time I needed a glass of water.)

(I think about what a glass of water means.)

I can't do this, I say.

Yes you can, he says. You're not a silly girl.

No, I'm not, I say. And I can't make up rubbish and pretend it's true. Those people in India. That water is their right.

Not so, my little Scotty dog, Keith says. According to the World Water Forum 2000, whose subject was water's exact designation, water is not a human right. Water is a human need. And that means we can market it. We can sell a need. It's our *human right* to.

Keith, that's ridiculous, I say. Those words you just used are all in the wrong places.

Keith spins the chair round with me in it until it's facing him. He stands with his hands on the arms and leans over me so I can't get out of the chair. He looks at me solemnly. He gives the chair a playful little warning jolt.

I shake my head.

It's bullshit, Keith, I say. You can't do that.

It's international-government-ratified, he says. It's law. Whether you think it's bullshit or not. And I can do what I like. And there's nothing you or anyone else can do about it.

Then the law should be changed, I hear myself say. It's a wrong law. And there's a lot I can do about it. What I can do is, I can, uh, I can say as loudly as I possibly can, everywhere that I can, that it shouldn't be happening like this, until as many people hear as it takes to make it not happen.

I hear my own voice get louder and louder. But Keith doesn't move. He doesn't flinch. He holds the chair square.

Your surname again? he says quietly.

I take a breath.

It's Gunn, I say.

He shakes his head as if it was him who named me, as if he can decide what I'm called and what I'm not.

Not really Pure material, he says. Pity. You looked just right.

I can feel something rising in me as big as his hard-on. It's anger.

It forces me up on to my feet, lurches me forward in the chair so that my head nearly hits his head and he has to step back.

I take a deep breath. I keep myself calm. I speak quietly.

Which way's the station from here, Keith, and will I need a cab? I ask.

Locked in the ladies toilet in the main prefab while I'm waiting for the taxi, I throw up. Luckily I am adept at throwing up, so I get none of it on my clothes.

(But it is the second time for months and months, I realise as the taxi pulls away from Pure Base Camp, that I haven't thrown up on purpose.)

I get myself back to London. I love London! I walk between Euston and King's Cross like it's something I do all the time, like I belong among all these other people walking along a London street.

I manage to get a seat in a sitting-up carriage on the last sleeper north.

On the journey I tell the other three people in the carriage about Pure and about the people in India.

English people are just as shy and polite as Scottish people really, under all that pretend confidence, and some of them can be very nice.

But I will also have to find a way of telling the story that doesn't make people look away, or go and sit somewhere else.

Still, even though I'm sitting here near-shouting about the ways of the world at a few strangers in a near-empty railway carriage, I feel – what is it I feel?

I feel completely sane.

I feel all energised. I feel so energised on this slow-moving train that it's like I'm travelling faster than the train is. I feel all loaded. A loaded Gunn!

Somewhere in Northumberland, as the train slows up again, I remember the story about the clan I get my name from, the story about the Gunn girl who was wooed by the chief of another clan and who didn't like him. She refused to marry him.

So he came to the Gunn castle one day and he killed all the Gunns he could find, in fact he killed everybody, family or not, that he happened to meet on his way to her chamber. When he got there he broke the door down. He took her by force.

He drove her miles and miles to his own stronghold where he shut her up at the top of a tower until she'd give in.

But she didn't give in. She never gave in. She threw herself out of the tower instead, to her death. Ha!

I used to think that story of my far-back ancestor was a morbid story. But tonight, I mean this morning, on this train about to cross the border between there and here, a story like that one becomes all about where we see it from. Where we're lucky enough

(or unlucky enough)

to see it from.

And listen. Listen, you other two remaining people asleep right now. Listen, world out there, slow-passing beyond the train windows. I'm Imogen Gunn. I come from a family that can't be had. I come from a country that's the opposite of a, what was it, dominant narrative. I'm all Highland adrenalin. I'm all teuchter laughter and I'm all teuchter anger. Pure! Ha!

We roll slowly past the Lowland sea, and the sea belongs to all of us. We roll slowly past the rugged banks of lochs and rivers in a kind of clearness of fine early morning summer light, and they're full of water that belongs to everyone.

Then I think to check my phone.

Seven missed calls – from Paul!

It's a sign!

(And to think I used to think he wasn't the right kind of person for me.)

Even though it's really late, I mean really early morning, I call him straight back without listening to any of the messages.

Paul, I say. It's me. Did I wake you?

No, it's fine, he says. Well, I mean, you did. But Imogen –

Listen, Paul, I say. First there's something I have to say. And it's this. I really like you. I mean, I really, really like you. I've liked you since the very first moment we met. You were at the water cooler. Remember?

Imogen –, he says.

And you know I like you. You know I do. There's that thing between us. You know the thing I mean. The thing where it doesn't matter where you are in a room, you still know exactly where the other person is.

Imogen –, Paul says.

And I know I'm not supposed to say, but I think if you like me too, and if you're not gay or anything, we should do something about it, I say.

Gay? he says.

You know, I say. You never know.

Imogen, have you been drinking? he says.

Just water, I say. And I mean, it's not the same thing at all, I know, but you seem quite female to me, I don't mean that in a bad way, I mean it in a good way, you have a lot of feminine principle, I know that, I know it instinctually, and it's unusual in a man, and I really like it. I love it, actually.

Listen. I've been trying to get hold of you all night, because –, he says.

Yeah, well, if it's about the print-outs, I say, there's no point. The print-outs were irrelevant. I wasn't phoning you about print-outs anyway. I was just trying to get your attention in the only way I could think of without actually telling you I fancied you out loud. And they really don't matter any more, not to me, as I'm no longer a Puree.

It's not the print-outs, Paul says.

And maybe you don't like me, maybe you're embarrassed that I said what I felt, well, never mind, I won't mind, I'm a grown-up, I'll be okay, but I needed to say it out loud, to tell you anyway, and I'm tired of feeling things I never get to express, things that I always have to hold inside, I'm fed up not knowing whether I'm saying the right thing when I do speak, anyway I thought I'd be brave, I thought it was worth it, and I hope you don't mind me saying.

Words are coming out of me like someone turned me on like a tap. It's Paul. He – turns me on!

But as soon as he gets the chance, Paul cuts in.

Imogen. Listen. It's your sister, he says.

My heart in me. Nothing else. Everything else blank.

What about my sister? What's happened to my sister? I say.

★ ★ ★

Paul is waiting for me at the station when the train pulls in.

Why aren't you at work? I say.

Because I'm here instead, he says.

He slings my bag into the boot of his car then locks the car with his key fob.

We'll walk, he says. You'll see it better that way. The first one is on the wall of the Eastgate Centre, I think because of the traffic coming into town, the people in cars get long enough to read it when they stop at the traffic lights. God knows how anybody got up that high and stayed up there without being disturbed long enough to do it.

He walks me past Marks and Spencers, about fifteen yards down the road. Sure enough, the people in the cars stopped at the traffic lights are peering at something above my head, even leaning out of their car windows to see it more clearly.

I turn round.

Behind me and above me on the wall the words are bright, red, huge. They're in the same writing as was on the Pure sign before they replaced it. They've been framed in a beautiful, baroque-looking, trompe l'œil picture-frame in gold. They say: ACROSS THE WORLD, TWO MILLION GIRLS, KILLED BEFORE BIRTH OR AT BIRTH BECAUSE THEY WEREN'T BOYS. THAT'S ON RECORD. ADD TO THAT THE OFF-RECORD ESTIMATE OF FIFTY-EIGHT MILLION MORE GIRLS, KILLED BECAUSE THEY WEREN'T BOYS. THAT'S SIXTY MILLION GIRLS. Underneath this, in a handwriting I recognise, even though it's a lot bigger than usual: THIS MUST CHANGE. Iphis and Ianthe the message girls 2007.

Dear God, I say.

I know, Paul says.

So many girls, I say in case Paul isn't understanding me.

Yes, Paul says.

Sixty million. I say. How? How can that happen in this day and age? How do we not know about that?

We do now, he says. Pretty much the whole of Inverness knows about it now, if they want to. And more. Much more.

What else? I say.

He walks me back past the shops and up the

pedestrian precinct into town, to the Town House. A small group of people is watching two men in overalls scouring the red off the front wall with a spray gun. IN NO COUNTRY IN THE WORLD RIGHT NOW ARE WOMEN'S WAGES EQUAL TO MEN'S WAGES. THIS MUST CHA

Half the frame and the bit with the names and the date have been sprayed nearly away but are still visible. It's all still legible.

That'll take some shifting, I say.

Paul leads me round the Town House, where a whole side wall is bright red words inside gold. ALL ACROSS THE WORLD, WHERE WOMEN ARE DOING EXACTLY THE SAME WORK AS MEN, THEY'RE BEING PAID BETWEEN THIRTY TO FORTY PERCENT LESS. THAT'S NOT FAIR. THIS MUST CHANGE. Iphis and Ianthe the message boys 2007.

Probably Catholics, a woman says. It's disgusting.

Aye, it'll fair ruin the tourism, another says. Who'd be wanting to come and see the town if the town's covered in this kind of thing? Nobody.

And we can say goodbye to winning that Britain in Bloom this year now, her friend says.

And to Antiques Roadshow ever coming back to Inverness and all, another says.

It's a scandal! another is saying. Thirty to forty percent!

Aye well, a man next to her says. It's no fair, right enough, if that's true, what it says there.

Aye, but why would *boys* write *that* kind of thing on a building? a woman is saying. It's not natural.

Too right they should, the scandal-woman says. And would you not have thought we were equal now, here, after all that stravaiging in the seventies and the eighties?

Aye, but we're equal here, in Inverness, the first woman says.

In your dreams we're equal, the scandal-woman says.

Nevertheless, equal or no, it's no reason to paint it all over the Town House, the woman's friend says.

The scandal-woman is arguing back as we walk up round the side of the Castle. In gilted red on the front wall above the Castle door it says in a jolly arc, like the name of a house painted right above its threshold, that only one percent of the world's assets are held by women. Iphis and Ianthe the message girls 2007.

From here we can see right across the river that there are huge red words on the side of the cathedral too. I can't see what they say, but I can make out the red.

Two million girls annually forced into marriage worldwide, Paul says seeing me straining to make it out. And on Eden Court Theatre, on the glass doors, it says that sexual or domestic violence affects one out of every three women and girls worldwide and that this is the world's leading cause of injury and death for women.

I can make out the *this must change* from here, I say.

We lean on the Castle railing and Paul lists the other places that have been written on, what the writing says, and about how the police phoned Pure for me.

Your sister and her friend are both in custody up at Raigmore, he says.

Robin's not her friend, I say. Robin's her other half.

Right, Paul says. I'll run you up there now. You'll need to arrange bail. I did try. My bank wouldn't let me.

Hang on, I say. I bet you anything –

What? he says.

I bet you their double bail there's a message somewhere on Flora too, I say.

I can't afford it, he shouts behind me.

I run down to the statue of Flora MacDonald shielding her eyes, watching for Bonnie Prince Charlie, still dressed in the girls' clothes she lent him for his escape from the English forces, to come sailing back to her all the way up the River Ness.

I walk round the statue three times reading the words ringing the base of her. Tiny, clear, red, a couple of centimetres high: WOMEN OCCUPY TWO PERCENT OF SENIOR MANAGEMENT POSITIONS IN BUSINESS WORLDWIDE. THREE AND A HALF PERCENT OF THE WORLD'S TOTAL NUMBER OF CABINET MINISTERS ARE WOMEN. WOMEN HAVE NO MINISTERIAL POSITIONS IN NINETY-THREE COUNTRIES OF THE WORLD. THIS MUST CHANGE. Iphis and Ianthe   the message boys   2007.

Good old Flora. I pat her base.

Paul catches me up.

I'll nip down and get the car and pick you up here, he says, and we'll head up the hill –

Take me home first, I say. I need a bath. I need some breakfast. Then maybe you and me can have a talk. Then I'll take us up to the police station on my Rebel.

On your what? But we should really go up to the station right now, Imogen, he says. It's been all night.

Are you not wanting to talk to me, then? I say.

Well, I do, actually, he says, I've got a lot to say, but do you not think we should –

I shake my head.

I think the message boy-girls'll be proud to be in there, I say.

Oh, he says. I never thought of it that way.

Let's leave the police on message until lunchtime, I say. Then we'll go up and sort the bail. And after that we'll all go for something to eat.

Paul is very good in bed.

(Thank goodness.)

(Well, I knew he would be.)

(Well, I hoped.)

I feel met by you, he says afterwards. It's weird.

(That's exactly what it feels like. I felt met by him the first time I saw him. I felt met by him all the times we weren't even able to meet each other's eyes.)

I definitely felt met by you this morning at the station, I say.

Ha, he says. That's funny.

We both laugh like idiots.

It is the loveliest laughing ever.

(I feel like we should always be meeting each other off trains, I think inside my head. That's if we're not actually on the same train, going the same way.)

I say it out loud.

I feel like we should always be meeting each other off trains, that's if we're not actually on the same train travelling together. Or am I saying too much out loud? I say.

You're saying it too quietly, he says. I wish you'd shout it.

It's raining quite heavily when we make love again and afterwards I can hear the rhythmic drip, heavy and steady, from the place above the window where the drainpipe is blocked. The rhythm of it goes against, and at the same time makes a kind of sense of, the randomness of the rain happening all round it.

I never knew how much I liked rain till now.

When Paul goes downstairs to make coffee I remember myself. I go to the bathroom. I catch sight of my own face in the little mirror.

I go through to Anthea's room where the big mirror is. I sit on the edge of her bed and I make myself look hard at myself.

I am a lot less than an 8 now.

(I can see bones here, here, here, here and here.)

(Is that good?)

Back in my own room I see my clothes on the chair. I remember the empty clothes on that memorial, made to look soft, but made of metal.

(I have thought for a long time that the way my clothes hang on me is more important than me inside them.)

I hear Paul moving about in the bathroom. He turns on the shower.

He turns everything in the world on, not just me. Ha ha.

I like the idea of Paul in my shower. The shower, for some reason, has been where I've done my thinking and my asking since I was teenage. I've been standing those few minutes in the shower every day for God knows how long now, talking to nothing like we used to do when we were small, Anthea and I, and knelt by the sides of our beds.

(Please make me the correct size. The correct shape. The right kind of daughter. The right kind of sister. Someone who isn't fazed or sad. Someone whose family has held together, not fallen apart. Someone who simply feels *better*. Please make things better. THIS MUST CHANGE.)

I get up. I call the police station.

The man on the desk is unbelievably informal.

Oh aye, he says. Now, is it one of the message girls or boys or whatever, or one of the seven dwarves that you're after? Which one would you like? We've got Dopey, Sneezy, Grumpy, Bashful, Sleepy, Eye-fist, and another one whose name I'd have to look up for you.

I'd like to talk to my sister, Anthea Gunn, please, I say. And that's enough flippancy about their tag from you.

About their what, now? he says.

Years from now, I say, you and the Inverness Constabulary will be nothing but a list of dry dusty names locked in an old computer memory stick. But the message girls, the message boys. They'll be legend.

Uh huh, he says. Well, if you'd like to hang up your phone now, Ms Gunn, I'll have your wee sister call you back in a jiffy.

(I consider making a formal complaint, while I wait for the phone to go. *I* am the only person permitted to make fun of my sister.)

Where've you been? she says when I answer.

Anthea, do you really think you'll change the world a single jot by calling yourself by a funny name and doing what you've been doing? You really think you'll make a single bit of difference to all the unfair things and all the suffering and all the injustice and all the hardship with a few words?

Yes, she says.

Okay. Good, I say.

Good? she says. Aren't you angry? Aren't you really furious with me?

No, I say.

No? she says. Are you lying?

But I think you're going to have to get a bit better at dodging the police, I say.

Yeah, she says. Well. We're working on it.

You and the girl with the little wings coming out of her heels, I say.

Are you being rude about Robin? she says. Because if you are, I'll make fun of your motorbike again.

Ha ha, I say. You can borrow one of my crash helmets if you want. But you might not want to, since there's no wings on it like there are on Robin's helmet.

Eh? she says.

It's a reference, I say. To a source.

Eh? she says.

Don't say eh, say pardon or excuse me. I mean like Mercury.

Like what? she says.

Mercury, I say. *You* know. Original message boy. Wings on his heels. Wait a minute, I'll go downstairs and get my Dictionary of Mythical –

No, no, Midge, don't go anywhere. Just listen, she says. I've not got long on this phone. I can't ask Dad. There's no one Robin can ask. Just help us out this once. Please. I won't ask again.

I know. You must be desperate to get out of that kilt, I say and I crack up laughing again.

Well, when you stop finding yourself so hilarious, she says, actually, if you *could* bring me a change of clothes that'd be great.

But you've been okay, you're both okay up there? I say.

We're good. But if you could, like I say, just, eh,

quite urgently, justify half an hour's absence to Dominorm or whoever, and disengage yourself from the Pure empire long enough to come and bail us out. I'll pay you back. I promise.

You'll need to, I say. I'm unemployed now.

Eh? she says.

I'm disengaged, I say. I'm no longer Pure.

No! she says. What happened? What's wrong?

Nothing and everything is what happened, I say. And at Pure, everything's wrong. Everything in the world. But you know this already.

Seriously? she says.

Honest to goodness, I say.

Wow, she says. When did it happen?

What? I say.

The miracle. The celestial exchange of my sister for you, whoever you are.

A glass of water given in kindness, that's what did it, I say.

Eh? she says.

Stop saying eh, I say. Anyway I thought we'd saunter on up in a wee while –

Eh, can I just stress the word urgent? she says.

Though I thought I might drive out to a garden centre first and buy some seeds and bulbs –

Urgent urgent urgent urgent, she says.

And then I thought I might spend the rest of the afternoon and early evening down on the river bank –

URGENT, she yells down the phone.

– planting a good slogan or two that'll appear mysteriously in the grass of it next spring. RAIN BELONGS TO EVERYONE. Or THERE'S NO SUCH THING AS A SECOND SEX. Or PURE DEAD = BRILLIANT. Something like that.

Oh. That's such a good idea, she says. Planting in the riverbank. That's such a fantastic idea.

Also, you're being too longwinded, I say. All the long sentences. It needs to be simpler. You need sloganeering help. You definitely need some creative help –

Does that creative have a small c or a big C? she says.

– and did you know, by the way, since we're talking sloganeering, I say –

Midge, just come and help, she says. Like, now. And don't forget to bring the clothes.

– that the word slogan, I say, comes from the Gaelic? It's a word with a really interesting history –

No, no, no, she says, please don't start with all that correct-word-saying-it-properly-the-right-way-not-the-wrong-way stuff right now, just come up and get us out of here, Midge, yes? Midge? Are you there?

(Ha-ha!)

What's the magic word? I say.

all together now

Reader, I married him/her.

It's the happy ending. Lo and behold.

I don't mean we had a civil ceremony. I don't mean we had a civil partnership. I mean we did what's still impossible after all these centuries. I mean we did the still-miraculous, in this day and age. I mean we got married. I mean we here came the bride. I mean we walked down the aisle. I mean we step we gailied, on we went, we Mendelssohned, we epithalamioned, we raised high the roofbeams, carpenters, for there was no other bride, o bridegroom, like her. We crowned each other with the garlands of flowers. We stamped on the wine-glasses wrapped in the linen. We jumped the broom-stick. We lit the candles. We crossed the sticks. We circled the table. We circled each other. We fed each other the honey and the walnuts from the silver spoons; we fed each other the tea and the sake and we sweet-ened the tea for each other; we fed each other the borhani beneath the pretty cloth; we fed each other a taste of lemon, vinegar, cayenne and honey, one for each of the four elements. We handfasted, then we asked for the blessing of the air, the fire, the water and the earth; we tied the knot with grass, with ribbon, with silver rope, with a string of shells; we poured water on the ground in the four directions of the wind and we called on the presence of our ancestors as witnesses, so may it be! We gave each other the kola nuts to symbolise commitment, the eggs and the dates and the chestnuts to symbolise righteousness, plenty, fertility, the thirteen gold coins to symbolise constant unselfishness. With these rings we us wedded.

What I mean is. There, under the trees, on a fresh spring day by the banks of the River Ness, that fast black backbone of a Scottish northern town; there, flanked by presbyterian church after presbyterian church, we gave our hands in marriage under the blossom, gave each other and took each other for better, for worse, in sickness or health, to love, comfort, honour, cherish, protect, and to have and to hold each other from that day forward, for as long as we both should live till death us would part.

Ness I said Ness I will Ness.

Into thin air, to the nothing that was there, with the river our witness, we said yes. We said we did. We said we would.

We'd thought we were alone, Robin and I. We'd thought it was just us, under the trees outside the cathedral. But as soon as we'd made our vows there was a great whoop of joy behind us, and when we turned round we saw all the people, there must have been hundreds, they were clapping and cheering, they were throwing confetti, they waved and they roared celebration.

My sister was there at the front with her other half, Paul. She was happy. She smiled. Paul looked happy. He was growing his hair. My sister gestured to me like she couldn't believe it, at a couple standing not far from her – look! – was it them? – sure enough, it *was* them, our father and our mother, both, and they were standing together and they weren't arguing, they were talking to each other very civilly, they clinked their glasses as I watched.

They're discussing the unsuitability of the wedding, Midge said.

I nodded. First time they've agreed on anything in years, I said.

All the people from the rest of the tale were there too; Becky from Reception; the two work experience girls, Chantelle and her friend Lorraine; Brian, who was going out with Chantelle; and Chantelle's mum, who wasn't in the story as such but who'd clearly also taken a shine to Brian; a whole gaggle of Pure people, including the security men who first arrested Robin; they waved and smiled. Not Norman or Dominic, were those their names? they'd been promoted to Base Camp, so they weren't there, at least not that I saw, and not the boss of bosses, Keith, I don't remember seeing him either. But the whole of the Provost's office came, and some officials from other places we'd written on; the theatre, the shopping mall, the Castle. A male-voice choir from the Inverness Police Force attended, they sang a beautiful arrangement of songs from Gilbert and Sullivan. Then the Inverness Constabulary female-voice choir sang an equally beautiful choral arrangement of Don't Cha (Wish Your Girlfriend Was Hot Like Me). Then the Provost made an eloquent speech. Inverness, she said, once famed for its faith in unexpected ancient creatures of the deep, had now become famous for something new: for fairness, for art, and for the art of fairness. Inverness, now world-renowned for its humane and galvanising public works of art, had quadrupled its tourist intake. Thousands more people were coming especially to view the public exhibits. And not just Antiques Roadshow, but Songs of Praise, Question Time, Newsnight Review and several other tv programmes had *all* petitioned the council, keen to record themselves in front of the famous sloganned walls. The Inverness art may have spawned copycat art in other cities and towns, she said, but none so good as in the city whose new defining motto, inscribed on all the signposts at all the entrypoints to the city, would be from this day forth *A Hundred Thousand Welcomes And When You See A Wrong, Write It! Ceud Mile Failte! Còir! Sgriobh!*

Really terrible slogan, I said privately to Robin.

Your sister thought it up, Robin said. Definitely in line for a job as Council Creative.

Which is your family? I asked Robin. She pointed them out. They were by the drinks table with Venus,

Artemis and Dionysos; her father and mother were cuddling the baby Cupid, which was problematic because of the arrows (in fact there was a bit of a fuss later when Lorraine cut her finger open on an arrow-tip, and even more problems when Artemis and Chantelle were found down the riverbank in the dusk light firing arrows at the rabbits on the grass at the side of the Castle and, Chantelle being very short-sighted, the damage to four passing cars had to be paid for, and Brian had to be comforted after Chantelle swore eternal celibacy, so it was lucky that Chantelle's mum had come with her after all).

Then we had the speeches, and Midge read out the apologies, including one from the Loch Ness Monster, who'd sent us an old rusty underwater radar scanner, some signed photos of herself and a lovely set of silver fishknives, and there was a half gold-edged, half black-edged telegram-poem from John Knox, sorry he couldn't make it to be there with us even in spirit:

Here's tae ye,
Wha's like ye?
Far too many
And ye're all damnt to Hell.
But whit can I say,
It's a weddin day,
So come on, raise your glasses now,
And wish the damnt pair weel!

We had the blessings then, and the toasts. Honour, riches, marriage-blessing, Love, continuance, and increasing, Hourly joys be still upon us, Juno sing her blessings on us, till all the seas gang dry, my dear, and the rocks melt wi' the sun. May our eternal summer never fade. May the road rise up to meet us, and may God always hold us in the palm of His hand. A dog on two legs was drinking too much whisky. A goddess so regal she must have been Isis spent the whole reception making fine new guests out of clay. A beautiful Greek couple came graciously up and shook our hands; they were newlyweds themselves, they said, and how had the run-up to the wedding been? was it as nervewracking as it'd been for them? They'd never thought they'd make it. But they had, they were happy, and they wished us all happiness. They told us to honeymoon in Crete, where their families would make us welcome, and that's exactly what we did, Robin and I, when the wedding was over, we hotfooted it to the hot island, its surfaces layered with wild flowers, marjoram, sage and thyme, its rocks split by the force of tiny white and pink and yellow flowers and everywhere the scent of herbs and salt and sea. We stood where the Iphis story had originated, we stood between red-painted pillars in the reconstructed palace, we went to the museum to see the ancient, pieced-together, re-imagined painting of the athlete, the acrobat, boy or girl or both, who was agile enough to somersault right over the top of the back of the charging bull. We stood where the civilised, rich, cultured, Minoan cannibals had lived before nature had simply flooded them into oblivion, and we thought about the story that arose from their rituals, the story of the annual sacrifice of the seven boys and seven girls to the bull-headed beast, and the clever artist, the man who invented human wings, who devised the girls and the boys a safe way out of the bloody maze.

But back at the wedding the band had struck up now, and what a grand noise, for the legendary red-faced fiddler who played at all the best weddings had come, and had had a drink, and had got out his fiddle, he was the man to turn curved wood and horsehair, cat-gut and resin into a single blackbird then into a flight of blackbirds singing all the evenings at once, then into a spawn of happy salmon, into the return of the longed-for boat to a port, into the longing that waits in a lucky place for two people who don't yet know each other to meet exactly there, where the stones grass over, the borders cross themselves. It was the song of the flow of things, the song of the undammed river, and there with the fiddler was his sidekick, who doubled the tune and who, when he played alongside his partner, found in everything he laid hands on (whistle, squeezebox, harp, guitar, old empty oilcan and a stick or stone to bang it with) the kind of music that not only made the bushes and the trees pull themselves out of the ground and move where they could hear better, but made them throw their leaves and twigs up in the air, made all the seagulls clap their wings, made all the dogs of the Highlands bark with joy, made all the roofs dance on the houses, made every paving stone of the whole town tear itself up, stand itself on its pointed corner and do a happy pirouette, even made the old cathedral itself on its fixed foundations leap and caper.

Up the river it came, then, the astonishing little boat, up the river that no boats ever came up, with its two great fibreglass juts like the horns of a goat or a cow or a goddess held ahead of it, and its sail full and white against the trees and the sky. How it got from the loch through the Islands, how it did the impossible, got under the Infirmary Bridge with that full huge sail up we'll never know, but it did, it sailed the stretch of Ness Bank and it docked right below us, and there at the wheel was our grandmother, and throwing the rope to be caught was our grandfather. Robert and Helen Gunn, they were back from the sea, in time for the party.

We felt in our water that something was happening! our grandmother called up to us as she put her foot on dry land. We wouldn't miss this, no, not for the world!

Well, girls, and have you been good, and has the world been good to you? and how was your catch? have you landed fine fish? that was our grandfather, his old arms round us, him ruffling our hair.

They were younger than the day they left. They were brown and robust, their faces and hands were lined like the trunks of trees. They met Robin. They met Paul. They flung their arms round them like family.

Our grandmother danced the Canadian Barn Dance with Paul.

Our grandfather danced the Gay Gordons with Robin.

The music and the dancing went on late into the night. In fact, there was still dancing going on when the night was over, the light coming back and the new day dawning.

Uh-huh. Okay. I know.

In my dreams.

What I mean is, we stood on the bank of the river under the trees, the pair of us, and we promised the nothing that was there, the nothing that made us, the nothing that was listening, that we truly desired to go beyond our selves.

And that's the message. That's it. That's all.

Rings that widen on the surface of a loch above a thrown-in stone. A drink of water offered to a thirsty traveller on the road. Nothing more than what happens when things come together, when hydrogen, say, meets oxygen, or a story from then meets a story from now, or stone meets water meets girl meets boy meets bird meets hand meets wing meets bone meets light meets dark meets eye meets word meets world meets grain of sand meets thirst meets hunger meets need meets dream meets real meets same meets different meets death meets life meets end meets beginning all over again, the story of nature itself, ever-inventive, making one thing out of another, and one thing into another, and nothing lasts, and nothing's lost, and nothing ever perishes, and things can always change, because things will always change, and things will always be different, because things can always be different.

And it was always the stories that needed the telling that gave us the rope we could cross any river with. They balanced us high above any crevasse. They made us be natural acrobats. They made us be brave. They met us well. They changed us. It was in their nature to.

And there's always a whole other kittle of fish, our

grandfather said in my ear as he reached down and tucked the warm stone into my hand, there it was, ready for me to throw.

Right, Anthea?

Right, Grandad, I said.

Acknowledgements and thanks

I've adapted the story of Burning Lily from the account of the early life of Lilian Lenton in *Rebel Girls* by Jill Liddington (Virago, 2006).

The myth of Iphis originates in Book 9 of Ovid's *Metamorphoses*. 'Carry your gifts to the temples, happy pair, and rejoice, confident and unafraid!' It is one of the cheeriest metamorphoses in the whole work, one of the most happily resolved of its stories about the desire for and the ramifications of change.

The statistics in chapter four were collated by Womankind (www.womankind.org.uk), a UK charity whose raison d'être is to provide voice, aid and rights to disempowered women worldwide.

I've borrowed the rhetorical structure of one of Keith's talks from a paper given in 2001 by the sociologist

J-P Joseph about the global water corporation Vivendi Universal, quoted in *Blue Gold* by Maude Barlow and Tony Clarke (Earthscan, 2002). The writings of Vandana Shiva are another good place to help comprehend what's happening right now, worldwide, when it comes to the politics of water, as is *H20: A Biography of Water* by Philip Ball (Weidenfeld & Nicolson, 1999), which lets us know, among many other marvellous things, that 'water is bent'.

Thank you, Xandra. Thank you, Jeanette.
Thank you, Rachel, Bridget and Kasia.
Thank you, Robyn and Hiraani at This ASFC.
Thank you, Andrew, and everyone at Wylie's, especially Tracy. Thank you, Anya.

Thank you, Lucy.

Thank you, Sarah.